WE[...]
TIM[E ...]

The Warhammer w[...] of brave heroes, a[...] enemies. Now for [...] mythical events has been brought to life in a new series of books. Divided into a series of trilogies, each brings you hitherto untold details of the lives and times of the most legendary of all Warhammer heroes and villains. Combined together, they will reveal some of the hidden connections that underpin the history of the Warhammer world.

THE BLACK PLAGUE

The tale of an Empire divided, its heroic defenders and the enemies who endeavour to destroy it with the deadliest plague ever loosed upon the world of man. This series begins with *Dead Winter*.

THE WAR OF VENGEANCE

The ancient races of elf and dwarf clash in a devastating war that will decide not only their fates, but that of the entire Old World. The first novel in this series is *The Great Betrayal*.

BLOOD OF NAGASH

The first vampires, tainted children of Nagash, spread across the world and plot to gain power over the kingdoms of men. This series starts in *Neferata*.

Keep up to date with the latest information from the **Time of Legends** at *www.blacklibrary.com*

More Time of Legends from Black Library

Book One of the Blood of Nagash

NEFERATA

Josh Reynolds

BLACK LIBRARY

For Sylvie

A BLACK LIBRARY PUBLICATION

First published in Great Britain in 2012 by
Black Library,
Games Workshop Ltd.,
Willow Road, Nottingham,
NG7 2WS, UK

10 9 8 7 6 5 4 3 2 1

Cover illustration by Jon Sullivan.
Map by Nuala Kinrade.

A CIP record for this book is available from the British Library.

UK ISBN: 978 1 84970 213 3
US ISBN: 978 1 84970 214 0

See Black Library on the internet at

www.blacklibrary.com

Find out more about Games Workshop
and the world of Warhammer at

www.games-workshop.com

Printed and bound by CPI Group (UK) Ltd, Croydon, CR0 4YY

It is a Time of Legends.

Nagash the Usurper is dead, but his last revenge has devastated the once-mighty kingdoms of Nehekhara. As the city-states turn to dust and their kings moulder in their graves awaiting their promised rebirth, a new power rises.

Before the fall, in the city of Lahmia, Queen Neferata and her inner circle learned the secrets of eternal life from Nagash's unholy tomes, becoming the first of a brand new race – the vampires. Thirsty for blood and power in equal measure, each of these powerful creatures pursues their own goals with single-minded fervour.

Neferata, proud and vain, seeks to re-establish her empire and once again reign as queen. W'Soran, master of the magical arts, desires power over life and death.

Abhorash, a warrior born, battles to slake his bloodthirst and regain his lost honour.

But for all their plots and schemes, the vampires are nothing more than pawns in another, much larger, game – Nagash's influence weighs heavily upon all those of his blood, and one day, he will return...

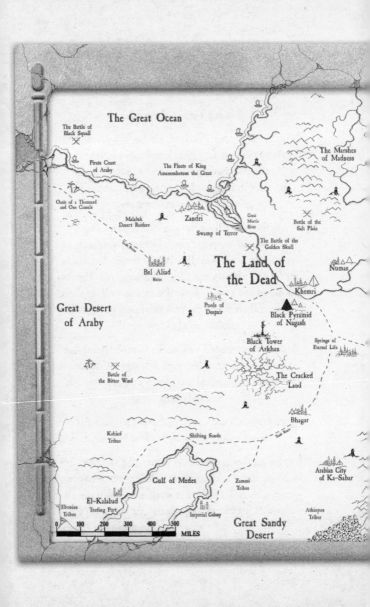

The Plain of Bones

Desolation
of Nagash

The
Sour Sea

Nagashizzar
Below which lies
the Cursed Pit

The Fortress
of Vorag

Battle of
the Grey Hag

Ruins

Misty Mountain

The Broken Teeth

Flight River

Red Cloud
Mountain

The Straits of
Nagash

N

Morrit Tarn

Cursed
Lahmia

S

Doom
Mountain

The Bitter Sea

Ash River

The Battle of
Phar's Legion

Battle of
Mighty Flame

Devil's Backbone

Lybaras

Gulf of
Fear

Mahrak
City of Decay

Resting Place of
Queen Khalida

Quatar
aces of Corpses

Charnal Valley

Doom
Glade
Swamp

The
Cursed
Jungle

Battle of
the Old Gods

Mount
Arachnos

Crater of the
Walking Dead

Temple of
Skulls

Lost Plateau

Rasetra

st Hold
Zorn,

KEY TO MAP OF THE LAND OF THE DEAD

🏛 Settlement		✕ Battle
⛩ Necropolis		⛲ Oasis
⛵ Fleet		🌴 Jungle
- - - Trade Route		🌋 Volcano
Tower Delineating Borders of Nehekhara		

◄ PROLOGUE ►

The Silver Pinnacle
(–15 Imperial Reckoning)

BONES RUBBED SOFTLY together within tattered scraps of armour as the skeletal sentries shifted aside their spears. Eyes burning with witch-fire, Arkhan the Black examined them for a moment, and then stepped through the archway, one fleshless hand resting on the pommel of his sword.

The place had belonged to the dwarfs once, and it showed in the design of the thing, though modifications had been made since. The majestic sturdiness of dwarf stone was consumed by the sumptuous decadence of lost Nehekhara. Draperies of Cathayan silk softened the stern arches of the corridor, as tile murals from Sartosa obscured the stones of the ceiling and fumes of exotic incense spilled into the halls from quiet alcoves. The statues of long-forgotten gods from dead lands squeezed into the spaces once reserved for the mighty stone forms of Valaya, Grimnir and Grungni, their marble eyes watching Arkhan's progress.

Dead men hovered along the path, toiling ceaselessly at labours that were beneath Arkhan's notice. Somewhere behind him, the vast doors of the hold crashed shut, causing the smooth rock of the path beneath his feet to tremble. From the outside, one would not even know that this place existed, unless one was familiar with the rune-markings of its former masters. In days long gone, the dwarfs had boasted of their dominion of these mountains and the gates would have been not only visible, but impressively so. But the dwarfs were no longer the masters here, and the hold's new mistress had a predilection for secrecy.

She had purged the routes and signs leading to this place in the intervening centuries since she had taken the throne. None knew the secret ways and means of Silver Pinnacle now, save those whom the hold's dark queen wished to know.

How Nagash had known was up for debate, given the circumstances. Gone were the days of shared counsel between Arkhan and his master. Dim though it was, the single guttering spark of humanity that remained to Arkhan – that made him who he was – served only to illuminate the rift between him and what Nagash had become in his time in the deep dark. Arkhan, fleshless as he was and driven by dark magic, was terrified of the nightmare thing that his lord had returned as: all brass bone and balefire, the Great Necromancer was a force unto himself, self-wrought and self-empowered, owing nothing to anyone or anything.

Nagash had sent him here to acquire the fealty of this place's mistress and her vassals, a task Arkhan was uniquely suited for, considering the connection between them. Or so Nagash had claimed. In truth, Arkhan thought it was because Nagash did not trust him. Not that he had any reason to. Arkhan had served Nagash well and faithfully for a stretch of time longer than his mortal life and had been rewarded with anni-hilation time and again.

In the thousand years since Nagash had last walked the land, Arkhan had tasted again the joys of independ-ence. He chafed now beneath Nagash's thumb, and he spun plots to free himself; all had failed, of course, or had never been implemented. Nagash was too strong and too in need of a lieutenant to let Arkhan return to Nehekhara and his conquests in the land of bones and dust.

Until such time as Nagash freed him, was destroyed, or was victorious, Arkhan the Black would serve him, however unwillingly.

The great stone gallery with its walls adorned by more murals and colourful tapestries from the lands of the Bretonni extended far ahead of him. It was lit by spe-cially constructed hooded braziers whose light set the shadows to dancing on the walls in shapes pleasing to the inhabitants.

Dark, low shapes prowled in the dark corners and alcoves, mewling softly amongst themselves in the debased tongue of the flesh-eaters. Above, clinging to the high ceiling like a living carpet of hairy flesh, were thousands of bats who watched Arkhan's progress and added their chittering to the background murmur of the ghouls' mewling. Arkhan ignored them all and moved steadily towards the raised dais at the end of the gallery.

The broad-boned skeletons of the citadel's former inhabitants waited for him there. They were arrayed in ranks before the dais, armoured and armed as they had been in life. Arkhan was not intimidated, but even so, the skeletal dwarfs gave him pause. His fingers tightened on the hilt of the black blade sheathed on his hip.

Perhaps it was a trap. He would not have put it past her. She would not bow her head to any creature, not even Nagash. The thought was a surprisingly pleasant one, and if he had still possessed the capacity to do so, Arkhan would have smiled. Instead, he simply stopped before the dais and its fearsome guardians and waited for the mistress of the mountain to receive him. As he waited, he studied the dais.

It sat at the apex of a set of circular steps that ringed around it, and was surmounted by great curtains of soft, dark silk that flowed down from somewhere far above like a black waterfall. Soft light lit the curtains from within, and the smell of strange spices and incense hung heavy on the air, hiding the stink of old blood that clung to the stones of the gallery. There was a cat as black as the shadows that clustered about the chamber lying on the steps, its yellow gaze fixed on him. As he waited, it rose languidly to its feet and trotted up the stairs and through the dark curtains.

There was a whisper of steel on the air and then a colony of dark shapes dropped from the bat-crowded ceiling of the gallery. Arkhan swept his sword from its sheath just in time to meet the downward stroke of a slim, curved blade. The liche stepped back, armour creaking, as more blades dug for his skull. He parried each blow with inhuman speed, ancient reflexes honed in countless battles carrying him through the tornado of steel that had descended on him.

Whispering voices reached him, sliding innocuously through the gallery inbetween the riotous meeting of swords. An audience of red-eyed courtiers had gathered in the balconies above, and they watched with ill-concealed delight as the liche defended himself.

He had expected a dozen perhaps or maybe twice that, at most. But there were hundreds of pale, hungry shapes looking down on him. Mostly women, but some men, scattered here and there. They were of all the races of man and none, bound as they were to a new, darker bloodline. Here was the army Nagash had sent him for: not the skeletons or the crouched, snivelling carrion-eaters, but this plague of nocturnal nobility.

They were as far removed from the vampires he remembered as he was from the gambler he had been centuries ago. Hundreds of red-eyed, blood-swilling predators, to be set upon the human who dared call himself emperor and who dared keep that which was Nagash's from him.

His attackers were red-eyed shadows, clad in dark jerkins and hoods. They moved with a fluid ease that part of him fondly recalled and envied. It was the ease of immortality, the suppleness that came with being separate from the world's ebb and flow and time's anchor. They danced around him like leaves in a strong wind, bending and twisting bonelessly around his half-hearted blows.

They made precise, lethal movements that would have killed a lesser being in a matter of moments. The gallery rang to the sound of steel on steel and agitated bats filled the air as Arkhan's mind raced. Was this indeed a trap? Or was it something more subtle… A test, or perhaps a game?

Arkhan caught a descending blade in his hand. Magically strengthened bone contracted and the sword blade cracked and shattered like an icicle. Its wielder blinked stupidly for a moment before leaping backwards to avoid Arkhan's own sword. The black blade hissed out, narrowly missing the vampire's midsection.

Another blade hammered down onto his shoulder. Arkhan barely registered the blow. The weapons were nothing more than common steel, and little danger to one as steeped in the raw essence of dark magic as he. They might as well have been hitting him with flowers. There was no need to even call upon his magics, save in the interest of cutting to the chase.

It was a game, then. He knew better than most how boredom crept up unawares and inexorably on the long-lived. Had it been her idea? Perhaps... She had been spiteful in life. There was no telling how much worse death had made her.

After all, look what it had done to him.

He stepped back, easily avoiding a blow that would have taken his head off, and lowered his sword. The vampires advanced cautiously. Arkhan flung out his free hand. Eldritch energies crackled, first in his palm and then beginning to crawl across his bony fingers. The vampires stopped.

'Enough,' a voice said. The curtains were swept aside by pale arms as a yellow-eyed woman looked down at Arkhan for a moment before indicating that he should approach. Arkhan closed his fingers and let his hand drop to his side. The vampires slunk aside and he stepped past them, sheathing his sword as he went.

'*You are either courageous or foolhardy to attack a representative of the Great Necromancer,*' he said, letting his words carry. '*Nagash does not forgive such insults.*' The whispering and chittering of the things in the shadows and on the balconies ceased at the mention of the name. The skeletal guard stepped aside in a rattle of bones and armour.

Arkhan started up the steps. The woman stepped aside, her robes swishing softly. She eyed him narrowly, the dark veins that ran beneath her pale flesh pulsing. Her lips curled, revealing delicate fangs. 'She has been expecting you,' she said softly.

'*Has she?*' Arkhan said. Looking at her, he recognised her dimly. One of the first of her mistress's get, turned back in those distant, happy days before Nehekhara had gone to dust. He didn't recall her name, only that she was a Cathayan, and had been a concubine, once.

'Or a messenger, at least,' the vampire said, shrugging.

'*Should I be insulted?*' Arkhan said.

'I thought you were dead,' a new voice said, from the throne at the centre of the dais, and the words held a familiar teasing note.

Arkhan bowed his head to the figure on the throne. '*I was,*' he said, his voice issuing from between his bony jaws like a spurt of smoke. The words hung on the air for a moment, echoing oddly.

'Yes… Several times over, I imagine,' the Queen of the Silver Pinnacle said, leaning forwards on her throne as he stepped inside. She gestured lazily to the woman. 'Leave us, Naaima.'

The vampire nodded and stepped past the curtains, letting them fall closed behind her. Arkhan looked at the creature that reclined regally in the throne, and the dim ghosts of ancient emotion stirred sluggishly. '*Neferata…*' he said. She was still as beautiful as he recalled, though that beauty no longer evoked the same desire. Even if it had, he no longer possessed the means to express it.

As pale and as cold as marble, her aristocratic features had sharpened from their former softness into something altogether more predatory. If Arkhan had been alive, he would have felt terror mingled with his desire, for Neferata of Lahmia was ruin in the flesh. Eyes like polished onyx stared unblinking at him and her great mass of night-black hair had been bound in thick serpentine plaits that coiled about her shoulders and across her décolletage. Despite the chill of the tomb, she wore nothing save a thin silk dress akin to the type she had worn when he had first seen her, so long ago. Golden armlets clung to her arms, and there were fine rings on her fingers and visible on her toes within her sandals; a belt of the finest wrought gold hugged her waist.

'Arkhan,' Neferata said. She gazed at him coolly, studying his emaciated shape with detachment. 'You are less than you once were.'

'*As are you,*' Arkhan said, gesturing to the stone floor. Neferata's eyes became slits, but Arkhan continued, '*You have gone from ruling a nation to hiding in a tomb.*'

'Hardly,' Neferata countered, leaning back. 'It is a fortress, dear Arkhan. *My* fortress.' She smiled. 'But it could be a tomb, depending on what message you came here to deliver.'

There was no sign as to whether the threat had registered save for the briefest flicker of Arkhan's eerie gaze. '*Nagash sends his regards,*' he said.

Neferata paused. There was no trace of the fear that the Great Necromancer's name had once engendered in the one-time Queen of Lahmia. Instead there was simply wariness. 'I was not aware that Nagash walked among us once more,' she said.

'*I have lost my flesh, Neferata, not my senses,*' Arkhan grated, his sword hilt creaking in his grip. '*You knew the day he awoke, as I did.*'

'Maybe not the day,' she said, smiling thinly. 'Have you rejoined him?'

It was Arkhan's turn to hesitate. '*Of course,*' he said.

'Why?' There was no malice in the question, only simple curiosity.

'*Why did you set your dogs on me?*' he countered.

She chuckled. 'To see what was left of you,' she said. 'To see whether you were merely a husk animated by Nagash's will, or something more...'

'*I should have thought Bel Aliad would have taught you better,*' Arkhan said.

'Oceans of time, dear Arkhan, have passed over that moment,' Neferata said, idly examining her fingers. 'Things – people – change, even those like ourselves who are, by definition, changeless.'

'*So I see.*'

'What does Nagash want?' she said.

'*What he always wants: servants.*' Arkhan said it flatly. There would be no lying to Neferata. She was too cunning for that and Arkhan had little reason to hedge. '*Vampire servants,*' he added.

'I would have thought his experiences with poor, unfortunate W'soran would have taught him better than that,' she said.

Arkhan made a grinding sound. W'soran had been a greedy fool, and Arkhan had paid for the vampire's overconfidence more than once during the war against Alcadizzar. '*I tried to find the sorcerer. He stole something of Nagash's and fled in the last days of Nagashizzar.*'

'He's dead,' Neferata said bluntly, 'and good riddance to him, the fool.' She sighed and met Arkhan's eerie gaze unflinchingly. 'Servants, is it?'

He inclined his head. She snorted. 'And I am supposed to – what? – throw open my gates and yield my divine right to his majesty, the King of Bones?'

'*If not, I am to take it by force,*' Arkhan said.

'Do you think you could?'

'*Yes,*' he said.

Neferata rose smoothly from her throne and pressed her hands to his chest. Her fingers rose, tracing the contours of his skull with delicate caresses. 'Oh, my sweet, savage Arkhan... You would, wouldn't you?'

'*As swiftly and as surely as I destroyed Bel Aliad.*'

She made a pouting expression and sniffed. 'Yes. And wasn't that a terrible waste.'

'*For you,*' he said.

'For both of us,' she said.

'*The dead can never rule the living, Neferata. They can only destroy them,*' Arkhan said, in a tone of one who has no wish to re-hash an old argument. She snorted and a slip of laughter escaped her.

'Yes, I know,' she said.

Arkhan paused. '*You have changed, then...*' he said. Bony fingertips brushed a strand of dark hair out of her face. Her own hand came up instantly and swatted his aside. The fingers of her other hand pressed deep into the metal of his ancient cuirass and suddenly he was flying backwards, out through the curtains and down the stairs.

Arkhan picked himself up slowly as Neferata stepped through the curtains, his sword in her hand. Automatically he glanced at his now-empty sheath and then up as she sprang towards him, aiming a blow at his skull. Arkhan twisted desperately, avoiding the strike. The sword crashed into the stone, cracking it. Neferata whipped the blade up and around with a skill he had not known that she possessed, nearly taking his head off as he bent back beneath the blow.

He backed away, raising his hands. She hissed, exposing inch-long fangs. Her form blurred as she moved, faster than the human eye could see. Fortunately,

Arkhan was no longer human. He slapped aside the blade and wrapped his fingers around her throat. She dropped his sword and suddenly a panther was raking its hind-claws across his torso. Surprised, he released the creature. Neferata resumed her shape and her blow caught him in the chest, rocking him back.

Magic crackled on the tips of his fingers. Nagash had taught him those first halting, clumsy spells but in the centuries since, Arkhan had become a sorcerer in his own right. Death and the loss of flesh had done remarkable things for his concentration. Neferata hesitated, a smile curling at the edges of her lips.

Snarls and shrieks suddenly echoed from every corner of the gallery. Vampires flung themselves at the liche. Pale fists and hooked talons tore at him and Arkhan spat hoarse syllables as he unleashed his magics. A vampire screeched as it was engulfed in black fire and reduced to a charred skeleton. He swept his arms out, creating a wall of flame between him and them, driving the creatures back in a spitting, hissing mass. But not all of the creatures retreated; through the flames came a black, feline shape, yellow-eyed and snarling.

The cat smashed into him, its claws raking his mouldy clothes and scraping bone. As he grabbed for it, its shape expanded, lengthening and stretching with a sound like butchery in reverse, until the vampire called Naaima was gripping his skull between two deceptively powerful palms. He felt his skull flex in her grip and prepared to flense the meat from her bones with a word. But, as suddenly as she had attacked, the vampire was again a cat, which eeled out of his clutches and padded away. Arkhan spun. Neferata lay sprawled on the steps, watching him as the cat climbed into her arms.

'Impressive,' Neferata said, stroking the cat. She

quirked an eyebrow mockingly as he stalked towards her. A dim flicker of anger pulsed through him, but quickly faded. He relaxed, letting the threads of magic he had bound to him unravel.

'Was that another test of my worth?' he grated, gesturing to his sword where it lay on the floor. It shuddered and shot towards his hand. He sheathed it with a flourish. Neferata clapped.

'No,' she said. 'It was a reminder of your place.'

Arkhan said nothing, waiting for her to continue. She sniffed. 'This is my place of power, liche. Not yours and certainly not Nagash's. He is old and brittle and not what he once was–'

'He is more,' Arkhan interjected.

Neferata paused. 'Perhaps… The fact remains, he holds no power here.'

'He will not accept that,' Arkhan said, looming over her. Neferata gazed up at him, unconcerned.

'He will have to,' she said, rising, still holding the cat. 'Neferata serves no man, whether he's dead or alive.'

'He will command you, as he commands me,' Arkhan said, his eyes blazing. *'You will have no choice…'*

'I have defied Nagash's will before,' Neferata said. 'I have defied and defeated his servants and I will do so again to hold on to what is mine.'

Arkhan stood silently, watching her. Then, in a whisper, he said, *'Tell me…'*

✦ ONE ✦

Lahmia, the City of the Dawn
(–1170 Imperial Reckoning)

Lahmia burned and Neferata ran.

Quicker than thought, with no more weight than a shadow, she ran, and the city died around her, one street at a time. Black smoke weighed down the air and hungry flames crawled across the stone and clay and thatch. There was an ache in her chest, though whether it was from the destruction of all that she had built or the dagger that had so recently been thrust into her heart by Alcadizzar she couldn't say.

Behind her, hooves thundered suddenly in pursuit. She heard the calls of the riders; they thought her easy sport, one more lost woman in a fallen city. One more woman to be served as always happened when cities fell. Pale lips skinned back, revealing teeth like razors, and dark eyes flashed. Rage, sudden and overwhelming, hammered at her temples, and she skidded to a stop, dust and smoke curling around her slender frame.

21

Clad in ragged silks and ruined armour, she spun to face the riders, fingers hooked like the talons of a lioness and her jaws wide, her fangs flashing in the light of the fires that curled and crackled around her. The lead horseman jerked back on his reins, his eyes widening in surprise. There were three more behind him, clamouring for a share of the spoils.

Then, in a whip-crack of startled air, she was moving. She swung low, letting a spear skid over her shoulder. It scored a trail of sparks across the back-plate of her iron cuirass as she drove her shoulder into the horse's chest. It bugled in surprise and reared, hooves gouging the air. Snarling, Neferata sliced open the animal's exposed belly with her claws. The horse screamed and toppled, carrying its rider with it. The man's screams joined those of his mount as he was crushed beneath its weight, but Neferata didn't stay to listen.

One foot on the dying animal's thrashing hindquarter was enough to propel her into the air. She swam through the smoke, piercing it like a stone from a sling. Her hands and feet caressed the long skull of the next horse as her weight broke its neck and knocked it down. The rider drew the curved blade at his side as the animal fell and her palm caught him in the jaw. Bone splintered and burst at her touch and he catapulted backwards as she snatched the sword from his hand.

A spear skipped across her pale cheek, releasing a trickle of black, sour blood, and she shrieked, battering the weapon aside with her new sword. She twisted and spun as the horseman charged past her, and caught the blade of his companion's spear as it dipped for her belly. She wrenched it and its wielder from the saddle and slammed him to the ground. Stamping on his throat, she yanked the spear from his grip and sent it slicing through the air towards the remaining horseman.

His horse bucked and kicked as it fled past her, back the

way it had come, dragging the body of its rider behind it. Neferata touched the wound on her cheek. It was already closing. Hunger flared through her, causing her vision to dim and redden at the edges.

She was tired. And hungry as well; she hadn't fed in what felt like days. Behind her, she heard the jangling rattle-call of a ram's horn and the stomp of marching feet. The riders hadn't been alone. She looked at the sword in her hand and her grip tightened. She had time. They were not so close that they could catch her. She could escape.

Or she could fight them. She could fight all of them. They would never find her, never catch her. She could kill them all, one by one, until they fled the city. She closed her eyes, imagining it. Then she snorted and shook her head.

'No,' she said. 'No, I couldn't could I?' Not alone at least. Alone, she was nothing more than a monster. The word pricked her like a hornet's sting and she growled. No, she needed to flee. To rebuild and regain what she had lost here, somewhere else.

A moan caught her attention. She swayed towards the first horseman she had downed. The animal was dead, but its rider lived, albeit crushed. He groaned and shoved at the beast feebly. One arm was pinned beneath the horse's weight, and his face was turning purple. Something in him had been broken, she knew. She could smell it rising off him like the sweet tang of roasted pork.

Neferata stabbed the sword down into the ground and sank into a crouch. The rider's eyes bulged as she crawled slowly across the horse's body towards him, her eyes gleaming like twin black suns. She drank in the rank musk of his fear as she reached for him, the tips of her fingers caressing his cheeks and chin. He was barely more than a boy.

Hunger spiked and her grip tightened. He squealed as she jerked his head to the side and exposed his pulsing throat.

Neferata laughed as she buried her fangs into the sweetness of him. The tang of his blood filled her nostrils, inundating her senses...

The Worlds Edge Mountains
(–800 Imperial Reckoning)

THE DREAM-RECOLLECTION evaporated, taking with it the memory of heat and blood. Its remnants were brushed aside by something cold and dark that reached out of the shadowy place between waking and sleeping for her. It was malevolence carried on musty wings of alien intent. There was a sound like crows on a battlefield in the dusk and a harsh whining moan that seemed to echo from everywhere and nowhere.

She saw the Corpse Geometries – though she did not know how she knew their name – rise and expand across the soul of everything, caging the rebellious *ka* and keeping them safe and bound from outer predation. All was silent. All was perfect.

Come, Neferata... Come, Queen of Lahmia!

Cold talons clutched at her, seeking to draw her back down into the dark of sleep. The foul taste of grave-soil filled her mouth and a voice like needles scoring bone spoke, scratching a litany of cold fire across her mind.

Neferata awoke.

Her eyes opened and she grunted. Gone was the sensation of being dragged down into unknown depths, replaced by the sting of cold and the gnawing ache of the bloodthirst. Whiteness filled her vision, gleaming in the moonlight. She rose to her feet, scattering the blanket of snow that had covered her and protected her from the harsh light of day. She wore white furs and her hair was bound back in a single thick plait that tumbled down her back like a glossy black serpent.

Neferata had not changed much since the fall of Lahmia. Indeed, change was now almost anathema to her. Her every fibre yearned for constancy, for the world to cease its inexorable march. But she had learned to her cost that to attempt to hold time frozen was to court destruction.

That was one of the reasons that things had ended as they had in Lahmia.

For a moment, she indulged in her memories, letting the illusion of peace drift across her mind. She could see the white stone of Lahmia's walls and feel the cool sea-breeze rolling in off the harbour. She could smell the exotic smells and hear the clamour of the Red Silk District, where men of a dozen nations revelled between voyages. She could hear the soft music of the celebrations held for the good and the great in the District of the Golden Lotus. She could taste the strong eastern wine which was poured into clay cups that held stubbornly to all of the tastes that had gone before. She could feel the pleasure-pain of the *hixa*'s sting.

The City of the Dawn had been the greatest and most beautiful of the cities of Nehekhara, guided by wise, undying kings into a golden age. She had been of an age, in life, to recall when kings lived for centuries before infirmity set in. Her own span had been measured in decades before Arkhan the Black had come to Lahmia. She had been the Daughter of Moon, then, and queen. For many before her, the latter had been, at best, a ceremonial title. The Queens of Lahmia were supposed to be removed from the mundane matter of politics, but Neferata had been a different sort of queen.

The king had been, at best, an erratic ruler and much of the burden of governing Lahmia day-to-day had fallen on her slim shoulders. It had been a burden she relished.

Arkhan had come in chains, with his heart cleft in two. Paralysed and trapped inside his form, Arkhan the Black had been dragged into Lahmia in the Hour of the Dead by Lamashizzar, her king and husband. The last of Nagash's immortals and the only one to survive that final, bloody war that saw the Great Necromancer flee into sour northern lands, much like the ones she now found herself in.

Lamashizzar had desired to rip the immortal's secrets from him by force and he had succeeded, to a degree. She looked down at her hand, noting the black veins that crawled beneath the pale skin. But she had learned so much more. And when that knowledge had threatened to destroy her, Arkhan had saved her life, though he knew it not.

She thought of the immortal, his lean face swimming to the surface of her mind. He had not been quite handsome, but arresting nonetheless. The image wavered and dispersed, leaving a skull in its place. Change took them all, in the end. Arkhan was no longer the being he had been. She thought of when she had last seen him, in the burning streets of Bel Aliad. A walking corpse, clad in black armour and red robes, dealing death with every step he took.

Arkhan's declaration of war on the living had been one of many things which had necessitated her abandonment of the caliphates for the primitive lands of the savage north. She looked around.

Trees surrounded her, clawing arthritically at the dark sky. Winter in the mountains was an ugly thing, she thought. Then, winter was ugly everywhere, but perhaps especially here, in these rough, wild hills, beneath the ghostly light of the black sun. Neferata turned north, her eyes searching.

The black sun was still there, as it had been every day and night for close to a decade now. It was not the real sun. Instead, it was more like an afterimage, a blotch of darker-than-dark, burned into the skin of the world. It rose at night in mockery of the moon and burned black over the mountains. Neferata felt the cold fire of its rays as it hung bloated and hungry for light below the moon, like some abominable beacon, drawing her towards it. At first, she had tried to resist. In Sartosa, it had been easy. She could ignore its subtle caress across the surface of her soul. But here and now, there was no escape.

It plucked at her thoughts, infiltrating them. In her dreams, she felt its gaze and in her waking moments it blazed at her from its northern nest. It called, and Neferata came. No matter how much she might wish otherwise. No one else could see it. It called to her and her alone, though she could not say why; it was a distant whisper that drifted just at the edge of her hearing, as annoying in its way as an incessant shout.

Angered, she looked south, towards Nehekhara, and a pang clawed at her chest. She reached beneath the heavy white furs she wore and let her fingertips drift over the spot where Alcadizzar's dagger had entered her flesh, seeking her heart. There was no scar there to mar her marble flesh, but she could still feel the traitor's blade.

Yes, she had been a queen once, centuries ago. Queen and goddess of a vibrant land, she had asked so little of her people and given so much in return and been rewarded with treachery and pain. Once, she had thought to go back, to re-take what was rightfully hers.

That was impossible now. Only the dead ruled Nehek-hara, and though she was not truly alive, Neferata was anything but dead.

No, Nehekhara – Lahmia – was dead and dust and there was nothing for her there, nothing but fast-fading memories of a different world and a different woman.

'Do you smell it?' a soft voice asked. Neferata glanced at the woman rising from the snow nearby and blinked in momentary confusion. Then she tilted her head and tasted the wind. Her eyes widened.

'Blood, freshly spilled,' the former Queen of Lahmia breathed. No wonder she had been dreaming. She stretched, thrusting her hands towards the moon. She felt no soreness or stiffness, even hungry as she was, but old habits were wont to die hard. She luxuriated in the feeling of powerful muscles pulling against one another. As a mortal, she had never truly indulged the limits of her body, but in the centuries since the tainted blood of Arkhan the Black had mingled with an assassin's poison in her veins, Neferata had come to derive a certain satisfaction from the raw physicality that immortality had conferred upon her.

She could run faster and longer than any beast and her strength was as that of the great saurians of the Southlands. She could follow the beat of a man's heart and track the sweet scent of his blood for miles. And all she required in return was what any predator required. Blood. Dollop or deluge, the blood was the life, and Neferata wanted to live. She looked at the other woman and said, 'Where?'

'To the north, I think,' the woman said, brushing snow from her shoulders. Like Neferata she wore heavy furs, though she no more felt the cold than her mistress. 'The cold dulls my senses, however,' she added hesitantly, with the wary modesty of a servant with a temperamental master.

'It dulls all of our senses, Naaima,' Neferata said, stroking the other immortal's cheek. 'But dulled or not, we will follow them. It has been too long since we last fed. Wake the others.' Naaima caught her hand and held it for a moment. Then she nodded and set about thrusting her hands into the snow to dislodge it and reveal four more huddled shapes. One by one the vampires snapped alert as the smell of blood invigorated them.

Neferata watched them awaken, a familiar sense of possessiveness rising in her. Each of them was a part of her in some way. They were all blood of her blood, having been gifted with her blood-kiss in the centuries since Lahmia had fallen. There had been more once, but these were all that remained. Neferata grimaced and turned away, looking south once more. It had been weeks since they had seen any sign of their pursuers. Perhaps they had given up.

No. Not her, not the little hawk. Neferata repressed a growl. Nonetheless, they had been wandering in the mountains for weeks now. With the coming of winter, the hills were barren of sustenance, and it was only their inhuman vitality that had kept the little group moving. But now, there was blood on the air.

'It smells like the greatest feast our father ever laid out, Khaled,' one of the vampires squeaked, her eyes wide as she stripped the snow from her glossy hair. Anmar bin Muntasir had been young when Neferata had delivered her up into immortality, only seventeen at most. Sometimes, Neferata regretted having done so, though she couldn't say why.

'Hunger plays funny tricks, sister,' Khaled al Muntasir replied. Anmar's brother had been given the blood-kiss within moments of his sister. Older by a decade before he had ceased aging, he was slender and handsome, and he had taken to an immortal's life with a relish that was almost unsettling. He sniffed the air and let his palm fall onto the pommel of the slim Arabyan blade hanging from his hip. His dark eyes found Neferata's and he smiled. 'My lady,' he said, inclining his head with courtly grace.

Neferata smiled, amused. She glanced at the final two members of her small coterie. Rasha bin Wasim, like Khaled and Anmar, was Arabyan, though she was a daughter of the desert rather than the cities as the siblings were and taciturn where they were talkative. Lupa Stregga, in contrast, had been a native of Sartosa in life. Where the others were dark, she was fair, and where they were subtle, she was loud. Stregga inhaled the air with a snort and reached into the snow to retrieve her sword. It was a short-bladed chopping thing, favoured by the sailors of her native land. 'Smells like *durra* to me,' she said, looking at Neferata. 'Then, it's been a dog's age since I've seen one.'

'What do they taste like?' Anmar said, looking at the taller woman. 'And what's a durra?'

'The little under-men,' Stregga said with a shrug. 'And I never thought to try and take a bite.'

'Probably wise,' Naaima said. 'The *dawi* are not men. There is stone in their blood.' She looked at Neferata. 'But it is not just dawi blood we smell, I think...'

'No, it isn't,' Neferata said. She licked her lips. She looked at the black sun and then away. The others looked at her eagerly, waiting on her command. They trembled like hounds straining at the leash, and hunger made their facades slip slightly, revealing the beast beneath the skin. Neferata knew that she was no different. Her human beauty had been replaced by something altogether more feline.

'We hunt,' she hissed.

They bounded through the snow like flickering shadows, shaking off the sluggishness of daylight torpor. The scent of blood curled and splashed through the air, teasing them on. Neferata took the lead, running wolf-swift through the trees. As she ran, she drew the short, heavy blade that was sheathed at her side.

She had been taught the art of the blade by Abhorash himself. The champion of the City of the Dawn had been a man of few words, but he was an unparallelled swordsman and a warrior without peer. Neferata could not match him – she knew of none who could – but thanks to his teaching she was better with a blade than many hardened warriors walking the world today.

She had not thought of Abhorash in many years. Not since his betrayal in Araby. The thought still sent a flush of rage spurting through her. They had all betrayed her, Ushoran and W'soran and Abhorash.

Every man betrayed her, in the end. Lamashizzar had tried to take her power from her, and reduce her to an ornamental queen. Arkhan had given her immortality and then died, again, before he could share it with her. And Alcadizzar had turned on her, and turned the other great cities against Lahmia.

A throaty laugh caused her to glance aside. Khaled had his own blade out and he was keeping pace with her, his eyes glowing with a ravenous hunger. The only man she had given the blood-kiss since Bel Aliad. She hoped she wouldn't regret it. Neferata leapt, her sandals scraping against bark as she ran up the trunk of the tree. The others followed. There were roads open to vampires that were denied to any other creature save birds or vermin.

She leapt from branch to branch, tasting the wind as she went. Sounds joined the smell. Weapons clashing and the screams of the dying rode the night-wind. Hairy shapes charged through the trees below, snorting and growling. Neferata stopped, perching in the crook of a branch. Her eyes narrowed.

She had encountered the twisted beast-men only once before, but she recognised them easily enough. They were hideous amalgamations of man and beast, with the worst traits of both. They stank of a dark corruption, though their blood was palatable enough.

The creatures spilled into a clearing, launching themselves with berserk abandon at their opponents. Neferata realised that they were seeing the final bloody moments of an ambush. She saw small, stocky forms littering the snow.

'Dawi,' Naaima hissed in answer to Neferata's unasked question.

Neferata peered closer at the broad bodies, nodding shallowly. Where had they come from? The dawi were dwellers in the depths. They rarely trod the open earth, and only then when it was absolutely necessary. Whatever they had been doing, wherever they had been going, they weren't going there any more. The ambush was done.

A large beast brayed in triumph and brandished its gore-encrusted axe at the dark ceiling of trees overhead. It was a massive creature, all simian muscle and taut sinew, with a belly like a stove and splay-hooves that ground the snow underfoot into slush. Scraps of armour and badly tanned hide struggled to contain its girth as it stooped and jerked the body of its opponent into the frosty air. All around it, similar scenes played out as its companions stooped to scavenge from the bodies that still steamed in the chill mountain air.

The dwarfs had fought bravely, but in the end, had been too few. The beasts' attack had been hard and wild, seemingly driven as they were by the talons of a desperate winter. Hunger gnawed at their bellies; some had already fallen to filling their gullets, slicing open the fine mail and jerkins worn by the dwarfs and burying their snouts in the tough flesh beneath. Others fought one another over the scraps and silver trinkets scoured from the bodies.

Wolf-teeth snapped behind goatish lips as the pack-leader drove back those who drew too close; it swung its axe wildly, and stamped its hooves as it tried to keep the body of its most recent opponent for itself.

The dwarf coughed and blood spattered his beard. Nonetheless, he grabbed the hand that held him and squeezed. Chaos-born bone popped and cracked and the beast screamed in shock and pain, releasing its hold. The dwarf fell heavily, his armour clattering. Blindly, he groped through the snow for a weapon. Talons speared through his hair and sank into his scalp and he was jerked backwards and sent hurtling spine-first into a crooked tree.

The dwarf groaned as he collapsed into the snow. Dwarfs were harder than most creatures, but even stone cracked if you hit it hard enough. He coughed again and tried to push himself upright. Blood drenched the dwarf's limbs and stained his armour, and the heady scent of it filled Neferata's nostrils as she looked down. The beastman stalked forwards, cradling its broken hand and swiping at the air with its axe. The others crowded around it, baying like eager hounds.

'Come on then,' the dwarf spat hoarsely, jerking upright, a rock in his hand. Pushing himself onto his feet, he hefted the rock. 'I'll match you stone for stone,' he said weakly. It was an empty boast, Neferata knew. The dwarf was dying on his feet, and his blood had turned the snow pink. The beastman roared and launched itself into an awkward charge, its axe cocked back for a skull-crushing blow.

Neferata moved.

She struck the tree above the dwarf's head and catapulted towards the beastman. Steel flashed and the beastman stumbled to a stop, blinking quizzically. Behind it, Neferata had landed in a crouch. One arm was stretched out, the crude steel sword held tight in her pale fingers. She glanced over her shoulder and her eyes met the dwarf's. The moment was broken by the hiss of hot blood sliding off the tip of the sword to *plop* into the snow. The dwarf's eyes rolled up into his head and he pitched forwards, unconscious at last.

The beastman made a curious sound as its head rolled off its shoulders to land in the snow near the unconscious dwarf. The other creatures drew back, whining and growling. Neferata rose smoothly to her feet, her arm still extended. She swept her gaze across the gathered beastmen and smiled. 'Take them,' she breathed.

A large beastman howled and lunged for her, swinging a spiked club. Something crashed down atop its head and shoulders, driving it snout-first into the snow inches from Neferata. Khaled rose, wrenching his sword from the pulverised skull of the twitching beastman. Black-haired and bearded, his hawk-like features twisted into a fierce expression as he gave a bark of laughter.

The remaining beastmen hesitated, their nostrils flaring. Snow drifted down from the branches above. A beast screeched as a figure dropped down beside it, cleaving through its shoulder and chest. Naaima spun, jerking her sword free of the dying beast and bringing it crashing around into the neck of another. She danced among them for a moment, leaving carnage in her wake, before she sprang to Neferata's side, blood coating her bare, pale arms to the shoulders.

'They smell foul and taste worse, I'd wager,' she hissed, her dark eyes narrowing.

'Needs must, when the gods demand, Naaima,' Neferata said, bringing her blade up and letting it extend in front of her. She grasped the hilt with both hands and chuckled. 'Their blood is red enough, regardless.'

'It's not the bottle, it's the vintage, Lady Neferata,' Khaled said, stepping to join them as the beasts pawed the snow and gathered their courage. He flung off his furs, revealing a tight cuirass of banded and beaten metal over a jerkin of thin, brightly coloured silk. He spun his sword with a flick of his wrist, his eyes meeting those of each of the beastmen in turn.

'And what vintage would these abominations be, Khaled?' Naaima said.

'Something unsubtle and northern,' Khaled said, grinning insouciantly at her.

'Silence,' Neferata said, and the pair fell quiet. She ran a finger along the thin runnel cut into the length of her blade, where the blood had collected. Delicately she licked the tip of her finger and grimaced. 'Sour,' she said.

'Needs must, Neferata,' Naaima murmured, her tone only vaguely teasing.

Neferata shot a glare at Naaima and then swung the sword, splattering the nearest beastmen with blood. 'Needs must,' she said. 'Twelve left.'

The beastmen had got over their confusion. They started forwards in a howling, stamping mass, drawing courage from numbers. Something snarled and sprang from the snow to the side, bringing down a squalling, goat-headed monster. The desert-leopard's fiery coat stood out in the snow as it shrieked a challenge at the beastmen before it casually bit the top of the goat-thing's head off.

'Ha! Cheat!' Stregga snarled, springing from a tree to wrap her long arms around a simian brute's head. She gave it a vicious twist as her feet touched the snow, snapping the creature's spine and nearly jerking it from its back. She finished the job with all the efficiency of a fish-wife and shook the bloody spinal column at the leopard. 'Cheat, Rasha! No points for you!' she said, and the leopard snarled in reply. Neferata smiled slightly at the sight of the beast. The changing of skins came less easily to those who had accepted her blood-kiss than it did herself or Naaima. It had taken Rasha almost a century to learn how to do it without agony or mistake, and only because Neferata had tutored her relentlessly in the practice. The others still couldn't; not even Khaled, quick study that he was. He might learn in time, if he survived.

A beastman spun and swung a crude hammer at Stregga's head. With a wild cry, Anmar interposed herself. Her sword pierced the hammer-wielder's gut and lifted it off its cloven feet, hurling it backwards where it landed limply near the leopard. Anmar panted slightly, her body shaking from blood-hunger and exertion.

'Nine now I think you'll find, my queen,' Khaled said, looking at Neferata, who said nothing. She and the others glided forwards. The six vampires surrounded the nine beasts, closing in on them from all sides. The battle that followed was brief and bloody. In moments, every beast was dead and their foul blood warmed the bellies of their killers.

'Tastes like goat,' Stregga said, sucking blood from a dollop of hairy flesh. Her eyes narrowed. 'Or like what I recall goat tasting like.'

'It tastes foul enough without you adding to it,' Rasha, now returned to her own shape, snapped, letting a beastman fall from her grip to thump into the pink-stained snow. She wiped the back of her hand across her jaw, smearing more blood than she removed.

'Needs must, children,' Neferata said, looking down at the crumpled form of the dwarf. He was breathing shallowly, and his blood smelled strangely acrid, like hot metal on a forge fire. She prodded his body with her sword, and he groaned.

'Tough little creature,' Khaled murmured, sidling up beside her. He cleaned his blade with a hank of beard torn from one of the dead dwarfs. 'Still… he won't last long out here, not like that.'

'No,' Neferata said, not looking at him. She prodded the dwarf again. The dawi had not been a common sight in Nehekhara. Indeed, she had not seen one at all until many years later, in Araby. And that one had been dead and stuffed as part of a caliph's trophy room. This one did not seem much healthier.

'Kill him,' Naaima said as she handed Neferata the top of a beastman's skull, stripped free of flesh, inverted and filled with blood. Neferata drank deeply, emptying the makeshift bowl in moments. She made a face as she handed the bowl back to Naaima.

The Cathayan vampire had strung up several of the bodies and was systematically draining them of every drop of their filthy blood, and collecting it in upturned shields and helmets collected from the dwarf dead. Anmar was busy filling the heretofore-empty water-skins the group had brought. Blood congealed quickly, especially in the cold, but a few stones properly heated and dropped into the skins would bring the blood back to something approaching edibility. It was a stop-gap measure at best – drinking old blood could be as debilitating as going too long without fresh blood.

Still, there was no telling how long they would be in these mountains. Neferata sighed and looked at Naaima. 'It seems a waste,' she said.

'We cannot drink from one of his kind,' Naaima said.

'That we know of,' Khaled said, squatting beside the dwarf. Naaima glared at him. He returned her glare with a raised eyebrow. 'Have we ever tried?' he said.

'Feel free, brother,' Anmar said. 'Show us whether your bravery extends to your stomach.'

Khaled grimaced as the others laughed. Neferata sank gracefully to her haunches. 'Enough. We must go. I will deal with him.'

She raised her sword in both hands and pressed the tip of the blade to the point where the dwarf's skull met his spine. It would be a merciful act – quick and clean. He groaned again, and muttered something in the language of his people. The words crashed together like rocks in a basket, unintelligible and meaningless.

All save one.

She did not understand it. Could not, for she did not know what it meant or to what it might refer. Nonetheless, it strummed a chord within her, and her spirit shuddered in its sheath of cold flesh.

Neferata rose smoothly to her feet, her face stiff and expressionless. She turned north, and the black sun blazed as if in answer to the question that swam to the surface of her mind. The others fell silent, sensing her disquiet.

'What are you?' she muttered, half expecting an

answer. As usual, none was forthcoming.

'Neferata,' Naaima asked, reaching out to touch her mistress's shoulder. 'What is it? What did he say?'

'*Mourkain*,' Neferata said, repeating the dwarf's word. She said it again, tasting the dark edges of it. 'Mourkain,' she whispered. And the black sun blazed with darkling joy.

⤙ TWO ⤚

The Shark Straits
(−1163 Imperial Reckoning)

The storm lashed the sea with whips of lightning. The sea, in its turn, did its best to return the favour, heaving and thrusting ever higher. The ship rode the thrashing waves as best as it could, but the hull groaned with something like agony and the sails were ragged strips of cloth.

The captain pressed his back to the mast and extended his sword. Rain pounded down, swamping the ship. It ran down his arm and across the blade, joining the ankle-deep water that splashed across the deck. The helm was unmanned, but he had other concerns. Namely, the two slim shapes that swayed easily across the deck despite the pitch and yaw. Eyes like dark lamps fixed on him hungrily and he swiped the sword through the rain, trying to force them back.

'Your service is to be commended, captain, but the time has come for a parting of ways,' Neferata said, glaring at the last living man on the ship through a veil of stringy, soaked hair. Blood stained her arms to the elbow and her pale shape was marred by the filth of the lower decks. The captain, a

Cathayan, shouted something defiant. Neferata's eyes flickered to the side.

'He is damning us to the six hells,' Naaima said.

'That's what I thought he said,' Neferata said. She was pleased in an almost child-like fashion with her facility with languages, but the Cathayan tongue was more complex than any she had ever encountered. 'Well, he's a bit late for that,' she said, snapping her fangs together.

The ship was bound for Araby, loaded down with silks and steel to trade for spices and slaves. In the years since her flight from Lahmia, Neferata had done well in Cathay. Too well, in fact. The powers entrenched there had not taken kindly to the former queen's predatory attentions.

If there was one thing that her final confrontation with Alcadizzar had taught her, it was when to become the memory of a thorn, rather than the thorn itself. The subtle politics of the east, as compared to those she had employed in Nehekhara, had been eye-opening. The great bureaucracy was composed of rings of power, each smaller than the next, spider-webs of steel influence and precision. Any man could be king, but to be the one who controlled the king – who controlled all kings – that was true power.

Unfortunately, those lessons had come too late to do her much good in the lands of the Dragon-Emperor. Now she was fleeing again, a fact which rubbed at her soul like a bit of grit caught beneath armour. Still, needs must...

The first absent crew member had been blamed on the sea and a sudden swell. The second had been blamed on the same, with the addition of drunkenness to explain such misfortune occurring twice in one voyage. By the third, the crew had been stalking the holds, weapons clutched in their sweaty hands. They had heard the stories of the gangshi – the stiff corpses that walked – that had come out of the capital in the preceding years, and like all sailors, were superstitious enough to believe those stories.

Neferata idly stroked the still healing spot on her belly where a bilge-hook had entered as she slept. The storm had been a gift from the gods, blacking the sky and setting the crew's minds to other, more pressing dangers. The Shark Straits were visible, and the storm seemed determined to drive the ship right into their jagged teeth.

'A parting of ways,' Naaima echoed. Her face was as expressionless as a porcelain mask. Neferata knew her hand-maiden well enough to see the storm of emotions hidden beneath the mask. As practical as she was, as ruthless as she could be, she lacked the stomach for slaughter. Killing had never sat well with Naaima. She preferred to sup in modera-tion, taking gentle nourishment from suitably docile partners or pets. Neferata recognised the inherent longevity of such a practice, but something wilder stirred in her at times, as now.

It was not quite hunger. Rather, it was a savage frenzy, a slaughter-lust that bubbled beneath her calm façade for months or years and then suddenly erupted. It was not only blood that she required; she needed death and pain and the screams of her prey as she clutched their throats between her teeth.

With a wildcat scream, she lunged through the sheets of rain that separated her from the Cathayan captain. With a yell he swung his sword, but Naaima was there, smashing his sword-arm to the mast and pinning it there. Neferata crashed against him, his armour digging into her flesh as her fingertips dug into his. He thrashed in a pleasing manner as she grabbed his topknot and yanked his head back, exposing his throat. She purred in pleasure as her fangs sank into his unshaven throat. Blood exploded into her mouth and the purr turned to a snarl as she gulped at the hot flow. His body gave a spasm and she stepped back, gesturing imperiously for Naaima to take her place at the still-gushing spigot.

The ship rolled beneath her feet as she glided towards the deck rail. The Shark Straits rose dark and hungry before her. The ship would run aground on them, and the scavengers said to lurk in their shadow would descend on the wreck when the storm had subsided. And from there, the caliphates of Araby awaited.

Neferata spread her arms over her head and laughed gleefully as the storm battered the ship towards the waiting rocks...

The Worlds Edge Mountains
(−800 Imperial Reckoning)

THE FIRE CRACKLED, casting twisted shadows across the snow. The flames rose like grasping hands. In her head, bones clattered across still vistas on a ceaseless, remorseless march. Words spattered across the surface of her mind, blotting out her thoughts. Eyes of green balefire stared at her from out of the heart of the fire, bright with predatory intent. They held her and pulled her into the dark. It was the needle-on-bone voice again, digging into her consciousness.

Neferata... The dead are stirring in their ancient tombs. They will rise and march across the world and force time itself to stop in its tracks...

Neferata...

'Neferata,' Naaima said.

Neferata blinked and her snarl rippled across the clearing. 'What is it?' she snapped, whirling on her handmaiden. Naaima stood her ground.

'The dwarf is awake,' she said.

Neferata shook aside the strange thoughts that clung

to her consciousness like cobwebs and looked over at the dwarf. He was a peculiar looking creature – all broad muscle and hair, wrapped up in armour more fine than that of even the kings of Nehekhara and leathers more skilfully tanned than any done by the hands of men. Such skill could be put to good use by the right hands. She stalked towards him and dropped down beside him.

She fingered one of the talismans attached to his armour and hissed as something snagged her. She sucked on her fingers and eyed the shiny silver amulet balefully. The dwarf groaned and his eyes cracked open. '*Bugrit,*' he said, stubby fingers reaching up to prod the crude bandage wrapped around his head. More bandages covered his arms and neck, and all were stained with crusted blood. The dwarf had lost much of the latter, and his flesh was the color of stripped bark. His eyes were dull with pain.

'Quite so,' Neferata said. She gestured and Naaima dropped to her haunches beside the improvised litter they had constructed out of a shield and two branches. The Cathayan gently probed the dwarf's skull and then moved on to his other wounds. The smell of his blood was less strong now, for which Neferata was grateful. The heat of it had aroused her thirst the way sea-water will seem like the finest wine to a marooned sailor, despite knowing the danger. True, there was no evidence save Naaima's assertions that his blood would sicken them, but Neferata didn't feel like taking the chance.

The dwarf glared at her suspiciously and spat a stream of crude syllables. Neferata shook her head. He frowned, and then said, 'Strigoi?'

'What's a Strigoi?' Khaled said. He had built the fire, more for appearances' sake than anything else. It wouldn't do to let their guest know the true nature of his rescuers, not while they needed him alive. Khaled spoke in Arabyan, as was his custom, and the dwarf blinked and replied in the same tongue.

'You're a long way from the desert, manling,' he growled, squinting at Khaled.

'You know our tongue?' Khaled said, surprised.

'I've been to the caliphates, and a beardling could pick up your speech in a few hours,' the dwarf said and sat up with a pain-filled groan. The smell of fresh blood suddenly filled Neferata's nose and she grunted. The dwarf looked at her. 'You're not Strigoi, then? You have that look…'

'Look?' Neferata said.

The dwarf ignored her question. 'I'm the only survivor, then?' he said, his voice turning harsh.

Neferata nodded. 'Thanks to our intervention,' she said.

The dwarf was silent for a moment. Then, with a grunt, he said, 'Then I owe you a debt. I am Razek Silverfoot.'

'And I am Neferata,' Neferata said, inclining her head. She motioned to the others. 'And these are my companions. We are heading north.'

'To Mourkain, is it?' Razek said. He slumped back. 'Have to be. It's the only place worth going out here,' he added, answering his own question.

'Mourkain,' Neferata said, letting the word roll across her tongue. Mourkain was a place. 'Yes, we are going to Mourkain,' she added, ignoring the looks her followers gave her. She knew that they could not see the glare of the black sun and even if they had, they would not understand it. They had followed her into the mountains because to do otherwise was to die on the spears of dead men, or because they felt loyalty to her. Her eyes met

Naaima's, and she nodded. Something howled hungrily in the darkness. Razek's hands flexed, as if itching to hold a weapon. 'Beasts,' he grunted weakly.

'But far enough away to be harmless,' Neferata said. 'Are you hungry?' She snapped her fingers and Anmar trotted towards them, holding a steaming skewer of charred meat.

Razek eyed the girl with something like surprise and took the meat, nodding in gratitude. 'Nothing to drink, by chance, is there?' he asked hopefully.

'Water, I'm afraid,' Neferata said. She crooked her fingers and Stregga sauntered over, holding a helmet full of melted snow. The dwarf frowned at the improvised cup. A muscle in his jaw jumped. It was a movement so slight that a human would have missed it, and Neferata knew at once that they had made a mistake. She rose and slapped the helmet out of Stregga's hands. 'Fool,' she snapped.

Stregga recoiled, stunned. 'Bring him a water-skin,' Neferata continued, her eyes narrowed. Stregga hesitated, and then nodded. She would empty one of theirs of blood and fill it with melted snow. It was a sacrifice, but a necessary one.

Razek watched her as he chewed the meat thoughtfully and then softly spat it out. 'I don't want to know what that was, do I?' he said, after wiping his mouth.

Neferata chuckled. 'No, likely not,' she said.

Razek caught the edge of the fallen helmet and picked it up awkwardly, his hands trembling with fatigue. 'This was my cousin's.'

Neferata hesitated. Several homilies swept across her mind's eye, pious sayings of comfort and kindness. But she also knew that they wouldn't be accepted by the dour, proud creature sitting before her. What could she say, then? What words would put him at ease? 'He died well,' she said finally. 'They all died well.' Then, 'They will not be forgotten.'

'No, they won't be.' Razek tried to push himself back up, but he immediately slumped back with a groan, the helmet slipping from his hands. 'I don't think I'll be so lucky,' he hissed, eyes squeezed shut. He gripped his chest and his breath slid through his teeth in whistling gasps. 'Feel like troll-leavings.'

Neferata leaned over him. 'You were badly hurt. The quicker we get you to shelter, the quicker you'll start to mend. Mourkain,' she pressed. 'Where is it?'

Razek looked at her, and the words dropped out of his lips before he realised that he was saying them. 'North. There's a pass, just over the next rise. It leads to Mourkain,' he said. She gazed into his eyes and felt the jagged edge of his will brush against hers. It felt less like the mind of a man than she had expected. As she pressed her thoughts down on his, she felt like water cascading into the crevices of a mountain. Eventually she would wear him down, but it would take more time than she was comfortable with. His current state helped, the pain of his wounds widening the cracks in his determination.

'Why were you going?' she said.

'I—' Dwarf stubbornness asserted itself. He shook his head. 'Dwarf business, eh?' he grunted. 'No offence, but it's not manling business.'

'Of course,' she said. Neferata stroked his brow and leaned him back. If her strength surprised him, Razek gave no indication. His eyes fluttered in his head, and she said, 'Sleep now. We will keep you safe, Razek Silverfoot. Sleep…' He resisted at first, stubbornly, but then he collapsed back, his eyes closing as pain and exhaustion dragged him under.

As the dwarf passed into unconsciousness, Neferata stood and wiped her hand across her furs. 'North then,' she said, looking at the others.

'And now that we know, what of him?' Khaled said. He smiled cruelly. 'A bit of sport, perhaps…'

'No,' Naaima said sharply.

Khaled looked at her and sneered. 'Why? He's no good to drink from according to you and he's slowing us down!'

'Quiet, Khaled. She is correct,' Neferata said, making a chopping gesture. 'We need him alive for now. We are in strange territory, and it would serve us well to have a guide, albeit an unwitting one.'

'But–' Khaled began.

'She said no,' Naaima snarled, and Khaled replied in kind, baring his fangs.

'I want to hunt,' he hissed.

'Do you?' Neferata said, the calm tone belying the fury that swept through her. 'Have you learned nothing from our troubles in Bel Aliad?' she continued, letting a snarl creep into her words. Khaled hesitated, his next words dying on his lips.

'It wasn't his fault!' Anmar protested, rising to her brother's defence. Neferata's gaze swung to her and Anmar stutteringly added, 'M-my lady.' She and Khaled were more alike than simply in appearance. Both were slaves to impatience and impetuousness, though Anmar was usually self-aware enough to recognise it. Regardless, it did not stop her from leaping to her brother's defence now.

Neferata felt a moment's sympathy. Then her sudden backhand caught the other vampire across the jaw and threw her to the snow. 'Must I discipline you as well as your brother?' Neferata said.

Anmar cowered, covering her head with trembling hands. Neferata turned away, her fangs snapping in frustration, and her followers fell back. Anger radiated off her at the best of times, like the warning of a storm. Now, a rumble of thunder slipped through her mask, striking all of them to their very cores. She fostered informality among her followers, and allowed them the freedom of initiative. Every so often they forgot that she was a queen. On those occasions they needed to be reminded, and forcefully. Examples were best taken to heart when they were inflicted suddenly and swiftly.

'But it was his fault, little leopard,' Neferata purred, looking at Anmar, who crawled away from her. Khaled tried to retreat, but she moved too quickly, and between one eye-blink and the next, her fingers gripped his chin. She leaned close. 'It was your fault, wasn't it, Khaled? I warned you, didn't I?' she said gently. Then, more harshly, 'Didn't I?' She shook him and his heels scraped the snow as he was jerked several inches into the air. 'But you didn't listen, did you?'

She flung him to the ground with a snarl. Bones snapped as he struck the ground, and he rolled onto his stomach, groaning as they re-knit. Neferata placed one sandalled foot to the back of his head and drove his face deep into the snow. 'I will not be questioned,' she said mildly, looking at each of them in turn. She released Khaled.

He spat snow from his mouth as he rose onto his hands and knees. Neferata guided him to his feet and shoved him towards his sister. Then she turned towards Naaima. 'Those packs we salvaged. Do we still have them?'

'Yes,' Naaima said. They had taken the packs from the dwarfs at Neferata's urging, though only Naaima had an inkling of why she would want them. 'There are papers. Ledgers, perhaps. My people know the dawi as great record keepers.'

'Perhaps,' Neferata said, rifling through the packs. Naaima recognised the look on her mistress's face.

'What is it?' she said softly, so the others would not hear.

'We did not run across them by accident,' Neferata said. 'They were going in the same direction we were.'

'I thought we didn't know where we were going,' Naaima said, teasing gently. She was the only one who dared do so, especially so soon after one of Neferata's 'lessons'. Naaima had known her mistress in life, and had guided her through the doors of death and undeath alike. She had seen Neferata at her worst and at her best. She had endured blows and curses and caresses and kisses. Neferata looked askance at her, wondering why Naaima had returned to Lahmia on the eve of its destruction, and why she had stayed since. She had never dared ask.

'No, we simply didn't know what it was called,' Neferata said, turning her attentions back to the matter at hand.

'Mourkain,' Naaima said.

'Mourkain,' Neferata said, smiling sharply. She held up a fistful of papers. 'You know the look of official documents as well as I, Naaima. These were no unlucky travellers. No, they had purpose.' She cast a lingering, contemplative look at the unconscious dwarf. Then she looked up. 'Night is fading. We must continue on. Let us go. Khaled, see to our new friend,' she said, gesturing for Khaled to grab Razek's travois. He made as if to protest, but Anmar's hand on his arm caused him to hold his tongue. Neferata nodded in satisfaction.

Perhaps they could be taught, after all.

Then the vampires were in motion, pelting headlong through the night, outrunning the sun. They travelled by night and rested by day. Someone was always awake to tend to Razek, but the dwarf slept through even the most difficult of travails.

Neferata knew now what the black sun signified, but the knowledge gave her no comfort. What awaited her in Mourkain? She had no answers. Indeed, it only raised more questions. The sun seemed to grow darker every time she looked at it, drawing the shadows of the night into its corona.

It was hungry.

She knew hunger when she saw it, even if the thing had neither mouth nor shape. A vast black all-consuming hunger crouched somewhere in the mountains, waiting for her to enter its maw. She had been a priestess as well as a queen in life, and she knew what portents were. Despite the misgivings, she did not turn around. And if the others had any worries of their own, they did not share them.

Granted, the sun wasn't the only thing that was hungry. More than once she caught Khaled staring thirstily at Razek's unconscious form. The beast-blood had turned rank quickly. Even Neferata felt a pang. And the beasts were certainly hungry.

The creatures they had killed had only been the scouts of a much larger herd. That herd was now in pursuit. Their cries were carried on the cold wind, and seemed to echo from every rock and tree. The snow began to fall again as they travelled. The vampires felt nothing, and even wounded, Razek seemed nearly as hardy. Nonetheless, they made sure to set small fires when they stopped to keep the dwarf warm. Razek rarely stirred. There were supplies in the packs they had salvaged, and when he needed to eat, he could.

By the fourth night, the distant howls of the beasts, ever-present, had caught up with them.

They ran on, the howls of their pursuers snapping at their heels. 'Why do we run?' Stregga barked, limbs pumping as she pushed herself through the knee-high snow. 'We'll butcher them as easily as the others, surely…'

'There are more of them,' Rasha said. 'Listen to the howls.'

'More to kill is all,' Stregga said, grinning.

'Feel free to stay behind,' Naaima snapped. She looked at Neferata. 'They will catch us,' she said. Neferata snarled in consternation. The beasts had tracked them, or, more likely, the dwarf.

They could leave him and keep moving. But Neferata knew that they would need him, and alive for preference. She couldn't say why, exactly, but she knew enough to trust her instincts when it came to such things.

Besides which, they needed blood, fresh blood. And the only palatable supply was charging towards them. She unsheathed her sword. 'We fight,' she said. 'Kill them all, and drain them dry.'

'Yesss,' Khaled said. The others echoed him. In the snow and shadows, they looked monstrous. Inhuman lust had burned away all pretence of humanity now, and only the blood-hunger remained.

Another howl rippled through the dusk and the harsh stink of the hunting horrors followed it. Something big crashed through the trees, its footsteps causing the ground to tremble. A moment later the trees immediately behind them disintegrated as a massive shape crashed through the curtain of flying wood and falling snow, bellowing. It was as big as four men and had the head of a deformed bull. Teeth like knives snapped together in a spray of froth and foam as the creature pursued them like an ambulatory avalanche.

'Ha!' Khaled crowed. He stopped and slewed around, his sword cutting across the beast's muzzle. It did not stop its charge, but instead crashed into him, catching him between its great curling horns. Khaled cried out as he was lifted off his feet and tossed into the monster's wake. It roared again and made to draw the great, primitive blade stuffed through the loop of its ratty loincloth.

Neferata struck out, her sword sinking to the hilt in the flesh of its forearm. It shrieked and reached for her with its good hand. She danced back and the claws closed on empty air. The others had joined the fray by then, circling the beast and striking at it like wolves bringing down a stag. Their swords left ragged bloody wounds on its thick, porous flesh and it grunted and howled, furiously lashing out at them.

Khaled had got to his feet and met the first of the creatures that had followed the big one through the trees. The goat-headed abomination chopped at him with a stone axe. Khaled ducked and weaved around its blows, toying with it for a few moments. Then, bored, he circled it too quickly for it to follow, grabbed one of its horns and kicked it in the small of the back, snapping its neck and spine with one jerk. More creatures boiled out of the dark trees and howling snow like ants. Several loped towards the dwarf, who lay unconscious and unawares on his litter.

'Khaled, Anmar, keep him alive,' Neferata said, avoiding an awkward blow from the dying giant. She stepped past it, leaving it to Naaima and the others.

'Do as she says,' Khaled said to his sister. He lunged

after Neferata, sword flashing through a hairy throat. Anmar made to call out to him, but she was soon too busy defending the dwarf to make any sound save an enraged snarl as her thin blade lopped off the crooked limbs that reached for her.

Neferata prowled among the monsters, letting her bloodlust have free rein and leaving bodies in her wake. There were dozens of the beasts, and she wondered where they had all come from. Had they inadvertently stumbled into the creatures' territory? Perhaps it was simply hunger. They all had the starveling look, with hairy hides shrunk tight to malformed bones.

'Look to your side, my lady,' Khaled said, sliding past her and bisecting a beast with a single graceful twist of his blade. Neferata glared at him.

'I told you to defend the dwarf!' she hissed.

Khaled didn't meet her eyes. He caught a heavy blow on his blade, turned it aside and grunted, shoving his opponent back. The creatures were stronger than men, and starvation had driven them to a frenzy that made them stronger still.

Neferata stretched past him, pinning the creature to a tree. 'Go back, fool,' she said. 'I need that stunted creature alive.'

'But–' Khaled began.

Before Neferata could reply, an arrow took a nearby beast in the neck, spinning it around. Hooves thumped on the snow. More arrows hissed between the trees. Neferata caught the sharp whiff of oil and leather and horse-sweat, and beneath that, the tang of blood rushing and pulsing in strong veins as she spun around a wailing beast, driving her sword up through its back. Still moving, she chopped an arrow from the air. She slid to a halt in a cloud of snow, nostrils flaring. Her eyes sank to slits and she tasted the air, her hunger stirring anew. It was not beast blood she smelled – this was human!

'Is that what I think it is?' Khaled whispered. His face was weasel-thin with feral hunger. His fangs splayed like the thorns of a rose.

'Back to the others,' Neferata snapped, struggling to contain her own sudden surge of ravenous need. The shapes of a score of riders became visible, weaving through the trees in a sure-footed gallop. The horses were smaller and hairier than those she had ridden in Araby and stocky by comparison, more like ponies than true horses. The men were equally stocky, with broad shoulders and wide jaws. Their hair was greased and bound in scalplocks, much like those worn by the warriors of Nehekhara. Their gear was rough and utilitarian – they wore furs over banded leather cuirasses and each man had a wide-bladed sword on his hip. Most of them had short bows in their hands and these buzzed like hornets as the men, knees tight on their mounts' barrel chests, fired as they rode with practised swiftness.

They gave brutal yells as they rode through the mass of beastmen, leaving trampled bodies in their wake. Neferata and Khaled retreated, leaving the beasts to the newcomers. Whoever they were, they were welcome to the creatures.

'If the dwarf is dead, Khaled, I will make you wish that you had never accepted my gift,' Neferata said.

'He'll only be dead if my sister is as well,' Khaled said tightly. Neferata looked at him. Vampires did not feel emotion as humans did, but certain bonds could not be broken, even by death and what followed. She thought briefly of Naaima, and then confronted the possibility of Anmar's death. Khaled was not the only one who would miss the girl.

Neferata moved more quickly, outpacing Khaled. She burst back to where she had left the others. A small surge of relief filled her as she saw Anmar standing amidst a number of contorted bodies. The girl was covered in blood, and she used her tongue to clean thick ropes of it from her blade.

'Greedy,' Khaled murmured. His relief was evident.

Beastmen lay everywhere and their corpses fouled the crisp purity of the snow and the air alike. 'I smell horses,' Naaima said, stepping over the body of the bull-headed giant. She looked at Neferata and sheathed her sword.

'We have guests to dinner,' Khaled said, striding towards his sister.

'Horsemen,' Neferata said. 'More than a dozen of them,' she added.

'Men, as in humans,' Stregga said, glancing at Rasha, who inhaled the air, her eyes mere slits. 'As in something other than the nasty juices of these hairy sacks,' the Sartosan went on, kicking one of the bodies.

'No,' Neferata said, slicing her sword through the air.

Stregga gave her a mutinous look, but held her tongue. The others hid their feelings better, even Khaled. Neferata smiled slightly and sheathed her blade. Horsemen meant civilisation. And Razek had said that the only civilisation nearby was Mourkain. She was close now. She could feel the heat of the dead black sun on her skin, but she didn't turn to see if it had risen.

Horses snorted. Snow crunched beneath heavy hooves. Neferata stepped towards the trees, her hands held away from her sides. Horses eased through the trees, the wary eyes of the riders taking her and her followers in. A voice barked what sounded like a command.

And the command was in Nehekharan.

Not true Nehekharan, but a debased cousin, a garbled brute-tongue that perhaps shared an ancient root with the language of home. Neferata hissed in satisfaction. It had been more than a century since Nehekhara had truly become a land of the dead. Had some of her people managed to escape the Great Dying?

Was that what this Mourkain was? Some last remnant of her people? Perhaps that was why she was being drawn there. The thought was a heady one: a new kingdom to rule, a new people to mould once more into a great empire.

A rider edged out of the trees. He was a big man, bigger than the others and even paler. His skin was the colour of a fish's belly and unlike the others he wore no furs, only a cuirass of boiled leather and brass discs, and his muscular arms were bare to the cold. Those arms were covered in looping scars, and a greased scalplock coiled around his neck. A wide, spade-shaped beard flared out from a jutting jaw. There was no light in him, no warmth.

'Neferata–' Naaima began.

'I know,' Neferata said. He was as dead and as cold as she was, though he was not like her. There was a grave-mould stink to him that offended her nose and she hissed as the stench invaded her nostrils.

The rider was a vampire. And as they recognised him for what he was, he recognised them. Neferata's nostrils flared and a glint of recognition sparked somewhere deep in her head. The smell of the warrior was familiar, though she had never seen him before. 'Well… what are you, eh?' she said loudly.

'Vorag,' the warrior barked. 'Vorag Bloodytooth, witch,' he continued in his crudely accented Nehekharan. 'Champion of Strigos,' he bellowed, thumping his chest with a fist.

Neferata blinked. She asked, 'Strigos – not Mourkain?'

Vorag cocked his head. He glanced towards the litter and Razek, his eyes narrowing. He seemed to recognise the dwarf. 'Who are you to speak of Mourkain? You are a barbarian.' He gestured to her furs.

Neferata laughed. 'No, I'm no barbarian.'

Vorag's face tightened. *Here is one who doesn't like the sound of laughter, especially when it's directed at him*, Neferata thought. 'Then what are you?' he barked.

'A question I might put to you as well,' she said.

Vorag grunted and slid off his horse. He stalked towards them, looking them over. 'I told you. I am champion of Strigos. These lands are mine, given me by right of battle, as a gift. These beasts are mine to hunt and kill.' He snapped his teeth together on the last word. Almost casually, he grabbed the limp arm of one of the dead creatures and wrenched it from the socket. He upended the shoulder stump over his mouth and greedily gulped the sluggish flow of brackish blood. He seemed to enjoy it. Neferata lowered her opinion of him accordingly.

His men, however, interested her more than their disgusting master. He stood in full view of them, openly feeding. Either they were so barbaric as to not be particularly squeamish or they knew full well what Vorag was. The latter suggested interesting times ahead. In Lahmia, they had hidden their secret, though not, in the end, well. But out here, with no civilised allies to placate, there was no need.

Finished with the stump, Vorag tossed it aside and

crossed his arms over his chest. 'I have answered your question, woman. Now answer mine – what are you?'

'A queen,' Neferata said.

Vorag snorted. 'There are queens aplenty in the wild lands. Every chieftain's woman is a queen, to hear her tell it,' he said. 'And that's not what I meant. Whose blood-doxy are you? Are you Strezyk's maybe, or that fool Gashnag's? Who do you belong to?'

Neferata darted forwards. Her face was inches from Vorag's before his sword could as much as twitch. 'I am no man's woman,' she said. 'I am Neferata of Lahmia, Vorag Bloodytooth. I am queen of our kind, little blood-drinker. If you bow to me, I will forgive this insult and I will not make your bones into combs for my hair.'

Vorag's eyes widened in shock, either at her speed or at her threat, and he inadvertently stepped back. A moment later, he roared and swung his sword up over his head.

⊰ THREE ⊱

The Great Desert
(–1158 Imperial Reckoning)

The raiders pushed their horses hard beneath the moon's idiot gaze. Sand made blue by the moonlight puffed and blew as the horses – famed for their stamina and stride – pounded along the bandit-road. Behind them, the caravan burned.

In a wagon swiftly being consumed by hungry flames, Neferata rose and pushed the collapsing canopy of the wagon aside with a growl of frustration. Naaima lay unmoving on the ground outside, an arrow jutting from between her breasts. Neferata knew that a simple arrow would do nothing worse to one of their kind than render them immobile but even so, the sight of her handmaiden in such a state drove her into a rage.

It had been nothing more than a lucky shot. But now the dogs of the desert were riding away, her treasures in their saddlebags. Gold and silver from Lahmia and the lands of the Dragon-Emperor, the wealth of ages, intended for greater things than being bartered for a drudge in some desert-rat's tent. Neferata snarled again and ripped an arrow from her shoulder, flinging it aside. She dropped down beside Naaima and plucked the arrow from her chest. Naaima's mouth opened and a rattling shriek escaped her lips as she sat up, eyes wild.

Neferata helped her to her feet and brushed a lock of bloody hair from her eyes. 'Can you walk?' she said.

'Y-yes,' Naaima rasped, rubbing the already closing wound with trembling fingers.

'Then you can run,' Neferata said, spinning and sprinting in the direction the raiders had taken. After a moment's hesitation, Naaima followed. The two women ran swiftly, more swiftly than any mortal being, and soon enough the horses came into sight. Neferata shrieked hungrily and leapt onto a horse's flank, her claws sinking into the animal's haunch. It squealed in fear and pain as Neferata swung up onto it like a lioness and pounced on the rider. She tore aside his scarf and headdress and sank her fangs into his throat, cutting off his scream. Sliding into a sitting position behind him, she ripped and chewed at the flesh of his throat, swallowing hot mouthfuls of pumping blood as she snatched the reins from his hand.

Naaima loped past, her jaws gaping, her delicate features stretching into something inhuman. A rider turned back and gave a yell as the vampire flung herself at him from a sand dune. She snatched him off his horse and hurled him to the ground, falling on him like a bird of prey. Neferata rode past and let the body of her victim tumble from his saddle.

She urged the horse on, conserving her own strength. The other raiders were pulling around, only just now realising that they had been pursued. Saddlebags bulged with ill-gotten loot. She rose in the saddle, letting the moonlight catch her bestial features. Men froze, hands quivering inches from sword hilts or bows. Her hair flared around her like a black halo and her jaws gaped wide, her tongue writhing in a nest of fangs. Eyes like hell-lamps blazed as she crashed among them, releasing *the reins to stretch her hands out. Almost gently, her fingers played across the chests of the first two men, crushing them at the instant of impact and bursting their hearts in their breasts.*

An arrow cut across her arm and she leapt from the saddle, bearing another rider to the desert. The archer fired again, skilfully controlling his horse with his knees. Neferata crouched over her kill, hissing as another arrow sank into her thigh.

Naaima leapt onto the archer's back, ripping at him. He fell from his horse and snatched at a dagger sheathed on his belt as the two vampires closed in. Naaima leapt back as the knife sliced across her belly. Her hands came away with the rider's mask. Neferata stopped suddenly, her grimace softening. 'Ha,' she said.

The archer was a woman. Fear had contorted her features, but it was easy to see that she was beautiful, albeit in a hard way. 'Daemons,' she spat, in the tongue of the desert peoples. She watched them warily, the dagger extended.

'No,' Neferata replied. 'Not daemons, little sister.' She rose to her full height and let her face soften back into its human semblance. 'Not quite, at any rate.'

The woman was young, and her heartbeat sped up as Neferata approached. In the moonlight, the young woman's face was almost familiar, and an old, remembered pang shivered up through her. 'She looks just like her,' she said softly. 'Doesn't she, Naaima? Just like my little hawk…'

'No,' Naaima said. 'Neferata – no, don't do this.'

'What is your name?' Neferata purred, ignoring her handmaiden, pressing a finger to the tip of the girl's blade and moving it aside.

The young woman's eyes had gone vague, their fierceness draining as Neferata's hypnotic voice and gaze insinuated itself into her mind, numbing her and dulling her thoughts. 'Rasha bin Wasim,' she said hollowly.

'Rasha,' Neferata repeated, rolling the letters across her

tongue. She brushed the dagger aside and it fell to the sand with a thump. *'You remind me of someone, Rasha. Should I tell you about her?'*

'Neferata, stop–' Naaima began, starting forwards.

'Her name was Khalida and I loved her very much,' Neferata said, fangs flashing as she plunged them into Rasha's throat.

The Worlds Edge Mountains
(−800 Imperial Reckoning)

NEFERATA HIT THE ground and bounced to her feet with a hiss. She swept her sword from its sheath and slashed wildly at her attacker. He snarled and met her steel with his own. They traded blows, reeling back and forth across the snow.

Bloody froth collected at the corners of his mouth as he snarled at her. She heard sinew-strings rub against wood as arrows were fitted into bows. She hissed in frustration. Then, with a wild cry, her opponent lunged, his sword descending towards her.

Neferata caught his thick wrist and held it. He mimicked her, grabbing her wrist as her sword dug for his heart. His eyes bulged and black veins stood out on his pale skin as he tried to match her strength.

'Neferata–' Naaima began, rushing towards her.

'Get the archers!' Neferata snarled.

Her handmaidens sprang to obey. Stregga and Rasha raced towards the horsemen as a number of arrows leapt to meet them. The women dived and twisted, their shapes blurring. The sound of bones snapping and skin ripping filled the air and then they were among the horses, setting them to bucking and squealing and their riders to clinging on for dear life.

Naaima set herself between Neferata and the other riders, her blade swatting arrows from the air. Neferata, free to ignore Vorag's men, concentrated on the other vampire. She was stronger, she knew. Indeed, it was all he could do to keep her at bay. No longer distracted, she smiled at him and easily jerked her hand free of his grip. She dropped her sword and placed her free hand against his face. 'Bow, Vorag of Strigos,' she said. 'Bow or die, such is the way of our kind. Has the one who made you not taught you that?' She leaned close. 'Submit, and I will teach you many things...'

Vorag frothed as he struggled. He snapped and whined like a wild animal in Neferata's clutch. She shook him slightly, with no sign of effort, and his sword fell from his grip. He grabbed for her wrist and her fingers stabbed into his head like bilge-hooks. Vorag screamed as she lifted him off his feet by the flesh of his face. His men sat frozen, awestruck by the sight of their leader being handled as if he were a dog.

'Enough,' someone said, then, louder, 'Enough, my queen!' Naaima shouted.

Neferata dropped Vorag and turned, licking blood from her fingers. 'Yes, quite so, Naaima. I think I have made my point.' She looked at her fingers. 'That tastes familiar.' She sank to her haunches, grabbed Vorag's scalplock and jerked his head up. 'Who gave you the blood-kiss, man of Strigos?'

Vorag spat a curse and she tightened her grip and slammed his head into the ground. Jerking him up again, she said, 'Who?'

'Ushoran, my queen,' a deep voice rumbled. Neferata froze. Then, she uncoiled and rose, still holding tight to Vorag's scalplock. She glanced over her shoulder. The others were standing near Naaima, separated from Vorag's men by a newly arrived trio of armoured figures on horseback who watched them all with red gazes. Their armour was cruelly ornate and stained red, with a heavy cuirass of flaring ridges and curved edges over a suit of long mail. The tallest of the three men urged his horse forwards. As one, the human warriors dropped from their saddles to kneel in the snow, heads bowed. Like Vorag and Neferata and her followers, the newcomers were vampires, though as different from Neferata's people as dusk from dawn.

Naaima and the others drew back, disconcerted by the sheer malevolent power radiating from the armoured man. The fanged visor of a winged helm was flipped up, revealing a noble, if brutal face. 'My queen,' he said again. There was no respect in his voice. The title was delivered grudgingly and the words were bitten off.

'Abhorash,' Neferata said harshly. And then, more softly, 'My champion...' Abhorash looked different than the last time she had seen him. Stronger, perhaps. As with herself, the years since the fall of Lahmia had burned him clean of imperfection. He was every inch the warrior; every movement spoke to potential violence, every word was a thrust of steel.

He had always been handsome, after a fashion, with solid features scooped to a point, like some great bird of prey wearing a human mask. In her youth, she had been enamoured of him, but childish fancy had faded into mature discontent as she grew to know him better. As she saw his weaknesses for what they were, rather than for the nobility he claimed to possess.

Her mind reeled at the sight of him. What was he

doing here? How had he got here? Was he following the black sun as well? Question after question splashed across her mind but with a shake of her head she thrust them aside; now was no time for questions.

'Surprised to see me?' Abhorash said grimly. His voice was strained, as if some great roiling fount of emotion were hidden beneath his façade of arrogance.

'Seeing as you were intent on dying gloriously the last time I spoke with you... no,' Neferata said. 'You always were a disappointment.' The jibe was meant to cut, and by the flicker of expression that flitted across his face, she knew it had struck home. He had never taken easily to immortality, though he had desired it strongly enough in the beginning. For a warrior he was surprisingly squeamish regarding the more practical aspects of eternity. Or he had been, at least. He looked hale and hearty enough now, and stank of blood as surely as she herself did. 'Ushoran made this?' she said.

'He has made many,' Abhorash said, faintly disapproving.

Neferata hesitated. She looked down at Vorag. He had said that this land was a gift. Whose gift, Ushoran's? He had mentioned other names as well... Strezyk and Gashnag. Were they more vampires? The implications were unpleasant.

Abhorash grunted and gestured to Vorag. 'Release him.'

'Who are you to give me orders, champion?' Neferata said, jerking Vorag's head viciously. The vampire groaned and she wondered at Abhorash's words – was this creature truly one of Ushoran's get? Had that conniving little rat made a nest for himself somewhere in these mountains?

'Not your champion. Not any more. Release him,

woman, or I will be forced to–' Abhorash rumbled, fingers caressing the serpentine pommel of the blade sheathed at his side.

'Die? Wouldn't that be a shame,' Khaled said, drawing his own sword and sliding between Neferata and Abhorash.

'Move, boy,' Abhorash grated, his dark eyes blazing. He blinked as if in recognition. Khaled hesitated, but stood firm.

'Ahhhhh,' Neferata breathed. 'I see you know my new champion, Abhorash.'

'You are as profligate as Ushoran,' Abhorash rumbled.

'I was only finishing the job you started,' Neferata spat, and Khaled twitched.

Abhorash shrugged, like a wolf shaking off an insect bite. 'Release *Timagal* Vorag,' he said again. Abhorash's two companions urged their mounts forwards, drawing their own swords. Neferata's eyes glowed like lamps, and her lips had writhed back from her fangs. Violence hung on the air, palpable and terrible. The humans had gone white and they trembled, like field-mice caught between duelling cats.

'Whose champion are you now, Abhorash?' Neferata said. 'Are you Ushoran's dog now?'

'I am no dog, queen of nothing,' Abhorash snarled, hunching forwards in his saddle.

Neferata abruptly released Vorag and stepped past Khaled towards the litter where Razek still slept, unawares. Abhorash blinked, surprise writ on his features.

'What–?'

'He said he was going to Mourkain,' said Neferata. 'He and his people were ambushed by a group of those twisted beast-men that seem to infest these mountains. They all died, save him.' She looked at Abhorash shrewdly. 'You were out here looking for him, weren't you?'

'What?' he said again.

'You were never fleet of thought, my champion. That these men should show up on the path the dwarfs were taking to Mourkain is too much of a coincidence,' Neferata said slowly, as if speaking to a child. She recalled Vorag's eyes as he had caught sight of Razek. 'They were looking for them, weren't they? An escort... and you were out here to escort the escort, but why? Oh, I smell Ushoran, and not just on that lout's blood...' She grinned. 'Does he not trust his own disciple?' Her eyes narrowed. 'Or perhaps it's you who doesn't trust him, hmm?'

Abhorash's face went still and stiff and Neferata knew that she had again struck a nerve. 'Well, regardless, I have saved you the trouble of finding him. Let's deliver him together, shall we? I should like to see my esteemed Lord of Masks once more.'

Abhorash's men looked to him for orders, and for a moment, Neferata wondered whether his hatred of her would outweigh his common sense. If so, she would be forced to kill them and perhaps him. The former was certain, the latter... not so much. Of all the first immortals, Abhorash was perhaps the only one who could match her. It was a shame that he was such a hidebound fool.

Abhorash snorted and waved his men back. 'Sheathe your swords, Lutr, Walak.' He looked at Vorag, distaste evident on his face. 'And someone help the Bloodytooth up.'

'Are you sure this is wise?' Naaima said, joining Neferata. Her fingers toyed with the hilt of her sword and she eyed Abhorash's broad back speculatively.

'Of course it's not, but the time for wisdom has long since passed,' Neferata said. 'She who hesitates is lost, after all.'

Naaima snorted. Neferata glanced at her, then away, choosing to ignore the jibe. 'The Bloodytooth,' she said, nodding to the brute as his men helped him up. He shook them off with snarls and curses.

'A barbarian,' Naaima said.

'And a vampire,' Neferata said, rubbing a drop of blood from the corner of her mouth and examining it between her fingers. Vorag, on his feet again, looked at her and his gaze became speculative. Then he grimaced and rubbed the still-bleeding wounds her fingertips had made in his face.

'He's not used to it yet. He barely knows more than Anmar. He is stupid,' Naaima said.

'Or Ushoran has not taught him all that he is capable of.' Neferata licked her fingers clean. 'Interesting, that...'

Naaima looked at her. 'What are you thinking?'

'You know me well enough to know that, sweet Naaima,' Neferata said, stroking the other's cheek briefly. 'I am seeking the advantage.'

As she turned away, she caught sight of the black sun and it seemed to pull at her more strongly than ever. It loomed large, larger than it ever had before, and seemed intent on swallowing the moon and the stars. Neferata blinked and looked away, but to no avail. It flickered and invaded her vision from every angle. She could hear it now, as well, a sibilant drone that invaded her thoughts. She shook her head, unable to discern the words she knew lurked within the sound.

The darkness at the heart of the sun squirmed and she was reminded of the great asps' nests that sat beneath the floors of the temple to Asaph. Slithering shapes coiled and pulsed in the belly of the black sun. They were vague things and stirred in her a fear such as she had not felt even when Alcadizzar's knife had plucked at her heart. They writhed like pain-contorted bodies in a fire-pit, or perhaps corpses trying to pull themselves from the earth.

Hurry, Neferata, the voice seemed to say. Watching the shapes, she thought of the dead men that W'soran had wrenched from their slumber of ages and set upon Alcadizzar's forces in that final, great battle. Something in the darkness seemed to latch on to this thought. The blackness stretched towards her from over the mountains, speeding towards her, faster and faster.

Neferata wanted to run, to flee, but she was rooted to the spot. The needle-on-bone voice was back, digging into her hindbrain like a butcher's hook into meat. It wanted something from her, something important. What did it want? What?

'What do you want?' she whispered.

'You hear it as well,' Abhorash said. He had dismounted, and led his horse by its reins.

She looked up. 'Hear what, my champion?' she said, forcing a smile as she shoved the sibilant, sharp whispers aside.

'Don't call me that,' he said. 'And do not play games with me.' He gazed steadily at her, as if searching for the answer in her face. 'Why are you here?' he said softly, rubbing his horse's nose. There was a wary look in his eyes, and a bubble of laughter rose up in her.

'Why am I not dead and buried beneath the Arabyan sands, you mean?' She glanced at Khaled. 'You taught him well.'

Abhorash said nothing. Neferata moved closer to him. 'Then, you did what you always do – you left.

You left those who were counting on you. And I stayed, and made the best of it.' She showed her fangs and Abhorash looked away. 'Is that shame, warrior? Or embarrassment?'

Abhorash's gaze snapped back towards her, hot and angry. 'Neither. It is disgust.'

Neferata hissed. 'It is I who should be disgusted!' She leaned close. 'If you hadn't left–'

'I left because I was no longer fit to stay!' he thundered. Neferata stepped back, blinking. The raw pain in Abhorash's voice was hard to ignore. 'None of us were,' he said, looking away. 'We should have all left. I should have made you. If I had…'

'If you had, Nagash still would have done as he did, and Nehekhara would still be dead,' Neferata said. 'And we would be dead with it.'

'We belong dead,' Abhorash said. Neferata said nothing. 'It is the pyramid,' he said after a moment, abruptly switching topics.

'And what pyramid are you referring to?' Neferata said, not looking at him.

'You'll see it soon enough,' he grunted, turning back to his horse. 'You want to go to Mourkain, after all.'

'Feel free to talk about it anyway,' she said. 'What is it, Abhorash? Did it call you as well?' An unintended note of pleading entered her voice and she cursed herself for the weakness. 'Does it come to you in your dreams?'

He shifted uncomfortably. She relented, seeing that he would not speak of it. 'Tell me about Mourkain,' she said. 'Tell me about Ushoran.'

'He has made himself king over these people,' Abhorash said. 'Savages mostly, though their culture is not as degenerate as some in these mountains,' he added. He was looking at Vorag as he said it.

'And Strigos,' she said.

'Their name for themselves,' Abhorash said. 'The Strigoi of Strigos, and Mourkain is their capital.' He looked at her. 'They are a hardy people.'

'They speak Nehekharan,' she said.

'A debased form, yes, I suppose they do,' Abhorash said.

'And you don't find that curious?'

'I hadn't given it much thought. Settra had outposts farther north than this in his time,' Abhorash said, as if that explained everything. 'In time, they might even be as our people are. Were,' he added, frowning. Neferata grimaced. The people of Nehekhara were dead and gone now. They were dust and bones, thanks to Nagash.

'And now Ushoran rules them,' she said. 'How did that come about, I wonder?'

Abhorash looked at her. 'Does it disturb you?'

'Doesn't it you? Oh, I forgot, you're his champion now, aren't you?'

Abhorash growled. Neferata met his glare and held it. 'It won't work, you know. Not with him. Ushoran is no more a king than–'

'Than you are a queen,' Abhorash bit out. 'Not now and never again.' He took her hand. 'Neferata…'

She yanked her hand free of his grip. 'No one touches me without my permission, my champion,' she said.

'As I have said, I am no longer your champion,' he said, letting his hand drop to his sword's pommel.

'Yes,' she said, smiling. 'You are Ushoran's champion now.'

Abhorash's lip curled. 'No. That particular honour goes to Vorag. I am a mere *ajal*.'

Neferata cocked her head. 'Ajal,' she repeated, tasting the unfamiliar word.

'It is the Strigoi term for a lesser lord. Ushoran is stingy with titles,' Abhorash said, smiling thinly.

'Why?' she said.

'Why?' He seemed puzzled by the question.

'Yes, Abhorash, why,' she said. 'Why serve him at all?'

His eyes shrank to slits. 'You wouldn't understand, my queen,' he said.

'No, I wouldn't.'

He turned and strode away, his cloak flaring about him. Neferata watched him go and snorted.

'He is frightened,' Naaima said. Neferata looked at her handmaiden. As ever, she had not heard the other woman's approach. In life, Naaima had been a shadow, and little had changed in death.

'Abhorash doesn't know how to be frightened,' Neferata said, albeit with more uncertainty than she was used to.

'Then he has learned,' Naaima said.

Neferata frowned. If Naaima was right, then that boded ill. What was Abhorash frightened of? Did he feel the same hungry pull that she did? Was that what had drawn him to Mourkain?

Do you feel it, Neferata? Do you feel the silent angles of the Corpse Geometries growing sharper about you? The charnel mathematics of Usirian have drawn you here, Neferata…

'Silence,' she hissed, closing her eyes. The voice withdrew. Usirian was the god of decay and death. The jackal-headed potentate of graveyards and dead-things; he was no more real than Asaph or Ptra. She pulled her furs tighter about her, suddenly, inexplicably cold.

Neferata and the others were given the horses of those of Vorag's men killed in battle with the beasts. The animals did not shy when the vampires mounted. Vorag met Neferata's questioning gaze and said, '*Hetman*

Ushoran instituted a breeding programme several years ago. He wanted horses that would be used to our smell.' He patted his own.

'That implies that there are enough of us to ride them,' she said. Hetman meant king, she thought, from the context.

Vorag smiled widely. 'More than enough, I should say. Everyone important got the bite.' He chuckled. 'And more than a few who weren't.'

'Which are you?'

Vorag's face reddened and then he grunted out a laugh. 'I'd be insulted, but I have a feeling you'd make me pay for it, Lady Neferata.'

'I would indeed, Timagal Vorag,' she said. There was much of Ushoran in this creature, or perhaps like simply called to like. She had proven herself the stronger and now Vorag would play nice. At least until her back was turned.

'I am important,' he said. 'The hetman gave me estates and men, which is more than he gave to some *agals*.'

'Agal and ajal,' Neferata murmured, filing the terms away for reference. Even among barbarians there was a hierarchy. 'Tell me more, Timagal… I would not appear ignorant.'

The ad-hoc column marched at night, out of deference to the immortals. Sunlight could be borne, at least by herself and Abhorash, but for the others it was tantamount to a slow death. They made good time regardless. Signs of civilisation had become more prevalent. Smoke trails in the distance spoke to the presence of villages and there were signs of the land being cleared. They passed by a number of mounted patrols, almost identical to Vorag's men. The Strigoi were taller and broader than the men of Neferata's homeland, and paler than many she had seen since. They wore rough, utilitarian clothing and leather armour covered in metal studs that jangled softly as they rode. Scalplocks like Vorag's were common and she wondered whether he had started the fashion. The riders gave Abhorash and his two warriors a wide berth, and Vorag glared openly at the other vampire, but only when his back was turned and only when he wasn't tutoring Neferata in the peculiarities of Strigoi culture. Such outright hostility could prove useful, if it were properly focused, she thought.

She kept close to Vorag, plying him with compliments and questions. One in particular she was most interested in getting an answer to. 'You mentioned others earlier…' she said. 'Like us.' She stroked his forearm as their mounts trotted side-by-side. 'It has been so long since I have met others of our kind, save those I brought into this life myself.'

'We are many,' Vorag said, smiling. 'It's Ushoran's idea of promotion.'

'Ah,' Neferata said. In Lahmia, they had purposely kept their numbers small, if only for safety's sake. 'Strigos is an aristocracy of the night, then.'

Vorag nodded. 'Too many, if you ask me. We were few, at first. Then…' He made a limp gesture. His smile turned feral. 'Granted, the younger ones don't last long.'

'No?'

'We are a fierce, proud people, my lady,' Vorag said, gesturing to his scars. He pulled a necklace out from beneath his cuirass and a number of fangs rattled on it. Neferata repressed a look of disgust. Vorag stuffed the gruesome trophies back beneath his armour. 'We fight as well as we f–'

'Yes,' Neferata said as Vorag urged his horse forwards, responding to a shout from one of his men. Personal combat wasn't unfamiliar to her. Such had been the law of the land in Nehekhara as well, though it had been a bit more organised in the case of her people. An old pain rose to the surface.

In her mind's eye, she saw the feast where it had all started to go wrong. She saw Khalida – her little hawk – stand up to accuse her of black magic and obscene rites. Only one of which was true. Khalida had demanded a trial by combat, and Neferata, trapped by her own words, had given in to her cousin.

She heard the clash of steel and felt that first gash beneath her left breast. She again felt that thrill of fear, so alien now more than a century after the fact. Again, she saw the blade in her cousin's hand looping out for her throat. She could feel Khalida's heart hammering through the thin material of her robe. And then she felt her die.

But she hadn't, had she?

Neferata opened her eyes. Khalida had come back. Again and again, she came back. She shook her head, driving the thoughts aside. She had left all of that behind. Let the dead stay in the land of the dead.

'Your fangs are showing, my lady,' Khaled murmured. Neferata closed her lips and glanced at the other vampire. He smiled at her. She didn't return the expression. He was never far away when she rode with Vorag. He was either overprotective or jealous, neither of which was useful to her at the moment.

'Where are the others?' she snapped. The forests had long since given way to the upper reaches of the mountains and the column of riders wound its way along a path into the high places. A few clumps of trees dotted the rocky slopes, but little else. They rode carefully. The Strigoi horses were bred for mountain travel, apparently, and displayed none of the skittishness she would have expected.

'Scattered through the column, as you requested,' he said. 'Your eyes and ears are open and among the cattle, milady. We learn their language and customs, as you commanded.'

'And why aren't you with them?'

'I felt it best to remain by your side, just in case…' he trailed off hopefully.

'Just in case what, my *Kontoi?*' she asked, not looking at him. The word was Arabyan, and meant 'noble rider'. In Bel Aliad, only men of noble birth rode horses into war, and clad themselves in the bronze and iron armour of the Kontoi.

She had learned, to her cost, of the power of a Kontoi charge. Especially when Abhorash rode at their head, as he had then. She looked at Khaled. 'Just in case I should require your protection, perhaps?' she snapped and her tone was as sharp as a slash of her claws. Khaled stiffened and dropped back as she rode on, and she cursed herself for her tone. Khaled required more reprimanding than her other servants, but honey had to alternate with vinegar sometimes. It wasn't his fault. Her blood-kiss seemed to affect men in certain unfortunate ways. She considered Abhorash's broad back and sniffed. Then, it always had, had it not?

Maybe Mourkain would provide answers to that as well.

She looked back at her followers, drifting through the column of riders with the feline grace that so characterised those with whom she shared her blood-kiss. They would return to her side, minds full of gossip, rumor and knowledge for her to sift through.

In life, she had employed the priestesses who served

as her handmaidens in much the same fashion. No one noticed women or slaves. And they always heard such useful things.

What would they hear in Mourkain, she wondered? Maybe the answer to what the black sun was. She looked up, wondering what had attracted Vorag's attention.

She looked ahead and the black sun seemed larger now; it had expanded in size, until its darkness swallowed all the stars and moon. Why hadn't she noticed it before? Why–

Something brighter than the light of creation's darkness flared into being around her, seared the air that filled her useless lungs and burned her pale skin to cracked and blackened scraps. She threw up her hands, but she was already blind and burning.

It rose over the mountains like some obscene beast crouching on the crags, its corona flickering through her thoughts like the tips of many knives. Cold heat slashed at her, chilling her bones even as it burned the flesh from them.

Neferata stood at the heart of the black sun and was consumed.

A world died.

Every living thing in this world died and then stirred, bones ancient and new alike shifting and rising. The Corpse Geometries flexed in the ocean of stars as the Kings and Queens of the Land of the Dead rose one by one from their mighty tombs and marched towards the black heart of the charnel kingdoms.

Familiar faces and forms stirred in the dust, rising and joining the march. She called out to them, but to no avail. They responded only to one voice, terrible and empty and cold. It was the voice like needles on bone. Simultaneously high and deep, like wind whistling through a ribcage, it spoke to her of the empire to come, the empire of ghosts and corpses, silent and perfect and eternal. The empire soon to rise…

Now that she was here. Now that she was in Mourkain.

Neferata opened her eyes and moaned. She swayed in her saddle as cemetery thoughts washed over her, seeking to pull her down. Again she tasted grave-dirt and smelled the rot of centuries. The concentrated essence of death filled her, making her light-headed.

'Neferata,' Naaima said, reaching for her. Neferata turned and saw the horror that hid beneath her handmaiden's beauty. Maggots writhed through the gaping holes in the Cathayan's cheeks and suppurating rents marred her nose and mouth. Teeth like razors flashed behind tattered lips. And in her chest beat a black sun just like the one in the sky.

Neferata felt her gaze drawn down. A similar pulsing mass of corruption throbbed in her chest. She looked at her hands in growing horror, seeing the sickly glow of her bones beneath the pallid, porous flesh. She looked up, and something impossibly massive and impossibly evil crouched between her and the sky, nestling in the dead stones of the mountains like a beast preparing to spring. It was a nightmare orchard of skewed minarets and thrusting towers, sprouting like broken spears from the bloody soil of a battlefield.

Hurry, Neferata! Come, claim your throne! You will be Queen of the World, Neferata. A queen of all that is, of all that ever will be for eternities without end. Come… come…

'Neferata,' Abhorash said from behind her. He grabbed her arm. She tore it free and spun, her fingers digging into the gorget that hid his throat. He crashed from his horse with a roar of surprise. Men's hands flew to their weapons as Neferata leapt from her horse and dived on her former champion. Worms moved beneath his skin and for a moment, she considered trying to dig them out.

There was corruption everywhere she looked, seeping into the rocks and strangling the life out of the crooked trees. And not just the trees; the Strigoi were bound by black threads that held them tight to their vampire masters, and they were shrunken, skeletal things to her eyes.

Swords hissed out and she twisted aside as Abhorash's men closed in on her from either side. She slid across the slushy ground on all fours, her jaws agape with a serpentine looseness. The red-armoured vampires advanced slowly, their blades extended.

'Walak, Lutr,' Abhorash gasped, pulling himself to his feet. 'Don't–'

They didn't listen. The one called Lutr came in fast, his sword chopping out towards her midsection. She caught the edge of the blade on her palm and drove it into the ground. Her fist connected with the vampire's helmet, crumpling the metal. Lutr dropped like a stone as Walak's blade sliced through her furs and the flesh beneath. The pain brought her back to herself, banishing the nightmare voice and its attendant phantoms.

'I said no!' Abhorash roared, grabbing his warrior and hurling the man aside in a prodigious display of strength. The warrior landed in a heap in the snow. The two vampires faced each other, fangs bared. Neferata was the first to let hers sink back behind her lips.

'I'm sorry,' she said, forcing herself to utter the words. She needed Abhorash. Whether or not he was a willing ally, she knew she needed him. She needed his strength, his staunchness. She needed her champion.

Abhorash hesitated, and then nodded brusquely. In his eyes, she saw that he knew exactly what it was that had driven her into such frenzy. Abhorash had seen it himself. 'Mourkain,' he said, pointing.

She turned, half fearing that the black sun would take her into its mad embrace once more, or that the foul mass she had glimpsed would lunge for her. Instead, she saw the land rise sharply into a crown of broken hills, through which slithered a dark and fierce river. And there, at the top, was Mourkain. The city rose up like tombstones over the hills and peaks and she knew that it was far larger than it appeared. It was not quite the abomination she had seen moments earlier, but she knew that it wasn't far removed.

'It is beautiful, is it not?' Vorag said.

'Yes,' Neferata said, not knowing whether she was telling the truth.

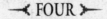

❮ FOUR ❯

The Great Desert
(−1154 Imperial Reckoning)

The desert tribesmen ululated wildly as they shook their weapons at the night sky. The victory had been swift and decisive. The Nehekharan pickets had never known what hit them, so swiftly had the tribes struck. Out here, on the edge of the Great Desert, the warriors of Nehekhara had grown lax and soft and they had paid for their inattentiveness with their lives. In contrast, the tribesmen were savages, clinging precariously to a harsh and unforgiving existence that had made them hard and fierce.

Neferata reclined on a pile of cushions, smiling benignly as she sipped from a cup of blood. She was clad in iron armour, bloodstained now. Naaima crouched nearby, speaking softly to Rasha. Neferata considered eavesdropping then dismissed the idea. There was no cause to suspect that Naaima was doing anything more than teaching her newest handmaiden some detail or other about her new existence. Neferata examined the young woman, smiling slightly. Rasha, a chieftain's daughter, had taken well to immortality. She had ripped out

her own father's throat and butchered her brothers for Neferata. Women, even chieftains' daughters, were not treated
well in the desert.

With Rasha's tribe beneath her thumb, she had swiftly
brought others to heel through similar methods – chieftains
and warlords torn to pieces by daughters and wives in nightly
orgies of long-repressed violence. She glanced around at her
new handmaidens; twenty in all, they reclined or supped on
the bodies of captives taken in the raid. The garrison soldiers
had been strung upside down from posts within the tent
and their blood dripped into clay basins. As she watched,
a woman lapped at the blood like a cat, her hair trailing
through it. What the tribesmen thought of the peculiarities of
their new mistress, she had never bothered to inquire.

Several thousand of the nomads flocked to her night-black
banners now. Some hailed her as the personification of the
Desert Snake, others called her Mother Night. It was all the
same to Neferata. As long as they served, they could call her
what they liked.

She looked over at the body of the young outpost warden
from whom she had been supping. He was cold now, and
blank-eyed. She clucked her tongue; she had taught Alcadizzar better than that, she had thought. The nomads of the
Great Desert rose and fell like the tides, and their loyalties
with them. It had been some time since some of their number
had given shelter to the fugitive Rasetran prince, and the
impositions he had made since – curtailing their traditions of
raid and plunder – had put many of them in a hostile mood.

Instead of bolstering the outposts, however, he had begun
to pull his troops into Nehekhara proper. Neferata took a sip
of still-warm blood. Something was going on. She could smell
it on the wind… There was a carrion stink that put her in
mind of old friends. There were rumours flying through the
camps, of dead men walking and plague and pox and old

evils newly returned. Black smoke had been seen belching from the mountains on the shores of the Sour Sea.

She closed her eyes, considering. Something had turned Alcadizzar's eyes away to the north. Now was the time to attack. Now was–

The shriek was a monstrous thing, loud enough to flatten men and tents. The wind whipped and curled, hurling sand and sparks into the air. Something massive crossed through the sky above the tent, titan wings beating thunderously.

Neferata leaped to her feet, tossing aside her cup and its dregs of blood and snatching up her sword. She drew the tulwar and tossed aside the goat-hide sheath as she bounded out of her tent, followed closely by Naaima and Rasha and her other handmaidens.

The shrieking thing landed in the centre of the camp. It was as large as three horses and eyes like campfires blazed at the scattering tribesmen as a great spear-blade nose quivered and needle-studded jaws gaped hungrily. Sharp ears unfurled from the square head and its wings were tattered sails. It shrieked again, and several of Neferata's handmaidens clapped their hands to their ears.

On the back of the bat-creature, a familiar figure sat, jerking the reins to control his obscene mount. Tattered robes did little to conceal the cadaverous nature of the rider and as his sunken features turned towards her Neferata snarled in recognition.

'W'soran!' she growled, loping towards her old high priest, murder in her eyes. She leapt up onto one of the great beast's wings as it slid across the ground near her and scrambled towards its back, her sword at the ready.

'I bring you greetings, mighty queen,' W'soran cackled. 'I bring you greetings from your lord and master, Nagash!'

Neferata sprang towards W'soran, her sword licking out towards his scrawny neck as the name of the Great

Necromancer struck a painful chord in her. Black lightning crackled from his talon-like fingers, catching her in mid-leap and flinging her back into her tent, which collapsed atop her. As she floundered free, she saw her handmaidens engaging the laughing maniac and his pet monster. One of her servants was slapped from the air by one of the beast's talons, her marble form disintegrating from the force of the impact. Neferata screamed and tore her way free of the tent.

As she made to return to the fray, something heavy struck her and flung her forwards. She rolled to her feet and slashed out with her sword, striking only shadows. 'He sensed you, Neferata,' Ushoran hissed, crouching some feet away. His bulky form was huddled beneath a thick robe, but she recognised her former advisor well enough. 'Nagash desires that you join him.'

'Join, or serve?' Neferata replied.

'One is much the same as the other,' Ushoran said, shrugging.

'You throw over your loyalties quickly, Lord of Masks,' Neferata said.

Ushoran growled, and his talons flexed. 'Lahmia is dead, Neferata. It is ruined and blasted and gone. Just like all of Nehekhara will be, when Nagash gets finished with it!'

Neferata lunged. Ushoran sprang backwards, narrowly avoiding her strike. 'Nehekhara and Lahmia are mine! Not Nagash's and not Alcadizzar's!'

'You cannot defy his will, Neferata,' Ushoran said, his claws skittering across her armour. 'He will have you, one way or another!'

'Then let him come for me himself!' Neferata snarled, backhanding Ushoran. He flew backwards, caught by surprise. She spun to see W'soran flinging magical blasts at her handmaidens. As far away as she was, she could smell his desperation. Her handmaidens were fast and strong, neither

*of which could be applied to the withered vampire. They had
expected to overawe her, to strike her dumb with Nagash's
name and their power. But she would not–*

YOU WILL.

*Neferata screamed as a mind like the cold of the tomb
invaded hers. The words echoed and re-echoed, shattering
her thoughts. She grabbed her head and staggered. The night
spun around her.*

YOU WILL SERVE ME.

*'No!' Neferata howled, clawing at her head. With a
despairing scream, she wrenched herself around and began to
run, away from the camp, and away from Nehekhara. Away
from her plans and hopes and desires, Nagash's thoughts battering at her as she ran.*

*The Worlds Edge Mountains
(–800 Imperial Reckoning)*

BEYOND THE THUNDEROUS crashing of the wild river,
Mourkain rose stark from the mountain. The city was
surrounded by a heavy wooden palisade in concentric
and ever-shrinking rings that jutted from the rocky
slope. Smoke rose from within, striping the air with
greasy trails. The decaying bodies of orcs and beastmen
had been impaled on great, greased stakes lining the
approaches to the palisade. The bodies, both bulky and
green and malformed and hairy, were in bad condition
and a flock of crows had claimed them for their own.

'They attack every few months,' Vorag said, swatting at
a dangling green leg with his sword. 'Not big on learn-
ing lessons, the *urka*.'

Neferata said, 'And the beasts?'

Vorag grinned, displaying his fangs. 'When the urka are thinned out, the beasts take their place.' He sheathed his sword.

'And vice-versa, I assume,' Neferata said.

'Ha! Yes,' Vorag said, laughing and slapping his thigh. 'The beasts are better hunting, but the urka have a better flavour. Or they did,' he said, frowning slightly. Neferata smiled knowingly. Vorag glanced at her and his frown deepened. 'You are strong. The Red Dragon is frightened of you.'

Neferata hesitated. 'Abhorash, you mean?'

Vorag spat a wad of bloody phlegm to the ground. 'Yes. That is what the people call him, "the Red Dragon". Wearing all that iron, like the scales of one of those beasts.' He shook his head. 'That's no way for a warrior to fight,' he said.

'You don't much care for him, do you?'

Vorag's only reply was to spit again. Neferata chuckled. Before she could reply, the strident groan of horns from the top of the palisade broke the air. Neferata looked to the gates, which were being pushed open by a line of men in dark jerkins and hoods. The smell of men and animals and the detritus left by both washed over Neferata.

'I've smelled nicer dung-heaps,' Khaled murmured, earning a baleful glare from Vorag.

'Surely you have not forgotten the smells of a military camp, son of Muntasir,' Abhorash said, urging his horse forwards. Khaled frowned. Vorag made a similar expression as Abhorash joined them.

'I forget nothing,' Khaled snapped. Neferata laid a hand on his arm.

'My followers do not, as a rule, often find themselves in such places,' she said smoothly. 'I have better uses for them than to waste them in battle.'

Abhorash grunted and Vorag laughed. The latter clapped Khaled on the shoulder. 'This will be a treat for you then, my lady!' he said as they rode through the gates. Neferata caught a strange, sweet stink from the men who had opened the gate. They stood as still as statues as the riders passed by, barely moving even when one of the horses came too close.

Beyond the palisade, ancient stones which might have been the remnants of some long ago destroyed wall rose up here and there, linked anew by more palisades. And beyond those stones... Mourkain. Neferata twitched the reins and her horse came to a halt. The crumbling stone walls of Mourkain rose up at an almost impossible angle, careening towards the sky.

Her first impression was one of age. Something had always been in this place, whether its name was Mourkain or not. It was a city in the same way that Lahmia had been, grown over centuries by generations, spreading first behind the river and then over it. Within the palisade, a great stone gateway rose, blocking access to a wide bridge of thick wooden logs that led to a second, smaller gate. Beneath the bridge, the river crashed and snarled, and even at this distance, she could feel the spray. She looked up at the first gate and saw that its bulk was punctuated by hundreds of alcoves packed with skulls. Some of the skulls were brown with age, while others glistened white and clean. Each of the skulls seemed to be looking at her and she recalled her first sight of the place, under the influence of whatever had called her here, and felt a chill caress her spine.

Neferata knew that Mourkain, for all that it might seem to be a living thing, was in truth a city of death.

With a squeal of fibre on stone, the stone gates swung

outwards. As they opened, Neferata saw a network of thick ropes connecting the hinges of the outer gate to the inner, and felt a brief burst of admiration. The outer gates could be controlled from within the city proper, as long as the ropes held. And if the ropes were cut, the stone gates would remain closed and the bridge sealed off.

She brought her horse to a halt and let the column move past her onto the bridge, until the stumping form of Razek came abreast of her horse. The dwarf's powers of recuperation had proven far more impressive than she had anticipated. The bleeding had stopped a few days earlier and scabbing had begun, and the wounds smelled clean. Privately, she was impressed with the dwarf's constitution. A human would have died from the wounds he had taken, but Razek was on his feet within a few days of the mauling, and had insisted on walking. She looked down at the dwarf. 'I believe we have arrived,' she said.

'Aye. Impressive, isn't it?' Razek said, his tone indicating that he thought it was anything but.

'Yes,' Neferata said. She kept her horse to a trot, so that she could keep pace with the dwarf. If he noticed the courtesy, he gave no sign. Then, he could have viewed it as an insult. They moved across the bridge, and she glanced down, at the river. It was no small thing, and seemed far deeper than she was used to.

'It goes down as deep as the mountain's roots,' Razek said. 'Dark things swim in it.'

They passed beneath the interior gate, and Neferata's nostrils flared. The smells of the city were intoxicating after so long in the wilderness. Thousands of warm, beating hearts greeted her, pumping the hot richness of human blood, and she sucked in a breath. 'How many live here?' she hissed. There were merchants stalls set up along the interior wall and the crumbling lean-tos of the *kmut* – the poor dregs of the city. Harsh accents barked offers to the teeming throngs and a wave of sound seemed to envelop her, as she was reminded of her youth and the days when she would sneak from her father's palace and mingle among the commoners on the docks, watching the great ships slide in on the tide.

'Who can say?' Razek said. 'You humans breed like lice.' He grunted, looking around. 'It's been a long time, as you manlings calculate it, since I've been here. Since any of my people have been here.'

'And with good reason, Thane Silverfoot,' a harsh voice said. 'But things are different now. You have our most humble assurances.'

Neferata turned. A broad-shouldered, broken-nosed man trotted towards them, thumbs hooked into a wide leather belt. He had a number of guards with him, dressed as Abhorash's men, in heavy armour and ornate helms. They pushed through the crowd like sharks through a school of fish. Neferata inhaled his scent and repressed an instinctive curl of her lip. Like Vorag, there was a grave-mould whiff to the newcomer. It was a deep stink that Razek either didn't notice or, perhaps, put down to a more human stench.

'Mourkain extends its greetings and its sorrows on your loss, mighty thane,' the man said, spreading his palm and bowing his head. 'We shall scour the hills for the beasts who–'

'Already taken care of, Strezyk,' Razek said brusquely, gesturing to Neferata.

'Oh?' Strezyk glanced at Neferata, who stood. The other vampire stepped back a half-step, his eyes widening slightly. 'Vorag mentioned newcomers, but–'

'I bear the Strigoi no grudge for this,' Razek continued, more formally. 'Our negotiations will continue as planned.'

Strezyk opened his mouth as if to admonish the dwarf for speaking in front of Neferata, but then closed it with a snap. Collecting himself, he again looked at her. 'And who might you be?'

'Neferata of Lahmia,' she said. Strezyk paused then shook himself.

'Hetman Ushoran has been waiting for your arrival,' he said, a patently false smile spreading across his broad features.

'He was expecting us?' Neferata said, slightly surprised.

'Oh yes, he has been aware of your coming for many weeks now,' Strezyk said smoothly. 'I shall escort you to the High Lodge.'

Neferata's thoughts crashed together fast and sharp. Was Ushoran then the cause of her visions? Was he compelling her to come to him somehow? Her hands clenched and her nails sank into her skin. The pain brought her back to herself a moment later. Was it Ushoran's voice in her head, crooning to her?

'He's a greased spoke and no two ways there,' Razek muttered, too low for Strezyk to hear. The armoured soldiers, the *vojnuk* according to what Vorag had taught her, formed up around them, not so close as to be insulting, but not so far as to be ignored.

'Who is he?' Neferata said.

'The new king's hearth-warden,' Razek said, distaste evident.

Neferata grunted, understanding what he meant, though she had never heard the term before. So, Ushoran had his own Lord of Masks now, did he? Maybe Strezyk was more cunning than his master, but Neferata doubted it. 'Tell me about the new king,' she said.

'Why don't you tell me?' Razek said, eyeing her. 'He seems to be a friend of yours, eh?'

Neferata looked at the dwarf, but said nothing. King Ushoran. The thought was neither amusing, nor pleasant. In Lahmia, Ushoran had served as her shadowed left hand, as Abhorash was her strong right one. It was Ushoran who had gathered those who were chosen to sacrifice their lives and blood to the Lahmian Court, so that the sun would rise and the world would turn and the city prosper. It was Ushoran who had failed to find Alcadizzar after the latter had escaped her clutches and it was Ushoran who had ruined everything by turning Nagash's eye upon them.

Ushoran had destroyed Lahmia. He had destroyed her kingdom and now, he welcomed her to his. One way or another, she was determined to make him regret it. She turned back to the city. The streets of Mourkain were like lines drawn on parchment, crossing one another over and over again. The city was a spiral of stone, with crude thatch huts and lean-tos giving way to more sturdy stone dwellings and finally the great buildings that seemed to form the heart of the city. The streets were choked with the smells and sights and sounds of a thriving, vibrant metropolis.

The Strigoi were an uncivilised-looking folk, but sturdy. Hardy, even, and their blood pumped bright in their veins as Neferata examined them. They all carried weapons, even the lowest among them, and they were a pale folk, with dark hair. A young people, as hers judged such things, barely out of the mire of the caves. But they had accomplished much in a short period of time.

And all, apparently, without the help of the gods; she saw no sign of temples or priests. The priestess in her rebelled at the thought... though she had long since turned from her own gods, the idea of them not even being represented was hard to grasp. Indeed, it was a weakness. A people with no faith were open to exploitation. She gave a soft laugh. These were thoughts for the future.

As they moved through the city, Neferata's followers rejoined her, slipping between Strezyk's men to form a barrier between their mistress and the armoured warriors. The column thinned as they approached the centre of the city; Vorag's men stayed behind, in the lower streets, but Strezyk led Neferata and her companions on. The burly vampire gave her a grin and a wave as he departed. He had noticed Strezyk's presence, and seemed to know what it meant. Abhorash and his two men, however, followed at a distance, staying a respectful distance from Strezyk's group. She wondered if her former champion thought that she might try and flee.

When she saw the pyramid, she knew that the answer was 'yes'.

Neferata was careful not to let her emotions show on her face as she looked up at the monstrosity of stone. It rose up suddenly, like a leopard springing from a tree. It was a massive structure, bristling with outcroppings and crude structural additions that seemed to serve no purpose save ornament.

It was a pyramid in name only; the resemblance was a superficial one. It was a crude mockery of the great pyramids of Nehekhara, devised by barbaric minds and built by unskilled hands. Heavy dark stones had been piled atop one another much like the grim barrows which dotted the northern lands. It careened high above the city, and stable growths of structure flourished along its length. There were narrow windows and balconies and things that might have been towers.

It crouched like a beast over the winding river which encircled and ran through Mourkain, and the rest of the city seemed to recoil from it, as if in fear. She knew at once, with an instinct honed by years of dealing with dark magics and ill omens, that this was the source of the black sun that had so tormented her.

'This is bigger than I remember,' Razek said, looking up at the pyramid. 'Old Kadon built it, the mad bugger. Back before we stopped coming here...' He trailed off, clutching his axe more tightly.

'This way, if you please,' Strezyk said, leading them towards the ornate doors that marked the entrance to the pyramid. As they neared them, Neferata felt something dark and beautiful surround her, like a bouquet of poisonous blossoms. The pain of earlier was swept aside by a rush of strange pleasure. She reached out to touch the rock and was rewarded by a pleasant tingle.

This, this was why she had come here. This place... Whatever was within called to her.

A clash of spears brought her back to herself. Men in ornate bronze armour blocked the doorway, their spears crossed over the aperture. 'I thought you said that Ushoran wished to see us,' Neferata said to Strezyk.

He nodded. 'He wishes to see *you*, my lady, and Thane Silverfoot as well, of course. But not your – ah – followers,' he said. He gestured, and his men moved to surround and separate Naaima and the others. Khaled had his hand on his sword and the others looked to Neferata. Strezyk's men weren't vampires, and the fight would be swift, if it came. Neferata looked to Abhorash.

'I will vouchsafe you,' he said. 'Not that you need it.' He rubbed the dent she had put in his armour and for just a moment, some of the humour of old was there in his eyes. 'It's tradition.'

Neferata sniffed and looked at Naaima. 'I will be fine,' she said, nodding sharply.

'Of course you will,' Strezyk said. He waved a hand and the spears were retracted. 'You are safer here than anywhere else, my lady. Hetman Ushoran has ensured it.' The oily unctuous tone put her teeth on edge, but she said nothing. Fuming, she followed Strezyk. Naaima and the others stayed behind, guarded by Strezyk's men.

Everything about the pyramid seemed to press down upon her as she entered, as if it sought to force her to crawl on her belly like an asp. The presence in her head was louder now, murmuring constantly, just behind her thoughts. It was stronger within than without, and an aura of darkness clung to the stones. It burned her eyes to look too long in any one direction and her bones felt brittle and cold within their envelope of weak flesh.

Death coiled waiting in this place. Death and something else; the faint odour of smoke filled her nostrils, and she pulled her fingers back from the walls and tried to banish the sudden surge of fear that tickled at the base of her mind. She heard screams and could not tell whether they came from within her mind or from somewhere in the pyramid.

'Are you well, my lady?' Strezyk said unctuously. He was looking at her knowingly and she resisted the urge to slap him from his feet.

'I am fine,' she said. 'Lead on.'

Great statues that reminded her of the ushabti of home lined the corridors, and ancient wall frescoes and paintings spread between them. The latter were immediately recognisable as being in the lost styles of Numas, Quatar and even Lahmia. She stopped at points, staring at them, yearning to touch them. She had never expected to see such concrete reminders of home again. Even the tiles in the floor were the same as those which had once lined the path to the Women's Palace.

Ushoran was trying to re-create Lahmia. The thought struck her like a hammer-blow. Rage followed a moment later. How dare he? He, whose actions had led to her city's destruction, dared to make a mockery of that lost paradise by hanging tapestries and encouraging these *savages* in aping Nehekharan ways?

The corridors themselves were crafted from slabs of stone and, like the pyramids of home, they moved across from east to west, and then up south to north in a zigzag pattern. It was like following a well-worn path. She knew where it would come out, as she recalled the holy routes of the temples of home. And with every step she took, the whispering in her head grew stronger. It was almost painful in its intensity, and she fought to ignore it.

The throne room crouched in the web of corridors that surrounded it, nestled like a cancer in the heart of the pyramid. Smoking, glowing braziers were scattered throughout the room, their light revealing the high balconies and great expanse of floor. At the other end of the room, a great flat dais rose, and on it, a throne. The throne was made from the ribcage of some great beast and spread across the rear wall, and on that throne... Ushoran.

The Ushoran she had known had had many faces. Brutish, handsome, plain, young and old; there was a reason he had been given the title of Lord of Masks. With Ushoran, there was no telling whether or not the face you were seeing, the voice you were hearing, was his own or a disguise he was putting on for one reason or another.

He sits in your chair, the voice hissed. She ignored it, trying to concentrate on the familiar-yet-not figure sitting before her. The man on the dais looked nothing like the man she remembered, but his body language, his expression was the same; those told the truth of him. He was handsome now, but the ugliness of old was there, in the curl of his lip and the twinkle in his eye. If he saw her, he gave no sign. He sat on his throne, lounging like a Cathayan potentate, dressed much as his nobles – trousers and a jerkin belted at the waist with a strap of beaten gold, and golden armlets and bracers on his heavily muscled limbs. A sword lay against his throne, still sheathed. He had never been one for weapons; it was just for show, most likely.

The throne room was crowded with courtiers – men and women whose clothing, while crude by the standards of any civilised nation, was fine enough to speak to their relative position in Ushoran's new hierarchy. In the sea of warm veins and throbbing pulses there were one or two spots of ugly cold. Vorag hadn't been exaggerating. The men were swaggering bullies, not much different from Vorag – a warrior aristocracy, not long removed from the saddle. The women interested her more. They had the look of she-wolves barely broken to the leash. They had grown sleek on their husbands' new statuses, but the hunger, the drive for more, lurked below the smiles and laughter. And, even more interestingly, none had been given the blood-kiss.

Of course, Ushoran had never been all that fond of women, beyond their more obvious qualities. A trait he had shared with her husband, Lamashizzar. It was a blind spot that a king could ill afford, let alone a spymaster.

She restrained a smile. It wasn't hard. The situation

was designed to annoy. One of Ushoran's more prized abilities was being able to insert his hooks into the most painful soft point on psyche or physicality and to twist.

Ushoran wanted her to see him this way; to see him enshrined in glory. Or maybe he wanted her to do something foolish. That would be like him. His mind was crooked, and if Neferata was a leopardess, Ushoran was a spider. He wanted her to fly into his web.

Well, two could play at that game.

Razek stumped forwards at a gesture from Strezyk, cradling his axe in the crook of one brawny arm. It was a calculated insult, she knew, though whether by Strezyk or his master, she couldn't say. 'Hail, Ushoran, King of Strigos,' Razek boomed, raising his free hand in greeting. 'I, Razek Silverfoot, Thane of Karaz Bryn, bring you the greetings of my father, Borri Silverfoot, King of Karaz Bryn, which manlings call the Silver Pinnacle.'

Neferata blinked. That explained *that*. What little she knew of the dawi suggested they wouldn't have sent just any warrior to open delicate negotiations, but a king's son? That implied that this was something special or else that they took even the most routine political engagement extremely seriously. It also explained why he had been so secretive. Her mind spun off in new directions. Had the beast attack truly been what it seemed, or had something else been behind it?

'You bring more than greetings, I trust, especially considering what you went through to get here,' Ushoran said, chuckling. Dutiful laughter rose from the gathered court. Razek's expression was like stone and Neferata hid a smile. Ushoran was a fool. In Lahmia, jape and jest had been the way of such things; informality hid the true currents of negotiation. But Razek was not human. And his greeting had told her everything about his view of such things. The dawi were a formal people, and Ushoran had just inadvertently insulted their official representative. *Fool*, she thought again.

'Aye,' Razek said as the sounds of amusement died away. He cleared his throat. 'I offer you our hand in friendship, and oaths of trade and alliance.' He proffered his hand in a ritualistic fashion.

'I'd wager that hand is hoping to be filled with good Mourkain gold,' Strezyk murmured to Ushoran in a too-loud voice. Razek's face tightened and Neferata shook her head, amazed. It boggled her mind. How did Ushoran expect to do anything with fools like Strezyk serving him? It was disappointing. Whatever his other flaws, the Lord of Masks had at least been cunning while in her service. Perhaps he had lost his edge here in these uncivilised mountains.

Pay attention, she thought, focusing on the dais. Ushoran had been offered a truce and had launched an attack, though not a successful one. Contrary to popular opinion, it wasn't always the weaker party who offered terms first; it was simply the party with the most to gain. Razek was talking again. She was impressed that the dwarf had held his temper; Naaima had said that they could be a volatile people. 'Aye,' Razek agreed. 'We want your gold, as you want our artifice,' he said bluntly. His temper might be holding, but it was definitely frayed if he had discarded formality, Neferata judged. 'It seems a fair enough trade to us,' Razek went on, setting his shoulders and raising his chin. 'What about you, King of Strigos?'

Ushoran frowned. He had never liked being shown up, Neferata recalled with a flush of humour. 'That is perhaps a conversation for a later time, Thane Silverfoot,' he said, leaning back in his seat. 'We have other matters to attend to this day.' He waved and Strezyk clapped his hands. Men stepped forwards, surrounding the dwarf. For a moment, it looked as if Razek wasn't going to move. Then, with a grunt and shrug, he turned to allow his escort to remove him from the hall. He glanced at Neferata as he stomped past. His face was unreadable. Regardless, she knew that it was a warning.

Strezyk clapped his hands again and she stepped forwards, leaving her own escort stumbling after her, trying to catch up. The crowd of backwoods nobles murmured. She ignored them.

'We bid you greetings, Lady Neferata,' Ushoran said, holding out his arms and stepping down the dais towards her. As she had noted before, the bland, innocuous Lord of Masks she remembered was gone, replaced by a handsome creature that seemed to have stepped straight out of a hero-myth. Even so, she caught a flickering glimpse of something else, a monstrous phantom shape superimposed over Ushoran. Which was his true form, she wondered?

'Lady,' she repeated, stepping forwards and flinging back the edge of her furs. 'You forget yourself, Lord of Masks.' She could sense the faint tremors in his web. What gambit would he employ? Would it be courtesy?

'Neferata–' Abhorash growled, making to step forwards. Ushoran gestured for him to remain where he was. He smiled at his former queen with apparent good humour.

'No, my lady, I do not think that I do. Much has transpired since our last meeting,' he said.

Neferata looked around the room, taking in the gathered faces. Though she did not know them, she recognised them well enough – the great and the good who clung like parasites to any throne. 'So I see,' she said.

'I am hetman here, Neferata,' Ushoran said, striding the rest of the way towards her. 'From Mourkain, I rule the mountains of Strigos. Here is the seat of empire...' he said grandly. A sudden burst of applause made him stop and raise a hand.

No, not courtesy then. He wanted her angry. That was her weak point.

'Oh, well done,' Neferata said. 'Delightfully stage-managed, oh Lord of Masks.'

'I am not the Lord of Masks any longer,' he said, looking into her eyes. 'There are no masks in Mourkain. I am king. And it is only fitting that you should bow.'

Neferata burst out laughing. It was an obvious ploy. He *had* gone soft.

'Impudent wench,' Strezyk snarled, dragging the mace from his belt. He swung it at Neferata, intending to batter her off her feet. She whirled, ripping off her fur cloak as she did so and flinging it over his head. He roared and stumbled and then she was behind him. She sank into a crouch and her claws plunged into his legs, ripping through the leather of his boots to get to the flesh within. Strezyk screamed as he fell, hamstrung. Ushoran stepped back as his servant's mace crashed to the floor.

Neferata rose and stepped over Strezyk's thrashing form. The vampire was already healing, but he would be out of her hair for a few moments at least. She looked at Ushoran. Had that been planned? Was it a tug of the web? Ushoran retreated slowly up the dais, smiling insufferably at her. 'As impressive as ever, my lady,' he said. 'Truly you are first among us, in power if not in status.'

'The latter can be easily rectified, Ushoran,' Neferata said, flicking blood from her fingers to the floor.

'Implying what? Would you kill me?' he said, laughing

as he plopped back down into his throne. Abhorash's men moved forwards warily. Neferata ignored them.

'Kill you? No… You have proven yourself useful in the past, Ushoran. Perhaps you will again. But I am a queen. I do not bow.' *Two can tug on a strand, Ushoran,* she thought.

'And I am a king!' Ushoran snapped. Ah, there it was. He had lost that mask of servility, at least. He had grown used to being master.

'No, you are a fool and a fraud, clinging to a throne no doubt won through treachery and deceit,' she said. His flinch told her that she had scored a point. She grinned. 'I think it only fitting that you give me your kingdom, since you destroyed mine.' *I see your offer and raise, cunning one,* she thought. A nervous titter rippled through the throne room.

Ushoran hissed. 'Lahmia's fall was not my fault, woman.' His mask of civility was gone now too, to join the servility, replaced by a rage that was tinted more than a little with something that might have been madness. The armrests of his throne cracked in his grip, the stone turning to powder. 'It was your madness! Your obsession with that puling princeling Alcadizzar! That was what damned us!'

It was Neferata's turn to flinch. Too close to the truth not to hurt. She exposed her fangs and lunged up the steps, claws out. If he wanted her in the web, now was the time to dive in. Abhorash stepped forwards, placing himself between her and her prey as she knew he would. Predictable Abhorash, dependable Abhorash, still protecting her, even if he didn't realise it. Her claws dug furrows in his mail and he grunted in shock as she sent him reeling. He countered by drawing his sword and forcing her to drop back down the step. Abhorash rose to his feet, the tip of the sword just beneath Neferata's chin. She backed away slowly, arms held out. She could have pressed the matter if she had wished and he knew it.

'Get out of my way, Abhorash,' she said. 'I would hate to kill you as well as him.'

'Are you so maddened that you think you could get away with it?' he said, looking at her with reproach. 'Do you think that you can win a kingdom this way?'

Neferata looked around. Horrified eyes that belonged to human and vampire alike watched her much like a flock of birds might watch a snake slithering through the grass below them. Her face hardened as an icy calm replaced the only partially false fury that had filled her only moments before. Her own earlier words to Naaima filled her head – *seek the advantage.* 'Maybe not hold one, but win one? Oh yes,' she said calmly.

'You've learned nothing in your years in the wilderness, I see,' Ushoran growled.

'Oh, I've learned much,' Neferata said. 'I've learned that thrones are like horses. They always throw their rider at the first sign of weakness.' She reached up and pressed two fingers to Abhorash's sword and pushed it aside. 'I've learned that it is far better to be the one holding the reins than riding the horse.'

'I thought you were a queen,' Ushoran spat her words back at her.

'I am, but not all queens sit on thrones,' she said. She nodded to Abhorash, who stepped back. 'You've given Abhorash a position within your new Lahmia, Ushoran. So why not do the same for me?'

'You?' Ushoran said, incredulously. Even Abhorash looked taken aback.

'You need me, Ushoran,' she said. 'You know nothing

of ruling a kingdom, nothing of statecraft or diplomacy. If you would be more than a petty warlord squatting in a tomb of stone, you will require someone with… finesse,' she said.

'I have more than enough advisors,' Ushoran said suspiciously. She could see the wheels turning in his mind.

'Yes, but what you do not have is a Lady of Masks,' Neferata said, her foot on the first step of the dais. 'Someone to shape your policy and be the dark left hand of this… paradise you have made.'

'Strezyk serves me admirably in that capacity,' Ushoran said slowly, gesturing to Strezyk. The vampire had got to his feet and reclaimed his mace. His face was flushed purple and his fangs jutted from his mouth like tusks. He sweated rage. Neferata glanced at him dismissively.

'Strezyk is a fool. He insulted the dwarf and nearly cost you a potential ally. He allowed me to get within a hair's breadth of you. He is foolish and vain and stupid, Ushoran. That is why you picked him. You never could stomach subordinates who were smarter than you.'

'And you could?' Ushoran said, glowering.

'I chose you, didn't I?' she said smoothly. The flattery did not go unnoticed. Ushoran stiffened, his eyes alight with speculation. She could almost hear the thoughts rattling through his head: *Can I trust her? Is this some gambit? Why? Why?*

'I am tired of the wilderness, Ushoran. I would rule again, even if it is at your side,' she said, bowing her head. 'Make me your Lady of Mysteries, if Masks are no longer to your liking.'

Ushoran laughed. The sound started as a low purr that burst out as a rumbling growl. 'Strezyk might have something to say about that, eh, Strezyk?'

Strezyk's mace caught her in the hip. Bone crunched and she nearly fell. Abhorash cried out, but Ushoran lunged to his feet and grabbed him. Neferata snapped upright and slapped Strezyk off his feet. The Strigoi slid across the stone floor and scattered nobles who hopped awkwardly aside. He struck a column and lay for a moment, panting. Neferata tested her hip and then faced him, her features lit with a predatory fury.

Strezyk rose, mace in hand, his own face twisting into something bestial. With a growl, he charged forwards, his weapon clasped in both hands, its head trailing behind him. Neferata lunged to meet him. She slid, ducking under his wild swing. Her claws dug into his belly, releasing a spray of sour black fluid. He screamed and gave her a glancing blow on the side of her head. Stunned, she awkwardly dodged his next blow.

His mace thudded down again, cracking stone. Strezyk was strong and fast, like all vampires. But as she had noted with Vorag, he had no idea of his true potential. He saw power only in terms of his human frame. Neferata had evolved beyond such preconceptions.

She had been the first of them. And she was stronger than any pale shadow that had come after. The mace dropped towards her head again and she caught it, her fingers squeezing the stone head so hard it cracked.

Caught up as he was in a berserk fury, he jerked at the weapon and kicked at her belly, trying to dislodge her. She slapped a hand to his leg and swung him into the air, hurling him into the dais hard enough to shatter one of the steps. Strezyk rose with a screech, his head flattening and expanding as hair burst from his pores and his clothes tore. Humps of muscle rippled across his widening frame and the mace looked like a toy in his bulging claw as he came at her again, howling.

She sprang past him, her claws leaving red trails across his hide. He spun, but she was faster. Like a cyclone of teeth and claws, she leapt and circled him, cutting him to pieces bit by bit. Soon he was gasping and the floor of the hall was slick with his blood. His fangs gnashed and he stumbled. In contrast, Neferata felt nothing – neither exhaustion nor even the slightest hint of fatigue. She circled him like some great cat of the veldt waiting for its chosen prey to give in, lie down, and accept death.

No vampire, even one as pathetic as Strezyk, would do that, of course. Persistence was built into them. When the last living breath fled, a will to persist like that possessed by no mortal creature filled them in its place. They could not surrender to death, not willingly.

Neferata stopped. Strezyk's eyes had gone half-mad and feral and the grave-stink rolled off him in waves. There was something tainted in Ushoran's blood, some feral weakness it seemed, an inclination to the bestial.

'Come then,' she purred, crooking a finger, 'one last time, Strezyk.'

The mace looped out, and her body became as mist, swirling and coiling up his arm as he gaped in shock. The mist seeped into his flattened, triangular nose and open fang-filled mouth and red eyes and hair-choked pores. Strezyk dropped his weapon and clawed at himself as he staggered back. He opened great canyons in his own flesh, trying to dig her out, but to no avail. Strange bulges began to form on his body, like flowers seeking the sun, and he groaned. His tongue and eyes protruded grotesquely as his body began to shake. He made a strangled sound and then gave an agonised scream as he abruptly burst in a shower of gore. Men and women screamed and there was a stampede to the doors as the ruin of Strezyk tottered a few steps and fell at the foot of the dais.

Silence fell on the hall as Neferata stepped out of the ruins of the former major-domo, picking her way delicately over the lumps of quivering meat and bone that littered the steps. Blood drenched her, turning her pale skin the colour of rust. She gazed up at Ushoran and licked her lips. She held his gaze for a moment. Then she dropped to one knee, spread her arms and bowed her head.

'My king,' she said, 'how may I serve you?'

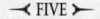

◄ FIVE ►

The City of Bel Aliad
(−1152 Imperial Reckoning)

Bel Aliad burned as Neferata led her warriors over the hastily erected barricades. She wore thin black robes and a voluminous hood and scarf to hide her from the sun, and light leather armour sewn with hammered copper discs over the former. The horse she rode was a sleek desert stallion, ungelded and almost as savage as its rider. She drummed her heels into its glossy black flanks and it leapt over the fire-pots the defenders had lit without hesitation. Her sword snapped out like a scorpion's stinger, and a man screamed as she split both a spear and the hands holding it.

She jerked the reins and her horse spun, lashing out with its hooves as she chopped at those defenders who had not retreated at her arrival. Wildcat screams heralded the arrival of her handmaidens. Like her, they rode the pride of the nomad herds and wore flowing black robes and hoods to pro-tect them from the merciless attentions of the sun that played witness to the ensuing slaughter.

'Drive them back!' she howled, waving her sword over

her head. 'The city will be ours!' As she said it, the words burned like bitter poison in her mouth. Bel Aliad, for all of its vaunted splendour, was not Lahmia. It was a shadow of the great tomb-cities of Nehekhara, a sad attempt by the Arabyans to ape their betters.

It was not Lahmia. It was nothing. But it would be hers. If Lahmia was lost to her, then she would have Bel Aliad. She would be a queen again, despite Alcadizzar and despite Nagash. At the thought of his name, a nauseated shudder ran through her. Nagash had demanded her servitude, but she had defied him. Let the others sup from his scraps like the dogs they were. She would make her own way.

She slashed and thrust about her as spears sought her vitals from every corner. The defenders had grown complacent; they had not realised the size of her army. Though W'soran's attack had scattered many of the tribes, enough had remained to create a force large enough to threaten more than just the trade routes between Bel Aliad and Khemri.

She snarled and sent a man spinning away, his face opened to the bone. She was painfully aware that even this attack served Nagash in some way, preventing any outside aid from reaching Nehekhara in time. She had seen the first few refugees of the Great Plague, and knew that it was without a doubt Nagash's doing.

Nehekhara was dying, as Lahmia had died. Part of her felt a vicious satisfaction at the thought, but another, more practical part knew that Nagash would not be satisfied with the throne of Khemri. No... the Great Necromancer wanted the world, and he would crush the thrones of the earth beneath his feet to get it.

As an immortal, she had become used to having a wealth of time to contemplate such gambits, but now, time was at a premium. How long would it take her homeland to die? How long until an army of rotting, plague-infested corpses *stumbled across the sea of sand and scratched at the walls of the Arabyan caliphates?*

If she could take Bel Aliad – and from there the other caliphates – and unify them into a mighty kingdom, then she might be able to stop him. She might be the only one who could. Ordinarily, pitting herself against Nagash would be the last thing on her mind. But her experience in the desert had taught her that there was nowhere to run. Nagash was the wolf at the door of the world.

Then, there was the fact that the Great Necromancer had insulted her. And no man, alive or dead, insulted Neferata and lived.

She would take Araby and her peoples and forge them into a sword to thrust into Nagash's sour, black heart–

The arrow caught her by surprise, sprouting as if by magic from her thigh. Another slapped home in her chest, nearly wrenching her from her saddle. She looked up. Archers made ready on the sloping rooftops of the buildings nearest the barricades. She gestured with her sword and Naaima kicked her horse into a gallop, leading Rasha and a few others towards the closest of the bowmen. Naaima leapt from her mount to the edge of the roof. Arrows sped towards her and her sword knocked them from the air as she attacked the unprepared archers. Men screamed and died as the other handmaidens followed suit.

Neferata growled in satisfaction. She urged her horse forwards. The defenders were falling back now, though not in an organised fashion, and retreating towards one of the city's many market squares. Men trampled one another in their haste to escape the attacking tribesmen. Bloodlust stirred in her and she gave herself up to it gladly. She had restrained herself for months now, whetting her appetite for the coming bloodletting. Now she unleashed the pent-up aggression, flogging her horse forwards after the fleeing warriors. She *hacked at their backs and upraised limbs, sheathing her arm in a sleeve of red.*

She was laughing when the first lance caught her horse in its chest. It squealed and fell, forcing her to dive from the saddle. She sprang to her feet, sword licking out. The armoured Kontoi of Bel Aliad had arrived. The lancers wore robes sewn through with flat iron plates and heavy helmets that covered their faces. Their lances were weighty spears of wood that could bring down even the heaviest horse. They met the nomads in a tangle of metal and flesh, and the Kontoi's greater mass began to prevail. Neferata found herself buffeted by horses and she leapt upwards, her claws snagging a Kontoi's armoured coat. She snarled into the man's helmet and then snapped his neck.

The sword nearly chopped through her arm as the dead man fell away from her. The Kontoi wore a finer coat than the others and brightly coloured silks dangled from his helmet in a rainbow halo. The sword seemed to writhe in his hand like a thing alive, and the sigils inscribed on the blade hurt her eyes. What was this? What was it–?

She fell back as the warrior swung at her again. The blade sizzled as it cut the air and it seemed to shiver. She fell from the horse and slid between its legs. She slashed the warrior's saddle strap with her claws, sending him crashing to the ground. The square was filled with heaving, stamping horses and men and the sky was growing dark. Night was falling.

She rose, flinging back her hood. The Kontoi scrambled to his feet. He had lost his sword in the fall. With a yell, he dived for it even as she lunged for him, catching it up as she landed on him. She spun him around and hurled him into a wall hard enough to crack the brick. The warrior staggered, but remained standing.

Neferata eyed him warily. Her arm was slow to heal, and black froth collected in the open wound as steam rose from it.

It ached abominably. She had been hurt in such a way only once before, when she had faced Alcadizzar before the gates of Lahmia and he had driven a knife into her heart. The sword was something fell and old. It was of foreign design, reminding her of the weapons she had seen in the marketplaces of Cathay, brought from the forges of the lands beyond the Great Bastion. Perhaps it was a daemon weapon of some kind, then. She would have more time to study it after she had torn it from the dead hands of its current wielder.

She stood up straight and stalked slowly towards him. 'You fight well, warrior,' she said, extending a hand. 'Tell me your name, won't you?'

The man hesitated. Her eyes caught his, holding them. She pressed her will down the length of the distance between them, hammering his. Slowly, almost grudgingly, he pulled his helmet off and tossed it aside, revealing a handsome, hawkish face. He was young. 'I am Khaled al Muntasir, witch, and I am your death!' he said, raising the sword. The blade shook ever so slightly, straining towards her like a dog on a leash. Khaled was sweating from more than just exertion. She could taste his fear, not just of her, but also of the weapon he held.

'If you fear it so much, why not lay it aside, Khaled al Muntasir?' she said. Her voice caressed him, piercing his mind and soul. She could do much with her voice. It had allowed her to conquer without raising a single weapon. But it took time to do it properly, and time was something she did not have. She reached out towards Khaled. 'Put the blade down, boy,' she purred, letting the soft tones envelop him. 'Put it down…'

He blinked and trembled. She was impressed. His resistance was remarkable. Then, perhaps that was the influence of the sword. She would have to learn where he had obtained it. Such a potent weapon might be useful in the coming days–

He lashed out. She narrowly stepped aside and hissed as she felt the foul heat clinging to the blade. She slashed him *across the face and he cried out. She grabbed his sword hand and pushed the blade away. Her other hand found his throat and forced him back against the wall. She looked into his eyes, flattening his will beneath her own. The sword was loose in his grip. She made to shake his arm, but a shout stopped her before she could.*

'Neferata, look out!' Naaima screamed from somewhere above.

Neferata spun, only to catch a lance full in the chest. She was slammed backwards into the wall. A scream burst out of her as the lance buried itself in her ribcage and burst out through her back, pinning her to the wall. Her screams pealed wildly as she thrashed and struggled like a bug caught on a pin. She clawed at the wood desperately. Her feet were too far above the ground and her mind was too disordered by the pain to effect a shape-change.

Khaled chopped down on the lance. He shattered it, but she was still pinned. Coughing, blood and foam running down her front, she reached for him. Horror in his eyes, he stepped back and readied the sword. It made a hungry sound as it pierced her heart.

It was only as the darkness closed in that she saw the hand that had wielded the lance that had pinned her. She carried Abhorash's frown down into the dark with her...

The City of Mourkain
(−800 Imperial Reckoning)

'IT WAS RISKY,' Naaima said, sipping delicately out of a cup. 'You are far too incautious, Neferata. He would have been well within his rights to have killed you. Abhorash–'

Neferata made a dismissive gesture. 'Abhorash is still my strong right hand, whether he knows it or not. His sense of honour is a trap none of us can escape.' She sipped from her own cup and looked around the apartment she had been given. It had once belonged to Strezyk, and was now hers by right of conquest. Apparently such was quite common in Mourkain, among the most rambunctious of the city's aristocracy.

It was located in one of the larger buildings of the city, a tower that was almost beautiful after a fashion, and through its great window the diverse and myriad smells of Mourkain infiltrated the chambers. Braziers of burning incense hid the stink of blood which emanated from the upside down, barely-alive figure dangling from one of the many hooks dangling from the ceiling.

He was a criminal, she had been told. It was Ushoran's practice to feed only from those accused of crimes, or from prisoners of war, a standard he held his followers to. Privately, Neferata thought it wise; nothing irritated a populace more than indiscriminate murder. She had learned that to her cost in Bel Aliad.

'My lady, we've rounded them all up at last,' Khaled said.

'Speak of the beast,' she murmured. Then, louder, she said, 'How many?'

'Six, my lady,' Anmar said, flopping down on one of the great cushions which lay scattered across the floor of the chamber. 'Not a fighter in the bunch. And one step above the great apes of Ind as far as brains go,' she added with a snort.

'Such sharp fangs, my little leopard,' Neferata said, rising from her own cushions. 'Intelligence and fighting ability can be taught. And if not, well…'

Khaled smiled. 'Well indeed, my lady. Strezyk had good taste as far as looks went.'

Neferata frowned. 'Careful, Khaled, your more unpleasant proclivities are showing. It is not a look which suits you.' She gestured imperiously. 'Bring them in.'

'What are you planning, if not to stock our larder?' Naaima said.

'I am planning to see that others stock it for us,' Neferata said. 'We need friends. Strezyk took the pick of the booty when it came to certain prisoners of war, something which won him no allies in Ushoran's little newborn snake-pit. We will not make the same mistake.'

Khaled brought the women in. They huddled together, stinking of fear. Barely-healed bite marks covered their arms and thighs and Neferata repressed a hiss of disgust. Strezyk had been a cruel master, that much was certain. And while cruelty had its place, practised on the helpless it was mere sadism, and as such worthless and, worst of all, pointless. For Neferata, cruelty was the tip of the blade you twisted to force action. To practise it on wretches like these was gross indulgence. Once again she reflected that Strezyk was no loss.

The women were as beautiful as Khaled had said. They were former barbarian princesses, the daughters, young wives and cousins of conquered chieftains and warlords. But the haughtiness had been beaten out of them, and at least one had been bled almost white. Broken in body and mind, Ushoran probably expected her to drain them and throw them away.

But she had other plans.

She took the chin of a red-headed beauty and turned her face to the light. 'Where are Stregga and Rasha?' Neferata said as she examined the woman's broad features.

'Stregga is where you sent her, courting that brute Vorag,' Naaima said. 'And Rasha is–'

'Rasha is investigating this edifice,' Khaled said smoothly. Naaima glared at him, and he smiled. 'As you requested, my lady,' he added.

'Yes,' Neferata said absently. On the ride to Mourkain, Vorag had displayed undue attention to the blonde Sartosan. Stregga had been only too happy to indulge those attentions. And Rasha, born raider that she was, was as cunning and stealthy as any beast of the desert. If anyone could sneak about without alerting the spies that Ushoran had undoubtedly already placed around her chambers, it was her.

She looked the red-head in the eyes. 'What is your name?' she said. The woman looked at her blankly. Neferata squeezed her cheeks gently, with only the softest of pressures. There was a flash in the woman's eyes, a buried spark of resistance. Neferata smiled. 'Never mind, we have time to get acquainted. Naaima, see that they are bathed and properly clothed and fed. Strezyk appears to have been a firm believer in keeping them hungry.' She released the woman and watched as Naaima led the girls out, considering. 'Khaled, I wish you to get acquainted to those men in Ushoran's personal guard. They're made up of the firstborn sons of the agals – the Strigoi nobles. Find out whether their loyalties lie to Ushoran, the throne or their families.'

'Of course, it would be my pleasure, but why?' Khaled said.

'You're questioning me again, my Kontoi. Is that wise, do you think?' she said without turning around.

'I merely wish to understand your grand strategy, milady,' Khaled said.

Neferata smiled briefly. 'My strategy, dear Khaled, is

to learn all that I can in order to ensure that our new kingdom survives longer than the last.'

The door thumped. Neferata turned. 'Ah. And here comes another source of information now. Stay here. I will see him alone.'

She left her private rooms and entered the audience chamber. She strode swiftly to the door and threw it open, startling the two guards Ushoran had posted in the corridor. They eyed her cautiously, having been part of her predecessor's guard. They had seen what she had done to Strezyk, and she could smell their fear.

'Milady, Thane Silverfoot–'

'Thane Silverfoot wants a drink. D'you fancy a drink, Neferata of Lahmia?' Razek said, stepping past her into the room. He looked at the barren chamber and snorted. 'Do you even have anything to drink?'

Amused, Neferata nodded to the guards and closed the door. One of them would doubtless be reporting to Ushoran. She turned to face the dwarf. 'I believe there's something in Strezyk's cabinets, yes.' She moved to the cabinets and plucked out a clay jug that sloshed promisingly. It had dust on it. She handed it to Razek, who pulled the cork with his teeth and took a swig. He made a face as he swallowed it.

'Terrible,' he said.

'Yes, I expect so. Strezyk seems to have been deplorably lacking in taste.'

'I heard he had an accident,' Razek said gruffly. He looked uncomfortable. Neferata knew that the dwarf was still feeling put out. Messages had been sent to Silver Pinnacle, via methods known only to the dwarf himself, letting King Borri know that his son yet lived. There were a number of dwarf traders and not a few itinerant miners in the city and Neferata suspected that one of them, or even several, had been bullied into taking word to Karaz Bryn.

'Yes,' she said.

'And you've taken his place.'

'Also yes,' she said. Razek looked at her. After a moment, he nodded.

'Good,' he said simply.

Neferata smiled. 'Gold,' she corrected. 'That is what this is about, I understand.'

Razek stared at the flames. 'My people are interested in opening proper trade with Mourkain,' he said.

'Is it your people,' she asked, 'or your king?'

'Not just him,' he said.

'You don't approve,' she said.

'I have a longer memory, even when it comes to gold. We used to trade with Mourkain many years ago as you manlings judge things. Back when Kadon was running the works,' Razek said. He shuddered slightly. 'Brrr, he was a bad one, old Kadon. Sour, like a bad patch of tunnel, and touched in the head.' He tapped his head for emphasis.

Intrigued, Neferata let him talk. Ushoran had been stubbornly close-mouthed when it came to his coup; at least she assumed that it had been a coup. He had always been a plotter, her Lord of Masks. It was just too bad that his plots always unravelled in the end.

'They said he found something down deep in the dark, and that it spoke to him and broke him,' Razek said in a faraway voice, as if reciting a children's bedtime story. 'Dwarfs know about that sort of thing. We know better than any man or elf what gnaws at the roots of the mountains and what coils in the dark beneath the world.' He tipped the jug and the contents dribbled into his beard. 'He used the dead,' Razek spat. 'That's what did it. He forced the dead to serve him. That's a power no mortal should have, let alone a creature like mad, bad Kadon.'

Neferata sat silently, digesting this new fact. She thought again of the black sun, and the voice like needles on bone. She suspected that it had spoken to Abhorash, but Ushoran? If he wasn't the cause, what was? The stones beneath her feet seemed to tremble like the flank of a purring cat. It wasn't a pleasant sensation. 'But things are different now,' she said, prodding gently.

He grunted. 'King Borri feels that what's done is done.'

'Not a very dwarf-like attitude,' she said.

Razek looked at her. 'Careful, woman, any other dwarf would have taken that for an insult. No, my father is practical. It's why he made me his hearth-warden, after all.'

'A prince and a spymaster,' Neferata said. 'Impressive.'

'I've always thought so. Besides, who can a king trust but family?'

'In my homeland, the answer was "anyone else",' Neferata said, smiling. 'Perhaps dwarfs are different.'

'We are. We are nothing like you, Neferata of Lahmia,' Razek said seriously. 'If your race survives for a million-million years you will never accomplish a third of what my people have forgotten.'

Neferata frowned. 'Perhaps. Or perhaps we will accomplish more.'

Razek chuckled. 'That's the spirit,' he rumbled. 'I owe you a debt, woman,' Razek added, handing the empty jug to her. 'That's why I'm here. I'll be doing all of my business with you.'

Neferata smiled. It was exactly as she had been hoping. 'You honour me, Thane,' she said, inclining her head.

'I've already sent messages off to that effect to King Borri, may his fundament warm the throne for centuries yet,' Razek said. 'And I'll be informing Ushoran as well.' He squinted. 'He's a weasel that one, but I trust you to keep accounts settled.'

'I've always had a head for figures,' Neferata said, upending the jug. It was her turn to raise an eyebrow. Razek grunted. 'Anything else I can do for you, mighty thane?'

'Get something better to drink. We'll need to keep our throats wet if we're to dicker properly,' he said, turning towards the door.

Neferata watched him go. She let the jug fall and laughed as it shattered. But it was only a brief noise. Sobriety returned quickly. 'Did you hear any of that?' she said.

'Of course,' Khaled said, stepping out of her chambers. Anmar followed him. 'Foul creature,' he said.

'But useful,' Neferata said, kicking aside a broken shard of the jug. She rubbed her chin, thinking.

'Yes, you are good at finding tools, are you not, my lady?'

Neferata spun, her eyes darting to the door to her private chambers. Khaled's sword sprang into his hand and he lunged smoothly, followed by Anmar. The siblings leapt for the bulky shape which had entered the audience chamber behind them on noiseless feet. Taloned paws caught the blades of both swords and sent the two vampires crashing to the floor in a heap.

'You left the window open,' Ushoran said through a thicket of fangs. He had forsaken his guise from earlier, revealing his true monstrous visage. He was covered in so much muscle that he was forced to stoop over. He balanced on his knuckles and his bat-like face had lost all traces of humanity. His fine clothes had been replaced by a simple loincloth that flapped alarmingly as he sank into a squat. Beady eyes fastened on Neferata and a tongue like a red worm darted out, dabbing at a bit of dried blood that clung to the lipless jaws.

'I wasn't aware I would be receiving visitors through any other aperture than the door,' Neferata said, waving Khaled and Anmar aside. The two looked at Ushoran in horrified fascination. Neferata wondered what they made of the other vampire, inhuman as he was.

'I find the climb refreshing,' Ushoran said. His red eyes swivelled. 'You've broken a jug. How clumsy. Did I startle you?'

'No. I simply didn't like it.'

'You still have a propensity for breaking things you don't like, then?' Ushoran eyed Khaled and Anmar.

'Only jugs,' Neferata said. 'To what do we owe the pleasure, my lord?' she said, bowing snallowly.

'I wished to speak to you, away from prying eyes,' Ushoran said. He reached out, snagged a bit of the jug and scraped at the floor with it. Neferata looked at the shape he had cut into the floor and grunted.

'Go,' she said, gesturing sharply. They went, as silent as shadows. Ushoran watched them go. Then he grinned, displaying his mouthful of twisted fangs.

'You always did have an eye for the pretty ones,' he said.

'At least mine stay pretty,' Neferata said. It was a petty thing to say, but the abortive growl that rippled from Ushoran made it worth it. 'I suppose that someone told you that Razek visited me?'

'I needed no one to tell me he would,' Ushoran said. He snapped at the air. 'I need the dwarfs, Neferata. Strigos needs them. They have the artifice I need to pull this kingdom of apes up out of the muck.'

'And you offer them gold in return,' Neferata said, crossing her arms. 'Where does that gold come from, I wonder? Have you turned these barbarians into a productive society?'

Ushoran gave a fart of laughter. 'Productive? Ha!' He grinned and scratched at the floor with his talons. 'They were barely scraping by when I found them. In a few generations they would have been no better than the ghouls that haunt the tunnels beneath this place. Inbred cannibals!'

'And Kadon?' Neferata prompted.

'Pfaugh, Kadon,' Ushoran said, motioning dismissively. 'He was nothing. Old and weak, like all mortals become. But he had his uses.'

'He seems to have had something in common with an old friend of ours,' Neferata said.

Ushoran sat back on his haunches and gazed at her silently for a moment. Then, 'The dwarf said that, did he?'

'Not in so many words.' Neferata stepped past Ushoran and into her chambers. He followed nimbly. 'Kadon was a necromancer, like W'soran.'

'Like Nagash,' Ushoran said.

'Yes. And how did that come about, hmmm?'

Ushoran went to the dangling man and lifted him. A groan slipped from the man's lips. Ushoran fastened his lamprey mouth over the unfortunate's throat and, with a sound like ripping papyrus, began to drink what remained of his blood. Neferata sipped from her goblet, watching him.

When he had finished, he turned to her and said, 'I don't know.'

Neferata let the lie pass. Talking to Ushoran was akin

to swordplay. The obvious drop of the guard was a likely feint. Instead, she settled for a change of tactics. 'Where is the gold coming from?' she asked again.

Ushoran cocked his head. 'Mourkain has many secrets. Kadon collected much wealth during his tenure as het-man.' He licked his fangs. 'We are in the process of re-opening the vaults.'

'And where did Kadon get this wealth?' Neferata said. 'Did he steal it from the dwarfs, Ushoran?' *Even you would not be so foolish, would you*, she thought.

'Here and there,' Ushoran said. 'Kadon was a fool and a degenerate, but he was a miser of some distinction. Perhaps he collected some dwarf wealth in his more active years. What does it matter?'

'It matters quite a bit,' Neferata said. 'Show them to me.'

'What?' Ushoran said.

'The vaults, my king, show them to me.' She emptied her goblet. 'Razek is curious, Ushoran, as am I.'

'You think he may try to steal the gold?' Ushoran said, and she could see by the look in his eyes that he had never even considered such a thing. *Oh my cunning lord, your wit has abandoned you as thoroughly as your looks*, she thought.

'No, but I think that if he learns that you're paying the dwarfs with their own gold he will not be pleased,' she said. 'And if that happens, our newborn alliance could quickly become enmity and Mourkain could find itself once more at war with the dawi. Now show me the vaults.'

Ushoran wiped the back of his hand across his mouth. 'Very well. See if you can keep up.' Then, with a scrape of talons across stone, he was bounding towards the window. Neferata was after him a half-second later.

Even as she vaulted out of the window, Ushoran was plummeting downwards through the chill night air.

He struck an outcropping and twisted through the air as if he were swimming. His flesh snapped, ripped and spread with a sound like a rupturing melon, and wings unfurled from his broad back. Black blood, expelled during the transformation, splattered across the rooftops below as a winged shadow sped off. Neferata landed on the outcropping, her eyes wide. Ushoran had learned something during his time in the wilderness after all.

The game of skin-changing was a hard one, and it grew harder the younger and further from the source their kind was. Of Neferata's get, one in three could shift shape to any appreciable degree, and of those whom her handmaidens brought over, fewer still could manage it. For herself, she had never faced any difficulty with it, and if Ushoran wished to show off, well, two could play at that game.

She leapt down, aiming for the highest, closest roof peak. As she landed, she sank her claws into the flesh of her scalp. Things moved inside her as she ripped the pale flesh from her frame, and freed the sleek, wet, black-furred thing within. Shedding her human skin, she began to pursue Ushoran's gargoyle shape in the form of one of the panthers which occupied the jungles of Ind.

She bounded across the rooftops of Mourkain, her claws digging gouges in the stone and thatch. Ushoran was fast, but she was faster. She leapt from peak to peak, following the swell of the mountain that Mourkain occupied. Whoever had built the bones of the ancient city had wrought it from the very guts of the mountain, and it was into those depths that Ushoran led her.

The upper reaches of the city were absent of life,

save torch-bearing patrols of hard-faced Strigoi, who staunchly kept their eyes averted from the great stone doorway leading into the mountain's peak. The doors were open, and a foul effluvium emanated from within. Neferata's lean shape slithered past the guards and darted through the arch. The smell of death enveloped her, even more strongly here than in the pyramid. The ground vibrated with a steady, mechanical pulse. Echoes of steel on stone rang from the rocks.

Something heavy and leathery thumped down in front of her, balancing on wing-limbs. The great bat shrieked and shook itself, trading one brute shape for another. Bone cracked and ruptured and then Ushoran stood before her, grinning widely.

Neferata loped towards him, shedding fur and rising to her feet as she reached him. She combed blood and the matter of change from her hair with her fingers. 'I see I'm not the only one to learn how to move between shapes in these intervening years,' she said.

'We all like to keep ourselves amused,' Ushoran said, flexing his great hands.

'Yet you do not teach it to those whom you give the blood-kiss?'

'And why would he do that? Power is only valuable when it is held by as few hands as possible,' a thin, hissing voice said. The words tumbled weirdly from the rocks. Something thin and insect-like detached itself from the shadows and stepped forwards. Despite the lack of light, Neferata saw its features clearly. And she didn't like what she saw. The face was that of a corpse, with blackened, dry flesh pulled tight over sharp bones, and cavernous eye-sockets, one of which was occupied by a milky, unseeing orb. The other was as black as a chip of polished obsidian and it glinted with malign intelligence. A thin strip of colourless hair, bound into a single worm-like lock, hung down from the pointed skull.

'W'soran,' she said.

'Neferata,' W'soran said, his good eye narrowing to a burning slit.

Neferata gazed at her former councillor with undisguised loathing. 'The years have not been kind.' And indeed, they had not. W'soran had become even more cadaverous in the intervening years since she had last seen him. Clad in ragged black, a deep hood over his verminous face, the vampire resembled nothing so much as a mummy which did not have the good grace to decay in silence.

'Physical appearances were always more your purview, my queen,' W'soran said. 'I am concerned with higher matters than hygiene.'

'So I see,' Neferata said, repressing a gag. W'soran stank of rot and strange spices. 'And what higher matters might these be?'

'You asked about the source of Mourkain's gold?' Ushoran said. He extended a claw towards W'soran. 'There it is.'

'Well, technically, *there* it is…' W'soran said, indicating the stumbling, hooded shapes which had followed him out of the darkness. Neferata hissed as the shapes stepped towards her.

'Corpses,' she spat.

'More than just corpses, my lady,' W'soran gloated. 'Bone, muscle, sinew, all that is dead in these mountains is mine to command!'

Ushoran swung his bulbous head towards the other vampire. 'Even as you are mine,' he rumbled. W'soran grunted.

'Yes, yes,' he said testily. 'That is our bargain, Ushoran.'

'*King* Ushoran,' Ushoran corrected gently. The hint of menace lurked in those words and the dead reacted to it, even if their master didn't. They closed about W'soran protectively.

'I wondered where you'd got to, after Nagashizzar fell,' Neferata said, breaking the moment. 'It is a comfort to me that you're still cowering in dark holes.' W'soran hissed, his pointed ears flattening against his long skull. Before he could reply, she went on. 'Show me,' she said.

W'soran led them deeper into the mountain. Great stairs, crudely carved and decorated with bas-reliefs of skulls, spiralled down into the darkness at the heart of the mountain and vast edifices of unknown purpose and alien beauty hove to out of the gloom. Corpses wove in and out of rough tunnels and smooth corridors, carrying tools.

'Kadon built all of this?' Neferata said, awestruck despite herself. Conglomerations of bone and wood braced the tunnels and great stone dips, containing burning lumps of coal and bone, lit their descent. Curtains made from the hair of bats and men draped the landings of the stairway and tattered shrouds hung from the sides of the stairs like tapestries. Braziers exuding the smell of embalming spices were scattered randomly and W'soran inhaled their stink as he passed them.

'Perhaps,' Ushoran said. 'Regardless, he extended it, century upon century. I watched him do it.'

'You always were good at spying,' Neferata said. Ushoran's lip curled, exposing a fang, but he said nothing. The stairs wound down through the mountain, and as they moved deeper, Neferata caught the mildew-stink of ghoul nests and saw dozens of scuttling white simian shapes scaling the rocks to either side of the stairs.

The scrabbling ghouls dislodged piles of bone, sending browned skulls rattling down into the depths.

'Largest nest of the vermin I've seen outside of Nagash-izzar,' Ushoran grunted. 'I feasted on them for decades before I revealed myself to the Strigoi. They hold hunts, sometimes, into the dark places. It used to be a rite of manhood, before I found better use for the creatures.'

'I believe that they are all that remain of the tribes that the Strigoi once warred with for control of these mountains. Kadon apparently enslaved thousands to build Mourkain, and when he was finished, the survivors were driven into the darkness, where they fed on the blind things swimming in the deep pools and gnawed the marrow from centuries of bones,' W'soran said. He chuckled. 'Mortals degenerate so swiftly. I have undertaken a study of it, and the results are–'

'Unimportant,' Neferata said.

'I would beg to differ,' W'soran said. He threw back his head and uttered an inhuman screech. A moment later, claws clattered across the stone. Neferata, prepared for treachery, was already turning as the ghouls scrambled up over the edge of the landing and bounded towards her. The first ghoul died, its skull shattered and driven into its spine by a blow from her fist. The second was opened like a fish, from groin to gullet. Behind her, something horrible gave a deep, rumbling cough.

Neferata spun and looked up into the dead, black eyes of something that stank of a battlefield. It was larger than the pitiful pale maggot-creatures milling about below, with a bloated musculature and infected, weeping sores through which protruded lengths of filthy yellow bone. It gave a cursory grunt as it stared down at her with a look of glazed ferocity.

Shock hammered through her. 'What–'

'Isn't he lovely?' W'soran cackled. He glanced at Ushoran, who was watching the confrontation calmly. 'Watch, Ushoran. Watch and see!'

The creature coughed and then rose up and threw back its head, uttering a soul-chilling howl. The howl was answered by the ghouls that clung to the walls. The corpse-eaters scuttled down like foul white spiders, their eyes gleaming with mingled fear and hunger. A few held bloody lumps of meat torn from the two ghouls she had just dispatched.

The big creature grunted and its claws spread. It licked its broken fangs and eyed her hungrily. It made a slurping sound as it started forwards. Confused, she almost didn't avoid the first lunge. Normally, ghouls were frightened of her kind, as foxes fled from wolves, but this thing – this *horror* – seemed almost enthusiastic to come to grips with her.

'What is the meaning of this, you old monster?' she snarled.

'Testing a hypothesis, my queen,' W'soran chortled, clapping his hands. 'Best pay attention, Neferata!'

The monster gave a thunderous hog-grunt and swiped at her. She leapt back, landing lightly on the shoulders of a surprised ghoul, and then vaulted over the giant's next blow. The unfortunate ghoul was bisected. Neferata landed behind the creature and it spun with a roar. It launched itself at her, slobbering grotesquely.

She backhanded it, putting every bit of muscle she had into the blow. The creature staggered, its jaw shattered and possibly its neck as well, but it didn't stop. Instead, it latched on to her and hooked her forearm with its teeth. She screamed, more in shock than pain, as it savaged her arm and lapped greedily at the blood that poured forth. She yanked her arm free of its vile grip and kicked it away.

'Look! Look,' W'soran said, gesturing excitedly. 'See! I told you, Ushoran.'

'I see,' Ushoran said.

The beast scrambled to its feet and, moaning, leapt at Neferata again. She ducked under its extended arms and jumped up swiftly, her palm striking its throat. Before it could worm free of her grip, she ripped its throat out in a welter of gore. It sagged with a sigh, falling to all fours. Neferata tossed the lump of flesh aside and glared at the other flesh-eaters, giving them a snarl. They slunk away, whining.

Neferata turned her glare on the other two vampires. Ushoran shrugged, but W'soran shook his head. 'Almost, almost,' he muttered.

Neferata leapt onto him, quicker than either of them could react. Her hands found W'soran's scrawny throat and she wrenched his bony body into the air and brought it down on the stone with a resounding *crack*. W'soran squealed and grabbed her face. His strength was surprising and she felt her flesh tear as she jerked him up again and flung him onto the steps hard enough to shatter one. W'soran shook his head and tried to climb to his feet but she was on him before he could, her claws hooked into his scalp.

'Neferata,' Ushoran growled.

Neferata hissed, tempted to throw off the masquerade she had only so recently taken up. Instead, she released the other vampire and stood. 'Was that a test, Ushoran?' she said.

'Not the kind you are thinking of, no,' Ushoran said. W'soran heaved himself up, his eyes incandescent with fury.

'I should flay your pearly flesh from your treacherous bones,' he rasped, glaring at Neferata. He clenched his fists, as if contemplating unleashing a spell.

'But you won't,' Ushoran said, interposing himself. 'We will put aside old grudges.' He looked at Neferata. 'There was no treachery here. You were in no danger. W'soran merely wanted to test his newest creation's abilities.'

'What was it?' Neferata said, tentatively touching the already healing bite-mark in her arm.

'A ghoul,' W'soran said.

Neferata blinked, surprised. W'soran laughed. 'Oh yes. I told you that I had been studying them.' He grinned at her. 'I have learned much, Neferata. Things that would make even your blood curdle.' In that moment, Neferata was reminded again of the fear she had once felt when in W'soran's presence. There was a horrible hunger in his eyes, a hunger that went beyond simple bloodthirst into something else. Nonetheless, she held his gaze until he looked away.

'If there are no more tests, perhaps I could see the vaults. Where are they?'

'Scattered all up and down the spine of the mountain,' Ushoran said, gesturing. 'I've had W'soran's maggot-addled minions digging them open. Kadon was like a jackal with a bone. He hid his wealth in random places. When he needed a new vault, he merely made one, using the dead to claw it from the rock.'

'Nagash employed similar techniques in Nagashizzar,' W'soran said.

'Which is where I got the idea,' Ushoran added. W'soran shot him a look, but said nothing. Neferata smirked. The two – the spy and the sorcerer – had never been friends. They were allies of convenience at most, and spiteful allies at that. If that spite were ever unlocked... She filed the thought away for future consideration. There were other levers and locks than just those crafted by the dwarfs in their palaces of stone.

The numbers of corpses increased the lower they went. Stumbling bodies covered in dried flesh walked alongside things that were nothing save bone and scraps of cloth. They came to what could only be an observation platform. Neferata leaned over the stone barrier and peered down into the inner workings of the mine. The dead moved like ants in their thousands, scurrying this way and that. Great machines, the likes of which she had never seen in all her years, ground away at the deep stone, manned by the squat, desiccated shapes of long-dead dwarfs. These latter corpses were even more unnerving than the humans, orcs and beasts that served as labour. Mangy beards, plaited with ancient jewellery, hung from fleshless jaws. Ragged suits of mail dangled from broad bones and strange lights danced in empty eye-sockets.

'Where by all the devils in the dark did you get those?' she hissed.

'Kadon took prisoners as well as gold in his war with the dawi,' Ushoran said. 'He forced them to craft him machines of great and fell purpose, down here in the dark.'

'The mummified corpses of the dwarfs retain a significant amount of muscle memory,' W'soran mused, eyes guttering like embers.

'Once we have strengthened the roots of this place, we can begin to build a fortress here. A true fortress, fit for an emperor,' Ushoran said. 'It will be a palace of bone and stone, from which I may rule our ever-growing empire.' He spread his arms as if greeting the jubilant throngs she thought he must be imagining.

Neferata shook her head as W'soran continued to prattle. Idiots, the pair of them. No, worse – Ushoran knew damn well what the end result of this would be. She looked at him and he gave her a hungry smile. 'You disapprove?'

'I'm told that the only thing the dwarfs value more than gold is their dead, and you are making a mockery of both. How long do you expect the alliance to last?' she said.

'Long enough,' he said.

'You intended to irritate Razek earlier, when you greeted him. Why?'

'Isn't it obvious? I need to know how practical my new allies really are. What are they prepared to overlook to get this gold?' Ushoran said. 'It wasn't just Kadon's necromantic inclinations that set Mourkain and the dwarfs at each other's throats, after all. They declared war on him for a variety of insults.'

'He offended them,' Neferata said.

'He was a fool, as we've said.' Ushoran crossed his arms. 'I have plans, Neferata. And to accomplish those plans I will need more troops than are currently alive within the boundaries of my kingdom.'

'You intend to use the dead,' Neferata said. A sickening sensation had settled in the pit of her stomach, like a bit of sour blood stuck in her craw. 'Just as we did before,' she said.

W'soran rubbed his hands together in pleasure. 'Not just the dead. There is much raw material here,' he said, and Neferata glanced at the dead brute in understanding.

'Imagine it,' Ushoran said. 'An army of the dead, sweeping over these lands, from this citadel, and making them fit for my coming...'

All is silent. All is perfect, the voice whispered in her head. *The charnel legions will march and bring silence to the world.* She shook it off, wondering if the others heard it as well. From the expression of fear that passed swiftly across W'soran's face, she suspected that he had.

'You think the dwarfs will tolerate that?' she said.

'You will see that they do, my Lady of Mysteries,' Ushoran purred. He was gloating. He thought he had her in a trap of her own making. 'At least until it is too late for them to do otherwise.'

'Double the guard,' Neferata said finally, turning around. 'No one must see this. No one not of your inner circle,' she said.

'Do not worry,' W'soran said, his fangs flashing. 'There are more defenders for this place than you have seen.' He gestured upwards. Neferata looked up and saw vast, loathsome shapes holding tight to the cavernous ceilings. Bats, bigger even than the creatures that she had seen in deep mountain caves, squirmed there. 'They hunt the wild horses of the plains. I heard stories of them in the Southlands, where it is said they pluck the great flying reptiles from their mountainous perches and feast on them beneath the moon,' W'soran said, as a man might speak of beloved pets.

Neferata shuddered. It wasn't fear, exactly, but she knew that such creatures would drain her dry as easily as she had done to so many men and women down the long, thirsty years. 'So I see. Fine,' she said, turning to Ushoran. 'You seem to have things well in hand, Ushoran. I can see now why you allowed an incompetent like Strezyk to serve you.'

'Strezyk served his purpose,' Ushoran said, flicking a claw. 'But I need a more competent left hand for the future.'

'You're truly planning a war, then?' Neferata said.

'For a variety of reasons,' Ushoran said.

'They wear out quickly down here,' W'soran said. 'The conditions are not conducive to maintenance, regrettably.' He looked at Neferata. 'I need more bodies. Fresh ones.'

'I'm sure you can always find more,' Neferata said.

'When the time comes, an expedition to the Silver Pinnacle will be invaluable,' W'soran said, rubbing his hands together in evident glee. 'The dwarfs are masters of the preservative arts and it is said that their crypts go on for miles. I have a theory that it was the dawi who first taught our peoples–'

'Our peoples are gone,' Neferata said automatically. The other two vampires looked at her, blank incomprehension on the face of the one, and anger on the face of the other. Ushoran grabbed her arm in his claw.

'Yes, and whose fault is that?' he snarled. 'Nehekhara is dead. Lahmia is dead. But we will build a better Nehekhara, a better Lahmia *here*!' He released her and turned. 'And this ruin and its secrets will help us do it!'

'Our history is dust, Ushoran. Would you use gold to buy it back?' Neferata said.

'Not just gold,' Ushoran said, his eyes blazing.

'Then what?' Neferata said, locking eyes with him. A feeling of anticipation filled her. W'soran laid a hand on Ushoran's arm and the light in his eyes faded. He shook his head, as if regaining some measure of control. The look of fear was back, pulling at the edges of W'soran's face like hooks. What was the old jackal scared of? What did he know that she did not?

'None of your concern, my Lady of Mysteries,' Ushoran said. Neferata frowned.

'No, I suppose not. What are my concerns, then?' she said.

'Preservation and expansion,' Ushoran said. 'I have promised my people an empire worthy of the great barrow-kings of awful memory, or that of the dwarfs at their height. And Ushoran does not break his promises.'

'No. And neither do I,' Neferata said.

⟨ SIX ⟩

The City of Bel Aliad
(−1151 Imperial Reckoning)

'Beautiful,' Khaled al Muntasir breathed, stroking the surface of the ornate sarcophagus that leaned at an angle against the wall.

Inside, Neferata raged silently at the gloating tone in his voice. She yearned to split the iron body of the sarcophagus and strip the meat from his face a piece at a time. But such was not to be, not while the shaft of broken lance remained in her chest. The sword had apparently been too dangerous to leave in her, and someone had replaced one with the other. And not just any shard of wood, but one treated with strange unguents and ointments, so that its very touch leached the strength from her and rendered her immobile. Now she stood in darkness, a prisoner of her own body, unable to even seek respite in oblivion or madness. And all thanks to her once-champion, Abhorash.

She remembered his eyes, watching her die. For that was what this was – a living death. Why had he done it? He had not visited her afterwards. Indeed, from what little she had

gleaned from her captor, Abhorash had departed as myste-
riously as he had arrived, wandering to the coast with his
coterie. He had been in Bel Aliad only long enough to help
train their Kontoi.

W'soran, Ushoran, Abhorash... The names hissed through
her mind like spilling sand. They had all betrayed her, and
for what? Spite?

She would show them spite.

But first, she had to escape.

Even locked in the darkness like this, she could feel the
faint touch of Naaima's mind. Her handmaiden prowled
through the dark places of Bel Aliad even now, searching for
her. Loyal Naaima, if she could but call out to her–

Light stabbed her eyes as the lid of the sarcophagus was
shifted. Khaled stared at her, his dark eyes wide. He licked
his lips. He reached out a trembling hand, and then yanked
it back. Beyond him, she saw his chamber; it was strewn
with mystical-looking bric-a-brac, preserved monkey's paws
and shrunken heads. There were tiny ushabti standing at
attention in silk-lined boxes and strange, formless shapes
squirming in glass jars. Khaled was not only a warrior, it
seemed; he was also something of a scholar. 'I know you can
hear me, witch,' he said, after a moment. 'Lord Abhorash
said you would be able to, at any rate. He said that you
cannot die. That you are immortal and ageless and evil.'

Evil! Neferata snarled in her head. How dare that self-
righteous fool call her evil! She would take great pleasure in
hunting her former champion down and flaying him from
the soles of his feet to the crown of his head. She would wear
his treacherous skin as a cloak and make combs of his bones!

Khaled blinked and stepped back. 'Yes... I see the hate in
your eyes, witch. The Sand Snake, that was what those dogs
of the desert called you. I wonder why you were squatting
with savages in the wilderness. Could you tell me, if I jostled

that stake of wood, ever so slightly? If I nudged it from your heart, just by the length of a fingertip, would you share your secrets with me, Sand Snake?'

Neferata watched him, unable to do anything else. Khaled chuckled. *'Or would you kill me? Yes. You would, wouldn't you? You'd butcher me like a goat. Sleep now, Sand Snake. We will talk more, later.'* He closed the lid, and she was once more left in darkness.

But she didn't rage. She had seen something in Khaled's eyes. A greed that she recognised easily enough; he wanted something. Something she possessed. In the darkness and the silence, she began to plan...

The City of Mourkain
(–750 Imperial Reckoning)

STEAM ROSE OFF the stones scattered across the bronze grill of the oven set into the far wall of the *bana* as Naaima poured a dipperful of water across them. The rocks were heated by a rack of red-hot coals which were occasionally stirred by whoever was closest. A series of long bronze pipes carried the heat from the oven into the water of the communal bath, heating it to a temperature that would have boiled a mortal alive. The vampires didn't notice. For them it might as well have been an icy pond.

Neferata sighed as steam filled the bathhouse, drawing forth sweat and the smells buried in the wooden planks that made up the roof. The bronze plates set into the stone walls reflected the heat back at the women soaking in the bath. The Strigoi *bana* were, for all intents and purposes, overlarge ovens, lacking the graceful function of similar structures in Sartosa or Araby. The art of the bathhouse was yet to infiltrate these savage climes, Neferata mused. Yet another thing she would be forced to remedy in the coming years. Still, for the moment, the bathhouse had its uses.

Vampires, unlike men, neither sweated nor secreted the oils that clung like pernicious perfume to the skin of the living. That did not mean, however, that they could not stink just as badly as any unwashed peasant. The odour of old blood never quite went away. But the scalding baths, followed by a splash from a bucket of perfumed water, hid the predator's odour quite well.

The bana were sacrosanct in Strigoi society. They were places where one could be at ease. It was not unusual for violence to occur in one, but it was frowned upon. It was also one of the few places that Ushoran's spies could not follow her.

Neferata settled in the water, letting it envelop her. Ushoran's spy apparatus was like an onion; the more layers she stripped and tossed aside, the more there seemed to be. Then there was W'soran, who had his own methods of spying. Not to mention that every Strigoi ajal and agal had at least one spy in their retinue. Most of those she had co-opted, but there was always another somewhere.

But not here, and that was why they had come.

'You should have seen the look on that greenskin shaman's face,' Stregga chortled. Her palm came down, slapping the still, steaming waters of the bath. 'Eyes bulging and tongue waggling as Rasha crushed his throat.' She gave a bark of laughter. She and Rasha had just returned from a routine expedition into the lands to the east, where the great orc migrations originated.

'Tasted foul, that one,' Rasha muttered, leaning back

against the edge of the communal bath. 'Their blood tastes of mould and mushrooms.'

'We all make sacrifices, my sisters,' Neferata said.

'Some more than others,' Naaima added, drawing the bone comb through Neferata's hair. Neferata ignored the comment.

'Continue, please,' she said, gesturing languidly.

'You were right, my lady,' Rasha said. 'They thought it was an omen, a leopard killing their shaman like that. Uzzer's lot are in control of the tribe now, and they're moving east, towards us. The timagals in that region are already squawking for help. The orcs will press them hard over the winter.'

'Good,' Neferata said, tracing circles in the surface of the water. The greenskins were pawns of prophecy and omen, at the beck and call of their feather- and bead-bedecked shamans. And the shamans took every leopard-mauling or giant-bat attack as an omen to wage war. It was a simple enough matter to stir them up. 'We'll see to the defences in the region. Perhaps Vorag…?' She glanced at Stregga, who made a face.

'Aye, he wants to fight, that one.' The blonde vampire sank down until the water brushed her chin. 'He's still upset that Ushoran banished him from court.' She cocked an eye at her mistress. 'A bit harsh, wasn't that, my lady?'

'I need the Bloodytooth on the frontier. Not at court,' Neferata said mildly. 'And I need him upset.' The Court of Strigos was a snake-pit; the nobles strove in a never-ending game of one-upmanship beneath Ushoran's watchful gaze. Only the most cunning and treacherous survived. Vorag would have been staked in his bed had it not been for Neferata's careful shepherding of him. And she had done the latter for one reason only – Vorag's influence among the hereditary nobles and military commanders was great and rivalled only by the acclaim the common herd gave to Abhorash.

It had been easy enough to get the former champion temporarily exiled. Ushoran's disfavour was easy enough to garner, and Vorag had begun making himself a nuisance; if it had gone on, Ushoran would have had Abhorash end Vorag's troublemaking permanently. But exiled, he was safe from Abhorash's sword and he would serve an invaluable purpose.

Through Vorag, she had begun to disseminate the first faint stirrings of resentment among the Strigoi nobility who were not tied to Ushoran's apron strings. The Strigoi were not unused to long-lived rulers, but Kadon had been a sorcerer. Ushoran was not. But he was seemingly immortal, and though many members of his inner circle knew what he was, not all of them had truly understood what an immortal king meant.

Neferata could have told them, had they asked. Even Kadon had had the good grace to step back from direct rule eventually. The stagnation was already creeping in. Men who had been turned when the Strigoi were horse-raiders with grandiose dreams of empire now ruled said empire, but could not shake the petty perspectives of those far-gone times.

And as the Strigoi people advanced, their hidebound, atavistic nobility became ever more out of step. The world moved on, no matter how much creatures like Ushoran and – yes – even herself at times wished it wouldn't.

'Besides, he'll enjoy fighting the orcs for a few years. He seems to enjoy the taste, at any rate.' She looked at Anmar. 'On to other matters… Tell me of the dawi, little leopard.'

'They left this morning, my lady,' Anmar said.

'You are certain?'

'I followed them myself,' Anmar said.

Neferata sat back and sighed. Razek had been a disappointment, in more ways than one. He was too observant. And he was too determined to discover the source of the gold that formed Strigos's wealth, and to lay claim to it for his people. The attempts had been made via human mercenaries – thieves and bandits, paid through third parties. All had died, or been paid off, but the attempts had become an annoyance, not to mention distracting. Razek, she was certain, knew that Ushoran was paying the dwarfs in their own gold, stolen by Kadon so long ago. And if he ever found proof, that would be it for the current amicable state of affairs.

Dwarfs were not given to plotting, but Razek seemed to break the mould. A quiet word in Ushoran's ear had resulted in Razek being recalled to the Silver Pinnacle once the trade between the two peoples had settled into a comfortable rhythm after a few decades. Still, there lingered the suspicion that Razek's influence was not entirely gone from Mourkain. The dwarf traders and merchants who came by the Silver Road all carried the stamps and seals of King Borri, but she suspected that they had Razek's gold in their pockets, and that gold went into the hands of yet more thieves and spies. He was more than just Borri's thane – he was the king of Karaz Bryn's hearth-warden. He was her opposite number and equally determined to accomplish his goal.

That alone necessitated his eventual death. *But not yet*, she thought. Razek was a known quantity now, and the dwarfs might yet come in handy, beyond the obvious. Tapping her lip, she glanced at Iona. The red-headed former concubine had flourished since being given the gift of Neferata's blood-kiss. She had transformed from a starveling wretch into a magnificent creature, her bedraggled looks amplified into feral beauty. 'And how are the gods, Iona? Are they satisfied with their offerings?'

'So their priestesses assure me, mistress,' Iona said, curling a lock of fiery red hair around one pale finger. 'The *sangzye* is collected without comment. Our people place little value on blood,' she added, shrugging. Neferata smiled in satisfaction.

The transplantation of the Nehekharan cults had taken close to thirty years of effort on her part; something to keep her interested during her idle moments. Small temples to Djaf, Phakth and Ptra now occupied the central plaza of Mourkain, and their priestesses had all been gifted with her kiss. Granted, those temples and their practices would be unrecognisable to any inhabitant of the Great Land.

Blood was the holiest of sacrifices, and each god accepted their due in the temples of Mourkain. The sangzye was a tax of blood, levied on the devout; it served to keep the growing population of vampires in check.

'Ajal Djazk,' Neferata said. She looked at Rasha, who smiled thinly. Djazk was the latest troublesome nail in need of hammering down: a minor lordling who'd attempted to subvert several of Neferata's handmaidens through bribery and other, less subtle methods. He was a brute and a slave to his passions. He was not alone in such, but he had made his intentions known in too blatant a fashion.

The memory of what Neferata had done to Strezyk was fading fast, even among those who'd witnessed it. Few of the Strigoi could accept that a woman, vampire or not, was something other than a servant or a concubine. She had made good use of that blind spot. Ushoran used Abhorash for public executions. But it fell to Neferata to eliminate those of Ushoran's inner circle who grew too free with their blood-kiss or otherwise machinated against him. Few saw it coming, and those who did rarely ran far enough to escape her growing reach.

'He never returned from his last beast-hunt,' the other vampire said. 'The beasts must have killed him. We'll find his remains strapped to one of their ugly stone idols somewhere, I'd warrant.' Her eyes glinted with pleasure.

'Would you,' Neferata murmured. 'Good. What of his concubines?'

'He only had a few who were in any decent shape. Of those, I pulled aside two or three that might be of some use. The others I sent to the temples. The priestesses will find some use for them,' Rasha said.

'Excellent,' Neferata said. The Strigoi nobility were profligate. They turned women, and sometimes men, without regard, like children hoarding toys. When a situation like Djazk's arose, those creatures were often left without a master. Those whom she could not find a use for, she had killed quietly, and without unnecessary pain. It was not the victims' fault that creatures like Gashnag had a taste for women and no self-control. Some, however, were only too happy to be of service. These she sent out and away from Mourkain, to be her eyes and ears among the brute tribes of men in the north and west and east.

She cocked her head back, looking up at Naaima, who had set aside the comb and was now tightly braiding her hair. Even now, centuries after the fact, Naaima refused to let any of the others touch Neferata's hair. Neferata, for her part, saw no reason to complain. 'W'soran,' she said.

Naaima frowned. 'He's up to something.'

'And the moon is made of the skull of a god,' Stregga snorted. 'Tell us something we don't know.'

Naaima glanced sourly at the other woman, but continued. 'Whatever it is, it's connected to his trips to the pyramid on certain nights. But we can't get close enough to follow him. Not with his guard dogs.' W'soran had taken to travelling with a pack of ghouls at his heels. The loping beasts were excellent watchdogs, if one didn't mind the smell. Clad in their black robes and hoods, they moved through the streets at night, spread out around the old monster like a flock of crows.

'Keep trying. He and Ushoran are keeping something from me, and I want to know what,' Neferata said. There had seemed to be no pattern before to W'soran's comings and goings in regards to the pyramid, but what she had learned from her spies over the years had put paid to that supposition. There was a pattern and a reason for that pattern. A reason she was one step closer to discovering.

A familiar scent stung her nose and she hissed in disgust. 'Who is watching the door, Naaima?'

'Layla,' Naaima said automatically. Neferata grunted. The girl was human. They had a number of human servants, all picked by Naaima, who had a way with the lower orders. 'Why?' Naaima said, a moment before she too caught the scent. Her eyes widened.

The door to the bathhouse opened, and grinning figures strode in, boots crunching on the delicate tiles. Neferata caught a glimpse of others outside, crouched over a too-pale shape. The girl had tried to bar their way and paid the price for her loyalty. Neferata kept her face expressionless as Naaima hissed in rage. The others reacted similarly, surging up out of the waters and surrounding her.

'Well, here we all are. How lovely,' the Strigoi purred, gazing at them with undisguised lust. He was tall and broad-shouldered and his name was Zandor. There were other Strigoi behind him. They were, like Zandor, minor nobles. Neferata recognised them all as Ushoran's lapdogs, sniffing at his table scraps, always trying to curry favour where they could.

'These are the ladies' baths, Ajal Zandor,' Neferata said blithely.

'Do forgive me, Lady Neferata, but I was pining for your beauty,' Zandor said, leering. The other Strigoi chuckled appreciatively. 'We would speak with you,' Zandor added sneeringly.

Neferata sighed. 'Very well, Naaima, take the others outside.' Naaima looked at her in horror. Neferata frowned. 'Go. I'm sure I will be perfectly safe here, with Ajal Zandor and his… companions.'

'Oh yes,' Zandor said. 'Perfectly safe, I assure you.'

Neferata restrained the urge to roll her eyes as her handmaidens left the bathhouse. Zandor, like the unlamented Djazk, was infamous in Mourkain for his ribald exploits. He thought a woman was only good for one thing and Neferata irked him to no end, though she had rarely spoken to him. Zandor sank to his haunches, eyeing her. 'I'm given to understand that you convinced our mighty hetman to spare that oaf Vorag, after he made such a mess of young Feyz at the Midsummer banquet.'

'Vorag was exiled,' Neferata said.

'He should have been staked out on the slopes,' one of the other Strigoi growled. He was a handsome creature, dark-haired and thin-featured. He wore gold, and polished brass discs adorned his furs.

'Hello, Gashnag,' Neferata said. 'I wonder, did Vorag demand the same when you took Ergat's fangs last month?'

Gashnag blanched. Zandor chuckled. 'It is not the deed, but how it was done, my lady. Vorag is little better than one of those beasts he so enjoys hunting.' He leaned forwards, his features assuming a predatory cast. 'Why do you support such a brute, I wonder? Are there benefits to a grateful monster?'

Neferata frowned. 'You go too far, Zandor.'

'I apologise,' Zandor said. 'I merely wondered why you backed one like the Bloodytooth when there are other, more influential friends to be had.'

Neferata laughed. 'Do you not have enough friends, Zandor?'

'None like you, my lady. Hetman Ushoran speaks highly of you,' Zandor said, stirring the water with his hand. 'And Khaled as well, though he is, perhaps, biased.'

Neferata was silent for a moment. 'You were Strezyk's get, weren't you, Zandor?' she said.

Zandor stiffened. 'And so,' he said. 'May a man not expand beyond his horizons?'

'Not if he is wise,' Neferata said softly.

Zandor stood. 'I am sorry that you feel that way. I had hoped to avoid a scene, but obviously you will not heed wisdom.' He turned. 'Kurven,' he said.

The vampire who entered the bathhouse was massive. There was too much beast to this one, Neferata knew. He had let himself slip into the permanent red twilight that creatures like Vorag danced along the edge of. Wide eyes bulged over a quivering, wet spear-blade nose, and a mouthful of fangs surfaced from a bramble-like beard. He was a hairy creature and fairly bursting out of his cuirass. A crooked claw pointed at her. 'I challenge you,' he growled, mangling the words into near unintelligibility.

Neferata's eyes flickered to Zandor, who smirked. Memories were short, even among immortals it seemed. Or, more likely, Kurven was a professional duellist. She noted the trio of necklaces that hung from the brute's neck, each one heavy with extracted fangs. 'Ushoran will be unhappy with you, Zandor,' she said, not moving from the water. 'I am his left hand.'

'Then maybe it's time he got a new one,' Zandor said. 'Women should not meddle in politics.' He looked at Kurven. 'Kill her. We all saw you challenge her. None here will say it wasn't fair and by the law.'

Kurven gave a howl that rattled the tiles of the bath-house, and sprang for her. Neferata sank beneath the water swiftly. The brute landed with a splash, his talons gouging the spot where she had rested. She rose behind him, fangs bared. Kurven spun, eyes blazing.

She ducked under the Strigoi's swipe and slashed him across the face, eliciting a screech. He was more angry than hurt. Quicker than she expected he lunged and caught her, shoving her beneath the water and driving her into the bottom of the bath. This one knew how to fight, unlike Strezyk. She brought her legs up and drove her feet into his belly.

Kurven released her and reared back. Neferata burst from the water, claws stretching for his hairy throat. The Strigoi were cheering, so certain of the beast's victory that they did not notice the door to the bath-house burst open to admit Naaima and the others.

With vengeful shrieks, the vampire-women dived onto the Strigoi even as Neferata launched herself at Kurven and buried her fangs in his throat.

Digging her claws into his chest, she whipped her head back, tearing his throat out in a welter of gore. Kurven gagged horribly and sank into the water, trying to hold his ruined throat together. Neferata didn't let him slip far. She hoisted him up, her talons sunken knuckle deep into the meat of his chest. She gave a shove with one hand, and bone buckled and splintered as she dug out Kurven's heart. Wrenching the organ loose she stared at it for a moment before she buried her fangs in it, swallowing its final, plaintive beat. She let Kurven sink into the darkening water and climbed out, still holding the heart in one hand.

The fight between her followers and the Strigoi had been quick. Only Zandor and Gashnag had remained to fight, while the others had fled as soon as they realised that Kurven was dead. Gashnag lay groaning on the ground, Stregga's foot pressed to the back of his skull and his blood dripping from her hands. Naaima was far stronger than a puling creature like Zandor and she had him on his knees, his arms twisted behind his back and his scalplock jerked tight, forcing him to stare up at Neferata as she swayed towards him, trailing Kurven's blood behind her.

'Somehow, I think you thought that this was going to go differently, Ajal Zandor,' Neferata purred, sinking to her haunches. She held up Kurven's mangled heart and showed it to him. 'I want you to remember this moment, Zandor. Remember my hand on a Strigoi heart, and I want you to recall that it could just as easily have been yours.' She clenched her fist, crushing the lump of meat. 'Let him go.'

'We should kill him,' Naaima hissed, leaning close to Zandor.

'Aye, let's take his fangs,' Stregga said.

'We already have,' Neferata said, gesturing curtly. 'Let him up, and Gashnag as well. Let's not keep these fine ajals from their business, shall we?'

Zandor left, his glare hot with rage and not a little fear. Neferata smiled, satisfied. 'The memory of Strezyk was getting stale. Now there's a new memory to dampen the fire in their bellies,' she said, looking at the others. Only Naaima wasn't listening. Instead, she was crouched over the girl who'd been guarding the door. Neferata saw at once that the Strigoi had been at her. Some of them saw humans only as cattle. She looked at Rasha and Stregga. 'Did you see the ones who did this?'

'I did,' Rasha growled.

'Find them and bring me their fangs.' Neferata looked at Iona and Anmar. 'Follow Zandor and see where he goes. I want to know who convinced that jackal that he could get away with this.' The vampires moved quickly, faster than the human eye could follow. Neferata watched them go and then turned back to Naaima. 'Is she dead?'

'Not yet.' Naaima looked mournfully down into the girl's features. 'But she will not survive these wounds. Not unless we do something.' A note of pleading entered her voice.

Neferata looked down at the serving girl, her body marred by great slashes and gouging, sloppy bite-marks. Her blood dripped down Naaima's arms. Her eyelids fluttered and a quiet moan escaped from her mouth. Something that might have been pity stabbed at Neferata. Pragmatism reared its head, crushing pity beneath its relentless tread.

She looked at Naaima. 'I have no need of her,' she said. 'Not with Djazk's women.'

'She was wounded in your service,' Naaima said, stroking the girl's brow. A fever-sweat had broken out, and Neferata could smell death congealing in the girl's wounds. 'You owe her…'

'I owe her nothing. She failed, and she has paid for that failure. Besides, of what use would such a creature be to me?' She knew it was the wrong thing to say even as she said it.

'You forget who you speak to,' Naaima said, and her voice was iron. 'What was I, but a maid? I was a concubine, Neferata. I was a lower possession than a horse or hound. And you found use for me.'

Neferata looked at her handmaiden, eyes narrowing. 'Are you challenging me?'

'Yes,' Naaima said simply. She neither bowed her head nor looked away. Between them, the girl moaned again, piteously.

Nonplussed, Neferata hesitated. She brushed a lock of the girl's hair out of her face. 'It is too late. I cannot save her,' she said.

'You can.'

Neferata met Naaima's eyes and the former Queen of Lahmia was the first to look away. 'What is her name?' she asked hoarsely.

'Layla,' Naaima reminded her. 'Her father was killed by the orcs. She used to work in the kitchens of Ushoran's palace. The other girls accused her of putting on airs, and the cook beat her for being disrespectful. She does not know her place, and she does not fear the dark. That is why I took her.'

'More fool she,' Neferata said. Tenderly, she took the girl from Naaima and tilted her, so that her head lolled against Neferata's shoulder. Then, with a sigh, she sank her fangs into the girl's throat, drinking deeply and stabbing to the root of the girl's life.

The blood-kiss was a sacred thing. It was a gift from Neferata to her chosen followers. As much as she took, she gave as well. It was a bond, forever linking her to them and vice-versa. Holding the girl, she extended her arm and Naaima took her wrist and forearm and bent her head. Her lips brushed the inside of Neferata's wrist and then, with a sharp, bright flash of sweet pain, she opened her mistress's veins. Neferata raised her bloody mouth from Layla's throat and pressed her wrist to the girl's slack lips. Her fingers curled as her hand flexed and blood rushed out, black and thick, into the girl's mouth. 'Drink, Layla,' Neferata crooned. 'Drink, scullery maid, or die.'

'Drink,' Naaima said, stroking the girl's throat with light fingers. 'Drink,' they said together, quietly. And Layla coughed and gasped and began to drink. Weakly at first, and then desperately, clutching Neferata's wrist tightly. She began to shudder and jerk, and a black, noisome fluid began to weep from her wounds as Neferata's blood began to circulate through her veins.

'What is happening to her?' Naaima said, looking horrified. Neferata had no answer for her. Layla jerked and groaned as her skin lost what little colour it had and her hair turned silver. Finally, the girl lay quiet in her arms, almost as if asleep. Neferata could see the cold darkness in the centre of her that marked her as a vampire.

Layla was not the first vampire she had made within the city, nor would she be the last, but nonetheless this time had seemingly awakened something – something which spoke to her out of that darkness, startling her.

The voice used no words, but memories. Crashing, slashing images of times long past.

Alcadizzar's breath, harsh in his lungs, washing over her as they crashed into one another. He was her child, though she had not borne him. He was of her blood. And now he yearned for her end. His dagger pierced her chest, seeking her heart with deadly intent.

She screamed, more from the agony of betrayal, of dreams hammered to dust, than from the pain. But as she crouched, bent over the blade jutting from her chest, Alcadizzar stared at her sadly as the wind wiped him away, one grain of flesh at a time. His eyes were the last to go, pain-ridden orbs that begged, even as they condemned.

A shape that was as black as the spaces between the stars stood in his place, its outline writ in green balefire. A voice that seemed to echo in the marrow of her bones rattled across her ears, speaking deplorable words, and inflicting a night-mare cancer of alien sound on the world. Around her, the sands shifted and slid, revealing spear-points and sword-tips and the curved, flayed-smooth skull caps of the tomb-legions.

A hundred generations rose from the howling sands and began to march on clattering, fleshless feet. Kings and queens and priests and nobles and peasants marched without complaint or identity forever through the darkness, drawn on by the needle-on-bone voice of the black shape.

THEY ARE MINE. NOW AND FOREVER, THEY ARE MINE, it said. *EVEN AS YOU ARE MINE, QUEEN OF THE CITY OF THE DAWN. COME TO ME. COME–*

'No!' Neferata shrieked, clutching at her head. Naaima darted forwards, grabbing Layla as she slid from Neferata's grip.

'Neferata, what is it?' the other woman said.

Neferata's claws dug into her scalp and black blood rolled down into her face. She turned away from her handmaiden, and fought to control the emotions that raged across her normally serene features. Something tugged and tore at the back of her mind, but with brutal, practised effort, she forced it back and deep.

Blood coated her hands – hers, Layla's – and it seemed to form the features of a man, proud and arrogant in her cupped palms. The human face rippled and melted, becoming something else entirely. Something that was not human in the least, and it gazed up at her as if looking through a gauzy sheet. A name seemed to swim to the surface of her thoughts, but she could not see it, not clearly, and the unfamiliar syllables died on the base of her tongue before she could even utter a breath. Swiftly she brought her palms together and wiped the blood across her robes.

'Neferata,' Naaima said.

'Nothing,' Neferata said. 'It was nothing.'

And in her head, something laughed.

⪪ SEVEN ⪫

*The City of Bel Aliad
(–1151 Imperial Reckoning)*

In the months that she languished in captivity, Neferata learned much about those gifts that she had wrested from the sinister brew flowing in her veins. While she had always been able to control the minds of others, she now had a more precise control over lesser minds. She amused herself by bringing insects to the sarcophagus. Beetles and worms and spiders now clustered around her in the dark, crawling through her hair and sliding every so often into her mouth, where her fangs closed on them like a trap and extinguished their tiny lives. Each of these provided her with the briefest surge of strength, which was quickly sapped away by the wood piercing her heart.

She needed something larger than spiders and flies. It was a pity that there were no rats. Her flesh had tightened over her bones, becoming dry and hard like leather, and her hair, what she could see of it, had turned a filthy white. A long time ago, such changes might have tormented her. Now, however, she knew that flesh was much like a set of robes, changing to fit circumstance.

Besides bugs, she made the acquaintance of Khaled's sister, Anmar. She was a pretty girl, still gangly and in the dawn of womanhood. Like her brother, she was a child of the harem, and he doted on her. And she, in turn, looked up to him. Even as Khalida had looked up to her cousin Neferata, before–

The thought brought pain. Neferata shoved the errant memory aside. Khalida was dead, as Naaima never failed to remind her. Dead and entombed for over a century, after refusing the gift Neferata had offered her, the foolish, stupid girl.

But Anmar was more receptive to the whispers of Neferata's voice. The girl had taken to sneaking into her brother's secret chambers. Mere curiosity became something else as Neferata's psychic hooks sank into her mind.

Until, finally…

'What are you doing in here?' Khaled roared, grabbing his sister by the arm and wrenching her away from the sarcophagus. If she had been able to, Neferata would have hissed in frustration. The girl had been moments away from opening the sarcophagus and freeing her.

'I was just looking–' Anmar began, trying to yank her arm free of her brother's grip.

'Don't!' Khaled snarled, hurling her against the wall. The girl cried out and Khaled's rage evaporated. He stared at his hands for a moment, and then rushed to her side. 'I'm sorry little sister, I did not mean to hurt you,' he said, helping her to her feet.

Khaled, Neferata whispered.

He froze. He straightened and looked at the sarcophagus, his face pale and sweaty. 'K-Khaled,' Anmar began as she reached for her brother. 'What is it? It's been speaking to me. What do you have in there?'

'Nothing,' he said. 'It's nothing…'

Khaaaaled, Neferata purred. The tendrils of her mind unfurled, caressing his. He shuddered.

'Get out of my head, witch. I've told you before, I will not listen to you,' he said, grinding his fists into his eyes.

'Khaled, who are you talking to?' Anmar said. She glanced at the sarcophagus, and went as pale as her brother. 'Is it… is it her? Is what the maids said true? Did you really… keep her?'

Aaaanmaaar, Neferata hissed, as she felt the girl's gaze fall on the sarcophagus.

'Who is that?' Anmar said, looking to her brother for reassurance. 'What is in that box, Khaled?'

'Just an old dead thing,' Khaled snapped. 'It is of no consequence.'

No consequence, am I? Neferata said, vaguely amused. Then why do you stink of fear, my fierce Kontoi?

'Quiet,' Khaled shouted.

Perhaps it is because you fear yourself, and not this old dead thing, Neferata said. You fear your desires, Khaled… What do you want, my love? I will give it to you. All you have to do is–

'I said be quiet!' Khaled shrieked. He wrenched the lid open and glared at her. She could see herself reflected in his eyes, a mummified thing, covered with crawling insects, withered talons clutching the splintered shaft of wood that jutted from her heart. He fell back, gagging. Her jaws twitched, crunching a centipede between them. Anmar screamed.

Quiet, girl, Neferata hissed. Anmar's jaw slammed shut and her hands flew to her mouth.

'Leave her be, hag!' Khaled snarled. He grabbed the end of the stake and jammed it deeper into her. Neferata's withered frame shuddered. Her head slumped to the side and her staring eyes caught his, freezing him in place.

Why would I do that, Khaled? she said. Why would I do that when I am so thirsty?

Khaled pulled himself away from her. 'No!'

So thirsty, Neferata said, not letting him break eye contact with her. Her will crashed down on him like a black wave. For weeks, her mind had wormed its way into his, even as it had Anmar's. He had come incessantly to gloat over her, to speak of his dreams and plans and desires.

He wanted to be caliph, did young Khaled. But he was the son of a concubine and thus not in line for the throne, and besides, there were a dozen brothers ahead of him.

But I can change all of that, Khaled, she said, and he leaned close. *You know I can. Abhorash told you, didn't he? He told you what I am and what my kiss can give you, she continued.* Her thoughts became his thoughts, and trapped his mind in a fog of red.

'Khaled,' Anmar quavered, reaching for him. 'Please Khaled, close it…'

Free me, Neferata said. Free me!

'Khaled…'

Khaled's fingers tightened on the wood. Then, with a convulsive jerk, he ripped it free of her heart. Neferata sucked in a lungful of dry air and emitted a shriek, her long unused vocal cords flexing painfully. But mingled with the pain was the raw pleasure of life renewed. Life, so long denied her, flowed through her dry veins and she stretched, feeling the air and listening to the sound of her prey's hearts as their rhythm sped up. The sweet smell of fear filled her nostrils and she hissed in pleasure.

Khaled stared stupidly at the splinter of wood in his hand, then up at Neferata. Her eyes blazed with a hunger long denied. 'Yessss,' she said.

'Oh, no,' Khaled said, stepping back, horror suffusing his features. 'Anmar, get out of here!'

'Khaled – what–' Anmar began fearfully.

'Run!' Khaled screamed, lunging for Neferata with the wood. She uncoiled from the sarcophagus, leaping over him and landing between his sister and the door.

'Too late, my Kontoi,' Neferata rasped, claws flexing. She caught Anmar as the girl backpedalled. 'Too late…' Her fangs sank into the girl's neck as savagely as those of a starving jackal. She worried the girl's throat, tearing flesh and cracking bone, her tongue stabbing hungrily into the wound.

Khaled howled with loathing as he smashed the wooden spike into her shoulder. She snarled, dropping the half-dead girl, and batted his improvised weapon from his grip. Then, with sinister tenderness, she took his face in her hands and kissed him, smearing his mouth with his sister's blood. He grabbed ineffectually at her wrists as she pulled him close.

'Do not struggle, my love,' she purred. 'Soon you shall have all that you desire. This, I promise…'

The City of Mourkain
(–600 Imperial Reckoning)

THE SUN HAD been blotted out by thick clouds that spread like oil across the sky, as well as the surging, wheeling flocks of carrion birds that circled overhead waiting for the day's reaping to be done. Unfortunately, Neferata had no time to admire the graceful curve of the birds' flight.

The orc crested the palisade, venting a full-throated bellow of berserk murder-lust as it took off a Strigoi's head with its crude axe. Neferata wove around the tumbling body and impaled the orc on her blade, causing it to stiffen and scream. She jerked her sword free in a crescent of blood and spun, lopping off its head as she came back around.

Even as its twitching carcass tumbled to the palisade ramp, more of them were pushing to fill the gap. Daubed in brutal, blue tattoos and war-paint and animal skins, they came at her in a rush. Their minds were too dull to enrapture with her dark skills, and she settled for dealing out quicksilver death. Stepping over the bodies, she saw that the others were faring similarly well.

Khaled, clad in the armour of one of Ushoran's guard, cut and slashed in the wedge of metal and flesh that defended the master of Mourkain as he struggled with one of the warlords of the green horde that crashed like an ocean tide against his walls. Ushoran was wearing armour himself, eschewing his more bestial habits in order to play the hero for his people.

Like always when he was in public, Ushoran wore the face of a god. Painfully handsome, strongly built, he towered his guards and at times, he seemed to be protecting them, rather than vice-versa. The orc was a large one, a full head taller than Ushoran. The beast wore the skins of a dozen wolves stretched and stitched over its frame, and carried a length of crudely beaten and sharpened bronze like a sword.

It whipped the sword at Ushoran, seeking to decapitate him. Ushoran stepped back, letting the curved tip of the blade slice past his chin. As the orc staggered, off-balance, he slid close and drove his own sword into the creature's gut. It howled in agony and dropped its sword, grabbing Ushoran's head in its paws. Ushoran was slammed down hard enough to crack the palisade, but he showed no sign that the impact had hurt him. He reached up and grabbed the orc's tusk, jerking its head down. Their skulls connected with an audible *crunch*, and the orc staggered back, minus its tusk, which Ushoran still clutched.

The vampire sprang to his feet and lunged, jabbing the orc in the throat with its tusk, while simultaneously reaching for the hilt of his sword, still lodged in the orc's belly. He jerked the sword free and swept it up, chopping the orc's skull in half, jaw to brow. It toppled from the palisade, knocking a number of other green-skinned savages off in its descent.

He looked at her, his face a mask of blood, and grinned. He was enjoying the fight, she knew. 'How heroic,' she murmured, blocking a spear-thrust aimed at her heart. She flung out a hand and tore the orc's throat out, even as she pivoted and hurled it behind her.

As Neferata turned she saw Abhorash leap from the palisade and chop down through the bull-neck of the giant that had steadily been trying to uproot a section of the palisade for the better part of the last hour. 'Speaking of heroes,' she murmured, grabbing an orc by the neck and shaking it hard enough to shatter its bones. She hurled it from the wall with a disgusted grimace as its foul blood splattered across the ornate cuirass she wore. Abhorash had been recalled from the eastern frontier, where he had been dealing with the ogre tribes that infested the hills there, and he had thrown himself into this new war with as much enthusiasm as he ever showed for anything.

He chopped at the giant's neck as it staggered and fell, his sword rising and falling like a butcher's knife, and his aquiline face was twisted into an expression of bestial exultation. Abhorash lived for battle. He had a will of iron, until the sky darkened with arrows and the soil ran with blood and then his savagery put even Ushoran's to shame. She watched the decapitated giant sway on its feet before toppling forwards. It took the bigger ones a long time to realise that they were dead. She could practically hear W'soran's greedy chuckle now. The giant, even headless, would make excellent labour for the mines.

The giant slumped over the palisade, and Abhorash, ever at the forefront, bounded towards the orcs that swarmed up its bent body like ants. He crashed into the oncoming green wave like a rock set against the tide. An orc burst at the point of impact, Abhorash literally tearing through the creature as if it were of no more bother than a linen curtain. Other orcs were flung aside like gnats. Abhorash grabbed one as it flipped into the air, snatching it by one ankle and wielding it like a living, screaming flail against the others. Only when the creature had been reduced to a bedraggled mess did he toss it aside and continue his rampage.

'He plays the part well, whatever else he might be,' Naaima said, snapping an orc's arm as it swung an axe at her head. Like Neferata, she wore the black and red enamelled armour that Ushoran's smiths had gifted to them. It was far more ornate than that which they had worn in Nehekhara, being all flaring ridges and sharp edges. 'And speaking of playing parts, Khaled ably defends Ushoran, I see,' she added, frowning as she bent the orc backwards over the palisade and broke its back.

'He is magnificent,' Anmar said, leaping up to perch on the palisade wall even as she kicked an orc in the skull hard enough to crumple the bone and send it flailing to the rocky slope below.

'Referring to your brother or Lord Abhorash, little leopard?' Rasha said as she stabbed a wounded orc as it lunged awkwardly for the other vampire. She hefted the kicking, bawling beast and sent it spinning from the palisade.

'Both,' Anmar said simply, craning her head around to look at her blood-sister. 'Do not say you have not noticed,' she added, teasingly.

'Not my type,' Rasha said, sniffing, leaning on her blade. She brushed a lock of bloody hair out of her sharp face and looked at her mistress. 'Still, he is useful, in a rather blunt, unimaginative way, eh, my lady?'

'Sometimes a hammer is the right tool,' Neferata said. Down below, Abhorash had been joined by his 'Hand' – the four companions who had fought beside him since the fall of Lahmia. The four vampires were an aloof lot, bound to their captain by blood and honour. Regardless, they fought for Strigos with a vigour that few could match. Together, the five vampires carved a path through the heart of the orc horde, butchering the savages with abandon.

'Speaking of hammers,' Neferata murmured and looked away from the battle, searching for Vorag. The Bloodytooth was not at the forefront, as he would've liked. Instead, he and his riders waited behind the palisade. It was Abhorash's plan, of course. Wait for the orcs to break themselves on the palisade and then let Vorag's riders harry them as they retreated. It was an effective plan, and sensible, which meant that Vorag saw it as an insult.

She had convinced Ushoran to recall the timagal, despite the fact that Vorag's own lands were the scene of the harshest fighting. Ushoran even thought it was his idea. Vorag had been forced to leave his hard-won territories to be engulfed beneath the green tide, and Neferata could tell that he was seething even from a distance. And beside him, blonde and bloodthirsty, Stregga was whispering sweet nothings into his ear, calming him and simultaneously enflaming his hatreds even more. Neferata smiled.

She carefully wiped the expression off her face as the thud of armoured boots sounded and Ushoran approached, mopping at the blood on his too-handsome face with a ragged strip of cloth. 'They're close to breaking,' Neferata said.

'You had doubts?' Ushoran sneered. Orc blood had collected and dried in the grooves and swooping curves of his armour. 'They are beasts. We have more trouble with rats in the granaries.'

'Overconfidence is an attractive trait in a man, but not a ruler,' Neferata said mildly, resting the flat of her blade across her shoulder.

'And as always, I bow to your previous experience,' Ushoran replied blandly. He frowned. 'I grow tired of this. We should be expanding, not merely holding what we have.' He kicked petulantly at a green-skinned corpse. 'I want to do something about this, about them.' He looked at Neferata. 'Do something. Earn your keep.'

Neferata raised a delicately plucked eyebrow. 'I'll need men and gold, as well.'

'Yes, fine! Fine,' Ushoran said, waving a hand. 'You can have it all. I grow weary of slaughtering these creatures. I need a real war. And prisoners...' His eyes were unfocused and his gaze drifted towards the black pyramid. 'Yes,' he said, shaking himself, 'prisoners.'

It was only a gentle caress, but Neferata knew that Ushoran was hearing the needle-on-bone voice again, even as she herself sometimes heard it. It spoke to him more often, and she was still unsure as to whether she should be relieved or jealous.

You could be queen again. You could belong to Usirian,

*and not the jealous moon. Your charnel kingdom would
spread like rot through a fruit, and the whole world would
sing hymns to your wisdoms and mercies–*

Ushoran was looking at her, his eyes glowing like
balefire. She blinked and looked away. Whether she was
jealous or not, Ushoran certainly was. Why else would
he avoid all of her attempts to discuss the presence
which had drawn her to Mourkain? He knew that she
heard it, even as she knew that he heard it. Abhorash
heard it as well, and probably W'soran, though she
hadn't cared enough to inquire. It was a mystery, and
Neferata hated mysteries. Ushoran had the key, and one
way or another she intended to get it out of him.

Now wasn't the time to bring that argument up again,
however. 'A real war requires participants. And the orcs
have succeeded in putting paid to the ambitions of
every petty chieftain for two mountain ranges,' Neferata
said, attempting to allay suspicion with speculation.

'What of it?' Ushoran said.

'Those chieftains might be willing to do our work for
us,' Khaled said, from just behind Ushoran. The latter
glanced at him. 'Let the savages tear each other apart.
It saves us the trouble, my king,' he added, bowing
obsequiously.

'I see now why you kept him around,' Ushoran said,
smiling broadly. He glanced slyly at Neferata. 'He has a
good head for war.'

'Yes,' Neferata said, meeting Khaled's eyes over Ushoran's shoulder. *Don't get too comfortable, my Kontoi,*
she thought, *remember whose dog you truly are.* If Khaled understood the meaning of the look, he gave no
sign. Horns blew as the Bloodytooth's riders shot out
through the open palisade to harry the orcs. Ushoran
watched them go and grunted.

'Once Vorag has had his fun, we will hold council. There are plans to be made.'

'Oh yes, I quite agree,' Neferata said, as some strange sensation prickled at the edge of her consciousness. Suddenly, a shadow fell across the palisade. No, several shadows.

Perhaps the orcs weren't quite as beaten as she had thought.

Neferata spun as a raucous screech blistered the air. A wyvern crashed into the palisade, bat-like wings folding in and crooked talons flattening several Strigoi. A long serpentine neck shot out and jaws snapped shut on the arm of the warrior next to Ushoran.

Crouching atop the elephantine beast's squat body, a large orc, clad in scraps of salvaged armour, thrust a spear at the King of Strigos. He bore the war-paint of a warlord, and by his ornate headdress of animal skins, jutting fangs and golden trinkets, she judged him to be the current overlord of the horde.

The spear, for all its crudity of design, pierced Ushoran's armour with ease, thanks to the raw muscle behind the thrust. Ushoran staggered as the spear pierced his side and nailed him to the palisade, his mask of beauty slipping for a moment to reveal the beast beneath. Khaled sprang to Ushoran's aid with an alacrity that Neferata found somewhat disappointing. He grabbed the spear and tried to pull it loose, even as the wyvern snapped at him.

Two more of the beasts had crashed into the palisade. On one, a wild-eyed orc wearing a leopard-skull head-dress made grandiose gestures. Green, sickly lightning burped from its palms, striking men and turning them into whirlwinds of screaming ash. On the other was a large orc wielding a spiked flail, likely the warboss's bodyguard or champion, and as Neferata watched, the weapon slapped the head of one of Ushoran's vampiric bodyguards clean off his body.

Neferata gave a half-second's contemplation to letting the orcs finish the job they had started. Then, with a snarl, she said, 'Anmar! Help Khaled! Rasha, take the sorcerer! Keep Ushoran alive!' A moment later, lightning-swift, she raced across the pointed top of the palisade and flung herself at the lead wyvern and its rider. The wyvern sensed her before its master and a great wing flared out as it attempted to swat her from the sky. Her sword tore through the leathery web of the wing and the wyvern shrilled, flinging her back. She flipped through the air and landed in a crouch on the palisade.

The dragon-like maw dived for her, a wave of foetid air washing over her. Dagger teeth slammed shut inches from her face as she jerked back. Her hand shot out and she dug her talons into the meat of the wyvern's snout. It screamed and its head snapped back, yanking her with it. Neferata swung up and landed in an awkward crouch between its head and shoulders. With a snap of its wings, the agitated wyvern took off, rising above the palisade despite the angry howls of its rider. The orc had lost its spear in the sudden movement and clawed for the heavy chopping blade sheathed on its hip.

Air rippled past her, momentarily deafening her. A wave of vertigo threatened to overwhelm her as the beast beat its wings and ascended. The wyvern shrieked as it sped across the sky above Mourkain, scattering the carrion birds. Arrows arced towards it from the rooftops below, but none could penetrate the beast's scaly hide. Neferata pointed her sword at the orc. 'You want to fight the true master of Mourkain, brute? Then come, fight me!' she roared as she drove her sword towards the warboss. The brute half rose from its makeshift saddle and its shoulders bulged with muscle as it blocked her blow with its own blade and forced her back.

She wobbled, nearly losing her balance. Beneath her, the ground rushed past in a blur of dull colours. There was no room to manoeuvre on the wyvern's back. There was barely enough room for the orc riding it, let alone her. Tusks plated with beaten gold jabbed at her face and she grabbed one, yanking it out of the orc's mouth. The orc squealed like a pig and grabbed her throat. The serrated edge of its blade eased towards her face. It was stronger than she had expected.

The orc shoved Neferata back against the rough scales, the edge of its blade brushing against her throat. With a convulsive swipe, she pushed up and beat the blade aside. The orc reared back, arms wide, mouth open. Neferata drove her blade through its chest and twisted her wrist, cutting its heart in two. It fell from its saddle, plummeting into the streets of Mourkain.

Neferata had no time to celebrate her triumph. The wyvern shrieked again and spun in the air, trying to dislodge her from its back. Without its master, it had gone wild. Neferata jammed her blade between two of its scales and hung on as the creature jerked and looped through the air. Flattened against its back by its speed, Neferata began to wriggle forwards. She needed to dispose of the beast, and quickly.

Inch by torturous inch, she climbed towards the beast's head. Jerking her sword free and stabbing it in, she anchored herself against the creature's increasingly violent efforts to throw her off. Its wings brushed one of the higher buildings, sending a stream of shattered stone and dust cascading into the streets. She reached the base of its skull, grabbed its horn and gave a jerk, yanking its head around through sheer brute strength. The wyvern banked, if unwillingly, and squalled in fury. Gritting her teeth, Neferata gave the horn another yank. The beast was stronger than her, but it hadn't quite realised it yet.

It was also very, very angry. And she was going to make it even angrier. Neferata spun her sword and jabbed the point against the edge of the wyvern's eye-socket. It snarled in agony as she shoved the blade between its eye and the socket wall. Spasms of pain rippled through its body, nearly flinging her from her perch. But she had accomplished her goal – the beast twisted through the air and raced blindly back towards the palisade and its fellows. Neferata hunched up on its head, gathering her legs beneath her. She jerked her sword free of its eye as it smashed into the second of the wyverns.

In the chaotic moments before the two beasts collided, Neferata saw Rasha leap away, followed by a crackling column of emerald fire. The orc shaman turned and gaped comically as Neferata's wyvern barrelled into its own and both beasts toppled backwards from the palisade in a thrashing, crashing heap of scale and muscle.

The water of the river reached up for them greedily and Neferata leapt from the wyvern even as the water closed around them. She lunged for the orc shaman, attempting to disembowel it as they hit the water. Abhorash had insisted on digging a moat between the palisades and the rest of the mountain slope. It had taken a hundred men more than a hundred days of backbreaking labour to carve the winding scar and another month to properly divert water from the wild, dark river that surrounded and irrigated Mourkain into it. The moat was only as deep as three men standing one atop the other, but it had served its purpose, blunting the idiot ferocity of the first few orc assaults.

A thrashing wing crashed against her, sending her shooting through the water. She barely held on to her sword. The two wyverns were tangled together, snapping and writhing. Bloody clouds floated through the water as Neferata arrowed towards the floating shape of the shaman. The orc was desperately clawing for the surface.

She grabbed its thick ankle and yanked it down. Sorcerers were dangerous, even to her kind. Even if the sorcerer in question were a green-fleshed savage, the magic they wielded was one of the few things she knew of that could kill one of her kind.

Thus, caution was called for. She sank down to the river bottom and crouched, hauling the struggling orc after her. Its piggy eyes bulged as the shadows of the struggling wyverns fell over them, and it clawed for the distant grey light of the surface. A slew of bubbles burst from its bulbous jaw. Neferata grinned as the shaman slowly drowned. When she was certain it was dead, she let the body float to the surface and followed it.

As her head broke the surface, one of the wyverns followed suit. It crashed up out of the water, torn wings flapping and its jaws coated in bloody froth. Blinded and berserk, it screamed a challenge and lunged for her as she crawled up onto the bank.

Two swords punctured its brain pan a moment before it struck, driving its head down into the water at her feet. Anmar and Rasha rose from the water as the beast's death-throes ceased. Neferata laughed and hauled the dead shaman up, lopping off its head a moment later. Holding up the head by one of its tusks, she leapt lightly onto the dead wyvern. She extended her arm, holding the head aloft.

She shrieked out a challenge in the greenskin tongue, pitching her voice to carry across the clamour of the battlefield. Her words didn't need to carry far. They only had to kick the first pebble of the avalanche loose.

The orcs broke, as she had known they would. In the past two centuries, she had learned the intricacies of their ways. It had been child's-play for one used to dealing with the ambitious kings of Nehekhara to incite the orcs to mass and attack.

Now, keeping them attacking for close to two centuries had been the trick. Two centuries of constant invasion and retreat had created a massive horde of the beasts – a Waaagh! as they referred to it. As each small wave was destroyed, it had collapsed and been absorbed by the next, creating a perfect storm of bestial violence. With this last attack, she judged that the time would be right for another period of infighting among the various tribal remnants, especially with the current warboss and shaman dead; others would have to be chosen.

'Rasha,' she murmured as she looked up at the palisade. Ushoran seemed to have survived and he was occupied with his guards. The slim vampire looked to her mistress, water trickling down her face.

'Wazzakaz,' Rasha said, knowing what Neferata wanted.

'Yes. Go give him a sign, would you?' Neferata said, tossing the head into the water. Wazzakaz was the next-most prominent of the current crop of orc shamans, and a firm believer in throwing his followers at the holds of their ancient enemies the dwarfs, rather than the pitiful territories of the humans. Now, after this most telling defeat of his current rival, would be the perfect point for

Wazzakaz to see an omen which would encourage him to insist that whatever chieftain was listening to him this week press his right to control the Waaagh!

Rasha moved swiftly and departed down the slope, unnoticed by any of the others there. Neferata's followers had learned much about the arts of stealth over the decades. Then, it wasn't hard in the aftermath of a battle to move without being noticed, especially considering some of the others up and about. On the nearby slopes, dark cowled and robed figures prowled among the dead. To the people, they were simply the Mortuary Cult. It was a source of supreme amusement to Neferata that W'soran had chosen to co-opt the cult of the liche priests of the Great Land, and dedicate it to gathering the dead for his dark experiments. She climbed out of the river and shook her hair, trying to free herself of the slimy feel of the water.

'We will reap a great harvest this day,' a sibilant voice chortled.

Neferata turned. The speaker was draped in heavy robes, but even with the concealing hood, she could tell that his head was overlarge and oddly proportioned. 'Melkhior,' she greeted the robed man. 'Your cloud cover came in handy. You should be commended.'

Melkhior emitted a gurgling laugh. 'You would be the only one to do so, my lady,' he said. She caught a glimpse of the face in the hood and repressed a grimace. More bat than human and more corpse than bat, Melkhior was the most senior of W'soran's ever-growing supply of apprentices. The other vampire had apparently discovered a love of teaching. Thin-limbed and bloat-bellied, Melkhior looked and smelled like a corpse that had been left overlong in the sun. That was natural among W'soran's students. Melkhior was also a treacherous little worm, if what her spies reported was the truth, having murdered at least three of his rivals for W'soran's attentions. That too he had learned from W'soran, and Melkhior was nothing if not an apt pupil. 'And you deserve a commendation as well,' the apprentice continued, gesturing to the dead wyverns. 'Such heroism puts even mighty Abhorash to shame.'

'Speaking of heroes, where is your master? Cowering in the dark while the rest of us defend his hideaway?' Neferata said, using the tip of her sword to pull the edge of Melkhior's hood away from his face. The vampire jerked back.

'He is above such petty concerns as mere warfare,' Melkhior said.

'Yes. So he has said on numerous occasions. What is it he is *not* above, I wonder,' she said, frowning. She traced the bloated sack of Melkhior's cheek with the sword tip.

'Ask him yourself,' Ushoran said.

Neferata turned and looked up at the palisade as Melkhior scurried away. Ushoran gestured sharply, as if to a dog. 'Come, my Lady of Mysteries. Your king requires your counsel.'

Neferata sheathed her sword without flourish. She refused to give Ushoran the satisfaction of reacting publically to his needling. She and Anmar stepped through the broken section of the palisade. The third wyvern lay there, gutted and cooling. Spears and arrows sprouted from every inch of its body and its rider lay in several pieces some distance away. Anmar preened slightly as they stepped over the orc's head, which still had a surprised look on its face.

'Well done, little leopard,' Neferata murmured as they joined the others.

'I live but to serve, my lady,' Anmar said.

'If only all of my servants were so accommodating,' Neferata said. Anmar made a face.

'He's only doing as you asked, my lady,' she said diplomatically. 'As he always does,' she added.

'Do you think I'm too hard on him, my child?'

Anmar paused, sensing the danger in her mistress's tone. 'I think he is devoted to you. We all are.'

'Devotion is no substitute for obedience. And your brother is anything but obedient. See that you do not follow his example, little leopard,' Neferata said, without looking at Anmar. She left the other woman standing there as she joined Ushoran's entourage.

Mourkain had weathered the orc attack as it always had. The palisades which covered the lower slopes and approaches took the brunt of any attack. Only occasionally, when the brutes gathered the sense to hurl some form of flying beast, like the wyverns of lamentable memory, at the city, did Mourkain itself suffer from battle.

Still, there were other ways to suffer. Fresh water was easy enough to come by, but food was almost impossible to grow in these high reaches. Thin, pinched faces filled the streets as Ushoran's panoply rode into the city. Rationing had been instituted early on, and with the coming of the Waaagh! food supplies had been limited to what could be brought in between assaults.

W'soran was waiting for them in the council chambers of the black pyramid, alongside another of his apprentices, the Strigoi nobleman Morath. The latter gave her a sickly grin. She felt some small pang of sympathy for the mortal – or not so mortal perhaps, considering that he had unnaturally lengthened his own span, albeit not in the usual fashion.

Morath was unusual. The only breathing man in the

room, the Strigoi was slim, with the look of a poet, rather than a warrior. He was as dangerous as any member of the Strigoi nobility, however, having been schooled in the arts of blade and bow since childhood. If he lacked Vorag's obvious muscle, he more than made up for it with a subtlety of wit that Neferata found refreshing. He was perhaps the only civilised man in Mourkain. It was a shame that he had been pledged to W'soran's service by Ushoran. Then, that was perhaps one of the few intelligent decisions that his majesty had made. Ushoran knew that W'soran couldn't be trusted, and that it was only a matter of time before he vanished or tried something, and left Strigos bereft of his magics.

But Morath, above all else, was loyal to Strigos; the ideal, if not the men who made it. He sat near his master, looking distinctly uncomfortable. Neferata could understand that as well. W'soran grew more inhuman-looking every year, with pronounced bat-like ears and a face out of nightmare. Thin, gangly arms protruded from the too-tattered sleeves of his robes, clutching tight to a messy pile of parchment, which he thrust at Ushoran as the latter entered the room. Ushoran scanned the parchment and grunted.

Shoving it back into W'soran's hands, he said, 'Abhorash, the map.' Abhorash unrolled a large bear-hide. On the opposite side from the fur, a great map had been inked in painstaking and impressive detail. 'Cartography is a rare skill, and one I have cultivated among my servants,' Ushoran said. He swept a hand across a section of the map. 'Orcs, barbarians and beasts – those are the enemies we face, my friends.'

Abhorash snorted. 'Those are not enemies. Those are obstacles.'

'Nonetheless, I need them not to be,' Ushoran said.

He looked at Neferata. 'I need them gone.'

'Orcs are easy,' Vorag said. 'If we can hit them hard enough and fast enough…'

'We don't have the men,' Abhorash said, arms crossed. 'It's all we can do to hold the mountain passes…'

'We don't need them!' Vorag snapped. Abhorash gazed at him steadily, but said nothing.

'The barbarians are trickier,' Morath spoke up, tapping the map. 'The tribes are constantly changing size as they fight amongst themselves, and they change chieftains almost as often. We never deal with the same one twice.'

'One barbarian is much the same as another,' W'soran said dismissively.

'And because you think that is why I am here.' Neferata studied the map. 'How big an empire do you desire, Ushoran?' she said after a moment.

'Why?' Ushoran said.

'Merely defining the limits of my authority,' she said. Ushoran looked at her. She smiled. 'The orcs are a problem. Diplomacy will be useless. But there are other ways of countering their numbers.' She flattened her palm on the map and looked at Abhorash. 'How would you describe the creatures, champion?'

'A force of nature,' he said.

'Like a flood, say, or an avalanche?' Neferata said. Abhorash nodded. Neferata patted the map. 'The mountains form a natural culvert, and the orcs have, by and large, filled that culvert. They attack, because they have nowhere else to go. And the more they attack, the more of them are drawn into the culvert, seeking the battle they crave.'

'Every time we force them back, it's like dumping water into a leaky bucket,' Abhorash said, nodding more fiercely. 'We have to plug the hole.'

'What hole? What are you talking about?' Ushoran snapped.

'I'm talking about ridding your lands of the orcs forever. We need to break their spine, to harry them out of the places they congregate and pulverise them as they are forced out into the light,' Neferata said, making a fist. 'They will eventually regroup, but we can buy ourselves several generations at least before their numbers swell to such proportions again.'

'And how will you do that? As he's pointed out,' Vorag said, gesturing to Abhorash, 'we don't have enough men for the job.'

'Perhaps not living men, no,' W'soran began, eyes alight with interest. 'I could–'

'No,' Neferata said flatly. 'We have an opportunity here that must not be squandered simply for expediency's sake.'

'You spoke of the wildling tribes earlier,' Ushoran said, stroking his chin.

'Not just them. If you desire expansion, we'll need closer ties with the Silver Pinnacle.' She tapped the marker for the dwarf hold. It had taken her spies years to discover its whereabouts; the dwarfs used trading posts to ferry their goods to Mourkain, so protective were they of the whereabouts of their hold. 'We must share more than gold with them...'

'Blood,' Abhorash said.

Neferata nodded. 'They're pressed just as hard as we are by the orc migrations. If we were to offer them a more proactive alliance...'

Ushoran sat back in his chair, a thoughtful expression on his face. Finally, he said, 'What would you need?'

'Vorag,' Neferata said immediately. Vorag blinked, and then slowly grinned. 'We'll need to move quickly.

The tribes will do our heavy fighting for us.'

'Yes, you still haven't said how you intend to accomplish that,' W'soran said. 'The Draesca and the other wildlings have no love for Strigos.'

Neferata smiled. 'You have your secrets, sorcerer. Let me have mine.'

When the council had ended some hours later, Neferata returned to her chambers. Naaima waited for her there. 'It's time,' she said.

'I sent the girls out at sunset,' Naaima said.

'As always, you predict my needs,' Neferata murmured, sipping her second goblet more slowly. 'They have their instructions, then?'

'Yes, and the tribes await their coming. Beautiful daughters of the high agals of Strigos, wedded to the chieftains of the tribes.'

'Blood is a stronger bond than gold. Longer lasting as well,' Neferata said, falling into a hard stone chair. 'The girls will choose handmaidens of their own from the high women of the tribes and those women will control their husbands and the tribes...' Neferata gestured with her free hand and smiled. 'Has Rasha returned?'

'Yes,' Naaima said. 'The orcs are moving west, towards the ranges where the Silver Pinnacle sits. It will be a year at least before they attempt to mount an assault, or try and return here.'

'Like water sloshing in a bowl. First one side and then the other,' Neferata said. She added, 'The trick being to get the water to slop out without getting wet.'

'It sounds like quite the trick, then,' Naaima said. 'And how will you do it?'

Neferata smiled. 'Why, by letting someone else hold the bowl, of course.'

⫸ EIGHT ⫷

The City of Bel Aliad
(−1150 Imperial Reckoning)

Neferata reclined in her palanquin, protected from the sun by curtains of muslin and silk. Cushions of all shapes, sizes and colours decorated the interior and she smiled as Anmar lounged across them like a cat. The corner of the girl's mouth was streaked with blood and her eyes held the dreamy gleam of one who had fed well and deeply.

She was so like Khalida, albeit lacking in the natural ferocity that Neferata's long-dead cousin had possessed. Tenderly, Neferata reached out and rubbed the drying blood from Anmar's mouth. 'Your brother has been up to something,' she said.

'My brother is always up to something,' Anmar said lazily. She pushed herself up. 'You are not angry, are you, my lady?' she said.

'I encourage initiative,' Neferata said. 'Don't I, Naaima, my sweet?'

Naaima snorted. She sat at the back of the palanquin with Rasha. Neferata had been both impressed and pleased to

find that both her oldest and newest handmaidens had sur-
vived the debacle of the attack on Bel Aliad, among others.
Abhorash had taught the warriors of Bel Aliad well, and they
had shattered the desert tribes in the months of her captivity,
scattering them to the four corners of the Great Desert. But
Neferata's handmaidens, like their mistress, were made of
sterner stuff.

'When it suits your plans,' Naaima said.

Neferata chuckled. 'True.' Her smile faded. 'But the
privilege of initiative must be earned, and your brother, little
leopard, has yet to do that. He has, if anything, earned himself a short leash.'

'We are simply eager to explore the power you have gifted
to us,' Anmar said.

'Your brother is eager to be caliph,' Neferata retorted. 'And
as a consequence, he endangers my plans for this city.' She
leaned back and looked up at the ribs of silk that made up
the ceiling of the palanquin, and then looked out through
the side curtain. The men who carried the palanquin were
devotees of the Cult of Mordig, the Great Ghul. Their brawny
forms were covered in scrawling tattoos composed of the cult's
holy writ – each devotee was a walking book, carriers of Mordig's word into the daytime world. They wore funerary purple
robes and silver skull masks.

Khaled had been a nominal supporter of the cult, as he was
one of many noblemen whom the cult supplied with esoteric
bric-a-brac. Neferata had used his connection to ingratiate
herself with the cult's high priests, and then, swiftly, to take
control. They were corpse-eaters and blood-drinkers already,
and her undead nature had only served to impress them.
They worshipped her now as the Charnel Bride, and Queen
of the Night.

As rumours drifted across the sandy expanse separating
Araby from the Great Land, the cult had grown in influence.

Many saw the servants of the Eater-of-the-Dead as the best defence against the walking dead which were said to now haunt Nehekhara. Whether that was true or not was something that had yet to be tested. Neferata intended to be ready regardless when the inevitable occurred.

'Thinking of home?' Naaima said.

Neferata shook her head. 'My home – our home – is the future. The past is dead. Best we leave it as such.' And the future, right now, was making Bel Aliad into a true power. The cult had adherents in each of the caliphates, and through them, Neferata was slowly weaving a web of subtle control. She had infiltrated the harems of the mighty with her followers – survivors from among the tribes as well as new converts. In these lands, where women were almost property, the giving of a beautiful woman as a gift was a common form of diplomacy.

It might take decades, but soon, the Cult of Mordig would control every nobleman from Bel Aliad to Copher and through them, Neferata would command the might of Araby. She sighed in pleasure.

That pleasure was wiped away in a flash of pain as an arrow pierced the curtain and smashed into her shoulder, hurling her to the other side of the palanquin. The palanquin tipped and then fell as the cultists carrying it sprouted arrows. People screamed as the streets were suddenly filled with armed men. Neferata hissed in pain as she jerked the arrow from her shoulder. 'What is the meaning of this?' she snarled.

'It's Al-Khattab!' Naaima said, narrowly avoiding a sword thrust that shredded the curtain. Sunlight boiled in, blistering the flesh of her arm. Neferata's hand snapped out, grabbing the blade before it could retract. She gave it a yank, heedless of the way the edge shredded her palm. She dragged the swordsman inside the palanquin and Rasha and Anmar *fell on him, growling. His screams echoed across the street, mingling with those of the market day crowd. Through the curtain, Neferata could see more men approaching.*

'That treacherous dog,' Neferata said, half admiringly. Al-Khattab was an opponent of the cult and the commander of the city's Kontoi. He had the caliph's ear, a situation that Khaled was attempting to rectify. She hadn't thought him capable of even contemplating outright assassination, but here they were. His men were clad in insignia-less armour, but they moved with training and speed. And the sun stood strong in the sky.

Men surrounded the palanquin, readying their spears. 'Come out, priestess of the corpse-king,' someone called. 'We will make your death as swift as that of that fool princeling…'

'Khaled,' Anmar gasped. 'No!'

Neferata snatched up the dead man's sword and looked at her handmaidens. 'Prepare, my daughters,' she said. Then, with a shriek, she lunged to her feet and sliced through the curtain. As the sunlight streamed in, she leapt out to meet the assassins…

The City of Mourkain
(–550 Imperial Reckoning)

HORNS BLEW LOUD enough to rattle the branches of the trees as the hunters followed the bloody trail left by their prey. Neferata leaned over the neck of her horse and tasted the wind. The musky, rotten smell of the fleeing beastmen was strong. Thirty of the beasts at least, maybe more; they had attacked a village on the northern frontier, putting it to the torch and eating the inhabitants. More and more of the creatures had been descending from the north of late. Abhorash and his men had undertaken an expedition to investigate, but that still left the mountains overrun with the cloven-hoofed vermin.

More horns blasted over the thunder of horses' hooves and the hunters whooped and howled in the light of the torches they carried. Neferata laughed as her horse leapt over a fallen log and galloped on. She could smell the cloud of fear that clung to their prey.

The riders were mostly Strigoi. Zandor was among them, and Gashnag as well. Those two had joined Ushoran's royal bodyguard in recent months, which Neferata had allowed. The two were cowed, more or less, and their feeble attempts to have her killed had trickled to nothing since she had not opposed their elevation to Ushoran's clique. It made sense to leave them where she could find them. After all, according to her spies, it had been Ushoran whom they had run to in the aftermath of their abortive assassination attempt. Whether Ushoran himself had set them on her tail, or whether they'd simply been attempting to curry favour, she couldn't, as yet, say. But she would find out eventually.

Nearby, Iona pressed close to her mistress. The henna-haired former concubine of Neferata's predecessor flashed her fangs in a smile. 'Volker is enjoying himself,' she said. Neferata looked past her handmaiden towards the burly chieftain of the Draesca tribe, as he awkwardly clung to his barrel-chested Strigoi stallion. Volker was hairy and gap-toothed, but cunning. Near him rode the chieftains of the Draka and the Fennones, as well as the savage Walds. Four of the largest tribes of the western marches and northern hills, and the four most dedicated opponents to the expansion of Strigos.

It had taken her decades of patient diplomacy to even

get them to the point where they would countenance accepting the hospitality of Ushoran. It never failed to amuse Neferata that she was first forced to build her enemies up before she could properly break them down. Fifty years ago, the tribes had been little better than the beastmen they now hunted. Now, however, their hill-forts dotted the hills and valleys of the badlands. Nomadic raiders had become farmers. War-chiefs had given way to hereditary kings, headmen to counts and bosses to barons.

And through it all, the Handmaidens of the Moon had whispered quiet counsel to the chieftains and their fathers and their father's-fathers. Religion was a subtle lever and the invented ones were the subtlest of all, Neferata had found. The Nehekharan religions were anathema to the wildlings, representing Strigos as they did in their eyes. She had been forced to come up with something innovative. Thus, the Handmaidens of the Moon; she had taken a minor hill-goddess called Shaya and crafted a more pleasing image for her, a goddess of healing and mercy, whose adherents were allowed to travel between the barbarian kingdoms without fear of reprisal. No man, no matter how powerful or paranoid, would willingly turn away skilled healers. Or, even better, skilled healers who were willing to act as messengers between men of status who could not ordinarily make contact without upsetting their bloodthirsty followers and rivals. And who would say a word about the Hand-maidens and their propensity for nocturnal travel, or the savage vengeance visited upon those who dared test the protection extended to them by their goddess?

She smiled. The Fennones, in particular, had taken to the new goddess. And their traders had carried the faith ever westwards, into the savage lands beyond the forests of their territories. The snort of a horse brought her out of her contemplative reverie.

The wildling chieftains were not natural riders, and it showed in their clumsy attempts to urge their horses to greater speeds. Their bodyguards were little better. In comparison, Neferata and her handmaidens, as well as the select few Strigoi allowed to accompany them for form's sake, rode as if they had been born in the saddle.

'Usirian's teeth,' Vorag swore. 'These hairy bastards ride like drunken urka.' The Strigoi's horse flew through the trees like a hawk, and its rider was fighting an obvious battle to control the inhuman savagery lurking within him. In the years since their first meeting, Neferata had noticed that Ushoran's blood-progeny had more problems in that regard than her own. Something bestial lurked beneath the skin of the vampires of Strigos, as if the dark magic which inundated the mountains had twisted them in some way.

'It was your idea to fill their bellies with wine before we started the hunt,' Stregga said, forcing her horse between Vorag's and Neferata's. Vorag barked laughter and followed after her, lust evident in his expression.

Stregga had pinned the Strigoi's ears back, and quicker than Neferata could have hoped. At least some things were going according to plan. Vorag's exile was no longer a topic of discussion at court, thanks to Neferata's agents. In the years since she had begun planning the extinction of the orc tribes that still squatted within the boundaries of Ushoran's ever-expanding empire, she had taken Vorag as her right hand, and bought his loyalty with her salt.

The Bloodytooth was no longer Ushoran's creature, if he ever had been. And he made a satisfactory replacement for Khaled, being both altogether more biddable and less prone to questioning her. Thought of Khaled made her frown. He was still playing shield-bearer to Ushoran, and was invited to all of the counsels and quiet meetings that her former Lord of Masks thought she was unaware of.

There was no question that Ushoran trusted her Kontoi. But should she?

A howl alerted her that their prey had come to bay at last. Horns bellowing, the hunters burst through the trees to confront the beastmen. The creatures screamed and howled as the riders flooded over them. Hunting spears pinned writhing, hairy shapes to the forest floor.

Neferata pulled her horse up short, letting the others indulge their bloodlust on the pathetic goat-things. 'Good sport, lady,' someone grunted. She turned and smiled serenely at Volker. Iona sat just behind him, her attention split between the object of her seduction and the dying beast-things. The crimson-haired vampire's face was twisted by feral hunger.

She examined the chieftain of the Draesca. He was broad, but short and gnarled. His beard was thick and tangled and his armour was of the crudest variety – beaten bronze plates sewn to a boiled leather jerkin with deer gut. His hair was held back from his leathery face by a band of gold that had probably belonged to a dwarf lord at some point in time. Dark eyes peered from beneath bushy eyebrows at her.

'I'm glad to see you enjoying yourself, great chieftain,' Neferata said. 'And I am glad to see you that you're enjoying my gift as well.' She nodded to Iona, who put her hand on Volker's brawny forearm. The chieftain gave a gap-toothed grin and patted the girl's pale hand.

'Truly the Strigoi are a blessed people to have such women spring from them,' Volker grunted, eyeing her speculatively. 'A shame that you yourself are spoken for,' he added.

'Yes, well,' Neferata said, looking over at the massacre that was occurring only a short distance away. One of the beasts had broken past the horsemen and, bleating, charged towards them, waving a notched and rusty blade. 'Your spear, if you please,' she said, extending her hand to Volker, who guffawed and handed the weapon to her. She bounced it on her palm and then, in one smooth motion, hurled it into the charging beastman. It folded over the spear and collapsed with a single, strangled whine. Volker nodded appreciatively.

'Yes, quite a shame,' he muttered. 'The Wald and the Draka are quite impressed with you.'

Neferata said nothing. Volker's previous cheer had disappeared. He frowned, his face becoming even more apelike. 'But the Draesca are not the Wald or the Draka. We are a proud people, and it will take more than Strigoi women or Strigoi wine to make us share blood and bone with you.'

'I know,' Neferata said. 'But if blood and bone don't serve, what about blades?' she asked.

'Are you threatening us?' Volker grunted incredulously.

'Nothing of the sort,' Neferata said, kneeing her horse towards the beastman she had spitted. Without a trace of effort she jerked the spear from its body and rode back towards Volker. 'You know of the dawi, I trust?'

Volker sat back on his saddle and tugged on his beard. 'Aye,' he said suspiciously.

'The dawi are the finest weapons-makers in the world,' Neferata said, extending the spear so that the tip rested beneath Volker's nose. 'This spear, for instance.'

Volker grabbed the weapon and looked at it as if seeing it for the first time. He rubbed his calloused thumb along the edge. His eyes flickered up to Neferata. 'You would trade us weapons?'

'I would.'

'For what price would you do this?'

'Blood and bone,' Neferata said, smiling.

Later, as the hunters, now satiated, rode back towards Mourkain, Stregga's horse fell into a trot beside Neferata's. 'Vorag is eager for the coming war, my lady,' the vampire said.

'Then he'll fit right in with these barbarians,' Neferata murmured. 'What else?'

'He's angry. The northern expedition–'

'The northern expedition is nothing.' Neferata shook her head. Vorag's temper was like a storm. It was a constant struggle to keep it in check and to keep it from upsetting her delicate web of schemes. Still, he was less disruptive than Khaled. 'Assure him that there will be glory aplenty in the mountains. He will once more be the saviour of Strigos, and Abhorash will not be around to steal his victory.' The Great Land was gone, and Ushoran's attempt to recreate it was doomed to failure. But there might be something worth saving from those ashes, Neferata thought. A society that could be moulded into something greater than it currently was. The way forward was not as the wolf or the leopard, but as the flea or the tick. A dead host was nothing but rotten meat. But a live one could keep her and her followers in comfort for eternity.

But a live host required careful pruning of anything that might endanger it. The orcs, for instance; but with the barbarian tribes, and Vorag's men, the orcs would be easy enough to destroy. She had learned much over the course of the past century, fighting and manipulating them. Now was the time to put all that knowledge to use. The orcs had outlived their usefulness and their violent antics were more hindrance than help.

Wazzakaz's Waaagh! had been crashing like a green ocean around the rock of Karaz Bryn for close to three decades now. The great shaman himself had gone from a vigorous, mad, bad bastard of an orc to a withered, hunched thing that cackled and rocked in its saddle. Her spies had kept tabs on the creature, and had watched the ebb and flow of the siege of Karaz Bryn.

She had sent messengers to the Silver Pinnacle, offering the aid of Strigos. Razek had yet to respond. Whether that was due to dwarf stubbornness or the war-effort, she could not say, though she expected that it was the former.

The next month was given over to the dull routine of preparation. Neferata stayed out of it for the most part – Vorag knew his own business, and she had no interest in second-guessing his preparations for the war to come. Instead, she concentrated on other, more important matters.

Namely, finding out what W'soran was up to.

She had spent decades rooting out the traitors and would-be regicides in the court of Mourkain; some, like Zandor, had been convinced to accept what scraps were offered. Others had been dealt with quietly. Nonetheless, one had escaped every trick and trap she had set. W'soran was plotting; she knew this as surely as she knew that he knew that she was doing the same.

But so far, she had caught not a hint or whisper of just what it was that he was plotting to do. He did not want to rule, such was not one of W'soran's desires. The urge to know what he was hiding had become almost unbearable.

Neferata stalked through the halls that W'soran had

claimed near the peak, ignoring the whispers and glances of W'soran's disciples as they hurried about in their cowls and robes even as she ignored the dead who moved stiffly about certain unwholesome tasks.

Even as her own numbers had increased, so too had W'soran's. Of them all, only Abhorash resisted the temptation to share his blood-kiss with others, save for his few followers. She did not know whether that suggested weakness or strength on his part. Perhaps it was simply the old familiar stubbornness that had so characterised her former champion in better, brighter times.

Not all of W'soran's followers were vampires, however. Like some virulent strain of plague, the vampire-disciples had taken apprentices of their own, creating a strange, semi-cultic hierarchy. Only one had not done so. And it was that one she was on her way to see.

W'soran's creatures went up and down in their master's favour like a fisherman's cog on the waves. Sometimes one would be the favourite and then another. Morath was out this week, it seemed. He was out often; refusing W'soran's bite was tantamount to spitting in the old leech's face.

She smiled. Morath had courage, of a sort. Not a physical bravery, but a mental fortitude that she admired. If circumstances had been different, she would have given him her blood-kiss. As it was, he could still prove useful, in the right circumstances.

Circumstances like these, for instance.

Finding out what W'soran was up to had become an itch that needed scratching. What higher matters, what concerns occupied the necromancer deep in his lair in the mountain? Why did he only go to the pyramid on certain nights? And why did he inevitably leave with fewer acolytes than he entered with?

The floor vibrated quietly with the rumble of the mine-works below in the guts of the mountain. More than gold was being dredged out of the dark now. She paused for a moment, listening. The gold would go to good cause. It could be used to open up trade routes to Cathay and Araby, and even Ind. Too, thanks to the whispered influences of her handmaidens, the barbarians over the mountains and to the north now desired it, though they had little practical use for it.

W'soran was even crafting a golden crown for the Draesca brute, Volker. Knowing W'soran, the crown would likely be more than just mere metal, but that was of little import. No, what was important was that the crown – that all of the gifts – would bind the savages to Strigos. Here in these wild hills she was perfecting the arts she had learned in Cathay and employed in Araby. War was a blunt tool, at best. Conquest could be achieved more easily by simply convincing the enemy that *they were more like you than they'd thought.* Familiarity bred more than just contempt, it also bred complacency. In a few centuries, the wildling tribes would fold easily and with little complaint into the Strigoi empire.

The same tactics could be applied personally. Seduction was more potent than fear, and took less effort to maintain. She had considered Melkhior at first, but found the idea of drawing too close to that creature repugnant.

But Morath was different. In his own way, the necromancer reminded her of Abhorash. Ushoran had forced him to accept W'soran's tutelage, wanting a man inside whatever spider's web the foul creature was sure to weave in his new lair. And it seemed only fitting that Neferata now take Morath under her wing.

She knew his scent now. It was stale, like crypt air, but lacking the rotten undercurrent that so many of W'soran's creatures emanated. The room was small as such places went in the hold. Bats fluttered in brass cages and jars of strange liquids sat on benches and shelves. Papyrus and scrolls were strewn everywhere, scattered amongst stacks of clay tablets from the South-lands and hairy books from the ice-lands far to the north. W'soran's agents had been scouring the world for centuries, hunting up precious bits of sorcerous knowledge for some purpose she did not yet fathom.

It all tied into the pyramid somehow. And the hunched figure sitting before her, with his back to her, would tell her how.

'My lady,' Morath said without turning around. 'The spirits bound to these old stones spoke of your coming.'

'Did they? And did they also impart my reason for coming here?' she said as she came up behind him.

'No, they did not.' Morath flinched as Neferata stroked his arm. 'Why are you here?' he said, not looking up from the scroll unrolled before him.

'Call it curiosity,' she said, peering over his shoulder. She clucked her tongue. 'Fell magics indeed.'

Morath looked at her. 'What would you know of it?'

Neferata shook her head. 'Me? Nothing, of course. W'soran's brood do not share their secrets with just any-one…' She traced his cheek with a claw, eliciting a thin trail of blood and a wince.

'What do you want, my lady?' he said.

'I should have thought that that would be obvious, Lord Morath,' she said, gently licking the blood from his cheek. He thrust away from her, knocking over the table and starting awkwardly to his feet. She could hear his heart thudding in his chest like a war-drum and see his blood pulsing in his veins. The smell of his fear was intoxicating. She frowned, restraining the urge to leap on him and feed until he had been bled white.

'No,' he said harshly. 'No, no. I've been around your kind too long. I'm not as foolish as that oaf, Vorag, panting after that–'

'Careful,' Neferata said mildly, looking at the scroll. Morath swallowed then snatched it away from her.

'This is not for your eyes,' he said. Neferata looked at him. Morath was handsome, in a way. He was no brute like Vorag, but there was none of the lean beauty of the men of her people either. He was hard-faced, all flat planes and angles and sharp words and edges.

'It could be, if you gave it to me,' she said, holding out her hand.

'And why would I do that?'

'Because only I can protect you from the trap you find yourself in. Ushoran can't – or won't. And W'soran is the cause of your nervousness, unless I miss my guess.' She took his abandoned seat and leaned back against the desk, smiling slightly.

Morath swallowed. 'You see much.'

'I see everything,' Neferata said. 'He is angry with you, isn't he? Because you have chosen not to accept his kiss, I'd wager.'

Morath said nothing. Neferata nodded as if he had. 'Did you know that it was he who first convinced my husband Lamashizzar to search for the secret of immortality? Even then, far before your people had even grasped the rudiments of agriculture, W'soran was scheming to cheat death.'

'And why shouldn't he?' Morath said. 'Why shouldn't we all? Our empire could persist forever with that power at our disposal!'

'Then why have you not accepted it?'

Morath paused. 'It is not the same thing. What you are is not what I wish to be. I'll not be a slave to my hungers for eternity–'

Neferata shot to her feet, forcing Morath back a step. 'A slave, is it? Is that how you see me, Morath of Mourkain?' she said in mock anger.

'Are you saying you're not? A slave to your bloodlust, a slave to that black presence which–' he began, and then stopped abruptly.

'The presence which – what? – lies perhaps in that pyramid,' Neferata said, and gestured loosely in the direction of the pyramid. She swayed closer to Morath, trailing her fingertips across his robes. 'What is in that strange barrow, Morath? Why do I feel some black malevolence in those stones? And why does your master seek to hide it from me, eh?'

'Because Ushoran requires it,' he said, stumbling back. 'I think you should leave.'

'Are you afraid of me, Morath?' she purred, staring into his eyes. She prodded at the sharp edges of his will – it was a thing of razors and brittle strength. One flex and it would crumble like grit in her clutches.

He forced himself to look away, flinging out a hand. Something sparked between them and Neferata staggered. Smoke rose from her burned hand and she hissed. 'What was that?' she snarled, lunging for him. He avoided her grip, raising his hands. Neferata hesitated. She had allowed her anger and impatience to get the better of her once again. Even as she cursed herself, she sought to present a calm facade.

'Your power is far greater than I thought, Morath,' she said, stepping back.

'If W'soran were here–'

'He'd let me try and torture the secret out of you. Or kill you himself to spite me,' she said gently. She could see the truth of those words strike home. 'You know enough of him, of what he is, to know that whatever he is up to, it is not for the benefit of your people.'

Morath stiffened. His hands drooped. She resisted the urge to smile. Like Abhorash, he thought himself a hero, a man doing his best for his people, when really he was as much prey to his lusts as any of her handmaidens. The only difference was that his lust was for power rather than blood.

'And you have the welfare of my people in mind?' he said.

'I have spent too many years building your people up to want to see them torn down, Morath of Mourkain,' she said.

'Then what do you want?'

Now she did smile. 'I only want just a bit of information, my friend, nothing more.'

'What do you want to know?'

Neferata leaned close and bent down. 'What is W'soran afraid of?' she whispered. 'What does Ushoran desire that frightens even that old fiend?'

Morath was silent for a moment. Then, with a croak, he said, 'A crown.'

'What?' Neferata stepped back, uncertain.

'Mourkain's crown,' Morath said. 'Ushoran wants the crown of Kadon. And he will not rest until he has it.' The words stabbed into Neferata's head like nails of cold iron, each one tossing echoes into the depths of her being.

As those echoes faded, something that was coiled in those dark depths lifted its head and Neferata felt a crawling chill spread throughout her person. 'A crown,' she whispered.

And in the darkness, something both familiar and foul laughed.

NINE

The City of Bel Aliad
(−1150 Imperial Reckoning)

'What have you done, fool?' Neferata snarled, slamming Khaled against the pillar hard enough to crack the ancient stone. He struggled in her grip, but could not break it. For all of the power he now possessed thanks to her kiss, Neferata would ever be his superior. She lifted him up, and his feet dangled a heartbeat from the floor, his heels drumming help-lessly against the pillar.

'I-I had to act!' Khaled sputtered. 'He was going to kill us!'

'Fool!' Neferata snarled again, punctuating the curse with another smash of Khaled's spine against the pillar. 'Did you lose your wits, or did you have none to begin with? Al-Khattab only moved because you sought to assert direct control of the caliph!'

Khaled's expression of injured innocence was wiped away at those words. 'But–' he began. Neferata made a sound of frustration and hurled him aside. He slid across the temple floor and the others were forced to move aside. Anmar made to go to his side as he hit the far wall, but Rasha and Naaima grabbed her, holding her back.

'Let me go! She'll kill him!' Anmar shouted.

'I won't kill him, little leopard,' Neferata said dismissively. 'That would be both foolish and a waste. Your brother is, as yet, necessary.' She turned and strode towards Khaled as he clambered to his feet. 'Fortunately for you, I have no time to devise a suitable punishment. How many men in your father's court can we count on?'

'Many, my lady,' Khaled said. Neferata grabbed his chin.

'Define "many",' she said.

'A third, maybe more,' Khaled said reluctantly. 'The nobility is suspicious of the cult, save for those of us with – ah – certain interests.' His face hardened. 'He would have listened to me! I know it!'

'Why?' Neferata said contemptuously, releasing him. 'Because you are a hero?'

'Because I am his son!'

'He has many sons,' Neferata said, turning her back on him. 'No… You have tipped our hand, my Kontoi. You have shown the murder-lust in our hearts to our false friends. Al-Khattab is determined to exterminate us.' She lifted her head, scenting the air that blew through the temple. 'Even now, they come with fire and steel.'

'They will be as sand beneath our hooves,' Rasha said, swinging the sword she had taken from one of the assassins earlier.

'Yes,' Khaled said eagerly. 'What better way to prove our power, than to kill our enemies? We will show my people the might of our cult and sever the head of the snake who threatens us in one fell swoop!' He spread his hands. 'My queen, you will have a kingdom again…'

Neferata stiffened. She turned, her eyes burning. Khaled blanched and scrambled backwards. 'I wanted an empire,'

Neferata snarled. 'What need have I of some petty caliphate? We could have had all of Araby! More, even. And all for the price of pretending that we had nothing at all!' Her face lengthened and spread, becoming feline. Her slender frame rippled with animal muscle as she advanced on Khaled. 'And now we will have nothing – nothing!'

'But, Bel Aliad–' he began.

'Bel Aliad is a blister on the hide of the desert! Damn Bel Aliad and damn you, you waste of blood!' Neferata shrieked, slapping him. Khaled spun and fell. Neferata howled. The inhuman sound echoed from pillar to post, descending into the deep vaults of the temple of Mordig.

And something answered her.

Throughout the temple, the great stone wells that led down into the night-black abysses beneath the sands of Araby suddenly echoed with the sounds of scrabbling talons as the children of the ghoul-god responded to the summons of their queen. The tomb-legions burst into the flickering light of the torches, a pale cancerous horde of ghouls that flooded the corridors of the temple.

Neferata had tamed them, in the first years of her freedom. Alone, she had descended into the deep vaults and fought the ghast-kings for control of their subterranean empires. Alone, she had returned with the fearful loyalty of the ghoul-tribes assured and the heads of a dozen ghast-kings tied about her naked waist.

The ghouls swept about her, chittering and whining, their filthy claws timidly touching the train of her robes as she stalked to the doors of the temple. The human servants of the cult had responded as well, their black armour and robes making them look like shadows.

'What are you doing, Neferata?' Naaima said, rushing to keep up with her. 'We can fix this. We do not have to throw away a decade of careful planning for Khaled's stupidity.'

Neferata said nothing, her face like stone. Her patience was a veil, as much a mask as the human seeming she wore. In truth, Khaled had given her an excuse to indulge the bloodthirst that had been building deep within her.

She flung open the temple doors to meet her would-be assassins. But rather than fear and steel, what she saw was something black.

It swallowed the horizon and reached for the stars, as if to strangle them. Flickering shadow-tendrils, spreading up-up-UP into the sky from some place far away, but too close for comfort. Neferata staggered, clutching at herself. Pain-nails were hammered into her head, burning her thoughts. She howled again, and staggered, clutching at her head.

COME.

COME TO ME.

'No!' *Neferata screamed. It was Nagash. Nagash's voice, inundating her thoughts as slimy water slipped through unseen cracks.*

MINE. YOU ARE MINE.

COME.

The horizon screamed with her, and the earth itself seemed to heave in terror. Alarms were ringing throughout the city.

The sky was shot through with green cracks and she could feel the dead in the burying grounds stirring in their shrouds. Blood burst from her nose and ears and eyes, coating her face. The others suffered similarly, and the ghouls set up a wail as they stared gape-jawed at the sky. Tormented spectres hurtled through the air like leaves caught in a wind.

It was as if something were calling all of the dead of the world north. Neferata's flesh writhed on her bones, as if it wanted to give in to the call. She took a step and then another.

'There! There is the witch causing this!' *a voice bellowed. Neferata tried to focus through the blood. Al-Khattab* galloped towards her, his impressively moustachioed face split in a self-righteous snarl. He swung up a sword. Soldiers followed, carrying weapons and torches. 'Burn them out! Burn this nest of abomination to the stones!' he roared.

Maddened and terrified of something that only she could hear, Neferata screamed and sprang to meet them, teeth and claws bared. With a howl, the ghouls followed their queen into battle…

The Worlds Edge Mountains
(−450 Imperial Reckoning)

THE SCREAMS OF wyverns and the bellicose roars of giants and trolls mingled with the general cacophony of the massed horde as it moved like a wave through the narrow valleys of the mountains. The orcs moved at a steady trot, not from organisation, but from simple eagerness. They were drawn to battle. Some wore armour scavenged from the dead, while others wore headdresses of bone and scalloping sapphire tattoos. They scrambled through the low river valley, tumbling trees and setting up a cloud of dust that blocked out the dull light of the mid-winter sun.

'Wazzakaz is efficient. It only took him ten years to beat the horde into some semblance of shape,' Rasha said, crouched low on the slope that overlooked the river of green winding its way through the valley. 'The dwarfs look as if they intend to meet them at the other end of the valley, where it starts to rise.'

'They're trying to lead them as far from the Silver Pinnacle as possible. A horde that size could lay a siege for years, if not decades, and once it got in, they'd be impossible to root out fully,' Neferata said, lying near her handmaiden. Orcs were like mould that way. They always came back when you least expected it, and ruined the grain in the process.

Her forces had found that out, almost to their cost, over the past few months. She had accompanied Vorag into the field as she had promised Ushoran, and it had been as frustrating as she had feared. They had wiped out the stragglers, the outcast tribal bands and the wolf-riders who scavenged from the Waaagh!'s leavings, but it seemed that the Waaagh!'s progress left almost as many greenskins in its wake as it added to its strength. Water splashing in a bowl indeed, even as she had said to Naaima.

The question now was, were the hands she had chosen to hold that bowl strong enough and quick enough to do as she required? Impatience thrummed through her momentarily. Part of her longed to be back in Mourkain, but it was too dangerous now.

Though W'soran had never given her an indication that he knew that she knew about the crown of Mourkain, she would have been foolish to assume otherwise. In the decades since she had pulled the secret out of Morath, the shadow-war between her agents and those of W'soran had escalated. Mourkain was simmering with discontent, and the conflict between them was only adding fuel to the fire. Thus, to keep the pot bubbling, but not yet wanting it to boil over, she had left. W'soran would lower his guard, and then she would know why he and Ushoran were so desperate to get their claws on Kadon's crown.

The soft scrape of twine on wood brought Neferata instantly alert. She cut her eyes towards Rasha, who jerked her chin and blinked three times. Neferata exhaled and rose slowly into a sitting position. 'You may as well come out,' she said. 'We've been expecting you.'

'Have you then?' a gruff voice replied. 'Well, isn't that just dandy?' A broad shape moved out of the rocks. The dwarf wore a leather coat over a suit of blackened mail, and had a crossbow pointed in a general fashion at Neferata. A broad-brimmed floppy trader's hat cast the dwarf's face into shadow, and his beard was threaded through with orc tusks and rat skulls. 'And why might that be, manling? Want to pick our bones clean after the *urk* are done with us? Going to root through our *gruntaz*, hmmm?'

'Hardly,' Neferata said. 'We've come to offer aid.'

'Oh, have you now? Isn't that a blessed event?' the dwarf replied caustically. 'Stop moving or I'll pin your pretty ears to your skull.' This last was directed at Rasha, whose hand crept towards her sword. 'D'you take me for a *wazzok*, is that it?'

'You ask a lot of questions for one who sounds so certain,' Neferata said mildly. 'I assume that Thane Razek Silverfoot is in charge of your expedition?'

The dwarf's eyes narrowed. The crossbow rose a few inches. 'And if he is?'

'He'll want to see me.'

'Will he now?' the dwarf said. He gave a thin whistle, and several more dwarfs, all dressed in dark clothing and armour, rose from their hiding places, all carrying crossbows. Neferata blinked, impressed. She hadn't even smelled them. 'Well then, *rinn*, let's see about that, shall we?' The dwarf jerked his crossbow and Neferata and Rasha were surrounded by the other dwarfs. The whole group began to climb the slope.

They made good progress, despite having to stop when

the shadow of a wyvern skidded across the rocks nearby. Luckily, orcs weren't the most observant of creatures, and the outriders were more concerned with reaching the battle than with securing the horde's flanks.

The aperture was well hidden. It took Neferata, with all her superior senses, three tries to spot it, and only then because she caught the steady thrum of dwarf heartbeats as the stone that blocked the opening was rolled aside. She and Rasha were led into the darkness of the steeply angled tunnel beyond. The entirety of the slope had apparently been honeycombed with tunnels that went off in seemingly random directions.

There were a number of dwarfs in evidence; dozens, in fact. Not quite a fighting force, but more than just observers, judging by the weapons they carried. Many of them wore the aprons and padded clothing she had come to associate with the engineers' guild. Razek had had several members of that secretive organisation amongst his coterie in Mourkain.

'It's an *und* – a watch-post, you'd call it,' a familiar voice said. Neferata turned. Razek looked little different from the last time Neferata had seen him. A new scar decorated the side of his face, descending from his scalp line, down through his eye and disappearing into his beard. But he was the same bulky, tough-looking creature she remembered. He sat at a round stone table, his hands flat on its surface. His expression changed from curiosity to something more alert as he examined her. 'I didn't realise manlings lived so long, Neferata.'

'My folk are long-lived. We are well-made, as your people might say,' Neferata said.

'Perhaps you are at that. It's been some time since we shared a drink,' Razek said, fluffing his beard. He glanced at one of his warriors. 'Beer,' he said. The warrior hurried off with an alacrity that Neferata envied. If only her own servants were that quick to obey.

'I assumed you got tired of being shown up,' Neferata said, turning to examine the central room of the outpost. It was barren of ornamentation, as befitting a dwarf outpost. The rough stone walls curved in a fashion that Neferata knew no human artisan could accomplish, and the whole of the outpost put her in mind of an overlarge animal den. There were other tunnels splitting off from the main chamber, leading to other hidden apertures, perhaps. Racks of weapons were mounted on the walls, including a few whose design and purpose escaped her completely. 'I did out-drink you, after all.' She looked at Razek.

Razek grunted. 'Only because I took it easy on you,' he said. 'Why are you here? This is of no concern to Strigos.'

Dwarfs could be touchy about matters of honour. They weren't a folk to accept aid gladly, or even at all. Neferata knew that she had to tread carefully in the next few minutes. 'I come to offer aid to our allies,' she said formally. 'We humbly ask that you accept what small help we can give to the throng of Karaz Bryn.'

Razek scratched his chin. 'And what form does that aid take? Surely it's not just you two...'

Neferata made a face. 'And if it was?' she said, in mock anger. 'Am I of no consequence, then? Is my ability in question?' Dwarfs respected one who was quick to defend their honour. In this case, it was more for the benefit of the other dwarfs in the outpost than for Razek, who was cunning enough to recognise her ploy for what it was. It was that same cunning which had necessitated the ending of their association, so many years ago. She pressed on. 'My forces wait in the reaches to the east, and our allies to the west and the south.'

'Allies, is it?' Razek said. He looked at the dwarf who had brought Neferata in. 'Ratcatcher, feel free to chime in, eh?'

Ratcatcher grunted and gnawed on one of his plaits. 'Aye, there are manlings massing in those regions right enough. But they're tribesmen – barely a step above the orcs themselves. We figured they were just preparing to defend themselves against the orcs, same as we are.' He looked at Neferata with newfound respect. 'If she's got them working together, they could punch the urk right in the belly.'

Razek looked back at her. 'And how'd you do that, then?' he demanded.

She shrugged. 'I have my ways.'

'You promised them weapons,' Razek said grimly. Neferata blinked. Momentarily nonplussed, she studied Razek and said nothing. He glared at her. 'Dwarf weapons, Neferata, sold in good faith to *our allies*.' His emphasis on the last two words was tinged with bitterness. What did he know, she wondered? Obviously her people had not been as efficient at ferreting out Razek's spies as she had assumed, but that was a problem for another time. Right now, she had to convince him to work with her.

'And paid for with our gold,' Neferata said softly. It was a calculated insult. Dwarfs lived by the law of debts, and to remind a dwarf of that was, Neferata had come to learn, the equivalent of questioning his competency. The bitter odour of dwarf anger filled her nostrils as Razek continued to glare. 'We do not play foul with you, thane of the Silver Pinnacle. But it is not your remit to tell us whom we may do business with,' she said.

Razek held her eyes. It was impossible to tell what was

going on behind his stony gaze and Neferata didn't even bother to try. Finally, Razek gave a snort. 'You know they'll take those weapons and stick them right up the Strigoi's fundament, don't you?'

'Yes, but not any time soon,' she said. 'The orcs are here now.' Razek grunted, though whether in agreement or otherwise, she couldn't say.

'We don't need them,' Ratcatcher said, looking at her contemptuously. 'Our warriors would only be hampered by the presence of manlings.'

'True enough,' Neferata said, throwing off her cloak and taking a seat at the stone table. She gestured. 'Then, this isn't about "need" but about debts owed, isn't that correct, Razek?' She leaned forwards. 'Have we not been good allies, Razek? We have helped you, and you have helped us, but is it not meet that allies shed blood as well as gold and beer?'

Razek raised an eyebrow. 'Are you saying we owe you a debt?' he said slowly. Then, 'Or perhaps it's the other way around?'

'Neither,' Neferata said. 'Or maybe it is both.' She made a fist. 'We would show you how much we value the friendship of Karaz Bryn, Razek.'

'We don't need your blood, woman,' Razek said dismissively. 'Manlings die too easily for it to be worth much.'

'Strigoi die harder than most,' Neferata said. She stood and drew her sword with a flourish. The dwarfs reacted much as she expected, some drawing weapons, others racing to the wall where crossbows and other deadly tools waited. Razek, however, didn't move so much as a muscle. 'Part of that is due to the benefits of our alliance,' she said, ignoring the startled dwarfs and laying the sword down on the table between them, its hilt towards Razek. 'Good dwarf iron,' she said. 'It is wielded by the hands of men.'

Razek's hand settled on the hilt and he lifted the blade as if it were a toy. He examined it with a critical eye and then set it back down. 'And what is that to us?'

'Progress,' Neferata said. 'The Silver Pinnacle is the wheel and we but the spokes. Together, we can move mountains.'

Some of the dwarfs muttered at that. Progress was a dirty word to some dawi. Change, that inevitable task-master, was their enemy as much as the orcs. Razek's expression remained the same. Then, abruptly, he leaned forwards. 'I'm listening,' he said.

The discussion went on for hours. Others dwarfs joined in, mostly to disagree with her in Khazalid, likely assuming she wouldn't understand. For the purposes of peace, she pretended that such was the case. It had taken her a decade to even gain a working knowledge of the language and two more to become fluent. It might take her another three to learn the strange, soft subtleties of the dwarf tongue. But she knew it well enough to know when she was being insulted.

The one called Ratcatcher was the most vociferous in that regard. The ranger had little love for humans, it seemed. Razek nodded brusquely at times, his eyes never leaving Neferata. When she spoke, he listened, but only grunted in reply.

If she had been human, her voice would have given out. Even so, she pretended to wet her throat with the beer they'd brought for her. The arguments were easy to make, for she had practised them for months prior to arranging this meeting. Years, in fact; one did not enter into negotiations with dwarfs lightly. In Mourkain, their merchants were known to haggle for days over the price of a single dollop of iron ore. But the dawi had arguments of their own.

At its heart, it all came down to trust. Mourkain had lost the trust of the dwarfs of the Silver Pinnacle centuries ago, and they had yet to gain it back. Trade was merely business. A true alliance could only exist between two equal partners.

Ushoran could never understand such a thing. He thought the dwarfs were pawns, when in truth, they could never be such. At the first hint of treachery or deceit, they would tear Mourkain apart stone by stone. And Neferata could not allow that to happen. Not until a time of her choosing. Eventually, Mourkain would need to be shattered, so that she could rebuild it into something stronger, but not now.

So instead, she spoke, her words hammering against dwarf stubbornness. There was no eloquence to it, no art, only those parts of the truth which she had hammered into the proper shape to fit her needs. And, finally, 'What's your answer? Will Karaz Bryn and Strigos fight together?'

Razek was silent. He tugged on his beard, his shrewd eyes on hers. 'Aye,' he said, after a moment. 'Aye, Neferata, we will at that.' Razek grunted and sat. 'Somebody bring me a map.'

Neferata sat for a moment, stunned slightly by the abruptness of Razek's decision. Instead of asking the obvious question, she merely inclined her head. Where dwarfs were concerned, silence was always the safest option. Razek had agreed, but not due to her words, that much she was sure of. But the why of it wasn't as important as the fact that he had.

Two dwarfs brought the map and unrolled it on the table. It was a beautiful thing, drawn with an eye for

detail that escaped even the most dedicated of Ushoran's cartographers. Strange marks that she had never
seen in relation to a map before littered the depicted
terrain. She made an assumption and said, 'These are
your cities.'

Razek frowned. 'Yes,' he said slowly, as if uncertain
whether or not he should be answering. Neferata noted
that there were far more dwarf holds in the near mountains than she had thought.

'Your people seem to have better claim to these
mountains than the Strigoi,' she said.

'We have better claim to the world,' Razek said grimly.

'If your people are so numerous, perhaps I was over-
eager offering our aid,' Neferata said.

Razek closed his eyes, as if in pain. 'Perhaps,' he said.

Neferata's eyes narrowed. She looked at the map
again, considering. She had learned little of the dwarfs
beyond some smattering of their customs to go with
their tongue, but what she did know implied that the
map was, if not wrong, perhaps old, older even than
herself, or Mourkain or even Nehekhara. There had
been a war, she knew, a war to shake the world, between
the dawi and some race from across the sea. The druchii,
perhaps, though she couldn't be sure.

It struck her then, that her kind were not the only ones
for whom nostalgia was a burden. The dwarfs clung to
their past as fiercely as Ushoran clung to the tattered
memories of the Great Land. It poisoned them just as
surely, and crippled them. She looked up from the map
and saw Razek looking at her.

'We cherish our past, too much perhaps. We hold
tight to ancient claims and grudges, nursing them,' he
said. 'More, we seek them out, to add to our burden of
miseries.' There was poignancy to his words that struck

her to the core. The desire to turn back the world was strong, even in her. She could only imagine how strong it must be in this creature before her who was immeasurably older. Then, the implication of his last words struck her and all at once, Neferata knew that she must tread carefully, even more carefully than before. Razek was no longer speaking in the general. He had a specific misery in mind, and she knew what it was. 'Honour is a two-edged blade,' she said delicately.

'Pah, what would a people as young as yours know about honour?' Razek said dismissively. 'No, it is not about honour, but about debts and accounts, as I have told you before, Neferata.' He splayed a hand on the map over the symbol she knew marked the sprawl of Mourkain. 'Debts must be paid and accounts balanced.'

'Regardless of the cost to both parties,' she said. It wasn't a question, and Razek didn't take it as such.

'Yes. But some debts must be paid sooner than others.' He slammed his stein of beer on the table, producing a ringing sound that echoed through the outpost. 'Gather round! Gather round,' he bellowed. 'We've got a *grobkul* to plan!'

'Grobkul?' Rasha murmured questioningly.

'The hunting of greenskins,' Neferata said. 'An apt description, if I do say so myself.'

The dwarfs in the outpost gathered around. They were a motley lot, insofar as Neferata could tell them apart. Younger, she judged, than those dwarfs in charge of the throng waiting to meet Wazzakaz's forces; eager thanes looking to win glory.

'Why were you stationed here, if I might be so bold?' Neferata said.

'The grobkul can be conducted many ways, but the most traditional is the hammer and the anvil.' Razek dropped his hands onto the table and slowly slid one palm towards the other. 'Block off the exits and give the grobi only one way to go. Then crush them from that end. Only way to be sure you get them all.' The other dwarfs nodded and muttered in satisfaction.

'And you're certain that the force you've got is capable of playing hammer?' Neferata said, examining the map. She traced a line. 'What about the river defiles here and here? How will you block those?'

'We have our ways,' Ratcatcher said defensively. 'We see everything. No grobi will slip past us!'

Rasha snorted. 'Then how did we get up here without you seeing us?'

'Who says we didn't?' the ranger snapped.

Rasha made to reply, but Neferata raised a hand, stopping her. 'Peace, master dwarf. I assume then, that you are aware of the movements of Wazzakaz's rivals to the north and the east,' she said. 'Krumpaz and Murk, I believe, though it's possible Murk was killed in that skirmish last month between his tribe and that of Olgutz.'

Ratcatcher blinked and looked at Razek, who shrugged. 'You're the scout, cousin. You tell me,' he said.

'They're moving with Wazzakaz,' Ratcatcher said, eyes narrowing as he peered at the map.

'No, they're moving *in the same direction*, and not even that,' Neferata said. 'The Waaagh! is on the verge of splitting into conflicting factions again, if they don't get a fight soon.

'That would explain the sudden surge,' Ratcatcher said grudgingly. '*Bugrit*, we're giving them just what they want.'

'And so what?' one of the thanes said as he pounded hard knuckles into his open palm. 'Just because grobi want something doesn't mean it's good for them!'

'Yes, but in this case, the bastards won't be as likely to break as we'd hoped,' Ratcatcher said. Neferata reappraised the ranger. He had missed something, but he was already compensating, adapting his line of thought to encompass the new facts. She hadn't thought a dawi could be so quick of thought. Perhaps that was why Razek had chosen these particular dwarfs as his companions. 'They might just splinter and run early,' Ratcatcher continued. 'Or scatter entirely.'

'Or shatter your lines and push through,' Neferata said mildly. Silence fell. She ignored the angry glares the others were giving her and looked at the map. 'Sheer momentum will overwhelm even the stoutest defence.'

Razek's face was stiff and scowling. 'You're saying we miscalculated their numbers.'

'Not at all,' Neferata said. 'But numbers mean little if you do not understand the meaning behind them.' She stood and leaned over the table. 'For close to two centuries, these tribes have waged war, smashing themselves and reforming,' she said. *Thanks to me, in part*, she thought. 'The impurities have been beaten from them. Wazzakaz is one of the most cunning shamans to ever fondle a fetish pendant, and his rivals are not much behind.'

'They'll be looking to get their boots in first,' a thane muttered. Razek nodded and his broad fingers traced a line.

'They'll overrun our positions in their haste to come to grips,' he said, leaning back and taking a sip of beer. Wiping foam from his beard, he tapped the map. 'It'd be like trying to fight an ocean, unless…' He looked at Neferata. 'You mentioned something about aid.'

She restrained a smile. 'Yes.'

He grunted. 'It's like chopping a tree: you take it down

with a number of blows, rather than just one. We'll pull the throng back to… here.' He put a finger down. 'The Strigoi can catch them in the passes and bloody them a bit,' he said, glancing at her. She nodded. He continued. 'And then, the throng of Karaz Bryn will shatter what remains.'

'An excellent plan,' Neferata said.

Razek grunted and knocked on the table with a thick knuckle. 'We'll handle the bulk of the fighting, of course. There's an art to fighting *grobi* that you manlings will never master.'

'Of course,' Neferata said. She looked up at Rasha. 'Go and alert the tribes. They will soon be called upon to prove the prowess they so readily boast of.'

Rasha nodded. Razek snapped his fingers. 'Ratcatcher, go with her. See that she gets there safely.'

'Rasha needs no help,' Neferata said, feeling her hand-maiden stiffen in silent protest.

Razek frowned. 'No?' He shrugged. 'Fine,' he said. As Rasha vanished down the tunnel, he said something in Khazalid to Ratcatcher and the grungy dwarf nodded and headed for a different tunnel. Razek looked back at her. 'You, of course, will accept an escort back to your people, I trust. Ratcatcher will gather his rangers to see you to safety.'

'But of course,' Neferata said. 'Your rangers are competent enough. They must be invaluable in these climes.'

Razek took a swig of beer. 'Indeed,' he said, wiping foam from his beard. 'They can get in most places without being seen. I was a ranger, for a time, as a beardling. Best years of my life.'

'Was it better than being Borri's hearth-warden?' Neferata asked.

Razek set his beer down. 'I am no longer hearth-warden.'

Neferata sat back down. She said nothing. Razek continued. 'My father felt that I could spend my time better overseeing our trading relations with other holds. He felt I was spending too much time among you *umgi*.'

That meant 'poorly made', Neferata knew. It was the dwarf word for human. Anger stirred in her, but she forced it down. Razek was watching her steadily. 'Were you?' she asked.

'He felt I was endangering the trading relations.'

'Ah,' Neferata said, tapping her lip with her finger. 'How curious.' *Because you were, you stunted little rogue,* she thought. *Though you did your best to pretend otherwise, I admit.*

'He saw no reason to question where the gold you pay us in is coming from,' Razek said as the rangers arrived, Ratcatcher in the lead. Neferata stood and began to follow the group out. Razek continued to speak.

'But I did.'

She stopped. Razek stood and trotted after her, holding something. 'I have looked forward to meeting you again, Neferata of Lahmia. You keep the accounts balanced, just like me.' He took her hand, pressing something into it even as he released her.

Razek strode away, leaving her alone with the rangers, who led her out. Not until she was outside, safely beneath the moon once again, did she look at what Razek had given her. It was a gold coin, stamped with an old, faded image. It was a dwarf coin, she knew, and felt a slight chill as she glanced back at the outpost, pondering the meaning of Razek's gift.

'If we're planning to go, now is the time,' Ratcatcher rumbled.

'Lead on,' Neferata said, closing her fingers about the coin.

TEN

The City of Bel Aliad
(–1150 Imperial Reckoning)

Bel Aliad heaved in the throes of civil war. Kontoi warred on Kontoi, noble house on noble house. Neferata moved through the incense-shrouded corridors of the ghoul-god's temple, followed by a panting praetorian guard of half-armoured ghouls. These were the largest of the colony beneath the temple, the ones who feasted on the freshest flesh and felt no fear in battle. They carried tulwars and, remarkably, possessed some skill in their use. Khaled had seen to that, at least.

Neferata herself wore the flowing mail coat of a Kontoi, and had a jewel-hilted scimitar sheathed on her hip. She disdained the use of a helmet, having never developed a liking for the feeling of metal and wood enclosing her skull. Her armour was covered in crusted, dried blood and when she stopped, several of her whining guards licked at the stains. Neferata ignored their antics. She stood in the central plaza of the temple, where her handmaidens – those who weren't involved in the fighting – oversaw the control of those parts of Bel Aliad that they held. Neferata scanned the faces of her followers and the priests who bustled about.

'Where is he?' she snapped.

'Where do you think?' Naaima said. The other vampire sat on Neferata's throne, reading a report. She tossed the scroll aside and pushed herself to her feet. 'He took as many ghouls as we could spare and went down into the tunnels. He's heading–'

'For the caliph's palace, yes,' Neferata said, rubbing her brow.

'You should have killed him.'

'Possibly,' Neferata said. 'And possibly his bloodlust will serve our purposes. As long as Al-Khattab holds the caliph, he holds the illusion of legitimacy. Khaled will be hailed as a rescuer…'

'By whom?' Naaima asked. 'The people on whom he feeds openly or the nobles whom he seeks to topple? Both fight us now, as well as Al-Khattab's conspirators!' Naaima trembled with anger. 'I warned you! I told you–'

'Be silent!' Neferata snarled, her voice echoing from the pillars. Every living thing, and most of the dead, froze at the sound of those words. Naaima stepped back, as if slapped. Neferata fell silent. She looked around. 'Where is Anmar?'

'I sent her with Rasha. There is a force approaching the city… I thought it best to find out who they are,' Naaima said hesitantly.

'When did you send them?' Neferata said.

Before Naaima could reply, there was a crash. The roof of the temple buckled and a section fell, crushing a number of priests and trapping one of Neferata's handmaidens. The vampire writhed beneath the stone, her lower body crushed to a paste. She shrieked wordlessly, her fists battering at *the stone and her human face dissolving into a mask of animal pain.*

Neferata moved swiftly to her side. She knelt and took her handmaiden's head in her lap. The woman's screams quieted to whimpers. 'Find out what's going on,' she said, flinging out a hand imperiously. Then she leaned over the wounded vampire, whispering comforting nonsense into her ear. With time and care, she might survive, but Neferata had neither. But she could see that her ending was as merciful as possible. That much she could do. Stroking the vampire's head, Neferata took a firm grip on her skull and, with barely more effort than it would take to crack an egg, she crushed it; the vampire spasmed and lay still, her unnatural life leaving her.

As Neferata let the remains of the corpse's head slough from her hands, something rolled out of the rubble. The skull was shattered and burning, but it chattered nonetheless as it caught sight of her, its blackened teeth clicking together as it crept towards her on tendrils of flame. Neferata batted it away with a hiss, watching as it shattered.

Neferata stood, holding out her hands for her ghouls. The creatures grabbed her wrists with pathetic eagerness and their cold tongues washed her fingers clean. She turned as Naaima rushed back into the plaza. 'Well? Is it Al-Khattab?' Even as she said it, she knew what the answer would be.

'No,' Naaima said. 'It is—'

Screams filled the air, echoing from the stone, reaching the plaza and its inhabitants from all across the city. The temple rocked as more burning skulls, howling like a chorus of wolves, crashed through the roof, showering the plaza in stone and splintered wood.

A ghoul screamed as one of the skulls, half crushed by its descent, fastened its jagged teeth in its leg. It began to gnaw wildly. Neferata felt something dark and ugly on the wind as Naaima finally managed to spit out her answer.

'It's Arkhan! Arkhan the Black lays siege to Bel Aliad!'

The Worlds Edge Mountains
(−450 Imperial Reckoning)

BY THE TIME she reached Vorag and the others, the horsemen were looking impatient. The dwarfs melted back into the shadows of the hills and scrub pines almost as quietly as her handmaidens could have done.

'Well?' Vorag snarled. He leaned over his saddle horn, his muscles contracting and swelling as if there was a storm going on beneath his hairy skin. 'Is it to be war? Or do we leave the stunted little fools to it?'

Neferata smiled. 'War, of course,' she said. Vorag threw back his head and howled. Moments later the men of his personal guard joined in, followed by the common soldiers who clustered around the riders. The howl echoed up through the pines and washed across the hills.

Stregga led a horse out of the group towards Neferata and the latter climbed quickly into the saddle. 'I've already sent a messenger to the wildlings. They'll launch their attack by morning.'

'If they don't run home first,' Vorag grunted. 'They're cowards, the lot of them.'

'They won't,' Neferata said, thinking of Iona and the other 'priestesses' scattered throughout the seraglios of the headmen of the tribes, both large and small, that had come at her request. Her daughters held those men's hearts and minds close, even as she held theirs.

Like Stregga and Rasha and all of the others, they saw the truth of Neferata's vision. They saw that a quiet word was more powerful than all of the swords a tribe could muster.

Those women, hammered into shape to suit her purpose, would hold their kings, chieftains and masters to the sharp edge of her design. She glanced at Stregga, whose hand had found Vorag's thigh. She gently squeezed his leg and the big vampire looked at her, his eyes hot with lust and, perhaps, something deeper.

Neferata turned away, wondering if their kind could feel love. Lust, she knew. Longing too, though it was a hard, harsh desire rather than the softer, more romantic kind she had known in life. Anmar seemed to love her brother fiercely for all that he didn't deserve it, the fool.

All will love you, when all is silent.

The voice was thin here, this far from Mourkain. Just a sibilant whisper, pressing against the underside of her mind, clinging like lichen to each thought. It was easy to ignore. Easy… She shook herself.

'Mistress,' someone said. She looked down.

'Layla,' Neferata said kindly, pushing a loose strand of the former scullery maid's hair up beneath her helmet. She wore the light armour that all of Neferata's handmaidens preferred, and wore it well. Her hand clenched nervously on the hilt of the sword at her waist. 'Are you ready for your first battle, my child?'

Layla showed her fangs as she smiled. 'I look forward to it,' she said, drawing her sword slightly before slamming it home again. Neferata smiled indulgently. Despite her earlier protestations, the girl had become exceedingly useful, with Anmar occupied keeping her brother out of trouble.

'Keep your wits about you, my little she-wolf,'

Neferata said. 'It is easy to get lost in the haze of blood-thirst, but to do so is to court death.'

Layla nodded earnestly. 'I will be careful, my lady.'

'Stay close to me, pup, I'll see you through it,' Stregga said loudly, riding close. She shared a look with Neferata. 'We've got to blood these new girls, my queen – teach them to hunt and make a kill on their own,' she said. She grinned insouciantly and tossed her honey-coloured hair. Like Neferata, she preferred to fight bare-headed.

Neferata chuckled and turned in her saddle. 'We need to ride out, while we still have the cover of the night,' she said to Vorag. 'We need to get in position.'

'More beautiful words were never spoken,' Vorag rumbled, patting his horse's neck.

The ride was a long one, and though the strength of the barrel-chested horses of the Strigoi was indefatigable, that of the unmounted warriors was not. They were hill-fighters, and tough, but keeping up with horses in uneven terrain over the course of several days tested even the toughest among them. The vampires, in contrast, moved smoothly and swiftly. Neferata's hand-maidens ran like pale lionesses through the crooked trees, outpacing and ranging ahead of the main body of the army.

The army was made up of frontier troops, men tested in years of battle against the orcs and beasts. Every frontier lord, no matter how minor, had some number of troops, and this expedition consisted of a number of frontier nobility. Vorag's men, in the main, or those whom he was grooming in his barbaric way. Neferata knew, with the certainty of long experience, that Vorag was training an army. The frontier agals had long chafed at the demands Mourkain placed on them. Ushoran used the frontiers of Strigos as a dumping ground for those who displeased him or otherwise were not suitable for his court: the savages, the bloodthirsty and the rebellious.

In other words, they were the perfect tools.

On the third day, somewhere far ahead and to the east, Neferata's keen hearing caught a sharp bleat from a primitive horn. She growled in satisfaction. The wildlings were on the move as well. She urged her horse on to greater speed. They swept through the ragged valleys and up steep slopes, only stopping when they had reached a thickly forested hill overlooking a rock-strewn gorge. Neferata reined in her lathered horse and swung from the saddle as Vorag said, 'Here?'

'If all goes according to plan, yes,' Neferata said, walking to the edge of the treeline. 'Make camp, and set out the pickets. We could be waiting for some time.'

'Some time' turned into another day and a night. Beneath the dark trees, the vampires could hide from the ravages of the sun. Neferata herself felt nothing; she stuck her hand into the light, letting it play across her fingers. A momentary tingle, like a kiss of heat, but that was all.

'I miss the sunlight,' Layla said, joining her at the treeline, but keeping well back from the cruel light. The sun was setting, but there was still enough of it over the horizon to prove dangerous to the younger of her handmaidens. The girl looked none the worse for wear for her lengthy run. She was still fascinated with the abilities that had been gifted to her, like a child with a new toy.

'You will feel it again,' Neferata said, pulling her hand back. 'With age comes strength. For now, you must be satisfied with the moonlight.'

The girl frowned, but said nothing. Neferata turned back to the valley and the horizon. The evening breeze carried the wild cry of the war-horns of the tribes as they mingled with the brutish drum-beats of the orcs. The wildlings had thrown themselves into their fight with commendable ferocity. Surprising the orcs as they had, they would carve off portions of the horde leaving what continued on, drawn as it was by Wazzakaz's momentum, for the Strigoi to weaken further. An hour later, Neferata saw the moon rise and felt the soil shift slightly. The vibration was faint, but she recognised its meaning. 'They're coming,' she said loudly.

'It's about time. I thought this plan of yours was going to be fast,' Vorag groused before turning to bellow orders to his subordinates. Neferata summoned Layla with a crook of her finger.

'Get up that tree and tell me what you see,' Neferata said, gesturing. Layla obeyed with an alacrity that made Stregga chuckle as she joined Neferata.

'She reminds me of someone. Can't quite put a finger on it...' the Sartosan said. Neferata glanced at her and the chuckles died away. Stregga shrugged. 'Sorry, mistress,' she said.

'There is nothing to apologise for,' Neferata said. 'Simply watch your tone.'

'Of course, mistress, I'm good at that, me. Soul of discretion. Quiet as a mouse. Silent as a leopard. Soft, like a–'

Neferata looked at her handmaiden steadily. Stregga grinned cheerily. Neferata snorted and turned away. 'I knew I should have killed you in Sartosa.'

'Good thing you didn't, eh?' Stregga said. 'When the bone-kings came calling, I was invaluable, if I do say so myself.'

Neferata snorted again and tapped her fingers on the pommel of her sword. 'My tolerance is not limitless, Lupa.'

'But my usefulness is,' Stregga said. 'Besides which, Vorag would protect me, eh Vorag?'

'She's almost killed me once, she-wolf. I'll not risk that again, not even for a morsel as delectable as yourself,' Vorag said heartily, joining them at the treeline.

Stregga made a face and Neferata smiled. She looked aside at Vorag and said, 'You seem cheerful, champion of Mourkain.'

Vorag's smile dissolved. 'I'll not hold that title much longer,' he said.

'No, you won't,' Neferata said.

'Abhorash,' Vorag said, chewing the name of his rival like a piece of stubborn gristle.

'The people love him,' Neferata said. 'My people loved him as well, before he abandoned them.'

Vorag growled. Stregga moved to his side comfortingly. 'Ushoran wants him to take command of the armies. Says my ways are old-fashioned,' he said.

Which they are, Neferata thought. *You are an anachronism, Bloodytooth, even in these primitive lands. And Ushoran is smart enough to recognise the game you're playing.* 'He has replaced many of your comrades and peers as well,' she said, not looking at him. 'Men who should have received the kiss withered and died while arrogant play-warriors live forever in glory. Zandor, for instance, or that preening fop Gashnag, neither of whom are a match for you.'

He looked at her, one fang protruding as he sucked on his lip. 'No, they are not. Once, we were men. Now we are nothing but ticks or fleas on the carcass of a dog.'

'I wouldn't go that far,' Neferata said. 'I'm sure many feel as you do.' *Mainly because I have ensured that they do so, over the course of these past centuries. Not just other vampires either, but those noble families who have continually been passed over for induction into the ranks of the immortals,* she thought with satisfaction. The wives and lovers of the Strigoi nobles had fairly fallen over themselves to receive her kiss. Ushoran refused to 'waste' his on women whom he saw as little better than dogs in heat. And those women had had years to mull over that insult and remind their husbands and lovers of it, as well as every other petty hurt Ushoran had done.

'They do,' Vorag said softly. It was his turn not to look at her. 'They say Abhorash's time in the north will be longer than he first thought. That the northern daemon-lovers are proving stronger than he estimated.'

'Abhorash always did overestimate his own prowess,' Neferata said smoothly. The 'scouts' she had sent into the north prior to Abhorash's expedition had obviously done their job. Mourkain gold now filled the pockets of northern warlords, and they were more than happy to band together to stave off Strigos's encroachment into the wastes. They would not succeed... Abhorash was effective for all his arrogance. But he would be occupied for years; long enough to see Ushoran put in his proper place... at her feet.

'With him gone,' Vorag began carefully, 'Ushoran has few allies at court, though he knows it not.'

Neferata's expression did not change. 'Nor will he. Ushoran is remarkably blind for one who prides himself on his cunning.'

'He is no true Strigoi,' Vorag said.

'Neither am I.'

He looked at her. 'But you are not king.'

'Nor would I be,' Neferata said. 'I have ruled, in my time. I found it... tedious.'

Vorag nodded, taking her comment at face value. 'And you bear Ushoran no love.'

'No,' Neferata said, allowing herself a small smile. 'No, I do not.'

Vorag nodded, as if satisfied. He was silent for a moment, visibly marshalling his thoughts. Stregga looked at her mistress. Neferata nodded slightly. It had not been difficult to bring Vorag around. The Strigoi were barbarians despite the veneer of civilisation that they wore. And for barbarians, treachery was like breathing. All it required was time to contemplate and machinate, something which vampires had in abundance.

The difficult part had been making Vorag think it was his idea to approach her. But now that he had done so, she could at last pull tight the strands of her carefully crafted web. 'These are times of change,' Vorag said, finally. It was an obtuse way of saying 'coup', but Neferata understood him nonetheless.

'Sometimes, change is for the better,' Neferata said. 'This is a mighty army, Timagal. It could accomplish much.'

Vorag shot her a look. But before he could reply, there was a shout from above. Layla dropped down from the branches overhead, landing on all fours in a shower of pine needles. 'They come, mistress!' she said, visibly excited. 'The orcs, even as you said!'

'Ha!' Neferata smacked her palms together. 'Vorag, get the men in place and ready your riders! We shall have to time this perfectly.' They needed to shave the orcs, not shatter them or draw their full ire. She only had a few thousand men, and she needed to hoard their strength for future endeavours. Vorag hastened to obey her orders. Neferata grabbed Stregga. 'Stay by my side, Lupa. You as well, Layla,' she said. 'We will be needed here.'

'Lovely. At the sharp end again, eh, my lady?' Stregga said, drawing her sword and sighting down the length of the blade.

'It's where we belong,' Neferata said, flinging off her cloak. The tribes had done their job well; the orcs streaming into the valley were disorganised. They were still dangerous for all that, and there were still enough of them to prove troublesome for Razek's throng further up the valley. They needed to get their attention.

'Sound the drums,' Neferata shouted, her voice carrying across the slope. 'Form up the dragon's scales!' In answer to her cry, the war-drums sounded, bone striking stretched skin in a deep, thudding rhythm. A thousand heavy bronze and wood shields, each the size of the warrior wielding them, were slammed down onto the hard-packed soil of the slope. The spikes that lined the bottom of each shield bit into the earth and anchored the barrier even as the shield-wielders crouched low at the barked order of the ajal in command, bracing the shields with their bodies. The ajal roared out another command and the second line of men stepped forwards, extending the pitch-hardened wooden stakes they held over the top of the shields. The heads of the stakes were equipped with bronze cross-pieces, to prevent the surprisingly durable orcs from pulling themselves down the length of the spear. The Strigoi had learned over the decades that the best way to handle the urka was from a distance. Pin them and butcher them at leisure.

The drums continued to thunder dully as the Strigoi battle-line settled into the position they would hold for the entirety of the battle to come. There would be no retreat. 'Curious strategy,' Vorag grunted, eyeing the line. He was already mounted and his frame trembled with eagerness.

'Cathay is a curious place,' Neferata replied. Drilling the rambunctious Strigoi in Cathayan military manoeuvres had been a battle in and of itself – one she had only accomplished by pricking Abhorash's vanity. She needed soldiers, not warriors. He had grasped the tactics and strategies of the armies of the east and adapted them to the Strigoi's more brutal methods of warfare with instinctive ease, and she suspected that Abhorash had spent some time in Cathay, though he never admitted to such.

Indeed, Abhorash rarely spoke to her at all. He kept to his men, training his armoured riders in the arts of the Arabyan Kontoi and the Khazag riders of the eastern steppes, crafting an elite core for Ushoran's growing army. She wasn't offended. Far from it, in fact; the further Abhorash stayed away from her, the better. She knew the others felt the same way, especially W'soran. Abhorash's honour was an anchor around all of their necks. It weighed them down and reminded them of what they had once had, and what they would never have.

'The orcs are a flood, Timagal Vorag,' she continued. 'We must let them bleed themselves on our rocks rather than attempt to match them, savagery for savagery.'

'As long as I get a taste of that blood,' Vorag growled.

'Have no fear in that regard,' she said. Neferata swept her sword out, and the drums thudded. The third rank stepped forwards, raising their bows. The Strigoi bows were stubby recurved things, meant to be fired from horseback at the gallop. Crafted from wood, horn and sinew and bound together with animal glue, they possessed a startling punch for their size. She jabbed the air and the archers reared back, aiming upwards.

'You remember the plan?' she said, not looking at Vorag.

'Of course,' he grunted. 'Have no fear, Neferata. The Bloodytooth will not fail you.' He snapped his reins and wheeled his horse about. In moments, Vorag's riders began moving back around the hill, secreting themselves in the thick trees. Neferata raised her sword, letting the iron catch the moonlight.

The valley had become a vast, seething ocean of green beneath the moon. There were thousands of them, like ants fleeing an ant hill. Larger shapes moved through the tide, carried on savage currents – giants and trolls and howling, shrieking crimson things that were more fungus than beast.

Neferata's sword dropped. Bows twanged and a solid cloud of arrows momentarily blotted out the moon. The horde below heaved like a wounded animal biting its flank.

'That got their attention,' Stregga said.

'And now we need to keep it,' Neferata said, raising her sword again. Two more volleys followed the first, and the mass of orcs disintegrated, a huge wave breaking off from the main body to crash towards the slope where the Strigoi waited. Neferata hissed. There were more of them than she had thought. She cast a calculating eye over the battle-line. The Strigoi were orc-fighters without peer, save for perhaps the dwarfs, but even they could be overwhelmed.

'Sanzak, get them ready,' Neferata said. The ajal in charge of the closest section of the line nodded; his eyes were red in the gloom. He was one of Vorag's get and bore his master's brute stamp upon his features.

He began snarling out orders as the first line of Strigoi readied themselves, and his commands were echoed up and down the line by his fellow ajals. The men stank of nervousness and battle-lust. Neferata waited just behind the line. She signalled for another volley.

Orcs fell even as they ascended the slope, but the creatures pressed forwards. Their green flesh daubed with savage azure tattoos and hideous war-whoops on their lips, the orcs were a terrifying sight. They struggled up the hill hour after hour in a wave of grunting, howling bodies, each one striving to be the first to reach the crest of the hill where the Strigoi waited for them. The stakes were heavy with brackish orc blood and the men wielding them were exhausted. Replacements scrambled into position beneath the shields, to give their wielders a moment to rest.

Momentum alone would have carried the orcs up and over eventually, despite the rain of arrows that cut through their ranks time and again, and that same momentum would carry them over the line of spearmen. They were stubborn creatures, fond of battle and inured to setback.

The only hope in thwarting an orc charge was, therefore, to surprise them.

'We're running low on arrows,' Sanzak called out.

'Not surprising,' Stregga muttered. 'If we can't keep them off the line, they'll roll right over us.'

'I know. Now it's our turn,' Neferata said, looking at Layla. The girl bared her fangs and drew her sword with a flourish. Without another word, Neferata charged down the slope and leapt into the air, her sword flashing out. An orc's howl was cut short as her blade separated its head from its shoulders. As she landed, she gutted a second, nose wrinkling at the stench of its spilling innards. Crude stone weapons shattered as they struck against the armour she wore. Spinning, she bisected another of the brutes.

Neferata spun, and orcs died. Nearby, Stregga copied her mistress's action and bounded down the slope, unleashing months of repressed savagery on the hapless greenskins. The vampire shrieked wordlessly as her sword licked out, lopping off limbs and heads with abandon.

Layla was, if anything, even more vicious than the other vampire. Her flesh rippled, sprouting a coat of thick, dark hair, and her skull elongated into something more vulpine than human as she crashed into the orcs, singing a Strigoi death-song. Her claws raked out, gutting a goblin even as she cut an orc in two at the waist with her blade.

Several of the ajal followed suit, the Strigoi bounding out of the shield-line with red-eyed eagerness. They fought like animals, wielding massive hammers and swords that pulped bone and meat alike. All in all, a dozen vampires had crashed into the orcs and within moments they were wading through corpses and blood in a savage frenzy.

But savage as it was, it wasn't enough. Neither did it need to be. Neferata raised her sword as high as she could, and the drums set to with a ferocity that even outdid that of the orcs. Moments later, with a howling cry, Vorag's riders broke from cover and charged. The horses sprang across the slope speedily, their hooves setting the ground to trembling.

'Back,' Neferata shouted. 'Fall back!' The vampires broke away from the fighting and scrambled back towards the line of shields as the horsemen rode into the fray. The riders howled and roared, and the bows in their hands peppered the orc flank raggedly. Orcs fell, struck by dozens of arrows. Other riders, led by Vorag, carried heavy-bladed spears which dipped and punctured green flesh. But the Strigoi had other tricks than just these.

On each horse's haunch was a tough fibre net. At Vorag's bellowed command, his men slashed the nets and let what they contained tumble in their mounts' wakes. Soon, each horse was dragging a web of chains and thick ropes ending in spiked bars, hooks and blades which clattered loudly as the horsemen neared the orcs.

As Vorag's riders struck the flank, they did not slow. Instead, they urged their horses to greater speed and rode on, leaving a path of carnage in their wake. The blades and bars jumped and swung as the horses galloped and smashed into the orcs, knocking them off their feet or shredding them where they stood. A full two hundred riders struck the orc flank like a wedge of death and the orcs were ripped apart with almost clinical brutality, sectioned off from the main horde and dissected.

True to form, most of the orcs momentarily retreated from the slope as they sought to come to grips with the horsemen. Neferata could almost admire how quickly the creatures adapted to changing situations. She lazily blocked a spear thrust from one of the remaining brutes and looked around. There were only a few dozen of the creatures close to the Strigoi lines. The rest were heading back for Vorag's riders with eager roars and bellows. The spear-wielding orc lunged for her again and she chopped her sword down, splitting its skull.

Stregga snarled as Vorag's horse went down with a burst skull, courtesy of a lucky blow. The Strigoi hit the ground and rolled to his feet in a cloud of dust, even as an orc mounted on a snorting boar charged towards him, spear levelled. Vorag deftly avoided the spear and swept his arms wide as the beast rushed towards him. He caught the boar around its neck and veins bulged black in his pale flesh as he wrenched the beast up in mid-gallop and flung it over his shoulder, snapping its spine in the process. The boar fell, spilling its rider, and Vorag pounced, jaws agape.

The battle lost cohesion moments later, devolving into a swirling melee. The signal drums thundered, calling for the horsemen to retreat as they'd planned, but to no avail. Their blood was up and it was all the ajals on the slope could do to keep the ranks from charging into the fray.

Neferata swung the flat of her blade out, striking the shield of one of the men, and snarled. 'Back,' she snapped. 'Get back or lose your head! Get them in line!' The men fell back in haste, resuming their positions, their faces white with fear as their vampire masters snarled and snapped at them.

Satisfied that order had been restored, Neferata scanned the melee. If they could find the creatures' war-chief, they might be able to bring an end to the battle in one stroke. The former wasn't difficult. Orcs were simple creatures, with simple desires. They wanted the biggest, loudest fight they could find, and they'd kill each other to get it. Right now, that fight was Vorag.

Neferata couldn't help but admire the way the Strigoi fought. He lacked the precision of Abhorash or the sadism inherent in Ushoran's tactics. Instead, Vorag fought like an animal unleashed. His size seemed to increase as he waded through the orcs that sought to pull him down. His body swelled hideously, his arms and shoulders bulging with muscle. He stabbed an orc through the head with a shattered spear and swept the body out, knocking another creature aside. His face wrinkled into a bestial grimace, his lips rolling back from needle-studded gums. Claws sprouted from his fingers and he ripped apart his enemies with wild abandon.

Pulling a squalling orc in half, Vorag threw back his head and howled. A moment later, a ground-rattling bellow echoed in reply and sent orcs scrambling as something massive thrust its way through the press that now surrounded Vorag. A saw-edged blade the length of Neferata's leg smashed down, digging a trench in the rock of the slope and forcing Vorag to skip backwards. The orc boss was bigger than three men and its red, piggy eyes were bright with feral bloodlust. It bellowed again as its eyes fastened on Vorag. The big blade snapped out, and he sank down and it sliced the air above his head. Vorag roared and flung himself on the orc.

Neferata couldn't identify the beast; there were dozens of bosses among the Waaagh!, each with their own tribes. This one was bigger than most, however. 'Can he handle it?' she said, looking at Stregga. Stregga didn't reply. She watched the fight, her teeth bared and her eyes wide as she drank it in. Neferata growled and slapped her. 'Stregga! Can he win?'

Stregga shook her head. 'I-I don't know,' she grunted. Moments later, Vorag was knocked to the ground by a sweep of the orc's arm. The creature roared and raised its blade over the stunned vampire.

Neferata cursed. If Vorag lost his head here, her plans would be endangered. It might take centuries to groom another capable of heading a revolt. Centuries she might not have. *Hurry, Neferata! The stars spin faster and faster as dust is stirred by hollow winds. You will be a queen again and you will rule over silent, perfect cities, but only if you hurry,* the voice purred at the back of her head. Annoyed, she shook it aside. A moment later she was moving, driving her own sword into the orc's unarmoured torso.

It howled in agony. A green hand fastened on her head as she tried to pull her blade loose and she was smashed down against the slope. Bone cracked and splintered and blood burst from between her lips in an exhalation of agony. Stregga was there a moment later, hewing through the orc's arm. The orc reared back, squalling as Layla leapt upon its back and clawed at its eyes.

Neferata pulled herself to her feet, grimacing in pain as her wounds re-knit. She lunged upwards, her teeth snapping together in the meat of the beast's throat. With a jerk of her head, she tore its throat out. It toppled backwards, and she rode it down, crouching on it. Gagging, she spat out the foul-tasting lump of meat and hissed at the orcs who had stopped to watch the fight. Stregga joined her, snarling like a hungry tigress.

Clutching her wounds, Neferata shrieked. The sound of it echoed across the slope, bouncing from tree to rock. One by one, slowly at first, then faster and faster, the orc advance became a retreat. The green wave reversed itself and began to wash downhill, back into the valley below. The Strigoi sent a farewell of arrows to keep the orcs moving in the right direction.

The slaughter lasted for what seemed like hours and the darkness began to slip into the purple of dawn as it ended. Wazzakaz's horde had been cut into thirds and reduced from a juggernaut to something substantially less intimidating. The slope was carpeted in the bodies of slain orcs.

'Beautiful,' Vorag said, trotting towards them. The big vampire grinned widely and leered at Stregga, looking none the worse for wear despite the blood that coated him head to toe. 'I couldn't have done it better myself!'

'No, you couldn't have,' Stregga said, wiping her mouth.

Neferata spat – she could still taste the bitter tang of the orc's blood. 'Did you send riders?' she said. Her wounds had healed, though the ghost-ache of bones broken earlier lingered.

'Yes and the stunted ones are ready. We should be able to – there!' Vorag gestured. The brass-banded dragon-horns of the dwarfs harrowed the frosty dawn air from their position far down in the valley. The orcs no longer had the numbers to beat the throng; they would be annihilated. Vorag rubbed his hands together. 'Should I take my riders down there, just in case?' he asked eagerly.

'No,' Neferata said. 'I want you to stay put. We'll need you and your riders fresh for the morrow.'

'Why, what's tomorrow?'

'The dwarfs don't pursue beaten foes. The orcs will flee. We need to grind them up and ensure that it takes generations for them to ever prove a threat again.' Neferata kicked a dead orc and glared down into its slack features. 'It may take days or months, but we need them beaten.'

'But–' Vorag began. Neferata looked at him. The other vampire grimaced and looked away, unwilling to match her gaze. 'Fine,' he grunted. 'What now?'

'We wait,' Neferata said. 'We let the dwarfs wet their axes as we promised. We'll need to send a rider to Ushoran, to let him know how we've fared here.' She smiled slightly at the look on Vorag's face. 'He will become suspicious, otherwise. And we wouldn't want that, now would we?' Her smile grew wider and she added, 'At least, not until it's too late.'

ELEVEN

The City of Bel Aliad
(–1149 Imperial Reckoning)

The dead fought in silence, their weapons rising and falling with monotonous ferocity. They hacked their way through the living warriors of Bel Aliad without slowing or stopping, and those that fell were replaced by their victims in time.

Arkhan the Black watched it all from the roof of the temple of the ghoul-god, and found it good. Or so Neferata assumed. The withered liche-thing barely resembled the man she had once known and… What? She pushed the thought aside. That was in the dim past and this was the present and here and now, Arkhan endangered everything she had built.

'You can't do this,' she said, approaching him.

'Neferata,' Arkhan said in his hollow voice. 'You still live.'

'You sound disappointed.'

'No,' Arkhan said. Bones rustled as he turned, his glowing gaze sweeping over her without apparent emotion. 'Does this city hold some special place in your heart?'

'No,' Neferata said. Her armour hung from her body in ragged scraps; it had been battered and torn by Arkhan's

bodyguards as she had killed them. In the ruins of her once great temple, her followers battled his, even as her enemies battled the dead in the streets. It was a war on three fronts, fought by three armies. She raised the notched and dull khopesh she held and pointed it at him. 'But it is mine none-theless. You will not take it from me.'

'Would you match your strength against mine?' Arkhan said. 'You ran from Nagash. Am I so much less fearsome?'

'Infinitely,' she said.

'Nagash is dead,' Arkhan said suddenly.

Neferata hesitated. 'What?'

'He is dead.'

'Did you–'

Arkhan made a rasping, wheezing noise she took to be laughter. 'No. And neither did your old friend W'soran.' The glowing eyes dulled slightly. 'It was Alcadizzar.'

Neferata closed her eyes, just for a moment. The pain was faint now, but it was there. She swallowed it down. 'Is he…?'

'I know not. Nor, in truth, do I care,' Arkhan said. 'Nagash is gone and I have been driven from Khemri. I need a new fortress, a new place to rebuild my strength before my opponents follow me.'

'Your opponents – who were they? Nagash killed everyone!' Neferata said. She knew even as she asked what the answer would be. She had known since that night where the sky turned green and the dead had grown restless in the burial vaults.

'The Great Land is a land of the dead now. They rule it in the darkness even as they did beneath the sun.' Arkhan used two fingers to push aside her blade. 'The tombs of the mighty gape wide and the war-chariots of Settra rumble to war.'

'No,' she said.

'Yes, he brought them back. All of them unto the first generation,' Arkhan intoned. 'And they are angry, Neferata.

They curse my name even as they curse Nagash's... and yours.'

'What?' Neferata said, shaken.

Arkhan lunged, swatting aside her sword and grabbing her wrist. He pulled her to him, his skull pressed close to her face. 'They hate you. All of the dead of Lahmia hate you. They want to punish you and all your court for your crimes. And her voice is the loudest of all.'

'Her?'

'The little hawk,' Arkhan whispered, and his words were like a knife sliding across her sensitive flesh. 'Khalida of Lybaras hunts once more, Neferata, and she is coming even now across the sands of the Great Desert.' He grabbed her chin. 'And she is coming for you...'

The City of Mourkain
(–350 Imperial Reckoning)

THEY RETURNED TO Mourkain under cover of darkness.

Neferata rode through dark streets, and was reminded of times long past, and another city that held its breath by night. Rasha and Layla rode close behind her. Stregga, of course, had stayed with Vorag, who was in no hurry to return to Mourkain. Instead, he intended to visit the other frontier nobles. Men, like him, who were kept at arm's length from the centres of power. Men who, like him, all had among their trains Neferata's handmaidens, though most knew it not, thinking them mere concubines, or priestesses or slaves.

In contrast to how long it had taken to subvert the religions of Strigos, it had taken no time at all to take swift and decisive control of the burgeoning slave trade.

Now, her followers controlled the flow of slaves from the west and the north and of the latter, those who met a certain set of requirements were culled and sent to Mourkain to receive Neferata's blessings. As a result, her handmaidens numbered over a hundred these days, their numbers only exceeded by those of Ushoran's get.

Sometimes she felt a faint sense of displeasure at the thought of employing so many in such a capacity. She had taken living creatures, women much like she had once been, and turned them from beings with their own destinies into playing pieces on a board whose parameters she was still, as yet, uncertain of. But those thoughts were few and far between. Mostly, she concerned herself with the humming strands of plot and counter-plot that stretched from her black brain. With the orcs broken, the trade routes had blossomed into full flower, bringing new blood from the west into the lands of the Strigoi. She had spent almost a century seeing to it, visiting the wildling tribes and those from farther west whose representatives had heard of Strigos and wished to see its power up close.

But rather than exploiting that strength, Neferata had instead undermined it. She had moved from tribe to tribe, spreading not the story of Mourkain's majesty, but of its frailty. She had whispered of the decadence of its rulers, of the weakness of its armies, and of the great wealth which it had, but did not deserve.

She smiled slightly. The Draesca had wasted little time; the wildling tribes had already begun asserting their control of the rough country and taking what could charitably be called more than their fair share of the wealth from the trade routes. Too, the Draesca had begun to eye the Draka and the other large tribes askance. Ushoran was not the only would-be emperor in these mountains.

It would be war soon enough. A few years perhaps, maybe a decade, and by then the wild tribes would have become less wild and thus more dangerous to Strigos, which had already begun to stagnate in its superiority. She could almost smell the rot; she sniffed, tasting... 'Blood,' she said, suddenly alert.

'The air is thick with it,' Rasha murmured, riding just behind her.

Layla sniffed. 'Why is it so quiet? What is going on?'

'Halt!'

Iron-capped spear-butts thumped on the street as the armoured warriors moved into the open. They wore fur cloaks to protect themselves from the night's chill, and their armour was chipped and black. 'Curfew, strangers... Do you have a reason for being out tonight?' one grunted.

'Curfew, is it?' Neferata said, pulling back her hood. The watchmen seemed to hiss collectively. They knew her face. There was no woman in Mourkain who looked like Neferata, though many aped her style. 'On whose orders, I wonder?'

'Hetman Ushoran, my lady,' the watchman stuttered. 'From sunset to sunrise, all citizens are to remain indoors.'

Neferata urged her horse closer. 'Why?' she said, holding the man's eyes with her own. Rasha and Layla joined her.

'Spies, my lady,' Naaima said. Neferata looked up. Her handmaiden stood across from the watchmen. She had arrived silently. Or perhaps she had been waiting for them. 'I am glad to see you back. We need no escort,' Naaima added, touching one of the men on the arm. 'Continue about your business and be assured that your superiors shall hear of your dedication.' The man saluted gratefully and the whole lot slid around and past the mounted vampires with as much speed as the dignity of their office could allow. Neferata watched them go before turning back to her handmaiden.

'I see events have occurred in my absence,' she said.

'Someone tried to kill Ushoran,' Naaima said bluntly. 'He's blamed us. He has Anmar.'

'What?' Neferata snapped, jerking on her horse's reins. The animal whinnied and lashed at the air with its hooves. 'Explain yourself!'

'His paranoia has become a force unto itself,' Naaima said. She extended a hand and Neferata swung her up onto her horse. Naaima settled behind her, clutching her mistress. She answered Neferata's next question before she had a chance to ask it. 'It was not us.'

'Good,' Neferata said simply, urging her horse into motion. The others followed closely. *Perhaps Khaled has learned from his blunders in Bel Aliad after all*, she thought darkly. 'Who was it, then? Was it W'soran?'

'I don't know. I suspect so. It doesn't matter. He has her. He wanted to see you as soon as you arrived,' Naaima said.

'Where is Khaled? Did he have nothing to say about this?' Neferata growled. Naaima didn't answer immediately. Neferata tensed. She could sense her handmaiden's disquiet. 'What is it?' she demanded.

'Khaled is the one who took her,' Naaima said harshly. 'He and Ushoran's guards intervened in a brawl between five of ours and a number of W'soran's abominations.'

'What happened?'

'Four of ours are dead. Anmar was the only survivor. Those creatures… they tore them apart, right in the street. W'soran claims they were resisting his authority.'

'His authority?' Neferata spat incredulously. 'That

creature only has as much authority as I deem fit. Khaled as well. He forgets himself if he thinks to put himself
at cross-purposes with me.' Neferata cursed and urged
her horse to greater speed. In his years in Ushoran's
bodyguard, the former Arabyan princeling had become
too comfortable, she had known that. But it was that
very thing which had likely endeared him to Ushoran.
Was he merely playing the part she had assigned him?
Or was he now truly Ushoran's dog? It was a question
she intended to get an answer to tonight. One of many
questions, in fact, that the time had come to have
answered.

Since she had learned about the crown of Mourkain,
and Ushoran's desire for it, a number of previously
nonsensical elements had fallen into place. She sniffed
the air, tasting the dull black skeins of W'soran's magic.
It had permeated the stones of Mourkain over the centuries, like ancient damp rising anew. It tasted different
tonight.

Vorag had told her much of Ushoran's coming, and
how Kadon had ruled before then. How Kadon had
worn a crown of black metal, but how Ushoran seemed
to either disdain it, or have mislaid it. Or, perhaps, he
had been denied it.

There were only a few reasons she could think of for
Ushoran to give sanctuary to a treacherous serpent like
W'soran, and one of those was to make use of the old
monster's knowledge, but why? Ushoran could simply
have had another crown made. What was so important
about this one?

At that thought, something vibrated through her, its
ugly voice echoing eerily in her head. *Come to me, Queen
of the Dawn! Come, Beautiful Death! Run to me. Run
to my embrace*, it hissed, its words scraping across the

underside of her thoughts like the coils of some great serpent. She could feel its intangible presence pulling at her as she rode.

The horses galloped through the streets towards the pyramid. She saw more guards, but none tried to bar their way. The city was bristling with them, and here and there among them, she saw the black robes of W'soran's ghouls. *Hurry, Queen of Lahmia! The stars spin faster and faster as dust is stirred by hollow winds. The dead howl in their cages of breathing meat! Hurry*, the voice hissed in her ears. She bent her head, trying to ignore it. Her eyes found the dark shape of the pyramid and she heard a whisper of ghostly laughter. Naaima held her tighter.

'You're trembling,' she murmured, low enough that others couldn't hear.

Neferata controlled herself. The moon was fat and bloated in the black sky and it cast a yellow eye over the plaza in front of the pyramid. She tugged on the reins as they entered the plaza. More guards awaited them. Spears were lowered and warnings shouted, but Neferata ignored them, leaping from her horse and stalking towards the doors, the others hurrying after her. Her talons slid from her fingertips as the guards in front of the door held their ground.

'Stand aside,' a voice bellowed as the doors were pushed open from within. Khaled stepped through, shoving a guard viciously aside. 'I said stand aside, fools!' he roared. He met Neferata's gaze as she swept towards him, not slowing. 'My lady, let me expla–'

She didn't let him finish. She snatched him up by his throat and lifted him over her head, her eyes blazing like coals. 'Fool,' she snarled. Her voice echoed across the plaza and she smelled the sudden surge of fear from the guards. Khaled gagged and tried to speak as her fingers tightened about his throat. Cartilage popped and bone crunched and Khaled jerked and flopped like a broken-backed snake. She flung him aside and spun to face Naaima and the others. 'Come!'

She struck the doors with her palms, forcing them open with a thunderous boom which echoed throughout the pyramid. She stalked through the corridors, servants fleeing before her like chickens fleeing a leopardess. A duo of Strigoi moved to bar her way at the entrance to the throne room and she gazed at them with blank fury. 'Move aside,' she growled.

Both wore the heavy black armour of Ushoran's guard, and both were familiar to her. Zandor bowed mockingly, one hand on his sword. 'We must announce you, my lady,' he said. 'It is the custom.'

'You might have forgotten, what with all that time spent among the barbarians,' Gashnag added, glaring at her. Both Strigoi looked ready for a fight. They were no longer the parasitic courtiers they had been so long ago. Now they were warriors, or carried themselves as such. She wondered, in the moment before she hurled herself at them, whether Abhorash had had a hand in that.

Zandor reacted first, half drawing his sword before her talons opened his face to the bone. He screamed and reeled, clutching at his face even as she caught Gashnag's sword in her hand. Blood dripped down the blade as the tableau held for several seconds. Then she tore the blade from the startled Strigoi's hand and backhanded him into the great bronze doors of the throne room. The doors burst inwards, carried wide by Gashnag's weight. He slid across the floor, his armour clattering, and Neferata followed him, carrying his sword.

'My Lady of Mysteries, to what do we owe the

pleasure?' Ushoran said. He looked human and ordinary on the throne. Anmar sat at his feet. The chamber was empty save for the hooded figures which stood near the great throne like a silent court, and the bulky forms of several monstrous ghouls. She was reminded of the creature that W'soran had unleashed on her in the vaults and she hissed. He had made more of them, obviously, and he had got better at whatever dark process had been involved in their creation. These creatures were bigger than the other, and were not quite so patchwork. They gazed at her with dim hunger and she remembered how the other had attached itself, remora-like, to her arm.

She tore her eyes from the monster to the steps of Ushoran's throne where Anmar sat, head bowed and shoulders hunched. Neferata gazed at the girl for a moment before she addressed Ushoran. 'I come to reclaim what is mine,' Neferata said, gesturing to Anmar. *See how he sits in your chair*, the voice hissed. She ignored it.

'If you had been a few moments slower getting here you would have had nothing to reclaim,' Ushoran said idly. 'I intended to give her to W'soran's pets there. What do you think of them, hmmm? Much improved from the last time you saw one. They are quite striking and vicious as well. They have a taste for the blood of our kind, I'm told. Isn't that so, W'soran?'

One of the hooded figures standing near the throne tossed back his hood to reveal W'soran's desiccated features. 'Oh yes, as I'm sure Neferata realises by now.'

Neferata ignored him. 'Why have you taken my handmaiden, Ushoran?' she demanded.

'You mean to say that your little spies haven't told you yet?' Ushoran said, gesturing to Naaima as he pushed himself up from the throne. He spread his arms. 'Someone tried to kill me,' he said. He gestured to Anmar. 'This creature of yours was seen in their company.'

'By whom?' Neferata said.

Ushoran's eyes flickered aside, towards W'soran. 'A little bat,' he said.

Neferata snorted. 'Of course. Why else would he have sent his beasts, rather than alerting his king?'

'You would know all about that, would you?' W'soran spat. 'What secrets do you keep, Queen of Mysteries?'

Neferata ignored that. 'Anmar,' she said. 'Come here.'

'She stays, Neferata,' Ushoran said mildly. 'She must be punished.'

'Then I will punish her,' Neferata said, extending her hand towards her handmaiden. 'Come here.' Anmar rose hesitantly. When Ushoran made no move to stop her, she bolted towards Neferata. Neferata held her for a moment, examining her. 'Your brother has much to answer for,' she murmured, stroking the girl's hair.

'He saved me,' Anmar hissed. 'W'soran's monsters would have killed me, my lady! They'd have left me in the street like the others!' She grabbed Neferata's hand. 'It was the only way, my lady,' she said urgently.

Neferata hesitated. Then, anger overrode the brief spark of regret. 'He should have saved all of you,' she hissed. She stepped past Anmar and glared at Ushoran. 'Anmar and the others were following a conspirator, as you commanded. That is why she was in his presence. My people work at crooked angles, Ushoran, and must occasionally play friend to our – to *your* foes.'

Ushoran cast a lazy glance at W'soran, who trembled with rage. 'I told you,' Ushoran murmured. He looked back at Neferata. 'This is the throne room of Ancient Kadon himself, you know. And it was here that I killed him. Impressive, is it not?'

'Why should I be impressed because you managed to

throttle some elderly madman?' Neferata asked.

'Elderly, yes, but mad? No,' W'soran said. 'Kadon's knowledge was greater even than mine.'

'Many things are greater than you, W'soran,' Neferata said pointedly.

Ushoran laughed. 'Such venom you spit, my queen. Such raw red rage you display, and for what? What have we done to elicit it?'

'The night is short, Ushoran, and I lack the patience to go into the many perfidies that you and that sour old corpse-thing by your side have inflicted upon me and mine. Tell me why I should not take this latest insult as the last?'

'Because you're curious,' Ushoran said, grinning. He tapped his head. 'I am as well. Does it speak to you in the quiet moments, Neferata? I'd wager it does.'

She hesitated, struck by the sudden certainty that there was a deeper game here. She had intended to use this breach to bully Ushoran into revealing his secrets at a later time. But perhaps Ushoran was seizing an opportunity of his own. *Tread carefully,* she thought to herself.

'Ahhhhh,' Ushoran breathed, nodding knowingly at her silence. He glanced smugly at W'soran. 'I told you that it speaks to her and Abhorash as well, I'd wager. And you said that they lacked the spark or wit to hear it.'

'Hear what?' Neferata snarled, taking a step forwards. She knew the answer already, but she wanted to see the limits of the web Ushoran was spinning. *Dust falls from the eyes of heroes and kings, and the dead are stirring in their tombs,* the voice whispered. *They will rise and march and thrust the world into a silent, serene shape. The Corpse Geometries will bend and slide into formation for the dead, binding the fires at the poles and snuffing the stars themselves.*

'That,' Ushoran said, as the shriek of the nails-on-bone voice faded in her head. 'I thought I was privileged at first, to hear it. Like a lover's croon. But it's not,' he said, the humour fading from his voice. 'It's the command of a master to a servant.'

W'soran bridled, grimacing. 'It's an echo, Ushoran... I've told you–'

Ushoran moved so fast that Neferata barely caught it. He backhanded W'soran, catapulting the thin vampire off his feet and to the floor in a heap. W'soran's servants closed ranks, and the air was suddenly alive with the acrid odour of fell magics. Ushoran paid them no mind, instead focusing his attention on Neferata. 'It's like acid, isn't it? Etching its way into your thoughts. You never met him, of course. That's why you don't recognise it. But I did, and when I heard it...' He shook his head. He made a face. 'W'soran was his favourite. Like a child with a new toy. He barely noticed me, damaged as I was. He left me to his beasts.' His fingers curled into fists and his human seeming wavered. 'But it was I who answered his call first! I who came to him! Me!'

'Which is why we're still here, of course,' W'soran said, as his acolytes helped him to his feet. Ushoran tensed. 'All this time after the fact, we're still here, trapped in this primitive shadow of Lahmia, forced to grub in the dirt like peasants.' W'soran wiped a bit of blood from his lipless mouth. His eyes swivelled to Neferata. There was more than just disdain there. There was also a warning. Ushoran wasn't the only one spinning a web. 'Because the first to come wasn't strong enough to do what needed doing,' he added, still looking at Neferata.

'Silence,' Ushoran snarled.

'What are you yammering about, old leech? What secret are you dancing around?' Neferata said.

'Have you ever wondered why our king wears no crown? The savages he rules so admire a fine crown.' W'soran grinned.

'Kadon's crown...' Neferata said, a number of things falling into place. Both W'soran and Ushoran started at that, but Neferata drove on before they could recover. 'But that is not Kadon's voice I hear, is it?'

'In part perhaps,' W'soran said with a shrug. 'But as Ushoran said, there's a reason you didn't recognise it. Or maybe you did, but pretended you didn't, even to yourself. You have heard it before, haven't you, centuries ago? I know, because I was there when Nagash spoke to you.' He looked at Ushoran. 'We both were.'

Nagash. The name hammered into her brain like a nail. Nagash, the Great Necromancer. Nagash, whose name had been wiped from the historical records of the Great Land. Nagash, whose elixir of immortality even now pumped in altered form through her veins.

'Nagash's, not Kadon's... It is Nagash's crown,' she whispered.

'My crown,' Ushoran countered, his hands twitching slightly. 'And with it, I will rule even as he did. But my rule will extend unto eternity, as even his failed to do. I will not make his mistakes and I do not possess his flaws. But I will have all of his power...'

'But you don't. Not yet. Why?' Neferata said. 'Where is it?'

Ushoran hesitated, his smugness evaporating. He looked almost... afraid. W'soran answered her, and he sounded as hesitant as Ushoran looked. 'Here. Right here and yet it is so far away.'

Ushoran went to the wall behind the throne, towards an empty niche where a statue might once have stood. He placed a hand against the stones and a hidden door slid open, revealing a set of winding steps. 'There,' Ushoran said softly.

'Ushoran–' W'soran began.

'No. No, if she wants to see it, we shall let her.' Ushoran looked speculative. 'Perhaps... perhaps I was wrong. Perhaps this was the answer all along.' He looked at the dark passage. 'Perhaps this is the price he demands.'

'Neferata, don't,' Naaima said as Neferata stepped towards the passage. Neferata shook Naaima's hand off. Her handmaiden's voice was drowned out by the sudden roar of silence that spilled out of the darkness. It was an absence of sound which muffled everything. Ushoran stepped within and she followed, hesitant at first and then faster. Her instincts screamed warnings of treachery and deceit but not for the first time in her life, she ignored them. She had to see what lay beyond. She needed to confront that which had drawn her here, even if it endangered her very existence.

'*Come and see*, it said, and I came unto Mourkain and saw,' Ushoran whispered hoarsely as they walked. His words rustled in the narrow tunnel like bats and the stones of the corridor beyond the hidden entrance seemed to vibrate in tune to his voice. Gently, she brushed dust from the stones, revealing the crude pictograms which had been scratched into the walls by the ancient builders. Like the hieroglyphs of home, these told the story of the tomb. The body had been found in the river that curled through the mountains, a crown in one hand. The body of a mighty man, larger than any man of the Strigoi, though reduced to ruin by unknown enemies. His features had been obliterated by old marks, like those made by claws.

'Who was he, Ushoran?' she said.

'Can you feel it, Neferata?' he said, ignoring her

question as they reached the end of the corridor.

'What is it?' she said, shivering. There was a vibration in her bones. It echoed from the floor and the walls and ceiling, and it was as if she were inside some great, living organism.

'The echo of a heartbeat,' Ushoran said, not looking at her.

Neferata listened, and knew he was right. The thudding *boom-boom-boom*, echoing up from untold depths and seeping through the stone, had the regular rhythms of a man's heartbeat. Steady, strong… familiar. 'No,' she said as the sound caressed her ears.

Ushoran turned, his face twisted in a sneer. 'Yes. Listen to it, Neferata. Do you hear it? Do you hear his heart? Does it beat faster?' He made to grab her and she slithered back instinctively, out of his reach. 'Do you hear him?'

The air became cold and sluggish and damp. Neferata swiped instinctively at it, as if it were full of cobwebs. A hand grabbed her wrist, but dissolved into curling wisps of mist as she spun. Words bled through the rock, snippets of past conversations.

'Damn you, Ushoran, who is buried here?' she snapped.

'You did this,' Ushoran said. 'You made him this way!'

Neferata turned around and around as half-formed faces made to speak and dissolved in a silent storm surrounding her. All familiar, though they spanned swathes of time she had not been there to see. The faces were of a child, a boy, a man and – what? – a corpse or a wraith or wight? Regardless, he was a king.

Alcadizzar, the boy she had raised as her own. The man she had groomed to be king and the king who had died for Nehekhara. Neferata hissed and spat as the smoky fingers drifted across hers in a gesture at once familiar and abominable. 'Away, wraith,' she said, swiping her claws through the wisps.

'Mourkain is built on his bones,' Ushoran snarled, lunging through the mist. He grabbed her wrists and his human façade rippled and tore like wet papyrus, revealing the horror beneath. Grey dead flesh over an ape's skull, with a thicket of fangs spilling from a lipless mouth. Eyes like the embers of a dying fire glared at her as he tried to pull her close.

'W'soran cannot break his hold over the crown! And without the crown I cannot truly be king! But you – maybe you...'

Neferata bent and brought the soles of her feet sliding up between them. Catching Ushoran in the belly, she tore him loose and sent him flying back. He hit the rock and screamed, as if it burned him. She rose. The floor felt warm beneath her feet. She smelled the hiss of cooking meat and, a moment later, felt the pain.

She was burning, even as Lahmia had burned, as Khemri and Zandri had burned, at Nagash's command. Alcadizzar whipped her with a lash of fire and regret and she screamed in agony. Ushoran, driven berserk by pain, roared and charged and his massive talons nearly took her head off. She ducked and he cut a gouge in the rock face. She cut through his belly and chest and his growls became screams as she opened him to the spine. He fell and writhed on the ground, his skin bubbling and rupturing. Turning, she began to run even as the heat ate into her own limbs. She had to escape this place. Her feet were burned raw and an agony she hadn't felt since that first night of her new existence raced over her nerves, eating at them like acid. Still, she stumbled on, trying to escape the embrace of the tunnel. If she could get to the main chamber, perhaps the pain would stop. That was all she could think about.

She could hear Ushoran following her, his claws scraping stone. The corridor felt as if it was closing like a fist around her and the needle-on-bone voice of the crown was drowned out by the grim rumble of stone and the echoes of Alcadizzar's voice as it thrummed through her mind, evoking ancient memories and ancient pain.

She burst out of the tunnel like a bat from the depths, flames wreathing her slender shape. She screamed, and there was nothing human in her voice. Ushoran caught her in mid-air, his grotesque gargoyle shape having sprouted wings. He too was on fire and the flames congealed greedily as his talons sought her throat. Maddened by pain and need, the two vampires crashed down onto the floor.

Her hair crisped and crackled like cloth in a cooking fire and her face split and shrank against her bones as she sank her fangs into Ushoran's throat. He howled and bucked, pummelling her with burning fists. They thrashed and fought, rolling across the floor. She worried the flesh of his throat, the blood boiling from the heat even as it reached her mouth.

'Off – get off,' he yowled, muscles heaving beneath his charred skin as he slapped her aside. She spun through the air and struck the wall, dropping bonelessly to the floor. The flames winked out, leaving them both blackened wrecks. Neferata cracked a crisped eyelid.

More of the obese ghoul-things had come into the chamber while she had been gone, and not just them. Smaller ghouls and the dead men who served W'soran as his guard filled the hall, surrounding her followers.

Stupid. She had been stupid to come here. Ushoran coughed and scrambled to his feet, his charred flesh

cracking and sloughing off. He had been burned before
and he shook it off with the speed of experience. His
claws scraped the floor as he made his way towards her.
His previous berserk rage seemed to have left him, and
he looked deflated and weary.

'You see?' he croaked. 'Even in death, he denies us our
due. The crown is ours by right. With it, we can recreate
that which was lost.'

Neferata pushed herself to her feet. The voice of the
crown – Nagash's voice – was back, smashing at her
doubts and worries and fears. For an instant, she wondered if this was how others felt when she turned her
gaze upon them.

The instant was washed away by visions of a great
city, not quite Mourkain or Lahmia, but a blending of
both. It was a city of possibilities, a city of could-be
and will-be; a city ruled forever by a night-hearted
aristocracy, where she would sup on the blood of
princes and kings as all the rulers of the world bowed
at her sandalled feet, and on her brow, a crown.

Crown and throne, Neferata, it purred. *Goddess and
queen, Neferata – that is what you will be. All yours…*

Did Ushoran hear the same? Did it speak to him in
the same soothing tones? Did it make the same promises? Perhaps it had even done so for Kadon.

'You have done your best to keep me on my throne,'
Ushoran hissed. 'You have done this even as you have
schemed to supplant me in the minds of my subjects.
That is why I ask you this now. Help me, Neferata.' He
half-reached for her, with a trembling claw. 'You want
Lahmia back, just as I do, just as Abhorash does, and
W'soran.

'Help me,' he said again. 'Help me put the world back
to rights, Neferata.'

Take the crown and the throne and the WORLD…

The lessons of the past crumbled in an instant, like the dead flesh which drifted from her burned limbs like black snow. All that was left was desire.

'As my king commands,' Neferata said, taking Ushoran's hand with her own.

◄ TWELVE ►

*The City of Lashiek
(–1147 Imperial Reckoning)*

*Neferata led her handmaidens through the crowded streets of
the Corsair City, her robes and cowl pulled close about her,
and a veil of hammered gold discs hiding her face from the
sun. There was a ship waiting for them in the harbour. It was
to take them to Sartosa, across the sea. The streets were full
of merchants, mercenaries and refugees, all going in every
direction at once. Overhead sea-birds wheeled, croaking, and
mangy dogs trotted through the streets.*

*She stopped as a group of soldiers, clad in silks and bronze,
marched past in ragged formation, pennons snapping from
their spear-points. It galled Neferata to abandon Araby. Bel
Aliad was a smoking ruin, thanks to Arkhan, and the other
caliphates reeled under his continued assault. Armies of the
dead trod the Spice Road, harrying what forces the caliphates
could muster, and Araby was no longer a place for patient
schemes and subtle machinations. But that did not mean that
such would always be the case.*

She caught sight of a flash of red. 'There she is,' Naaima murmured a moment later, standing behind her mistress. She gestured towards a shisha house on the other side of the street. Naaima and the others were dressed much as Neferata was, all save Khaled, who wore the armour and full-face helm of a Kontoi. Ragged silk strips hung limply from the spiral point that topped his helm and his cloak was ragged and threadbare. His eyes were haunted behind the chainmail mask that covered his face.

The destruction of Bel Aliad had struck him hard. Every desire and dream that he had nurtured to his breast for the past decade had vanished like a wisp of smoke, leaving him empty of either ambition or energy. Anmar was equally shaken, but had chosen not to emulate her brother's apathy, instead throwing herself into Neferata's schemes with admirable abandon. For Khaled, Bel Aliad had been a kingdom to be won. For his sister, however, it had been little more than a cage.

Neferata led her followers towards the shisha house. Men sat on reed mats outside of it, inhaling sweetly scented smoke from a waterpipe. Anmar sat on a similar mat within, wearing a bright crimson robe. She looked up as they entered and laid a hand on the arm of the woman who crouched nervously beside her. The woman was a slave, and pale-skinned like the barbarian tribes who inhabited the far north. 'My lady,' Anmar said. 'The ship is ready whenever we are.'

Neferata nodded and glanced at the slave, who trembled and turned away. The woman stank of fear. Anmar gently stroked her neck, calming her. 'Ilsa here is a servant of the Dowager Concubine, aren't you, Ilsa?' Anmar said softly. The young vampire's eyes glinted. 'She has agreed to your offer, mistress, and has sent Ilsa as a gift. The girl speaks the language of Sartosa. The Dowager thought she might translate for us upon our arrival.'

Neferata smiled beneath her veil. Though she was leaving

*Araby for greener pastures, her influence would remain. The
Dowager Concubine was the ruler of the Corsair City in
all but name, and with her protection, Neferata's servants
would flourish. When she had re-settled herself, she would
re-establish her influence in the caliphates for as long as they
stood.*

*She knelt and reached out, taking the terrified slave-girl's
chin. Neferata smiled and held the girl's gaze, soothing her
and mesmerising her. 'I'm sure that she will come in handy
in one fashion or another,' she murmured…*

*Nagashizzar
(–328 Imperial Reckoning)*

THE AIR STANK of rot and swamp gas, and scavenger birds
spun through the overcast sky. There was no sun in these
lands, and there hadn't been for hundreds of years. In
the Desolation of Nagash, it was always grey and dark
and foul, a reflection of its creator's soul. Nagashizzar
was a twisted blend of mountain and fortress, and it
loomed above the dead land like a monolith to a forgotten god.

It had taken them the better part of a year to reach
the shores of the Sour Sea from Mourkain, and Neferata climbed swiftly, ignoring the tiny avalanches her
movement set loose. Her patience had worn thin over
the months of journeying and she was eager to reach
her goal. The others followed at some distance. Ahead
of her, Layla moved with inhuman grace, leaping and
climbing, marking the safe path. 'I smell ghouls,' the
girl called back.

'These mountains are filthy with them,' Morath said

from below. The necromancer climbed slowly and cautiously, lacking the grace of his protectors. 'There are thousands of warrens in these hills, thanks to Nagash.'

'I would have thought that they'd have left,' Rasha said, helping Morath climb. 'When he died, I mean.'

'Where would they go?' Morath said. 'When they were human, before Nagash corrupted them, Cripple Peak was their home. That ancestral memory keeps them here, lurking in the blighted shadow of Nagashizzar.'

'The question is not their presence, but their intentions. I would not fight unless we have no choice,' Neferata said, stopping to wait for the others to catch up. 'This journey has taken up too much time as it is.'

'It may take even longer, I fear,' Morath said, leaning on his walking stick. He looked bad, cadaverous even, as if his human vitality were being leached away by their surroundings and replaced by something else. 'Nagashizzar is massive, according to W'soran. It may be months before we find a safe way inside, let alone find that which we seek.'

'Which is?' Layla said, dropping down to perch birdlike above Neferata.

'You should listen more than you natter, girl,' Rasha said.

Layla stuck her tongue out between her fangs. Neferata chuckled. She reached up to yank on the braid of hair that dangled from the girl's head. 'We seek one of the Books of Nagash, child. One that W'soran seems certain is still hidden somewhere in this stinking pile.'

'Implying it's one that the old thief didn't manage to steal when he fled,' Rasha said.

'There were nine of them,' Morath said, looking up towards the high towers of Nagashizzar, shrouded in grey mist. 'Nine books in all, comprising all of Nagash's knowledge on the subject of death.' Morath raised a hand. 'W'soran stole one, as did Arkhan the Black. The other seven, however…' He gestured limply. For more than two decades, Neferata had aided the necromancer in hunting down every scrap of information about those books. Her agents had scoured Araby, Cathay and Ind, hunting stories and memories. Neferata herself had travelled to the decadent coastal cities of the Black Gulf and hunted a certain Abdul ben Rashid through the Street of Booksellers in Copher, where she had torn him apart in broad daylight after he refused to hand over his necromantic scribbling.

And in two decades, all signs had pointed towards Nagashizzar.

'Like as not, rats chewed them to rags and ghouls use them as loincloths,' Rasha said. Morath glared at her, but said nothing. Neferata smiled. Necromancers were precious about their parchments and papyri.

'We'd best hope not, my huntress,' Neferata said, turning to continue on. 'We need them.' *I need them*, she thought. W'soran had sworn that those books had the secret to binding Alcadizzar's angry ghost and freeing Nagash's crown from his clutches. And Neferata wanted that crown. It was the only reason she had agreed to Ushoran's mad plan of an expedition to Cripple Peak. It had taken them months to get here, and would likely take them months more to find those books, barring interruptions.

A shrill cry echoed from the rocks, rebounding down the spine of the mountain. Neferata's head jerked up, and her nostrils flared. She smelled sour blood and rotting meat. It seemed that someone had come to greet the visitors. They had been forced to fight more than once on their trip through the Desolation, battling mutant beasts and the degenerate tribes of savages who clustered on the shores of the Sour Sea, but it had been days since they'd left the territory of the tribes behind.

A tumble of rocks rattled down from above, nearly dislodging Layla, who yelped as she was struck. Rasha shielded Morath and Neferata swatted a rock aside with her hand. A group of men would have likely been discomfited by the rock fall. For vampires, it was barely an annoyance.

'Rasha, stay beside Morath!' Neferata barked, drawing her sword. 'Layla, get back here and help her!'

'But–' Layla began, searching for the creature that had dared to drop rocks on her.

'Now,' Neferata snarled, bounding up the slope with more speed than caution. 'Keep the sorcerer breathing, whatever else happens.'

Over the years, Neferata had become intimately familiar with the methods and manner of the corpse-eaters. Where there was death, there were the eaters-of-the-dead. They had a society of sorts, and kings and queens and lords and ladies. They were a mockery of the men they had descended from, but even mockery has a kernel of truth.

But these ghouls were not like the almost-tame creatures that scampered through the tunnels beneath Mourkain, or the organised tribes of Araby. No, these mountain-ghouls were a breed apart. It was akin to the difference between wolves and dogs. Hidden tunnel mouths suddenly vomited clay-crusted simian shapes. The ghouls boiled from their tunnel like wasps from a disturbed nest, their ape-like agility propelling them down towards her from all directions. They had painted their flesh with clay and filth, and some carried sharpened bones as weapons. Most, however, seemed to content to use their claws and teeth.

Neferata shrieked, casting her voice at them like a weapon. Several dozen stumbled to a halt, tripping up those immediately behind them. Neferata was on them a moment later. Her sword slashed across the front rank, gutting four of the creatures and lopping the arms from a fifth. She pressed her attack, aware that even with all of her strength the creatures could pull her down through sheer weight of numbers. She had to break them; they were scavengers by nature, and would retreat if their prey looked to be too strong.

Her elbow came down between the head and shoulders of a ghoul, shattering its neck even as her leg swept out. Her foot crushed a slavering jaw and the force of the kick spun the ghoul in place, dropping it dead to the rocks. Her sword darted out, chopping like a cleaver into grey flesh. Severed limbs lay heaped on the ground as she created a corridor of death through the ghoul ranks.

Alone, Neferata had blunted the momentum of the ambush. The ghouls scrambled back from her, yelping and howling. Many retreated for their holes, but more stayed. Greasy bodies crashed into her as they sought to drag her down. When she killed one, two more took its place. Hooked claws tore her flesh and she returned the favour. She was in constant motion, her feet and hands crushing skulls and splintering bones even as her sword removed heads and spilled intestines.

For a moment, the snarling creatures that swirled around her wore the faces of enemies new and old, of every obstacle that stood in her path – Razek and Al-Khattab, Lamashizzar and Khalida, Khaled and Ushoran. *Obstacle* and *enemy* were interchangeable concepts for Neferata and she wondered, in the bliss of bloodletting, when that had become the case.

Then the moment passed and she stood alone, drenched in blood. The survivors squatted around her, stinking of fear, their yellow gazes riveted on her. It was ever the way with the corpse-eaters; simply kill enough of them and they worshipped you. If only men were so easy.

Neferata stretched out her sword, catching one of the larger beasts beneath its jaw with the flat of the blade. It gurgled something. She frowned. 'Morath, I trust W'soran taught you whatever debased mewling passes for the language of Nagashizzar,' she called out.

Morath hurried towards her, flanked by Neferata's handmaidens. The blades of both vampires were dark with blood, but only a few ghouls had been opportunistic enough to attack them. Those creatures littered the slope below. Morath spoke in a halting, gurgling tongue that seemed to be less word than bark. The ghouls answered with barks of their own. Morath turned to Neferata, who was examining the blood dripping from her sword to the rocks. Several ghouls squatted low and snuffled at the spreading stain. 'You've impressed them,' Morath said.

'They will serve us, or I will hunt them down. Tell them that,' Neferata said.

'That's unnecessary. They know,' Morath said. 'You have a way with ghoul-kind. Even W'soran can only gain grudging service from them, and they flee at the first opportunity.' He made a face. 'They call him the Painfather.'

'The minds of ghouls are as the minds of men. They seek strong leaders,' Neferata said. The ghouls began to flow back into their holes in pairs and groups. A number stayed with them, as if to act as escort, a fact which Morath confirmed.

'They will show us the secret ways into Nagashizzar. But it is dangerous in the deeps. There are creatures there that even the ghouls fear,' Morath said as they followed the capering cannibals. 'Rat-things, such as W'soran once spoke of.'

Neferata nodded. She had heard similar stories in Cathay and then again in Araby; of chittering red-eyed shadows and stealthy paws in the dark. She had thought it a fable. But now, looking up at the crude walls of Nagashizzar where it sprouted from the mountain's peak, she could believe it. Where else would rats congregate, save in a warren such as this? This close to the fortress of the Great Necromancer, she could feel the evil that infected rock and soil. It sank greedy claws into her mind, and she felt a strange invigoration, similar to that which she felt when entering Kadon's pyramid in Mourkain.

The ghouls led them up the slope and into the warrens that honeycombed Cripple Peak. As they entered the foul-smelling hole, Neferata realised that Nagashizzar was very likely sitting atop a molehill. The trip through the cramped and crude ghoul-tunnels was tortuous and did nothing to improve her first impression. The creatures had clawed them from the very stuff of the mountains and they wound in seemingly no particular direction. Nonetheless, the ghouls led them unerringly on and they walked for hours, deeper into the darkness.

Here and there as they made their way through the tunnels they saw what remained of its structure and the delving of its former inhabitants. There had been more than ghouls in Nagashizzar once, and not all of the human tribes that Nagash had conquered had degenerated into the debased wretches guiding them. Some had simply died. There were heaps of bone – some gnawed and some not – clustered in corners and in nooks and alcoves, like offerings to some vast charnel god. Not Mordig, though, not here. No, the only god here was Nagash, and the ghouls prayed to him in the dark.

There were ghoul-women in the tunnels they travelled through, and squalling pups as well. They hissed and shied away as the males moved ahead, snarling and snapping, keeping the others away from their 'guests'. There was no sign of what they had once been in their behaviour or appearance. 'Is this our fate?' Morath muttered.

'What was that, necromancer?' Neferata said.

'These creatures were once men,' Morath said, gesturing to a cowering carrion-eater. 'Five or ten generations ago, they might have been the same as my own people. And now they are – what? They are nothing but cannibal beasts.'

'One cannot live in the bowels of death for so long without developing a taste for it,' Neferata said with a shrug.

'Is it inevitable, then?' Morath spat. 'Will the Strigoi become cowering apes, hiding in the dark and gnawing bones?' He glared at the vampires. 'Is that what awaits us–' Morath stopped as the tunnel blossomed into an uneven chamber. Strange lights seemed to move through the rock and, his rage forgotten, he dug his fingers into the soft, ashy rock, revealing something that wept a toxic green smoke. His hand trembled as he examined the stuff that rested on his palm. 'This is…' he hissed. 'I didn't believe… not really.'

'What is that foulness?' Layla whispered, her nose wrinkling.

'The stuff which nightmares are made of,' Morath said, letting it hiss through his fingers to the floor. 'It's called *abn-i-khat*. Nagash devoured it; it sustained and consumed him.' He looked at the ghouls. 'And likely these poor creatures as well,' he said.

'Much like magics in general,' Neferata murmured, her flesh crawling as she took in the shimmering veins of the weirdly glowing ore. Morath looked at her.

'Maybe, but it is a price some of us willingly pay,' he said.

'Yes, yes, so much the martyr,' Neferata said, peering into one of the dark tunnels. She sniffed the air as she spoke. 'You have sacrificed much for your people. And you think I have not?'

'You consumed your people,' Morath said quietly. 'And now you would consume mine.'

Neferata spun with a snarl, her lips writhing back from her razor-teeth. 'What did you say?'

'You heard me, leech,' Morath said, his pale features growing even paler. The ghouls began to whine and moan as Neferata stalked towards the necromancer. 'You and Ushoran and W'soran and even Abhorash, you are leeches, battening on the blood of the Strigoi. You are twisting us, the way W'soran twists flesh and bone, making us over in your damnable images!' He swept out an arm to indicate the ghouls. 'And you won't succeed. That is the saddest thing. You will simply make us into beasts like these!'

Trembling with anger, covered in dried blood, Neferata reached for Morath's head. Her talons scraped almost gently against his cheeks. 'You are lucky I need you, Morath. You are lucky that I do not see fit to tell W'soran of your part in my investigations into his schemes.'

'You think he doesn't know? Do you think my mind is proof against his sorceries?' Morath said, and in his eyes, Neferata saw the truth of his words. She could see W'soran's dark sorceries squatting in his student's mind and soul like some ugly spider. She had expected it, but to see it so plainly was startling. The old monster lacked subtlety.

She dropped her hands. 'What else does he know?'

Morath chuckled hoarsely. 'What makes you think he talks to me? If you are unique from your fellow monsters in any fashion, Neferata, it is in that you speak openly to your servants.'

'Servants hear everything anyway,' Neferata said, turning away. There was a sound in the darkness, of quiet steps on the shifting strata of the mountain. The ghouls were agitated. Morath barked something and they began to lope into the darkness, leading their 'guests' on. He looked at Neferata.

'We are wasting time. There are other scavengers in the dark than just ghouls and they are stirring. We should go. These tunnels are too dangerous to linger in for long.'

'The ghouls seem safe enough,' Rasha said.

'What makes you think that?' Morath said bitterly. 'They are hunted for sport here, even as in Mourkain.' He glared at the vampires, as if blaming them for that fact. Which, Neferata supposed, he did.

They left the stinking warren and its eerie glow behind. The ghouls led them up through the winding tunnels, and often Neferata's keen ears caught the quiet scuttling of something that was moving near them, perhaps just on the other side of the walls. After what could only have been a number of miles, the crude tunnels gave way to what, she judged, had once been mine-works. Vast wooden bracers held up the mine-tunnels, lending them a sense of stability that the more cramped ghoul warrens lacked. There were more piles of bones here, these mostly not gnawed or otherwise disturbed and surprisingly anatomically complete. 'Nagash's miners,' Morath murmured. There were hundreds of them, lying where they had dropped when Nagash had been destroyed.

'There are more dead here than in the entirety of the world,' Layla whispered.

The quality of the air had changed as well. There was a verminous smell to things now, a sort of musk that clung to the ancient support timbers and the bones that littered the sides of the tunnel. There were strange marks that glowed faintly on the walls. Neferata touched one and felt a tingle in her fingers. She grunted as she realised that some of the green stone had been used like chalk here, but as to the nature of the mark she couldn't say. It was unlike any writing she had ever seen.

The ghouls had drawn together in a huddle, their yellow eyes darting around. They grimaced and whimpered. Morath looked at them pityingly. He flicked his fingers and the beasts suddenly loped away, back the way they had come, running as if their lives depended on it.

'That was foolish, necromancer,' Neferata said. 'We need guides.'

'And blood,' Layla said.

'You would not want to drink the blood of anything which lurks in this place,' Morath said. 'And we need no guides, not now. Like calls to like, in the sour places.' Morath dropped to his haunches and dug through the closest pile of bones, extracting a nearly mummified hand. A thin shroud of flesh clung to the age-browned bones and Morath hissed in satisfaction.

He held up the hand and blew a soft breath across it.

The fingers stiffened and straightened with an ugly clicking sound. Morath held his hand flat over the fingertips and a burst of puffball light emerged from his palm like poison being drawn from a wound. He winced as the light split and settled on the fingertips, as if the bones were candles. He held it up by its wrist stump and the light slid greasily across the rocks of the tunnel walls.

'What is that?' Neferata said.

'A light to guide us in the darkness,' Morath said. 'Normally, we use them to find hidden barrows and tombs. The hand is drawn towards the largest concentration of the dark energies which we weave together to raise the dead and in this place, it will find Nagash's throne room much quicker than the shoddy ancestral memories of our ghoulish hosts.' He raised the corpse-light, his face pinched with strain. Neferata and the others followed. The faint skittering sounds followed them, though at a distance. It was as if their mysterious pursuers were travelling in a roundabout fashion.

The mines of Nagashizzar proved to be as vast as Morath had warned. Though the necromancer swore that they were travelling in the correct direction, Neferata found herself wondering whether they were going up or down. Time seemed to have little meaning in the ageless, suffocating confines of the mines and days blended into weeks. For Neferata and the other vampires, this was no hardship. They could go months without nourishment, though they preferred to feed as often as possible. Morath, however, was another story.

The necromancer had the lean form of a man on the edge of starvation, and he only grew thinner during their time in the dark. Part of that, Neferata knew, was due to the spell. Keeping his grisly candelabrum lit for so long seemed to take most of his strength, and they were forced to help him keep up more than once. He had brought supplies, but those were exhausted soon enough. Soon, the three vampires were forced to catch the fat black rats that scurried through the dark tunnels for Morath to feast on. A number of the vermin had mutations – extra limbs, scales or bone spurs – but the necromancer devoured them regardless, chewing the foul meat as if it were the greatest delicacy.

Every rock and tunnel seemed to pull at Neferata's very core as they travelled, sucking her down into a maelstrom of darkness that only intensified the longer they walked. It was like a trap, and she was the rat who had walked blindly into it. To distract herself, she wondered what was occurring in her absence in Mourkain. Everything now balanced on the sharp end. An action taken in haste might tip the whole affair one way or another and unravel every strand of her carefully crafted web. She should not have left. But the crown, and what it implied, was too great an opportunity to pass up.

She needed it. It had called her to Mourkain to claim it. She was a queen, was she not? And queens had more need of crowns than grovelling schemers like Ushoran. She saw it so clearly now, down in these dark tunnels. It had used Kadon to draw Ushoran, and it had used Ushoran to draw her and now, now was the time for it to be claimed by its true mistress. After all, was she not Nagash's rightful heir? Was she not a daughter of his blood, at least in the ways that mattered? Was she not a queen of the Great Land?

Yes, yes, you are all of this and more, it murmured, caressing her thoughts. *You will be a queen again and you will rule over silent, perfect cities. You will rule over a world of unchanging tides and unfailing devotion. All will love you. All will serve you.*

Even him, it hissed, *even Alcadizzar.*

She shuddered slightly, thinking again of Alcadizzar's face. He would be a ghost-king for a vampire-queen; what could be more appropriate? He would love her in death as he had not in life. Everything would be–

The blade stabbed down from out of the darkness above as the roof of the tunnel seemed to unfold like the membranous wing of a bat. Morath, caught unawares, could only stare upwards in stupefaction. Neferata's palms slammed together on the oily blade, trapping it inches from Morath's head. With a roar, she jerked the blade's wielder from its hiding place and dashed it to the ground. The cloak the small figure wore was the colour of the rock, and its hairy limbs were bound in leather and rags. It jerked its blade free of Neferata's grip and flipped up, lashing out at her as it chattered curses. It wielded two blades and they hummed as they cut the air. She had little room to manoeuvre in the cramped tunnel, but the creature seemed to have no such difficulty. It sprang into the air and bounced from wall to floor to ceiling, always stabbing and cutting at her.

Losing her temper, she shot a hand out, wincing as the blades chopped into her arm. She swung her arm, pulling the weapons out of her attacker's hands, and grabbed a hairy throat with her unwounded hand. The hood fell back, revealing the frothing, snarling snout of a great rat. With a cry of disgust, Neferata bashed the creature's brains out on the side of the tunnel, leaving a dark trail across the rock.

'What in the name of Settra was that thing?' Layla yelped, looking around. The scuttling sounds they had been hearing since they entered the mines were louder now, as if whatever was making them was no longer concerned with stealth.

Rasha spat a word in Arabyan. Neferata nodded as she pulled the blades from her arm. 'Ratkin, even as Morath warned us,' she said. 'Foul little beasts. Where there's one, there's a thousand. We should hurry,' she added.

'It might be too late,' Rasha said, pointing back the way they had come. Strange lights flickered in the darkness. Weapons rattled and a wave of chittering voices rolled down the tunnel.

'The throne room is near, it must be,' Morath said, rubbing his throat and looking down at the body of his would-be assassin. He sounded more hopeful than confident. 'If we hurry–'

'Hold them for as long as you can,' Neferata said to her handmaidens. Rasha grimaced and nodded. Layla hissed eagerly.

'I've killed rats before. It should be easy.'

Neferata didn't reply. She grabbed Morath and slung him over her shoulder. He squawked at the treatment, but fell silent as she broke into a sprint. She ran easily, despite the encumbrance. 'You said it was nearby,' she growled to Morath.

'I can feel it, like a weight on my heart,' he gasped. The skeletal hand flexed and the light that clung to the fingertips began to glow more brightly. She took that as a good sign. Behind her she heard the clash of weapons and smelled the musk-stink of the ratkin's blood as it was spilled. She sped up, moving like quicksilver. Anyone watching would have seen little more than a pale blur. The rough mine tunnels gave way to shaped corridors as she ran. The corpse-light was burning as brightly as a torch as she raced onwards.

She passed through vast, dark, deserted halls and echoing vaults. She loped through great, now-empty storehouses and silent, shuttered rooms that had once been the sites of Nagash's blasphemous rites. Morath gasped as she ran through the immense mountain crypt, barely able to breathe so swiftly did she move.

Neferata felt a strange sense of recognition and realised that Nagashizzar and Mourkain shared more than a legacy of death; Kadon, whether he had known it or not, had recreated Nagash's citadel in his own crude fashion. Thus, when they reached the antechamber to Nagash's throne room she knew it at once for what it was.

She barrelled through a thick curtain of spider-webs and dust, sliding across a rough stone floor on her feet and hand, her claws leaving thin canyons in the stone. She tossed Morath down. 'On your feet, necromancer, we're here.'

Morath climbed to his feet and held up the glowing hand. The corpse-light illuminated a great swathe of the massive chamber. It was a crude parody of the antechamber to the throne room of the great palace of Khemri. Even Nagash, it seemed, had not been immune to nostalgia.

The doors to the throne room were little more than unfinished slabs of bronze now gone green from verdigris and their hinges were braided sinew, long since fossilised into immobility. Morath hesitated, staring up at them. Strange char marks covered them, and he said, 'There was a battle here.'

Neferata looked at him. 'Can you open them?' she said flatly.

'W'soran taught me,' Morath said. 'It will take me a few minutes, however. I am weak,' he added, at her look. 'These past weeks have been difficult. I am merely mortal, woman, unlike you.'

'Why did you volunteer to come with me, Morath? W'soran wanted to send Melkhior, and in truth that might have been more convenient,' Neferata said, annoyed.

'W'soran is frightened,' Morath said, looking at the door. 'He fears the crown and its hold on Ushoran. Aye, and on him as well, and you,' he added. 'He is planning something. To flee, I think. And when he goes, only some of his students will go with him. The others will be disposed of.'

'You want protection,' Neferata said.

'Wouldn't you?' Morath looked at her. 'Isn't that why you came to Mourkain?'

'No,' Neferata said.

Morath grunted. 'No, I suppose not, eh? Well, you'll soon get what you want, won't you?'

'And you'll get what you want,' Neferata said. 'I'll need an advisor, Morath. A man who knows his people as well as you seem to would be invaluable.'

Morath looked at her. 'Do not offer what you cannot promise.'

Neferata sniffed. 'Can I not? When the crown is mine–'

'You will not be you any longer. Or so W'soran says,' Morath said darkly. 'Even Ushoran is not Ushoran. Not any more. He grows less and less like the man I once served, and more like the thing he is – bestial and rapacious and too hungry for this world.'

'But you could keep me from becoming that way, Morath of Mourkain,' Neferata said, clutching his arm. 'Unlike Ushoran, I know how to listen to those who serve me!'

'Really? Because you ignored the fears of your hand-maidens to undertake this journey,' Morath said. He jerked his arm free of her grip. 'I must concentrate.' He stretched out a pale, thin hand and stroked the air. A pall of dust rose, puffing from the edges of the doors. Then, with a groan as deep as the mountain itself, the long-immobile doors began to move. They rumbled inwards, shaking the ground beneath Neferata's feet.

Flagstones of black marble paved the path inwards, and the path itself was lined with elaborate and grotesque columns which stretched up into the darkness to support the arched ceiling. Morath's wheezing breath echoed strangely in the space. Neferata strode ahead of him, her eyes adjusting easily to the darkness.

The room itself had seen much activity, despite the sealed doors. There were great gaping holes in the stone walls and immense char marks scored the spots where there were no holes. The black marble on the floor had been seared to slag in places and more than one of the columns had tumbled into pieces. Intuition told her that the rat-men had likely burrowed through Nagash's throne room after the Great Necromancer's death, and they had left evidence of their presence, including piles of old droppings and huddled, miserable piles of gnawed bones.

The centre of the room was marked by the presence of more than a dozen ancient corpses, scattered haphazardly in a rough circle. Morath grabbed her arm as she started forwards. 'Abn-i-khat,' he whispered, pointing with the skeletal hand. A glowing stain marked the floor.

She kicked a body aside and it crumbled into dust. 'What was this?'

'A rite of some kind was conducted here. But it was interrupted,' Morath said, his eyes narrowed speculatively. 'Perhaps W'soran…?'

'It would not surprise me,' Neferata said. W'soran had been chased from Nagashizzar with his tail between his legs, and he was naturally reluctant to discuss it. Her eyes scanned the chamber and were drawn to an ominous presence occupying the far end.

She hissed, and Morath looked to see what had startled her. He swallowed thickly as he saw it and said fearfully, 'Nagash's throne...'

The throne of the Undying King occupied the far wall. It was, like the throne of Mourkain, a paean to barbaric splendour. But unlike Mourkain, its majesty was no pallid mockery. Here was the truth of which Mourkain was only a weak echo. The throne was crafted from great blocks of stone and petrified wood and lined with the bones of beasts and men. Ropes of now-brittle human hair had been woven into a cushion and glimmering strands of abn-i-khat ran through its form, casting a faint illumination over the floor all around it. In the first moment that Neferata glimpsed it, a massive shadowy shape seemed to occupy it, only to waver and vanish as Morath's spell-light passed over it.

'Magnificent,' she said, swaying towards it. It drew her in, as if it were calling out to her in a whisper that only she could hear. As she drew close, she felt something shudder through her, and abruptly, her stomach twisted into a painful knot. Pain slithered through her limbs and she staggered. It felt as if a hundred hands were plucking at her flesh, seeking to strip it from her bones. She squalled and felt her body contort and then she staggered, unable to stand.

'Neferata,' Morath cried out, grabbing her as she slumped. He dragged her awkwardly back, away from the throne. 'What–'

'It's *him*!' she shrieked, shoving him aside and scrambling away from the throne. The feeling of revulsion lessened, and the pain waned. She spat out the black blood that had suddenly filled her mouth, and looked at her arms, where black veins pulsed angrily.

'Nagash is dead,' Morath said, looking at the throne.

'So am I, necromancer,' Neferata snapped. 'He's there. Some part of him is in those stones, clinging like a leech. It's like a knife scoring my nerves.'

'I see something,' Morath said, stepping forwards. She resisted the urge to cringe as he drew close to the throne. 'Look,' he said, holding his corpse-light aloft to reveal dust-covered shapes which were spread out around the foot of the throne and spilled down the steps of the dais.

'What are they?'

'Tomes,' Morath muttered, dropping to his knees before the throne. 'How long have they lain here?'

'Does it matter?' She turned away from the throne and gritted her teeth. She could still feel the nauseating sensations. 'Do what we brought you here to do, and be quick about it!' As Morath set to clearing the dust and mould from the tomes, she strode towards the doors, wanting to get as far from the throne as possible.

The sounds of battle were growing louder. She felt no fear for her handmaidens. She knew from experience that even the most inexperienced of their kind was far tougher to kill than anything yet living in this mountain. Her blood was strong, and it made others strong as well.

It would make the world strong. She smiled softly at the thought, knowing even as she did so that the thought was not hers. Some small part of her rebelled then, angry. She would not do as Ushoran had done. There would be no aristocracy of the night, battening fat on the blood of mortals. That way lay stagnation and cessation. That way lay rebellion and danger.

No, she would rule softly and gently, from behind curtains and viziers. She would stand behind all of the thrones of the world and their politics and wars would be her parlour games, enacted for her amusement down the long, unending corridor of years. It would be a great game, that.

Bones clattered beneath her feet. She looked down. Piles of brown and yellow lay heaped in the corners, as if some great force had swept them aside. Rotted armour and rusting weapons lay amongst the piles, enough to outfit an army. Dust and cobwebs and the filth of ages provided a pathetic barrow for the dead. She glanced back at the throne.

'You failed, old skull. But Neferata will not,' she said, baring her fangs. She blinked. The veins of abn-i-khat had seemed to flicker in response to her words, and she felt a chill curl around her spine. Momentarily unnerved, she said, 'Morath, have you found anything useful in that rubbish?'

'I... don't know,' he said. He sat on the dais steps, a crumbling book in his hands. The glow from the hand had dimmed and it lay near his foot, discarded. He thumbed through the crumbling pages cautiously. 'They've just sat here for centuries...' he said, as if offended by the thought. 'Why wouldn't the scavengers have taken them?'

'Maybe they tried,' Neferata said, gesturing to the crumbling bodies. 'Have you found what we need, or not?' Before he could reply, the sound of swift footsteps on the stone echoed through the chamber. 'Prepare yourself, necromancer,' she said, loosening her sword in its sheath. She could smell the rat-musk now and she thought that she caught a glimpse of red eyes in the darkness of one of the holes which marred the wall.

'There are so many of them – so much knowledge,' Morath almost moaned, flicking through crumbling pages, his eyes widened as if to drink in the faded scrawling that covered each page. 'What we could do with all of this–'

Neferata glanced at him. 'I care nothing for Nagash's scribbling, Morath. Find the right damn one before it's too late–'

With a squealing cry, more than a dozen rat-things burst from one of the close tunnels, carrying short stabbing spears and rough wooden shields. They charged towards Neferata and she moved to meet them. Morath shot to his feet and spat harsh, croaking syllables, and a curling spike of dark, blistering energy carved a swathe of destruction through the horde. Neferata was hot on its heels and her sword smashed down through a shield and into the furry body cowering beneath it.

In moments the surviving rats were scampering back the way they had come. Neferata spun as Rasha and Layla entered the throne room through the doors, covered in blood, some of it their own. 'They're regrouping,' Rasha said. 'And more are coming besides. Morath was right – we've walked into a nest of the foul beasts.'

'More than a nest,' Morath said, looking longingly at the books and scrolls scattered across the dais. 'If W'soran was telling the truth, there's a damn city down there and enough troops to keep us busy until the world ends.' He snatched one of the books up and flipped through it. 'We could kill thousands and they'd still keep coming.' He clutched the crumbling book to his chest.

'Then it is best if we take our leave,' Neferata said. 'Is that what we came for?' She gestured to the book in his hands with her sword.

He hesitated. His eyes darted to the other tomes scattered about. 'I-I think so.' It was plain that he wanted to claim otherwise. Morath had a hunger for knowledge that rivalled the dwarfs' love of gold.

'Do you think, or do you know?' Neferata snarled, taking a step towards him. 'I have no time for games, Morath. There's an army breathing down our neck and we won't have a second chance at this!'

Morath hugged the book more tightly, but he met her gaze. His posture stiffened. 'This is the one,' he said more harshly.

'We won't make it ten yards past those doors, mistress,' Rasha said bluntly. 'I can hear them out there. They're all around us. We were under siege the moment we left the ghoul warrens!'

Neferata hissed in exasperation. So close and yet to be deterred by vermin was as complete an insult as she could conceive. Had this been Ushoran's hope all along? That she would fall here and her bones join those–

'Ha!' Neferata pointed to the bones that lined the hall. 'Here. Here is where we shall find our reinforcements.'

'It will take all of the strength I have left,' Morath said, not quite protesting. He was speaking the truth, she knew. He was paler than normal and looked shrunken, somehow. He cradled the mouldering tome to his chest as if it were a child.

'Do it,' Neferata demanded. 'Do it or be damned, Morath. If you want my protection, then make yourself worthy of it.'

Morath nodded, grim-faced. Neferata felt something like a caress across her heart, and then Morath raised his hands and black energies, painful to look upon, curled from his fingers. A strange smell filled the air, which would have choked the living.

To Neferata, however, it smelled like the sweetest of wines. The winds of darkness clamoured to be used, pressing themselves upon the world through Morath's ritualistic gestures. Neferata gulped down a greedy breath, drinking in the stray magics with instinctive abandon. They invigorated her more than even the headiest swallow of blood. Was this what W'soran felt as he employed his necromantic magics? She glanced to the side. It was obvious that the others were feeling it as well. Even as the living felt repulsed by the magic of the grave, the dead were seemingly drawn to it.

Morath spoke and his voice, while not deep, burned and echoed amongst the stones of the hall. Brown bones which had soaked in the grime of centuries burst upwards on tattered feet and clawed for the sky. Long-dead things lurched into the light of his spell, shedding dirt and immobility like water. Moans that were more a memory of sound than sound itself settled heavily on the air.

Neferata stepped forwards. Ancient weapons rattled as the dead raised them in salute. A hundred skulls, covered in veils of filth, returned her gaze with empty ones of their own. The floor and walls shook and shuddered as a cloud of cold, wet air and mist seeped from the pores of the stones. The mist swept about the feet of the dead and rose up before them like a wave, disgorging the emaciated shapes of warriors in ancient bronze armour, whose eyes glowed with a sinister light.

Morath stepped past them, face drawn and haggard. 'The Yaghur served Nagash for centuries. As they will now serve you, Lady Neferata,' he said. He slumped on the dais, his limbs twitching as if they ached. 'I've wrenched the dead from the guts of this place. Hopefully it will be enough.'

'It tires you,' Neferata said, looking at him.

'Of course it tires me,' Morath said. 'I am wrenching the dead out of their graves. It is like a game of tug-of-war, between them and me. If I set a foot wrong or make the wrong gesture, I'll join them in the darkness.'

'W'soran seems to have none of your difficulties,' Neferata said. She could hear the skittering of the ratkin in their holes. They were regrouping and regaining their courage in the sanctuary the darkness provided. She wondered at their hesitation. Were they that cowardly, or was it perhaps that they felt the raw essence of evil that lingered here?

'Your *kind*,' Morath spat the word, 'have no difficulties channelling the magic required to pull the dead from their sleep. Or so W'soran says, at any rate.'

'You don't believe him?' Neferata said, raising her sword. She glanced at Rasha, who nodded. Shapes moved in the darkness outside the doors to the throne room.

'Would you? He lies as a matter of course,' Morath said, clutching the tome he held more tightly. 'He doesn't care for Mourkain... only for his damned experiments. If he didn't have the captives from battles and raids he'd take my folk and make monsters of them!' His voice rose in pitch.

Neferata watched him reassert control of himself. 'Teach me,' she said. 'Teach *us*.'

'What?' Morath said.

Neferata sank down to her knees before him. 'Teach us, Morath. W'soran will not do it, the jealous old creature. But you can. Teach us your magics, these magics you say that we can do so well, and we will use them in defence of Mourkain and the Strigoi. We will take on the burden of death, even as we are meant to do,' she said, letting her will add weight to her words. His mind, normally silver-sharp and bright, was dull now, exhausted and weak. It crumbled beneath her subtle assault, her words and pleas mingling with his until Morath of Mourkain could no longer tell his own thoughts from what she had put into his head.

'I... yes,' he said hesitantly, his face crumbling. 'But first we must escape this trap.'

'Leave that to me,' Neferata said, rising to her feet. She looked at Layla and Rasha, both of whom still looked exhausted and weak, though that was changing as they bathed in the raw death-stuff dripping from the floating nightmare forms which surrounded them. 'Sisters, will you follow me?'

'Always, my lady,' Rasha said hoarsely. Layla nodded, her eyes blazing with hunger. Neferata looked to Morath, but he lay on the dais, barely breathing. The necromancer would be of no further help. The dead looked to her silently, their wills bound to hers by Morath's magic.

'Then it is time to remind these creatures that they rule here only at our sufferance,' Neferata said, raising her sword as small, vicious shapes scuttled into the throne room in a verminous tide. They came in a chattering wave, much as they had before, albeit in greater numbers. The front rank of the creatures halted as they caught sight of the newly risen dead and those behind stumbled into them. Neferata seized the opportunity and gestured sharply. 'Take them,' she snarled.

Before the vermin could react, Rasha and Layla leapt to the attack, and the dead moved with them in an eerie, creaking harmony. Rasha stretched out an arm and impaled a quivering rat-thing on her blade. With a growl she yanked it up and let the writhing, squealing form slide down her weapon's length. Layla chopped heads and tails with gleeful abandon, covering herself in the foul blood of the creatures like a child playing in mud. The dead men hewed and hacked at their scurrying enemies with something that might have been personal animosity. Though the creatures they had once fought were long dead and gone, the current generation of ratkin knew just who – and what – it was that they faced and long-buried fear burst through their veneer of menace, puncturing their courage and sending many fleeing into side passages and tunnels, their shrieks and cries adding to the cacophony of the conflict.

Neferata watched the slaughter unfold in satisfaction. The ratkin broke within moments; their organised ranks falling into a disorderly rout. They fled in all directions, and those who didn't do so fast enough were trampled underfoot. Neferata knew that it was only surprise that had allowed her tiny force to accomplish such a defeat. She also knew that it wouldn't last long. The rats had lurked in the walls of Nagashizzar for too long; they wouldn't give up that easily. It was time they took their leave.

She sheathed her blade and stooped, scooping up Morath as easily as a mother might lift a child. Her flesh quivered as she stepped back from the throne; again she saw the shadowy shape there, its skull wreathed in smoke and flame, and her heart, long since dead and still, shuddered in its cage of bone. Then the moment passed and the throne was empty.

She spun and moved swiftly towards the doors, followed by her handmaidens. The spectral warriors charged ahead in silence, clearing the path. For the first time in centuries, the dead marched in Nagashizzar, and they brought misery with them to those who had thought themselves secure in their mastery. As they made their way out of Nagashizzar, the whispers began again, stronger, as if the touch of dark magic had given them a strength they had previously been lacking.

'I am coming,' Neferata hissed in reply. And somewhere, in the darkness, something cried out in triumph.

⊰ THIRTEEN ⊱

*The City of Sartosa
(−1146 Imperial Reckoning)*

*The spear licked out, its blade surmounted by a halo of dust
and smoke. Neferata barely brought her sword up in time,
driving the spear-point into the mast behind her. It hammered home, cracking wood. The crack widened as the spear
was jerked free by its wielder.*

*The druchii hissed and lunged again, his lean body driving
the spear towards her belly with inhuman speed. Neferata
caught the haft, just below the blade, and guided it around
her even as her sword came up and pierced the druchii's side.
The elf bucked in agony and Neferata ripped her sword free,
letting her opponent fall.*

*Neferata stepped over the body and looked out over the
deck. The port of Sartosa was aflame as the druchii raiders
ravaged the city, looking for loot and slaves. More of the pale,
black-eyed elves charged across the deck towards her. They
had butchered the remaining crew easily, but were finding
Neferata and her handmaidens to be an altogether tougher
breed of opponent. She had faced the creatures before, in the*

Shark Straits. They raided the coasts of Araby with depressing regularity and had taken a number of vessels that she considered hers. She considered this to be a form of belated justice.

A white-haired elf woman ran towards Neferata, shrieking in what might have been delight. Curved blades connected with Neferata's sword, the force of the blow nearly knocking her from her feet. The elf spat something in her own liquid tongue and Neferata responded by shoving aside her opponent's swords and lunging, snake-swift, to clamp her jaws on the elf's throat. She was careful not to gulp down the blood that burst into her mouth, having seen the effects it had had on one of her handmaidens who hadn't been so cautious. The vampire had collapsed as if drugged, and had yet to awaken.

Neferata tossed her head, ripping the elf's throat out. The elf slumped, clutching at the spurting hole in her jugular. Neferata spat out what was in her mouth and shoved the dying elf to the side. The others, clad in scaly cloaks and dark armour, hesitated. Neferata smiled, blood staining her face. 'Kill them for me, my sweets,' she spat.

The ghouls burst out of the open hold behind the elves, their slimy paws tangling in the cloaks and their talons hooking the ornate armour. The druchii turned on this new threat with remarkable aplomb, but surprise and numbers were on the ghouls' side. The struggling elves were either torn apart there or they were pulled into the dank hold, to be devoured alive if she judged their screams correctly. The ghouls were hungry, having had little to eat beyond rats or the cast-off members of the crew once Neferata and her followers had finished with them.

The screams of the druchii ringing in her ears, she found her gaze sliding east, where distant mountains climbed into the clouds. In the tongue of the Sartosans, they were the 'Mountains-at-World's-End'. Something seemed to flash between those distant peaks and she felt a jolt. It had merely *been a reflection from the fire off the water, she thought.*

Yes, just a reflection.

Nonetheless, she continued to stare and before her aston-ished eyes, a vast black cloud seemed to rise up from the mountains, as if a flock of birds had suddenly taken flight. For a moment, the cloud seemed to take the form of a man – no, not a man, something worse. And then it was gone and it was once again just a reflection and Neferata turned back to the slaughter to drown her misgivings in blood…

The City of Mourkain
(−327 Imperial Reckoning)

NEFERATA STALKED THROUGH the hall towards the audience chamber. Naaima raced after her, fighting to keep up. 'Neferata, wait!' the latter cried out. 'You mustn't do this! It's over!'

Neferata stopped and spun, grabbing Naaima's throat. 'Understand me when I say this, Naaima, *I say when it's over!* No one else,' Neferata snarled.

'Abhorash is mobilising what remains of Mourkain's military,' Naaima said, grabbing her mistress's wrist. 'He will crush Vorag's rebels within months, if Vorag doesn't simply flee to Cripple Peak as he seems intent on doing!' She glared at Neferata, unafraid. 'Ushoran *knows*, Neferata. He knows it was you, even if he can't prove it.'

'He knows nothing,' Neferata said. 'All of his atten-tions are on the crown.' She released Naaima. 'Let Abhorash waste his time on Vorag. By the time he gets back, it will be too late. I will be queen again, with pow-ers undreamt of at my command.'

'Would you fight them both?' Naaima said. 'Would you fight both W'soran and Ushoran and their entourages? Our forces are scattered, and of those of us here, we are too few.'

'We have enough. The time to strike is now!' Neferata said, her form quivering with impatience. 'The web has been drawn tight. All eyes are on other sights and our fangs are at Ushoran's throat, though he sees them not.'

'Khaled, you mean,' Naaima spat.

'Ushoran trusts him,' Neferata said.

'You mean you trust him.'

Neferata laughed. 'Hardly, but I know him. He fears me and hungers for my touch. He will do as I command.'

'And if you're wrong?'

Neferata paused. 'Then I will kill him. We must go now, Naaima. W'soran's ritual will begin at any moment and we must strike as soon as he has completed it.' W'soran had been positively gleeful when he received the tome that Morath had discovered. Within a few weeks he seemed to have discovered what he needed to bind Alcadizzar's spirit, and tonight, with the Witch-Moon high in the air, was the night he had chosen to do the deed.

'And what then?' Naaima pressed.

Neferata looked at her in frustration. 'What do you mean what then? Then we will have a kingdom to rule, and an empire to build.'

'Remember what Abhorash said to you on our first day in Mourkain?' Naaima said desperately. 'Remember what he said about the difference between taking something and holding on to it?'

'With the crown–'

'You've seen what the crown has done to Ushoran.

Look at yourself! All of our plans, tossed over for impulse,' Naaima said, grabbing Neferata's arms. 'You endanger all of us, and for what – something that you neither need nor truly want?'

Neferata pulled her arms free of her handmaiden's grip and slapped her. Naaima fell, eyes wide. 'Who are you to say what I need? Who are you to question me?' Neferata hissed, looming over the fallen vampire. 'I will–'

Kill her. She is of no further use to us. Kill her for questioning you.

The voice was like a shiver of ice-water down her back. The voice – the damned voice! It had all begun to go wrong when she had first heard its whisper so many years before. And every decade, it grew louder and more insistent, like a maggot burrowing into her very brain. Its whispers had become demanding screams since her return from Nagashizzar, and now she could barely focus on anything else. 'I will… I will forgive you, this time,' she said, forcing herself to calm down. She stepped back, vision blurring as if her head were surrounded by a halo of flies.

It had all gone wrong in her absence, despite Naaima's best intentions. Someone had told Vorag that Ushoran had decided to rid himself of his more barbarous servants in an effort to quell the unrest that swept Mourkain and Strigos. Creatures like Zandor and Gashnag had turned on their fellows. Several of the frontier ajals had seen their holdings burned or taken, and those who did not flee were impaled in the ashes of their lairs. Vorag had made his move, fearing he would have no other time. Stregga had gone with him. Sometimes Neferata cursed the initiative of her followers.

Now Strigoi fought Strigoi in the east and the wildling

tribes had seized their opportunity. Savage hillmen attacked the outposts of Strigos and what forces had not been mobilised to fight Vorag now waged war on their former allies.

'We should leave. Tonight,' Naaima said, rising warily to her feet. 'We'll seek sanctuary with the Draesca. Or we could find Vorag. We could even go north, or west. Leave these mountains forever.'

'I'm tired of running,' Neferata said, not looking at her handmaiden. She clenched her hands and her claws extended like a cat's. 'I am tired of going poor into the night. It is the same game, over and over again, Naaima.' She growled. 'I want a new game.' She looked at her servant, the only being she could still, perhaps, call friend. 'Would you leave me again?'

'No,' Naaima said, after a moment of hesitation. 'No, for better or worse, our fates are bound together.'

'I've told you, there is no fate,' Neferata said.

'Prove it,' Naaima retorted. 'Let us leave.'

Neferata opened her mouth to reply, but no sound came out. She closed her mouth and turned, stalking towards the throne room of the black pyramid. After what seemed like an eternity, she heard Naaima begin to follow her.

The others were waiting for them in the audience chamber. Layla and Rasha and Anmar stood to the side, across from Ushoran's honour guard, who were at last allowed into the pyramid with their master. And in a half-circle before the open aperture that led down to Alcadizzar's tomb stood W'soran and his disciples, including Morath.

No others were in attendance, not even Ushoran's inner circle. Likely they were too busy trying to decide who to back in the civil war now brewing. Neferata's agents had made sure that it wouldn't be an easy choice. Most would sit on the fence until one side or the other looked to be victorious, and then they would make their move to curry favour.

It was all perfect. Ushoran, alone, save for a few guards, with her knife at his throat. W'soran would stay out of it. The old beast despised them both equally, and he had flee the first chance he got, if Morath was to be believed. No matter, she could always find him again, if she needed him.

'Ah, now the circle is complete,' Ushoran said as he spotted her. He smiled thinly at her. 'I trust I did not call you away from anything important?'

'Nothing that can't wait,' Neferata said. 'I am honoured that you invited me to – what is this? – your coronation? And with so few in attendance...'

'Jealousy ill becomes you,' Ushoran said.

'And condescension, you,' Neferata said. 'Vorag marches east. He has supporters there, on the frontier.'

'And Abhorash marches in pursuit?'

'As you requested,' Neferata said. 'It wouldn't do to have him here. Not for this.'

Ushoran made a face. 'No,' he said. 'You did well.'

'Your gratitude fills me with joy,' Neferata said.

Ushoran snorted as he watched W'soran and his disciples prepare themselves for the rite. 'I doubt that. Still, let it never be said that I cannot acknowledge the wit and worth of another.'

'Oh, I've never said that,' Neferata murmured. 'The war with the tribes goes badly, my spies tell me.'

Ushoran grunted. 'We are too few. But not for long.'

'And what if Vorag defeats Abhorash? This civil war may become a less than foregone conclusion,' Neferata said, not looking at him. 'There are too many nobles straddling both sides. They will turn on us, Ushoran.'

'Are you trying to upset me?' Ushoran hissed. He glared at her. 'Or are you simply so spiteful that you would seek to cast a shadow over this moment?'

'Neither,' Neferata said, meeting his glare calmly. 'I am merely doing what you have tasked me with. I am informing you of the threats which besiege this straw empire you have built.'

'Oh?' Ushoran's expression turned cunning. He gestured sharply. Khaled stepped forwards, carrying something wrapped in a bloodstained cloth. With a start, Neferata realised that it was a cloak. A dwarf cloak.

Ushoran was watching her face. 'If you were so intent on informing me of threats to my rule, I cannot help but wonder why you neglected to mention that our stunted neighbours have been scurrying about in our pantry.'

Khaled pulled back the edge of the cloak, revealing a bloodstained axe; Razek's axe, she realised in shock. Khaled did not meet Neferata's eyes as she glared at him. 'I did not want to worry you,' she said. 'I trust that you dealt with the trespassers?'

'Oh yes,' Ushoran said grinning. He traced the scrolling rune-work on the blade of the axe, wincing slightly. Neferata had never noticed before, but the runes were worked into the steel in threads of silver. 'I dealt with them myself. I have not hunted in some time. Sometimes I wonder whether my current laws regarding such are as wise as I am assured that they are.'

'We shall have to come up with some sort of explanation for the dawi,' Neferata said, momentarily nonplussed. Razek was dead. Some part of her felt as if she had been cheated. She looked at Ushoran. 'If they are aware of what he was—'

'Then you will deal with it,' Ushoran said, still watching her. 'Won't you?'

Neferata paused. 'What do you mean?'

'W'soran has said that the dawi work just as diligently and as well dead as they do alive. I think he exaggerates, but, well… he is the expert.' Ushoran's lips peeled back from the nest of fangs that inhabited his mouth. 'Imagine it, my lady. The Silver Pinnacle, working day and night in the darkness, crafting arms and armour for the glory of Strigos and all for the price of a bit of blood.' He snapped his fingers in front of her face. 'We will be as invincible in war as we are in matters of life and death.' He tapped the axe again. 'And this will be our last payment to our allies, I think. After all, what need have the dead of gold?'

As plans went, Neferata could see the efficiency of it. It was also mad. And Ushoran was mad for suggesting it. She could see an unhinged hunger in his eyes. He had always been a slave to his hungers, even as they all were.

The forges of the dawi of the Silver Pinnacle will ring in the darkness unto eternity and the dead will sheathe their bones in iron and march against sunrise and sunset alike, the voice purred. It showed her the dead, crawling across the earth like black ants, sheathed in metal, burying everything under their iron limbs, and she was reminded of scarab beetles crawling across a corpse and stripping it of all flesh. The world would be a gleaming, silent tomb.

She shook her head and Ushoran cocked his, looking at her curiously. 'You disagree?'

'I… no, no, it is a good plan,' she said, forcing the words out. 'I look forward to it.'

'Do you? I wonder,' Ushoran said, turning back to the ceremony. 'Now shush. History's epilogue begins now.'

Stung, Neferata stepped back and joined her

handmaidens. Naaima laid a hand on her arm and Neferata shook her off. Naaima looked afraid; it was the first time that Neferata had seen fear in her handmaiden's face since before Lahmia fell. Layla was trembling like a child or a frightened animal, her eyes red and wide. Rasha was less obviously affected, but there were signs of strain on her face and in the rigidity of her muscles. It was no longer just her. Something was stirring in the dark, and even lesser creatures could sense it. Her senses were screaming in terror. The throne room seemed to contract. Someone was sitting on the throne. For a moment, the shape was lean and immense, a rickety giant clad in armour such as she had never seen, with a crown on its skeletal brow and eyes of green balefire that burned her clear through.

She shook her head and the vision passed. She looked at Anmar. 'What is your fool brother playing at? I told him that Ushoran was to know *nothing* of the dwarfs until I decided to tell him!'

'My lady, I–'

'Don't try and protect him, girl,' Neferata said, grabbing Anmar's arm. 'What is he up to?'

Before Anmar could answer, W'soran and his followers began to speak, one after the other, their voices blending in dark harmony. The light of the braziers scattered about flickered and then blazed all the brighter, turning from a clean pale glow to something sickly and weird as the words echoed from the oddly vaulted reaches of the chamber.

Neferata stiffened as something reached out of the darkness of the tomb-corridor and caressed her. The chamber seemed to tremble with titan footsteps and the rock groaned and shifted. Smoke issued from the cracks in the walls and the floor and she could feel a heat pressing down on her from every direction, just as before.

Alcadizzar was coming.

W'soran spat something, and he flung out one gnarled limb. A weft of crackling onyx lightning stretched from his hand, splashing across the aperture. His disciples threw back their heads as W'soran pulled more power from them. Neferata blinked as she caught sight of what might have been obsidian webs spreading between the necromancer's acolytes and binding them all together. Her blood began to race as she sensed something coming. She looked around, seeing the same intent expression on the face of every vampire in the chamber – a feral lust that stripped from them even the most basic shred of human dignity and instead replaced it with the bald greed of a starving animal.

When the light came, it was painful. A curling wing of flame lashed out of the aperture, spattering across the line of necromancers, and one screamed, high and piteous, as his ragged robes caught fire. He tumbled from the line, thrashing and beating at himself with stick arms and wispy fingers. The flames simply consumed him all the faster for his attempts to put them out. He crawled across the floor, leaving a greasy trail in his wake, his flesh blistering from his bones.

'He comes!' Morath screamed suddenly. Neferata saw the Strigoi stagger, their hands clapping to their ears. A moment later she understood why. The voice screamed, rattling her brains inside her head. It was not the voice of the crown, not the thin whisper of Nagash's shadow, but the full-throated howl of the Prince of Rasetra and the last true King of Khemri as he was dragged from his tomb by W'soran's magics. There was nothing of her gentle prince in the mad, billowing shape which lurched from the aperture, its limbs ballooning and thinning like the smoke of a raging fire. It roared and its face became an elephantine skull as it squeezed itself into the chamber.

'Bind him, damn you!' Ushoran roared, fighting to be heard over the tumult. 'Bind his damned soul, W'soran! Do it now!'

W'soran did not reply. His dark parchment-like flesh had gone utterly pale from the strain of the great wreaking which he was attempting. The spirit swept one of Ushoran's warriors up and the vampire flailed like a leaf caught in an updraft. It was crushed against the ceiling of the chamber, reduced to a wreck of bloody meat and crushed armour. Alcadizzar turned, empty eyes seeking more prey. Neferata froze as his eyes lit on her. Her handmaidens dived aside as the spirit swept towards them, but she could not move. She heard them crying out, but she could not answer.

Alcadizzar stopped, his ethereal features inches from hers, his blank eyes staring into her dark ones. She felt the heat of him, and knew that he could burn her form to a cinder, should he so choose. In life, Alcadizzar had been magnificent. In death, he had become something so monstrous that she felt fear for the first time in centuries.

But he did not burn her, or dash her to the stones. Instead he hesitated, his face becoming malformed as it rippled with long-forgotten expression. Again she saw times past, spreading out around them like the wings of some great bird, a kaleidoscope of thought and emotion and lost moments. Of a child whom she had weaned on immortality, of a boy whom she had trained, of a man whom she had come to – what? Had it been love? Or simply desire writ large?

'I wanted…' she croaked, reaching up as if to stroke his cheek. 'I wanted things to be different.'

She saw his end. She felt the tremor of the hissing, smoking blade in his hands as it sheared through Nagash's upraised hand, and felt the foul heat of that same sword as it ate into him, burning his hands raw and black. She saw him stumble through the mountains, naked and broken, his shard-thoughts so sharp that they cut his soul to ribbons even as his body at last began to fail. She saw him clutch Nagash's crown tight to his chest as he sank to his knees in the freezing waters of the river, a living, screaming mummy, his flesh burned tight to bones made strong by the elixirs she had fed him as an infant.

She heard the crown scream as he carried it into the darkness, and how it ripped his soul free of his body, trying to force him to let go. She felt Kadon bind that monstrous soul-thing back into its shell, nearly killing himself in the process. And she saw him release those bindings even as red-eyed death closed in on him. And she knew, then, just what it was W'soran was trying to do and something she thought was sadness flooded her. 'Oh, if you had just given in to fate,' she murmured.

And what of you, Neferata, Alcadizzar whispered, *would you give in?*

Struck, she gaped at the spirit as it suddenly convulsed. Beyond it, visible through its cloudy shape, something horrible swayed in the aperture. It had clawed its way out of the deep places, invigorated by W'soran's magics. Alcadizzar's body, hungry for the return of its soul, was still a mighty thing, even shrunken by death. Withered muscles pulsed beneath cracked and dried flesh as it took a faltering step.

'No,' she hissed. 'No!'

'Yes!' Ushoran howled.

Alcadizzar howled as well, as his spirit was dragged into his corpse. Many of W'soran's acolytes were on their hands and knees, vomiting black blood as their master strained against the dead king's strength. With a shriek, W'soran thrust his arms out, and Alcadizzar's essence splashed against his corpse, seeping into it like an implosion. The thing rocked on its heels and its arms slowly spread, dropping the thing it held.

The strike of the crown against the floor sounded like thunder. 'Now,' Ushoran snarled. 'Now, I will have my vengeance.' He leapt for the wight, his claws sinking into its dried meat. 'Now, I will tear you apart, usurper. I am the master here! *Me!*'

Alcadizzar shrugged, slapping Ushoran to the floor. Though contained, the malevolent spirit yet possessed strength. It groaned, and there was an eternity of agony in the sound. It reached for Ushoran, grabbing his neck and hoisting him off his feet. His guards swarmed it moments later, Khaled among them, hacking and slashing at the undead thing. Bound as it was to a physical frame, it lacked the strength to face that many opponents. The wight staggered and spun as blows struck it. Neferata could only watch helplessly as Alcadizzar fell to his hands and knees, the flickering light in his eye-sockets fading even as Ushoran threw himself on the wight and ripped its head from its body with a massive twist of his shoulders.

'Behold,' Ushoran roared, 'the king is dead.' His eyes fell on the crown. 'Long live the king,' he said more softly. Khaled stepped close to him and Neferata tensed in readiness. Ushoran lifted the crown. It throbbed in his hands, screaming in triumph. Khaled's hand hovered over the hilt of his sword, his eyes on the crown and on its bearer. Tapestries were consumed in balefire along the stone walls and strange shapes seemed to walk between the ripples of otherworldly heat emanating from Ushoran's prize. 'Now,' Neferata hissed. 'Do it now – Khaled, now!'

Khaled's hand jerked away from his sword. The crown settled on Ushoran's head. Neferata shrieked and lunged. She tossed her traitorous servant aside and pounced on Ushoran, her features running like melting wax as they assumed a more daemonic cast. 'It is mine-mine-mineMINEMINEMI–' she shrilled as Ushoran fell over backwards with her on top of him.

The crown neither resisted nor aided her. In truth, it seemed pleased, though it didn't speak. Images and memories not her own washed over her in benediction, and she saw the truth of it all at once. She saw the unmasked face of what lurked within that iron circlet, and heard its lustful glee as it contemplated its future. Not her future or Ushoran's, but rather the future of the thing that it would make of them.

Ushoran howled as her claws found his eyes and he flung her over his head. She crashed into the floor hard enough to crack the stone. Ushoran turned, his body undulating as if it were trying to twist itself into a new shape. Neferata scrambled to her feet and yanked her sword from its sheath. She drove it with all of her might into Ushoran's chest, propelling him backwards up off the floor and against one of the columns in a cloud of stone chips and dust. His talons fell on her arms, lacerating her pale flesh and forcing her to stumble back. Ushoran writhed like a bug pinned to a board, his limbs wriggling independently of one another. He howled and snapped like a wounded wolf, his eyes weeping terrible energies which coruscated around his form.

'Treachery,' one of the Strigoi roared as he lunged for her.

'It's not treachery,' Neferata said, backhanding the vampire with enough force to shatter the front of his skull. 'It's a mercy killing.' But even as she said it, doubts rose fierce, stinging her. The crown seemed to reach for her as Ushoran thrashed, calling to her, crooning.

I will ride you through the gates of the world, it said, each word a dagger of pain. *You will be queen, Neferata, queen of Lahmia, queen of Mourkain and queen of the world, if you but take me up. Throne and crown, Neferata… TAKE ME UP!*

And Neferata, all at once, knew her answer. She spun, tearing herself away from the seductive voice, away from its promises of an eternity of powerful servitude, away from the dark fate laid out for her. She would be queen, but on her own terms.

'Kill her,' W'soran shrieked. 'Rescue your king!' Neferata turned at the necromancer's howl and saw shapes heaving in the weak light of the braziers, casting mutated shadows across the stones. W'soran's ghoul-creatures had entered the throne room on stealthy claws and now they loped towards her, slavering.

An arm, impossibly long, whipped towards her and the talons attached to the blunt fingers gouged the wall as she ducked and spun, plunging her sword into the hollow gut of the ghoul-thing. It screamed and staggered. Rasha and Layla were on it in the instant, hacking and stabbing at it.

Another of the beasts lunged, the bone spurs jutting from the ruptured flesh of its forearms scraping along the floor as it sought to snatch Neferata up. Recalling the strength such creatures possessed, Neferata leapt. Her feet touched its wrist and she bolted up the length of its arm. It reared back as she slid across its shoulders, weasel-quick. Taking her sword in two hands, she drove it through the back of the creature's skull, and the tip emerged between its jaws.

It grunted, coughed and slumped. She yanked her sword free and dropped to the floor before it. Anmar and Naaima had a third beast down on its hands and knees. It groaned piteously and fell, tongue protruding and the fire in its eyes guttering out.

Neferata glimpsed W'soran fleeing the chamber and prepared to follow him when she caught sight of Anmar and saw her handmaiden's eyes widen. Anmar screamed, 'No!'

Neferata turned and gasped as a tearing agony ripped through her. Blood burst through her lips. She looked down at Khaled's sword as it wriggled deeper into her belly. She grabbed the blade and looked at her Kontoi as he stared blankly at her. 'What–' she coughed.

'Why didn't you take it?' he rasped, staring at her accusingly. 'Why couldn't you *just take it*?'

Neferata staggered back, pulling herself off the sword. She pulled the blade as she went, yanking it from Khaled's hands. Around her, her handmaidens were battling Ushoran's guards, but she couldn't focus. The thwarted screams of the crown pounded on the surface of her mind, making it hard to think. She stumbled and turned, bringing the sword up. Ushoran... She had to kill him. He couldn't be allowed to wield the power she had felt.

Ushoran had freed himself, however. He glared at her, hand pressed tight to his belly. But it wasn't Ushoran, not entirely. Something else looked out from behind his eyes and it hated her now, because she had spurned it. Just as Khaled hated her, just as she had hated

Alcadizzar. She saw the whole story of it in Ushoran's eyes and she chuckled.

'You were right,' she said, grinning. 'Spite. It was all for spite.' Then she screamed as Khaled brought Razek's axe down on her shoulder, slamming her to her knees. She dropped the sword and fell onto her face as her flesh burned. As she screamed, her handmaidens raced to her aid.

Ushoran raised his hand and said, in a voice that was not his own, '*STOP.*'

And then Neferata knew nothing more, as the darkness that had once been so welcoming crashed down on her like the blows of a spurned lover.

⟢ FOURTEEN ⟣

*The City of Sartosa
(−1020 Imperial Reckoning)*

Neferata moved gracefully across the coloured tiles of the plaza, her robes trailing behind her. Her servants strode just behind her, shading her from the sunlight with a silk curtain held aloft on poles. 'The druchii can be bargained with,' she said, stirring the air with her hand-fan. 'Who will miss a few hundred fishermen, Abruzzi?'

'Their families, I would assume, Lady Neferata,' Abruzzi of Sartosa said. He was a stiff-necked, heavy-faced man, and he looked uncomfortable in his coarse robes of state. 'I do not know how things are done in Cathay, but here, we do not like to surrender our own folk to beasts from across the sea.'

'Nor do we,' Neferata said, touching his arm. 'But needs must, Abruzzi. Sartosa has no strength at present. The druchii control the seas where the Arabyans do not. We must change that. More, we must have the time to change that,' she said. 'What are a few innocents in comparison to an empire that controls the seas?'

'You say it so prettily, my lady,' Abruzzi grunted, eyeing

her. *'Are all women so cold-blooded in Cathay?'*

'Needs must, my lord,' Neferata said again. She sighed
and tapped her lips with her fan. *'Then, there are... things
that could be done.'*

'Such as?' Abruzzi said, stopping. Neferata paused before
replying. The palazzo was a monument to the alliance of
form and function. The walled garden was open to the sky
and water burbled in the aqueducts that ran along the top
of the walls. There were thick, fleshy plants and brightly
coloured flowers everywhere she looked, and caged song-birds
sang sweetly.

She wondered whether Abruzzi could smell the effluvium
of the dungeons beneath the garden, or whether the gruff
former-soldier knew what strange nourishment her garden
received. A few months after her arrival on a night of chaos
and fire, Neferata had used what wealth she had managed
to bring from Araby to set herself up as a noblewoman from
Cathay in the heart of Sartosa's wealthiest district. Now her
daughters and sisters danced with merchant-princes and
senators at moonlit galas and some had spread beyond, entering the lands to the west and the north.

Some few yet remained in Araby, lurking within harems
and as the young brides of old merchants and noblemen. The
news they sent her was invaluable in building her fortunes
anew, and she could now predict the activities of the pirates
of the gulf with a startling accuracy. She had increased the
wealth of Abruzzi as well, among others.

'There are... secrets, known to me, my lord,' she said,
feigning hesitance. *'We could provide the raiders with their
tribute without sacrificing a single Sartosan.'*

Abruzzi hesitated. He looked at her, but did not ask the
question she knew was foremost on his mind. For that she
respected him. Only a fool asked the obvious question. *'And
if you do this... what?'* he said.

'I would expect an appropriate compensation, commensurate with my standing,' she said prettily.

Abruzzi was silent for a moment, looking at an orange and yellow blossom that nodded in the breeze. He touched the flower and sniffed it. 'You have much aided the senate, my lady, in removing certain obstructions to the furtherance of our influence over the more – ah – short-sighted of our nobility.'

'Best to leave such thankless tasks to an outsider, I have always thought,' she said, fanning herself.

'Hmm.' Abruzzi looked at her. 'Not a single Sartosan, you say? You can spare our people from the bellies of the black arks?'

'Yes,' Neferata said.

'And your appropriate reward?'

'A seat on the senate,' she said. She raised a hand before he could protest. 'Not for me. For a... protégé of mine. His wife has done me many services, and I would see her – and him – rewarded.'

Abruzzi grunted. 'Easily done,' he said.

'Then we have an accord,' Neferata said, smiling...

The Silver Pinnacle
(−326 Imperial Reckoning)

THE SNOW FELL with a silent fury across the mountain. Ice gripped Neferata's hair, changing the once-lustrous mane into something resembling a nest of black snakes. Across her shoulders, the dark-furred cat stirred, its triangular, tufted ears twitching. Yellow eyes opened and a quiet chirp escaped its mouth. She stroked it with her free hand. She wore a heavy bearskin and the black, ornate armour of Ushoran's honour-guard, and the cat nestled between the pauldrons. Neferata moved through the waist-high drifts slowly but steadily, the haft of Razek's axe clenched tightly in her grip. His blood still stained the handle and hers stained the blade, but if there was some meaning in that, she had had little time or desire to contemplate it.

Instead, her eyes found the great stone dragon head that seemed to lunge down towards her through the storm of falling snow, from the heights of the peak. It was a large thing, and bore more than a passing resemblance to the craniums of the giant lizards she had seen in the Southlands. The artistry that had gone into the crafting of it boggled her mind; her people had been known far and wide for their craftsmanship, but even they had lacked the sheer attention to detail that the dragon head displayed. It seemed to have no purpose, jutting as it did from the tightly packed rocks. Her keen eyesight picked out distant outlines that were likely other, similar protrusions, encircling the apex of the peak in a crown of dragons. With difficulty, she pulled her eyes down to examine that which she had come for.

The great doors of Karaz Bryn rose over her, looming bulwarks of stone and ancient metal fashioned by the artisans of a dying race and controlled by mechanisms which mankind would still struggle to understand a thousand years hence. The doors were set into a massive archway that had been decorated with an intricate latticework of carvings that might have depicted anything from legends to episodes of historical significance. The doors themselves were decorated as well, with a profusion of glowering, stylised faces done in the sharp, blocky style preferred by dwarf artisans.

There was a faint glow to those faces and it was one

she knew would be invisible to human eyes. Even she could only glimpse it dimly. There was some magic worked into the very substance of those doors, and it bothered her to look at them for too long.

Even with the snow, her preternatural eyesight picked out the tiny holes where dwarf eyes watched her approach. She could almost hear their thoughts. And she certainly heard the whine of crossbows being readied. She stopped. Her muscles tensed and readied to propel her in one direction or another. Her hold on the axe tightened. The dwarfs had quietly moved to a war-footing in the year since Ushoran had taken Nagash's crown for his own. Trade had not quite dried up, but it was more guarded. Fewer merchants came bearing King Borri's seal. Fewer dwarf-made goods found their way to Mourkain. Even as she had warned Ushoran, the trust of dwarfs was a fragile thing and easily cracked. And she was here now to shatter what remained utterly.

'I request entrance to Karaz Bryn,' she called out, her voice echoing. Minutes passed. Snow settled on her shoulders and head. The cat chirped querulously, and she murmured soft nothings to it.

'Who are you to ask such?' It was a rumble of sound, echoing from the peaks that rose around her and sending small avalanches of snow tumbling from on high. Speaking tubes and amplifying flutes gave it such an effect, she knew. Nonetheless, it was impressive.

The voice spoke in Khazalid. Neferata replied in kind. 'One who has come to return something which was lost,' she shouted, holding the axe up to where the unseen speaker could see the runic insignia stamped on the swell of the blade.

Silence fell. She waited. Minutes passed into hours. Hours passed into days. The cat leapt down from her shoulders and trotted into the darkness, returning some hours later, as if checking on her. She could not fault it for its anxiety. Neferata stood for a time, and then sank to her knees, kneeling in the snow, Razek's axe in her lap. The cold was nothing to her, nor was the snow. It was nothing but an irritation. It was simply another indignity heaped upon the pile.

Ushoran had beaten her.

He had beaten her at her own game. Even as she had undermined him, he had worked a deeper game, breaking apart the bonds of loyalty that she thought unbreakable. She blinked a snowflake from her eye. No, he had not broken it. He had twisted it instead, turning devotion and desire into something altogether more vicious.

Pride was her curse. It always had been. She had too much of it, too much to see the obvious, at times. And she had paid for it again and again. That too she hadn't seen. Not for what it was.

Ushoran had made her bow.

That thought rattled around in her head as she waited. She grimly forced it down, and then it would stubbornly shoot to the surface, taunting her like a splinter beneath her thumbnail.

He had forced her to her knees. He had forced her to swear allegiance to Strigos, to Mourkain, and to him. He had forced them all, though some had gone more willingly than others. Some of it was the crown's influence. That was what Morath had tried to warn her of, what W'soran had been terrified of. Nagash's night-black will made manifest. It was impossible to resist.

That was the only reason she still lived. It stuck in her craw, that thought, but even she wasn't so blind as to pretend it was any other way. She had bowed and

Ushoran had let her live. She was more useful alive than dead. Abhorash was still occupied in the south. Vorag and his rebels had fled towards the Sour Sea, and her former champion doggedly pursued them. W'soran too was gone, fleeing in the months after Ushoran's ascension. Neferata suspected that the old monster was heading south as well, seeking Vorag's protection. That was what she would have done in his place.

That was what she should have done.

Instead, she was here, kneeling in the snow. Her features rippled with a snarl. The cat stiffened and nuzzled her throat, purring softly. She stroked it and fought to control the beast within. There were too many eyes on her and too much depending on her. Her web was stretched thin and fragile and one false move, one moment's surrender would render it so much ragged gossamer on the wind.

Ushoran's power had increased, but not his wisdom. He had unleashed her to do his will, but his will only reached so far. The farther she had gone from Mourkain, the less it had pressed upon her. Now it was barely a feather's weight. Now, she stood before a fortress, with an army, and Ushoran was in Mourkain, confident that he had her held tight in his claws. She closed her eyes.

She would not fail.

And she would not bow again.

On the third day, she heard the squeal of ancient machinery propelled to life and a loose curtain of snow fell as the great doors of the Silver Pinnacle began to swing open. Raising the axe, she strode forwards, the cat once more about her shoulders, the soft rumble of its purr damping the impatience she felt. The momentum of the doors had cleared a great swathe of snow from the path, leaving the ground bare and damp.

There was more magic awaiting her. It was worked into the welcoming sigils that marked the interior archway and as she passed beneath them, they caused Neferata's flesh to prickle. The magic struck at the heart of what she was, circling and trapping her in a ring of unseen fire. It took an effort of will not to slap at her flesh and beat out the invisible flames. On her shoulders, the cat shuddered slightly.

She took hold of herself as the dwarfs came out to meet her, clad in light mail and some carrying high poles with flickering lanterns which threw mad shadows across the rocks and snow. She stood in their light, axe extended, her other hand resting on the pommel of the sword on her hip. Other dwarfs carried crossbows, their bolts aimed unerringly at her.

'*Zanguzaz*,' one spat. That meant blood-drinker. Apparently her agents hadn't managed to hide certain facts from Razek as well as she had thought. It was another failure to set at Khaled's door when this was done. She inclined her head.

'What of it?' she said, meeting their hostile gazes with a bland one. 'I have come to return the ancestral weapon of the Silverfoot clan.' She let them see the axe.

'Where is the one who bore it?' one of the dwarfs barked. She could tell by the decorations in his beard that he was in charge. He bore a resemblance to Razek – he was a brother, perhaps, or more likely a cousin. It mattered little to her. Sympathy was no longer a vice she could afford.

'Dead,' she said simply.

The dwarf closed his eyes, as if the thought pained him. When he opened them, the banal hostility of the watchman had been replaced by something else. For a moment, Neferata thought he might order his warriors to fire, but instead he simply turned and gestured sharply. 'Come.'

The others fell in around her as she was led through the doors. Even as she passed through the archway the doors began to swing shut. She peered up into the gloom, spotting the ancient mechanisms responsible. Massive cogs and gears, the purpose of which escaped her, shifted and spun against one another, setting up a rumble that caused the stone floor beneath her feet to vibrate with a constant hum. She grunted. The cat stretched, yawning. It dropped to the floor silently and retreated into the gloom. If the dwarfs saw, they gave no sign. Their attentions were held with iron rigidity on Neferata, even as she had known they would be. They had not asked for her weapons, for what threat could one woman – even one who drank blood – be to a mighty hold?

The entry hall was massive, with vast fluted galleries that swept up into smooth balconies that looked as if they had been coaxed from the stone by the hands of a sculptor rather than a stonemason. Tiles lined the floors, each one a work of art in and of itself, depicting an act of heroism or courage by a member of the Silverfoot clan. Large ancestor statues, representing past generations of kings, thanes, and lords of the Silver Pinnacle, lined the walls, each ensconced in his own nook.

Glowing globes, containing luminescent liquid, hung from stone half-arches spaced evenly along the length of the hall, casting a soft glow across everything. At the other end of the hall was a second set of great doors. These were another defence measure, sealing off the remainder of the Upper Deep from invasion. She knew both from her conversations with Razek and from her own spies over the centuries that the hold had many entrances – not just the one she had come through. There were doors everywhere on this level and others, some hidden, some not.

Regardless of the size of the attackers' force, there was no way to lay siege to a dwarf hold. A mountain could no more be surrounded than it could be levelled by conventional means. It must be inundated and worn down from within as well as without. Both could take years.

She had months.

The weight of the hold seemed to press down on her as they walked. The thunder of the guards' heartbeats was like some harsh, strange music to her ears, and its tempo aroused a nervousness in her that she was not used to. It was like being close to the beating heart of the world itself, and she desired nothing more than to drive her fangs into it and drink the earth's life away and to leave the rocks grey and barren and the soil cracked and dry. She wanted to drink the world's lifeblood and leave it a husk.

Her knuckles popped as her hands clenched. One of the dwarfs eyed her and exuded the stink of nervousness. That wasn't her thinking those thoughts. It was Nagash's damnable crown. Nagash wanted to eat the world and ride its shell into the darkness between the stars, for an eternity of silence. And Ushoran would help him do it, if there was anything of Ushoran left.

The crown's weight had crushed him the minute he placed it upon his brow. It had shattered his personality into fragments, breaking him the way a man might break a horse. And it had nearly done the same to her. It wanted to break everything. It wanted to render the world a vast charnel pit, peopled only by the dead. And she would be damned to oblivion before she let that happen.

The world was hers; every scrap of dirt, every peasant and lord, human or otherwise. It was hers and Nagash – or his shade – would never have it. She would burn it to ashes before she let that happen. She had lost her city and her empire. She would not lose the world.

Dwarfs in armour marched past, some throwing curious glances her way. Razek had never spoken of the Silver Pinnacle's military might, but she knew that it was substantial. They had easily weathered an orc Waaagh! and Kadon's ill-fated incursions, among other perils. And King Borri had fought against the elves in that distant time when Ulthuan's armies had marched on the dwarf holds.

The Silver Pinnacle would not fall easily. Not to conventional tactics.

A dull rhythmic thudding filled the air. She brushed aside the reverie, concentrating on what was coming. She had been led into a vast chamber, larger even than Ushoran's gaudy monstrosity of an audience chamber. The first thing she saw was the glaring skull of a dragon.

She had never seen one. The closest she had ever come was a glimpse of the saurians of the Southlands, and they were as different from dragons as men were from her kind. The skull was large and studded with horns and it bent over as if in benediction.

Whatever force lingered within those bones, was unwelcoming at best and malevolently hostile at worst. In many ways, it reminded her of the cold malice of Nagash's crown. A vast, ancient presence that threatened to blot out her senses with the effluvium of its passage. *Even Nagash*, the voice of the crown said, *even Nagash would have hesitated to face that thing when it had lived.*

But it was dead now, and its skull and spine and

tattered wings were trophies for the dwarf king who sat glowering beneath it.

The throne beneath the bones was not large, but impressive all the same, as was the squat figure who sat upon it. Borri Silverfoot, King of Karaz Bryn, Lord of the Silver Pinnacle, looked like an ancient version of his son. He was broader, if anything, and heavily built. He wore no robes, only a sleeveless suit of fine mail, belted at the waist by a broad leather belt. On his white head was a simple circlet of office. His only decorations were the silver charms woven into his great beard and the silver bracers which enclosed his massive forearms.

Several figures stood to either side of him. One was a dwarf woman, clad in heavy, pale robes with her head hooded and her hands folded into her sleeves. She carried no weapons, but her eyes burned with something that Neferata could not identify beneath her steel half-mask. A burly bare-chested warrior, more squat than any dwarf she had ever seen before, stood a few steps down from the throne. He held an unadorned axe and his head was shaved, save for a swooping crest of rust-hued hair. His beard had been dyed the same colour, and it had been greased into stiff spikes that stuck out in all directions. Just behind the throne, an elderly dwarf stood, leaning against the haft of his hammer, which was taller than he was. His beard reached to the stone, and hundreds of rune-stones had been threaded through it. The sound they made as they clinked together set Neferata's teeth on edge.

Her escort fell back as she approached the throne and dwarfs in heavy armour with their faces hidden behind iron masks took their place. They carried heavy, but perfectly balanced, hammers in their gauntlets, and looked less like living things than stumping mechanisms. They escorted her to the foot of the throne dais and then formed a living palisade around her. It bore the air of formality and ritual, rather than caution, but she knew that even so, the warriors would be alert to any threat to their king.

'My son is dead,' Borri said, his voice shattering the silence like a hammer ringing on an anvil.

'Yes,' Neferata said. One of the guards took the axe from her hand and carried it reverentially up the steps to the throne. Borri's blunt fingers brushed the bloodstains on the handle and for a moment, his eyes clouded over with pain. Then they snapped back into focus and he flicked his fingers. The warrior laid the axe across Borri's lap and stepped aside to stand with his king.

'How did he die, and how did you come to bring me the news?' Borri said.

'He did not die by my hand, and I was commanded thus,' she said.

A hush fell over the audience chamber, as if every dwarf present had drawn in a breath at the same moment. Borri's expression didn't change.

'The manling lies,' the red-crested dwarf grated. He looked at his king and then at Neferata, and gestured with his axe. 'She lies! Razek was a mighty warrior!'

'Silence, Grund. I asked how he died,' Borri said hollowly. Grund fell silent, glaring at her.

'As a result of treachery,' she said plainly.

'Whose?' Borri said, his fingers curling almost protectively over the haft of the axe.

'My lord Ushoran's,' Neferata said. 'He struck down Razek and his followers.'

'As the runes foretold,' the old dwarf wheezed, his knuckles popping as he tightened his grip on his hammer. 'Razek's doom was writ long ago. This he knew.'

Borri gave a stiff nod. 'It does not mitigate the stain of the misdeed,' he said. Then, more loudly, 'Step forth, Grudgemaster! There is a record to be made!'

An older dwarf, clad in ceremonial robes, stepped forwards from the crowd, cradling a heavy book in his arms. The book was almost as large as the dwarf himself and nearly as thick, and he carried it forwards with difficulty as well as reverence. Its covers were made from thick plates of silver and bronze, and the spine was made of iron. As the book-bearer moved, the king's guard began to rhythmically pound the floor with the heads of their hammers, and a droning dirge rose from the throats of the gathered dwarfs. Neferata's hackles rose as the sound resounded through the hall and coiled around her like restraining chains.

'Be honoured, woman,' Borri said, his voice carrying easily over the dirge. 'You are to pay witness to something sacred.' His eyes were deep and dark and sad as they held hers, and Neferata was once more struck by the thought that the dwarfs would make better allies than enemies. Borri motioned to the bones that loomed over his throne. 'This beast took my father and my brother,' he said solemnly. Grund flinched, looking away. 'I took its life and made its lair into my home. The debt was thus paid. Debts must always be paid.' Neferata said nothing. Borri grunted. 'Good. Your words are neither needed nor welcomed.'

The Grudgemaster ascended the stairs towards the throne, and Grund joined him, sinking to one knee before Borri. The book was placed on Grund's broad back and he grunted as its great weight settled on him. He leaned on his axe for support as the Grudgemaster carefully opened the book. Ancient parchment crackled. The Grudgemaster barked something in Khazalid and a younger dwarf hurried forwards, bearing a heavy stone bowl filled with what Neferata thought might be ink. The Grudgemaster extracted a silver and leather writing implement from within his robes and handed it to Borri, who took it and dipped it into the bowl of ink.

Silence fell. As the echoes of the dirge faded, Borri began to write. And as he wrote, he spoke. 'Let it be henceforth recorded that I, King Borri of Karaz Bryn record this grudge before my people. I name myself grudgesworn against Ushoran, King of Mourkain. He is zanguzaz, and treacherous. By his hand did my son and heir, Razek, Thane of Karaz Bryn, meet his doom. Recompense and reparation are called for, and accounts will be settled in blood. Before my thanes, and my people, and with Grungni, Grimnir and Valaya as my witnesses, I swear this oath.'

The Grudgemaster sprinkled ground stone on the page and Borri carefully blew it off. Then he closed the book and looked up. 'Why did Ushoran do this?' Borri's voice grew soft, but it carried as easily as before. The Grudgemaster took the book up and descended the dais. Grund stood and cracked his neck, working the kinks out.

Neferata shrugged. 'Why ask, mighty king? The result stands. Razek is dead and I am here to demand the surrender of your hold.'

Borri was silent for a moment. Then he laughed. There was no humor in the sound; it was akin to the creaking of rocks just prior to an avalanche, and as he threw back his head, the avalanche fell. The laughter echoed through the silent audience chamber. Unlike in Ushoran's court, no one here picked up the thread and joined their voice to Borri's. The king laughed alone. As the echoes faded, he gazed at her steadily. 'Surrender it to whom, woman?' Borri rumbled.

'To me,' Neferata said.

'Mad as well as a liar,' Grund said. 'By Grimnir's beard, I'll have your head!' He raised his axe and started down the stairs.

'Stay,' Borri said. Grund halted. Neferata smiled. 'She has come under a flag of truce, and audacity buys her mercy. You may leave as you entered, woman. None here will stay you. Go, and leave us to our grief. In time we will meet again, and I shall not be so merciful.'

Neferata didn't move.

'Did you hear me?' Borri said, his voice taking on a menacing edge.

Neferata's reply was to draw her sword and bound over the heads of the hammerers. The dwarfs sprang into motion even as her foot touched the stairs. Her blade looped out, slicing through Borri's beard and sending one of the charms bouncing down the stairs. Borri's hand fastened on the blade and he jerked her forwards even as he drove the tip into the back of his throne. Razek's axe sliced out and she was forced to release her sword and flip backwards to avoid its bite. She landed in a crouch on the stairs, but not for long.

Grund crashed into her, nearly flattening her. His axe cut at her a moment later and she found herself surprised by the crested dwarf's speed. Even as heavy as he looked, he still moved almost as fast as she herself. With a joyful howl, he threw himself at her. 'Take my burden from me, witch!'

Neferata had no idea what he was talking about and she had no intention of finding out. She avoided his wild blows, reeling this way and that and once nearly bending double as he swung at her. Grund's eyes bulged and foam collected at the corners of his jaws as battle-fury swept him up in its embrace. His axe bore no runes or devices. It was simply an axe. But Neferata was loath to test its edge. She sprang back from him, putting a large span between her and the dais.

But even as she landed, hammers crashed into the stone, narrowly missing her as she danced and wove through the throng of guards that sought to bring her down. She caught a hammer on her palm. Even as her fingers curled around its head, she yelped. Smoke rose from her palm as she jerked it out of its wielder's grip and grabbed the haft, lashing out with the weapon. A dwarf flew backwards, his helm crushed and the skull beneath turned to paste. Another crumpled, his breastbone shattered despite the protection of his armour. Neferata's frenzied assault drove the hammerers back, and they spread out, surrounding her but staying out of her reach. She turned slowly in place, keeping them all in sight.

'What did you think to accomplish?' Borri said, rising from his seat. He jerked her sword from his throne and hurled it clattering to the floor. He stared at the blood welling from his palm and flexed his hand as if the blade had caused him no more pain than an insect bite. 'Did you think to assassinate me? Did you hope to remove the heart from my people?' He grunted. 'We dwarfs are not as men. We do not quail when our own die. We fight all the harder.'

He came down the stairs, still holding his son's axe. The robed woman and the elderly dwarf followed him, and Grund paced in front, trembling like a hound on a leash. 'This axe has tasted your blood, I think. It thirsts for it still, regardless,' Borri said.

'It shall have to work to get another taste,' Neferata said, shaking her palm. Something had burned her. She saw that the head of the hammer was shot through with threads of silver and growled. Razek's axe had been the same.

'Not as hard as all that, I think,' Borri said grimly. 'You are alone, woman. Outnumbered and surrounded. Surrender and I will be merciful. That offer still holds.'

'I think our concepts of mercy differ greatly, King Borri,' Neferata said, twirling the hammer in her hands. It was a good weapon, but too brutal for her tastes. She spun on her heel and sent the hammer flying towards Borri. She did not wait to see whether it struck its target. Instead, as all eyes followed the hammer, she leapt for an opening in the ring of flesh and steel that encircled her.

Behind her, she heard the ring of metal on metal and Borri bellowed a command. The floor trembled as the hammerers followed her. Crossbows thrummed and quarrels peppered the floor and walls. Neferata avoided each one with ease. To one with her senses, the bolts appeared to be moving in slow motion. She could see the very air split and twist as the bolts cut through it. Even as the bolts struck the archway of the audience chamber, she was into the corridor beyond and running. She had wasted enough time.

Horns sounded in the deeps, warning the hold of danger. She knew that the horns were not for her. The corridor trembled as the great gate began to open once more. Frigid air slithered into the hold, greeting her as she reached the entry chamber even as the doors began to spread wide.

Naaima stood before the doors, surrounded by dwarfs seeking to bring her down. Broad shapes stabbed at her, and her pale flesh was streaked with black blood. Neferata struck the gate-wardens like a thunderbolt. Her talons sank into the back of a dwarf's head and she jerked him backwards with savage force, snapping his neck and crushing his skull like an egg. More dwarfs flooded into the entry hall through the second set of doors.

'Did you get the gates?' Neferata snarled, snatching an axe from a dwarf's hand and burying it immediately in its owner's face. A moment later she was forced to use it to deflect a crossbow bolt.

'They're opening, aren't they?' Naaima replied, narrowly avoiding a blow that would have taken her arm off at the shoulder. Her rejoinder ripped the dwarf's face from his skull.

'Then we only have to hold on for a bit longer,' Neferata said. Even as the words left her lips, a trio of crossbow bolts sank into her back, puncturing her armour like paper and knocking her to the ground. She screamed in pain and surprise, and flopped around for a moment like a fish in the bottom of a boat, before pushing herself to her feet, the heads of the bolts scraping against her insides as she moved. She coughed blood and awkwardly plucked one of the bolts free.

'Shoot her again!' the watch-warden commanded. 'Bring her down!' He was the one who had escorted her into Borri's presence, the one who resembled Razek.

Neferata growled low in her throat and sent the bloody bolt flying into one of the crossbowmen, knocking the dwarf backwards with the impact. Naaima yanked the others free as she and Neferata began to back towards the widening portal. Gears groaned as the massive doors allowed a cold wind inside, and a flurry of snow.

More dwarfs filled the entry hall, all armed and seemingly intent on using those weapons on her. Horns sounded loud, low and long from the side-passages and the upper balconies. Neferata scanned the ranks of dwarfs; in minutes, a hundred or more crossbows were aimed at her. And behind the line, King Borri and his hammerers.

'Get that damned gate closed!' the king roared. 'She's trying to escape!'

'She won't get far,' the watch-warden roared. 'This is for my cousin, hag!' His axe licked out, gouging her armour. She swatted him aside, sending him crashing to the floor and his axe flying.

'Escape is for the defeated,' Neferata said, stepping back into the opening. With the air of a performer, she threw back her head and extended her arms. 'Enter, my loves, and be welcome!' she howled. Snow spun around her and behind her and the white expanse was suddenly shattered by black shapes that burst from it like abominable shooting stars.

The wolves were more carcass than carnivore, but they were dangerous for all that. Twice as savage in death as they had been in life, the large beasts loped into the hold, fleshless jaws agape and an alien hunger burning in their lifeless eyes. They stank of ancient places and secret crimes and the sight of them caused the closest dwarfs to hesitate, though only for a moment. But that moment was enough. The wolves hit the line, absorbing hastily-fired crossbow bolts as if they were no more than mosquito bites. They made no sound as they crashed into their prey, but the dwarfs screamed well enough.

Behind the wolves came Neferata's handmaidens, their armour crusted over with ice. Khaled sprang past her, his face tight and feral with pleasure as he tossed her a sword. 'You look as if you could use this,' he said nastily, his tongue writhing between his fangs like a red snake.

She snatched the blade out of the air without replying.

Khaled laughed at her silence and strode past her, as the handmaidens clustered about her. Anmar looked at her worriedly. The young woman had taken to staying by her brother's side in the weeks since they'd set out from Mourkain. Perhaps Anmar suspected that her brother's manner and method would see a Strigoi sword in his back, or maybe she feared that Neferata would attempt to wreak her revenge sooner rather than later. She hesitated, torn between her mistress and her brother. 'Lady,' she began.

'Follow your master, whelp,' Neferata hissed. Anmar stepped back, as if slapped. She spun and followed Khaled into battle. Neferata watched her go and then turned to Iona and the others. 'Help them. We need to drive the dwarfs back and hold this point. Everything depends on it. Go!'

The vampires sprang into motion, still one moment and then flashing forwards, shadows thick with kill-urge. The other end of the entry-hall was slick with blood as the organised ranks of the dwarfs crumbled into a melee. The wolves stalked among them, dragging dwarfs down and mauling them. The vampires flung themselves into the confusion with fierce glee, Khaled in the lead.

'He's heading for Borri,' Naaima said. Neferata frowned.

'Can't have that, can we? I need more time.' She looked at her handmaiden. 'See to the advance. Morath and the others need to hurry. I will see to the rest.'

'Are you—' Naaima began, casting a dark look at Khaled. She reached up, almost but not quite touching Neferata. Neferata grabbed her hand.

'Go,' she said. 'And hurry.'

Naaima nodded and turned, sprinting into the snow.

Neferata tightened her grip on her sword and threw herself into the red sea of battle. Khaled was carving a wet path to Borri, who seemed determined not to allow the invasion of his hold to progress further. A rotting wolf lunged out of the confusion towards the king, but Grund slapped it from the air and crushed its skull to powder with his foot. More horns were sounding now, so many that the stone seemed to vibrate with their sound. There were more guards in the high places, and crossbow bolts dropped like rain. Nearby, a wolf stumbled and fell, its unnaturally invigorated form looking like a hedgehog for all the bolts jutting from it. Neferata swatted a bolt from the air and searched for her former servant.

Khaled spat Arabyan oaths as his sword chopped down on a dwarf. He kicked the body aside and then the way was clear, save for the mad-eyed Grund. Nostrils flaring, the red-bearded dwarf made to face Khaled, but Borri stopped him with a look. 'No, this is not your doom,' Borri said. Grund cursed, his lips writhing back from rows of filed teeth.

'Let me have my doom, brother!' he shrieked, his muscles rippling with tension. The raw agony in his voice gave pause even to Khaled, who hesitated. 'Please,' Grund spat, as if the word were a razor, slicing his throat to shreds even as it escaped.

'No,' Borri said. He pointed his hammer at Khaled. 'This is my kill.' As Grund stepped back Khaled trotted forwards, more confident now, and Borri waited with his son's axe in one hand and a hammer in the other. 'Come on then, corpse-eater,' Borri said. 'Some of us have kingdoms to run.'

Khaled obliged, diving forwards like a bird of prey, his sword extended. Borri took a half-step back, his hammer beating the blow aside and his axe ringing off Khaled's pauldron, staggering the vampire. The hammer swam upwards, the edge of the head catching Khaled on the chin. Borri moved even faster than his son, Neferata realised. Then, Razek had been a diplomat, not a warrior. Borri was a king of the old style – a warrior down to his very bones.

He had fought elves once, in an age when men hid in caves, and likely worse things. Khaled, for all the inhuman ferocity that flowed from him, was as nothing to the things that Borri had seen in his darkest moments, Neferata knew.

Khaled staggered back, his shattered jaw re-knitting itself. Neferata tensed, hoping that Borri could finish the job. It would make things simpler in the long run. But such was not to be. Khaled, aware of what he faced now, avoided the next blow and his sword lightly stroked the side of Borri's face, opening a gash that stretched from jowl to brow. The dwarf didn't hesitate, barrelling into the vampire, who squirmed backwards, letting his sword dart out to prick the dwarf's face and uncovered arms.

Neferata hissed. Khaled was attempting to draw Borri away from his guard. Once out of the protective envelope of steel and muscle, he would be surrounded, cut off and brought down. Khaled wasn't playing champion, he was playing bait. With the king dead, it was very likely that the dwarfs would retreat. And with Borri dead, taking the hold would be an easier, quicker affair. And Neferata couldn't allow that.

She flew across the distance separating her from the combatants. She threw herself in among the hammerers, cutting down one with a grunt of effort. Even as strong as she was, cutting through the solid mass of an armoured dwarf was no easy task. A hammer connected with her hip, cracking bone, and she turned her stumble into a leap, crashing into Khaled and sending them both flying. Borri's guards raced to surround their lord and Khaled was forced to slither out of reach of their weapons.

Her former servant glared murder at her, but she pretended not to see. Her sword sliced out, cutting the head from a hammerer, and then she was up and limping back.

'What were you–' Khaled raged, grabbing her arm. Neferata shook him loose.

'Keep the gate open, fool!' she snapped, gesturing to the winch mechanism that controlled the gate. Several dwarfs were attempting to fight their way towards it. Khaled uttered a snarl and bounded towards them, his sword snicker-snacking out to relieve one of the warriors of his bearded head. Neferata grinned and turned back to Borri. The king's eyes met hers, and she knew that he knew that the dwarfs were going to lose control of the gate. 'Fall back, mighty king,' she murmured. 'Stall with all of your might. Make us pay in blood for every metre.'

As if he had heard her, Borri's eyes narrowed. Then he raised his hand. One of his hammerers put a curling ram's-horn to his lips and blew a single, sorrowful note. The remaining dwarfs in the gallery began to fall back, even as they attempted to pull themselves into something resembling a battle-order. The sound of great pistons shook the chamber and Neferata looked up. Some dwarfs scrambled across the balconies, moving pulleys and wheels into motion even as others covered the retreat of their fellows with another barrage of crossbow bolts.

'What in Usirian's name are they doing?' a vampire snarled as she plucked a bolt from her thigh. Neferata snorted.

'Exactly what I supposed they'd do. They're sealing the entry hall.'

'We have to stop them!' Khaled snarled, gesturing with his sword.

'No, not us,' Neferata said. She turned her face to the snowy wind. A thin black shape galloped through the doorway on a horse that was nothing but bone and balefire. Morath glared about him with hollow eyes as his arrival scattered the gathered vampires. The snow turned to steam as it touched him. Large leather-winged shapes joined him, swooping up towards the balconies with predatory shrieks.

'Just in time,' Neferata said, sheathing her sword.

'It took more than I suspected to keep the bats flying in the storm. Even dead flesh and necromancy have their limits,' Morath said, watching as the fell-bats attacked the dwarfs above. One by one, they either retreated or died, and soon not one living dwarf remained in the entry hall.

A moment later, the chamber resounded with the sounds of the inner doors of the hold slamming shut as one.

The siege of the Silver Pinnacle had begun.

⟡ FIFTEEN ⟡

The Tilean Coast
(-1020 Imperial Reckoning)

The village clung to the rocky coast, a swift wind from the shores of Sartosa. Neferata leapt from the galley even as it crunched into the soft sand. She wore dark robes over her armour, as did her followers. Naaima, having no taste for such things, had stayed behind. Khaled and Anmar, however, had been eager to come. The siblings followed her up across the shore, their expressions hungry.

'An exquisite plan, my queen,' Khaled murmured. 'We shall lull the druchii into complacency and then strike.'

'We will strike, won't we? I detest those creatures,' Anmar said. 'I detest handing people over to them even more.' The young woman looked pensive. There was no moon and a thick mist crept inland from the sea, obscuring them from anyone who might have been watching.

'Rather than feasting on them yourself, you mean,' Khaled countered, grinning.

'Among other reasons,' Anmar said primly.

'Yes, it is a detestable business, but it is necessary,' Neferata said. 'We must ensure our influence takes root in the senate, and we need allies among the old ruling class. Sparing their people the druchii levy will see to that.'

'I still don't see why we don't simply take power,' Khaled said. 'None could gainsay us.'

'As we tried in Bel Aliad, you mean?' Neferata asked pointedly. She turned on him. 'Only a fool does not learn the lessons of the past, my Kontoi. Are you a fool?'

'He meant no insult, my lady,' Anmar said quickly.

Khaled glared at his sister, but said nothing. Neferata sniffed and continued on. Regardless of the necessity of the thing, she had to admit that it had been too long since they had hunted properly. Murder and bloodshed were things that she had learned to avoid, following the events in Bel Aliad. No sense in alerting the hounds to the trail, was there? And there was even less sense in revealing yourself to the hawk.

She restrained a growl and instinctively searched the shadows, though there was no cause. The angry dead were an ocean away and her nemesis was with them. Let Arkhan waste his immortality fighting opponents who couldn't be killed. She had no reason to do so. The world was large enough.

And it's not as if you were frightened, said her treacherous thoughts. It's not as if seeing her again shook the very foundations of your sense of self.

There had been such hatred there, in her eyes. All-consuming and terrifying. Would she have hated so much, had she accepted Neferata's kiss? Neferata glanced at the siblings, wondering whether the same hatred lingered in their hearts. Did they resent her? Did it matter, as long as they feared her? Khaled looked at her, and in his eyes she saw only the same mingled hunger and desire that was always there. He was a yawning void of need, always wanting what he could not have, always demanding what could not be given.

She knew that he was mad, even as his sister was mad, and she herself was the maddest of them all. The world was mad; a world where the dead walked and the proper order had turned topsy-turvy.

Behind them, she heard the soft pad of the feet of the ghouls they had brought from Sartosa – the sad, tattered remnants of the great ghoul-cult of Mordig – as they slipped from the bellies of the galleys that had brought them. Over a hundred of the creatures followed them inland as they moved towards the sleepy village.

'Take them,' Neferata hissed. The ghouls swarmed past her, loping towards the village…

The Silver Pinnacle
(–326 Imperial Reckoning)

HEAVY MAULS STRUCK the massive interior doors that led into the hold. The mammoth ghouls who wielded them were even bigger than the creatures Neferata had faced. W'soran had outdone himself, fattening the beasts on the blood of her co-conspirators. Sticky protrusions of bone stuck out from their elephantine hides and their lungs flexed like bellows as they pounded unceasingly at the ancient portal, filling the air with thunderous groans as well as the reverberation of metal on metal. There were six of them, and Neferata knew that twice that number wouldn't have been enough to bring down the doors. Not with the enchantments woven into the very core of their creation.

Behind the beasts, the silent ranks of the dead, their number swelled by the disgorged inhabitants of the great barrows and mass graves that riddled these hills, waited. Hundreds of tribes had come and gone in the centuries since Kadon had first raised Mourkain from the rock, and the dead of those tribes yet remained, if one knew where to look.

Amongst the dead, Morath sat astride his skeletal horse, surrounded by a vanguard of Strigoi, all clad in the black armour of Mourkain's foundries. Ushoran had sent his most eager warriors to accompany her in her task. Or perhaps they were his most expendable ones. Some were fierce berserkers, like Dragoj or Racki, who had been among the first to turn on Vorag when he had faltered. Others, like taciturn Redzik and his clinging shadow Dzaja, were seasoned campaigners sent to keep hold of the reins. And then there were the overly-ambitious fence-sitters like Zandor and his cronies; they had sat out the coup, waiting to jump to the side of the victors. Now they sought to prove their loyalty with the over-enthusiastic fanaticism of the new convert.

Neferata and her handmaidens waited off to the side. 'We're not getting in this way,' she murmured.

'Then what would you suggest we do? Talk them into opening those doors?' Khaled said, striding towards them through the ranks of skeletons. He looked at Neferata. 'Then maybe you could, at that,' he added.

'I wouldn't dream of interfering,' Neferata said smoothly.

'You're supposed to be leading this little sortie, or had you forgotten?' Khaled growled, not quite meeting her eyes. He didn't dare, not even now.

'You're quite the one for determining what I'm supposed to be doing, aren't you, my Kontoi?'

'Horns,' Naaima interjected.

'They've been tootling for all they're worth since this began,' Khaled snapped. 'What matters a bit more noise?' He shot a glare at Naaima for daring to interrupt.

Neferata looked at Naaima. 'Different horns,' the former said. 'Different signals, but to whom–'

There was a sound like stone snapping and then a wave of heat blew through the open outer doors, heralding the arrival of a downpour of molten rock. The bubbling, burning brew struck the lead elements of the undead army. Though the dead seemed unconcerned, the magma dissolved animated bone and ancient armour alike, reducing far too many of them to slag. Morath jerked his mount's reins, forcing it to back up as the seeping edges of the spillage crept into the entryway. Nonetheless, the sudden rush of heat caused the skin of his face to blister and Morath grunted in pain. One of the Strigoi shrieked as a bit of the burning substance spattered him, and he staggered and fell, clawing at flesh which had suddenly assumed the consistency of stewed chicken.

'Them,' Anmar said, her voice filled with horror.

Neferata suddenly recalled the odd stone dragon head which had protruded from the lofty upper peaks of the mountain. It had seemed out of place at the time, but its purpose was plain now. 'Clever, clever creatures,' she snarled. Then, 'They're cutting our forces in half!' she said, gesturing towards the ceiling with her sword. 'We have to destroy that thing.'

'The dead don't mind it,' Khaled protested, his eyes wide as he stared at the hissing, bubbling rock.

'Of course not, they're dead,' Morath nearly shrieked. One hand was pressed to his face. 'But they can be destroyed by it easily enough! I can't revivify melted bone.'

Khaled snarled and shared a look with Redzik. The Strigoi was rangy and hawk-like and was a seasoned warrior, lacking Vorag's bluster or Gashnag's pomposity. He nodded and gestured to two of his fellows. 'Jirek, Dinic, get up there,' he growled. The two vampires hesitated, looking at their fallen fellow, who had been dragged from the burning liquid but whose healing was slow to begin. He mewled piteously, and his face looked like one overlarge raw wound. Redzik grunted and cast his gaze at Zandor. 'What about you?'

'I think not,' the ajal said, stepping back, his hands raised.

Neferata snorted. 'The courage of Strigos is legendary,' she said. 'I'll go.'

'Not alone,' Anmar said. Neferata looked at the girl for a moment, and then nodded. Khaled growled.

'Foolishness. Fine, Jirek, Dinic, come with me, the rest of you organise some sort of defence – the dwarfs won't sit idle. They'll try to crush us between the hammer and the anvil. We'll soon have every warrior in this rat-hole at our throats.' For a moment, Khaled shed the lethargy of the predator and was once more the Kontoi he had been in life. He looked at Neferata. 'After you, my lady,' he said.

'Too kind,' Neferata murmured. The magma had cooled into a black splotch across the snow. Bone limbs twitched as it hardened. She stepped lightly across it and began to ascend towards the peak, moving as swiftly as she was able. Anmar followed close at her heels and the others just behind. The snow had been melted away, revealing the carefully crafted runnels which had been installed to conduct the flow of the magma. The ingenuity of the dwarfs was impressive. They were a people who thought defensively, preparing for onslaughts which might never come. Neferata could respect that sort of cunning.

The wind smashed against them as they climbed, and the snow fell in great clumps. They didn't feel the cold, but it played merry havoc with their senses, rendering sight, smell and sound unreliable. Nonetheless, the vampires climbed quickly, following the runnel. Neferata caught a scrape of stone on stone and reached out to touch the edge of the runnel. It trembled slightly. 'Take cover!' she shouted, throwing herself to the side. The others did as she did even as a blistering explosion of fiery liquid sluiced down from on high, throwing up fumes and steam. The Strigoi, Dinic, wasn't fast enough and he howled as the magma caught him.

Neferata watched as Dinic staggered to his feet, enshrouded in burning liquid. The magma seemed to reach out and enfold him in molten fingers. The vampire's screams rose in pitch as his flesh crumbled off his bones. Tearing at himself, Dinic stumbled back and fell into the runnel, dissolving even as he hit the magma flow.

'That's done it,' Neferata said. She sprang to her feet as the last of the magma slid away and dropped into the runnel. 'They know we're coming – hurry!' The stone of the runnel was painfully hot and her flesh reddened and blistered as she ran. She ignored the pain. It was an easier path than climbing the mountain, and more effective. The stone maw of the dragon rose over her. She leapt up, slithering between its char-black fangs and down its throat.

She only had moments before what she was doing would go from a brilliant idea to a bad one. She hoped the others were following close behind. She hurtled through the dragon's throat and a very surprised set of features filled her vision. The dwarf jerked back with an oath that was cut short as her sword found his throat.

She whipped the blade out, decapitating him even as she emerged from the tunnel and into the hidden tower.

It was a circular stone room, with flues set into the walls and a number of heavy pipes and sluice-works crisscrossing the walls and ceiling. It stank of sulphur and raw heat. Five dwarfs were there to greet her. Only one reacted quickly, grabbing a handy hammer and swinging it towards her head. In the cramped confines of the tower, she had little room to manoeuvre and was forced to let the weapon connect. Her skull rang and she swung wildly, driving the warrior back. He spat something in Khazalid and one of the others dived for a crossbow leaning against the wall. Neferata hurled her sword, pinning the would-be crossbowman to the wall in mid-flight. With a snarl, she dived on the hammer-wielder, bearing him to the ground, her vision still swimming from the force of the hammer-blow. The others closed in.

The rock ceiling cracked and shuddered above them, causing the dwarfs to look up in shock. Neferata concentrated on her prey, bashing the dwarf's skull against the floor until his head cracked like an egg and what was within slopped out. Even as she rose, the ceiling came away in great chunks, ripped apart by Khaled and Jirek. Anmar dived in through one of the newly-made holes, and her sword flashed in a tight arc, gutting one of the dwarfs. The others reacted by fleeing for the trapdoor which led down from their perch.

'Grab them!' Neferata spat. Khaled sprang past her, his talons tangling in one of the dwarf's braids and hair. He hauled the burly shape off its feet and swung the dwarf around, hurling him out through the gap in the roof to smash himself lifeless on the mountain-side below. Jirek caught the other even as he descended, tackling him with a scream like a hungry tiger. Dwarf and vampire tumbled down into whatever was below. Khaled almost followed, but Anmar grabbed him.

'Wait!' she said.

There was a concert of screams from below. Neferata ducked her head down, and her lips writhed back from her fangs in disgust. Jirek and his prey had blundered into the delivery system for the magma. Specially treated pipes had burst and the room swam with heat as magma sprayed and dripped, coating walls, floor and combatants liberally.

Neferata retreated. 'Fool,' she said, kicking the stone trapdoor into place. The floor was already growing warm. 'That artifice would have been useful.'

'Jirek was more useful,' Khaled said, glaring at her.

'Debatable,' Neferata said. 'Nonetheless, we must make sure that there are no other surprises waiting for us. The dawi are cunning, and I'd rather they didn't find a way to make the mountain vomit its guts all over us.' She jumped lightly onto the wall and climbed out onto the roof.

The panorama of the Worlds Edge Mountains spread out around her, vast and uncaring of the war begun in its depths. Above, the sky was the colour of tar and the snow spiralled down like tears. She reached out, setting her talons on the horizon, even as she had done as a girl, visualising what would be hers. With a grunt, she drew her hand back. Tossing her head, she brushed her windblown hair out of her eyes and spotted the black shape of a river slithering out away from the mountain. She smiled.

Khaled and Anmar joined her a moment later. 'We destroyed the pipes and devices. This thing is no threat now,' Khaled said.

'Oh, well done, dog of Mourkain,' Neferata said. 'You do your master proud.'

Khaled grabbed her arm. 'I would have done the same for you if you had let me,' he said. 'I would have served you forever,' he continued, almost pleadingly.

'You serve none but your own lusts, my Kontoi. I saw that clearly in Bel Aliad, before I first kissed you,' Neferata said, placing her fingers along his cheek. 'And I will acknowledge no desire save my own.' Her claws scraped his face, opening the flesh to the kiss of the cold wind. Khaled stepped back, releasing her. His eyes hardened.

'Ushoran says different,' he sneered, gesturing to her throat.

Neferata smiled softly and licked his blood from her fingers. 'What he says and what you hear are two different things, my sweet, savage, sad son. And that you never saw that is one of the reasons why I am glad to be rid of your tedious love.'

Khaled snarled, but Neferata turned away and leapt off the tower. She dropped into the snow and started back down.

The dwarfs did not remain idle after the failure of their dragon-weapon. Neferata soon found herself wishing that they had, if only to provide respite from the dangerous tedium that followed. Two weeks passed in the wake of the dwarfs' flight into the lower regions of their realm, but, like all vermin, they refused to stay in their holes.

Instead, they had displayed the unguessed intricacies of their craftsmanship. There were apparently innumerable hidden passageways and concealed doors and the dwarfs had sallied forth three times in strength, pummelling the dead before retreating into their hidden enclaves. Others had crept from unseen points to set off explosions and fire crossbows into the vampires and ghouls. They had already lost four of the Strigoi vampires to such tactics, and the remaining warriors were becoming unsettled and impatient. When not fending off these attacks, Neferata and the Strigoi passed the time in fruitless debate.

'There must be more than one way in,' Morath said testily. He looked half-dead, and weird lights flickered beneath his skin. He sagged in his saddle. The stink of exhaustion seeped from his pores.

'There are a number of ways in. Finding them, however, is another matter,' Neferata said, resting on her haunches, her chin pressed to the pommel of her sword, her fingers draped over the hilt. It was not the most regal position, but it suited her mood. She stared out at the blizzard.

'Who says we have to find them, eh?' Zandor said. 'We just set those bone-bags we brought with us to chipping away at this anthill until we make a passage.'

'Do you have any concept of how much power and time that would require?' Morath snapped. 'No, of course you don't.'

Zandor growled at the necromancer, his normally handsome features lengthening into something lupine. 'Watch your tone, meat, or I'll–'

'You'll what?' Neferata said, without turning from the snow. 'In case you had forgotten, Zandor, I require Morath's services more than yours, indispensible as they are.'

'And you'll hold your tongue, witch,' Zandor said, grinning at her in a lopsided fashion. 'You're only here because Ushoran still professes to respect your abilities. But if you give us trouble–'

'Your head will be the first to touch the dust,' Anmar

said, tapping Zandor's throat with the flat of her sword. The other Strigoi snarled like a pack of dogs. Neferata's handmaidens drew closer to her. She herself neither moved, nor paid attention to the ongoing confrontation.

'Quiet!' Khaled roared. He looked at Neferata. 'What are you thinking?'

'The river,' Neferata said. 'The river is the way in. It travels beneath the mountain.'

Morath's eyes lit up with realisation. 'It might be possible, yes. A small group, no more than a hundred,' he said. Then he frowned. 'No. No it won't work. My abilities are great, but the strain...'

'Not you. Me,' Neferata said, rising to her feet.

'Your grasp of the necessary magics is incomplete,' Morath said slowly.

'Then complete it,' Neferata said. 'Teach me, Morath. You will find me a most apt pupil...'

'No!' Khaled barked.

'Quiet, Arabyan,' Zandor snapped. 'Why shouldn't we? If the witch wishes to leave the glory to us while she sneaks in the back door, let her. A few tricks might help her distract the dwarfs for more than a few moments before they take her traitorous head.'

'Your support is noted and appreciated, Zandor,' Neferata said. 'It will take time, of course.' She looked at Khaled. 'But I'm sure we can find something to occupy our days and weeks, no?'

He made a face and looked at the immense inner doors that sealed the rest of the hold away from the entry-chamber. The Upper Deep was theirs, but getting into the lower levels would be difficult. More than difficult, in fact; near impossible, even with the forces at their disposal, unless something tipped the balance in their favour.

Neferata inclined her head as Khaled glared at her. 'What would you suggest?' he grated.

'Come, come, my Kontoi, surely you have taken part in sieges before?' Neferata said. 'There are things which must be done.'

His eyes lit up with understanding. 'As ever, my queen, you are correct,' he said. He grimaced a moment later as he realised what he had said. Neferata gave no sign that she had heard.

In the days that followed, the dead fell easily into old routines formed in life. Roving patrols of skeletal horsemen rode through the claws of the weather that gripped the mountains, their ancient bronze armour green with verdigris and sheathed in ice. Corpse-wolves loped through the scrub forests of the mountain slopes, hunting for the merest whiff of warm blood. And the ranks of the numberless dead swelled day by day as Morath pulled them from their crude graves.

Neferata had made her camp out of the grip of the blizzard that continued to batter the region, within the entrance hall. A pavilion tent had been erected by fleshless hands and filled with luxuries, brought specifically for that purpose from Mourkain. Even if she was being forced to play general for Ushoran, there was no reason she couldn't do so in comfort. She studied the old scrolls while lying on a pile of cushions, handing them to her handmaidens when she had finished. Of them all, only Naaima seemed to have grasped the art of the magics as well as she, but the others would learn in time.

Morath stood in the centre of the tent, warming his hands over a brazier. He wore heavy furs over his slender form and dark circles weighted down his eyes. The tent flap was opened and Redzik, one of the Strigoi, stepped in, snow falling from him in clumps. 'We've found it,' he said.

Neferata tossed aside a scroll. 'Where is it?'

'Just where you said,' Redzik said. 'The wolves sniffed it out. The river goes right into the mountain's guts.' He hesitated. 'It's iced over, though. Probably why there's no guard on it. No telling how deep the ice runs...'

'It doesn't matter,' Neferata said, stretching. 'It's time.' She looked at Morath. 'You know what to do?'

'Knowing and accomplishing are two different things,' the necromancer spat. He shivered. Neferata reached out and gently stroked his cheek with the edge of her palm. Morath shuddered. She smiled gently.

'I have faith, my sweet Morath, as should you. After all, does not a god stand at our side?' Like the rest of them, he had stood frozen as Ushoran became something terrible. Morath's prediction had come true, and he had done nothing to prevent it.

'I'm... I am sorry,' he croaked, after a short silence. He looked away.

'Men are always sorry, after the fact,' Neferata said, running her fingers across his shoulders. 'But it is not you from whom I will accept an apology. You're a dog, Morath, and a dog can be forgiven biting at the whim of its master.'

He jerked as if she had struck him. 'Mourkain–' he began hoarsely.

'Mourkain would have been a paradise,' she said, turning to follow Redzik out of the tent. Naaima and her handmaidens paced after her, checking their weapons and armour.

'You do not have to do this,' Anmar said as Neferata approached. 'Naaima could go, or even Layla,' she suggested, taking Neferata's hand.

Neferata was silent for a moment. Vampires could not feel regret; or, rather, none she had known had ever displayed such. But what was writ on Anmar's face was as close to it as she thought that they could get.

'And what would I do, little leopard?' Neferata said. 'Would you have me sit and sulk in my tent? Or would you rather me sit and ponder the intricacies of your brother's betrayal?'

The remark was spiteful, and Anmar took it as such. She pulled back. Neferata hesitated, wanting to reassure her, but knowing that there was no purpose to such a gesture. She was going to kill Khaled and Anmar too, if she interfered. She would kill all of the traitors and fools. Instead, she said, 'You have made your choice, little leopard. You have chosen your brother over me.'

'Could I do otherwise?'

'Only you can say,' Neferata said, turning away. 'Blood calls to blood and like to like. I made a mistake with your brother. I should have left him dead on the floor of his secret room, and taken only you. But even then, I knew I could not separate you. It seems nothing will.'

She strode away, noting Khaled approaching as she did so. She wondered whether he had heard. From his expression, she guessed that he had. A momentary surge of satisfaction lifted her mood as she stepped outside. The wind and cold enveloped her and she welcomed it.

Besides her handmaidens, a troop of skeletal horsemen and spearmen, their bones coated in glistening ice, accompanied her. A token force and one she intended to leave near the river. There would be plenty of dead within the hold for her to manipulate, if she were right.

The dwarfs entombed their dead, as W'soran's studies of Mourkain's depths had shown. There were generations upon generations, going back to the first inhabitants of the hold, all waiting for her gentle summons to march to war against their kin. They would catch the dawi in a pincer, between two walls of bone and metal.

When they reached the river, she found that it had indeed frozen solid, just as Redzik said. Neferata stood on a bluff overlooking the river, Naaima and Iona beside her. They had left the others below, out of sight, with the dead. Neferata sniffed the wind. Several of the corpse-wolves were prowling nearby, their gait awkward and uneven.

'We'll set the dead to shattering the river. Once we have a hole, we'll go down,' she said. 'We will awaken the dead of the hold even as the Strigoi batter their way in. If need be, we will of course open the doors for them again. Eventually.'

'Are you certain that this is wise?' Naaima said.

She was eyeing the river distrustfully, but Neferata knew she wasn't actually talking about that. 'No,' Neferata said. 'But we face two enemies here, not one. And we cannot strike until they are both properly weakened.' She looked askance at Naaima. 'Or would you have me remain a slave?'

'I would have you live,' Naaima said, not looking at her.

Neferata stared at her for a moment longer. Then she looked at Iona. 'Gather my handmaidens. We will descend as soon as possible.'

'What about Anmar?' Naaima said suddenly.

'She has chosen to remain by her brother's side. I have chosen to allow her to do so.'

Naaima said nothing, but Neferata caught the soft susurrus of her thoughts nonetheless. She knew exactly what her handmaiden was thinking. She glanced at the other woman. 'You think that was a mistake?'

'I think that even though we are immortal, that even though we are no longer human, something yet remains for us of mortality and humanity. And for some of us more than others…' Naaima brushed a loose strand of frost-stiffened hair out of her face. 'Khaled's betrayal hurt us all.'

'Not you. You never liked him to begin with.'

'Nothing good comes from men like that.'

'Nothing good comes from men,' Neferata corrected. 'Lamashizzar, Alcadizzar, W'soran, Ushoran, Abhorash… *Nagash*.' The last name was said in a bitter snarl. 'All of them men and all fools and monsters. They seek to bind us to their destinies, as if we have none of our own. As if we should be *thankful*.' She spat the last word. She looked at the river, her eyes dark and far away. 'Our destiny is here, Naaima. Here in these cold stones. The dawi worship death, even as the people of the Great Land did, before Nagash – before *we* – perverted it. There is old death, old strength in the bones of the mountain and it is upon that strength that I shall build…' She trailed off.

'Build what?' Naaima said.

Neferata spun. 'How many wolves did we bring?'

'What?'

The bullet took Naaima in the shoulder, crunching through her pauldron and shoulder joint alike and spinning her around and off her feet. Neferata made to grab her, but too late. Naaima plummeted off the bluff. The ice shattered at the point of impact and the vampire slipped into the dark water.

The wolves she had seen before had shed their reeking skins, revealing the squat shapes of a number of dwarfs, who'd been wearing them. One was recognisable, even at a distance and with his beard turned silver. Orc tusks and rat skulls still dangled in his beard, though more than the last time she had seen the ranger called Ratcatcher. He grinned at her and tossed aside a long-barrelled fire-stick to one of his men as another was shoved into his hand. He took aim and fired even as Neferata leapt from the bluff after Naaima.

The rangers had been waiting for them. That was the only thing that made sense. They had been waiting for them to eventually stumble across the river. Days, weeks, months – she knew that none of it would have mattered to the taciturn and eccentric Ratcatcher. There was no guarantee that the rangers had even been in the mountain when they'd attacked.

Neferata hit the water not far from where Naaima had crashed through. She plunged into all-encompassing darkness. The cold wreathed her bones, and though it did not bother her, she could feel it. The blood pumping through her limbs turned sluggish and she caught the sharp, familiar tang of Naaima's blood floating on the current. Like a shark, Neferata arrowed downwards, following the scent of her handmaiden.

Even for one who could see in complete darkness, the depths of the river were near impenetrable. Neferata was forced to rely on her other senses. When she felt the brush of a flailing hand, she latched on to the attached wrist and began to swim for the surface. It was an instinct, to seek succour on the surface. Neither she nor Naaima had a need to breathe, nor did the glacial current hamper them. Regardless, Naaima's body was dead weight.

Neferata hauled Naaima up until they collided with the ice. Neferata punched through it with a single blow, driving her fist up into the open air. Using her shoulder and elbow, she widened the hole and forced an opening big enough to accommodate them both. Naaima gasped like a beached fish, and blood spurted and sizzled in the hole in her shoulder. A foul-smelling steam issued from the wound and Neferata gagged. 'What–' she began.

'Burns,' Naaima gasped. 'It burns!'

Neferata drove her fingers into the wound and shrieked as something as hot as any fire caressed her fingertips. Steeling herself, she plucked the offending object from the wound. It was a lead ball, shot through with veins of silver. She growled and hurled it away.

'Silver, blood-hag,' a voice called out. She looked up and saw a firing line of dwarfs trudging across the ice towards them. All carried the long fire-sticks and had great two-handed axes strapped to their backs. Ratcatcher was chewing on a lit fuse, and a stinking tendril of smoke wafted up around his head. 'You can thank Grund for that, the sad bastard. He saw how you blood-drinkers shrivelled around it. And if there's one thing the Karaz has plenty of, it's a pretty bit o' shine.' Ratcatcher let the fire-stick swing off his shoulder and he dipped his head, touching the hissing fuse clenched between his blackened teeth to its back.

The fire-stick roared and Neferata was hit by a hammer-blow that took her off her feet. She landed on her back on the ice and heard it crack beneath her. The silver-threaded ball burned through her arm and she gasped as she tore at the wound. The ball fell out and rolled across the ice, steaming and bloody.

The dwarfs had stopped some distance away. Ratcatcher was unhurriedly reloading, even as he continued to speak. 'The engineers call 'em handguns. Don't trust them myself, but I must admit they're a mite handy when it comes to this sort of thing.' He looked at her. 'Quite a few dead ones you brought with you. They might have made a mess if they'd got in. Lucky we figured you'd try this eventually.' He chuckled. 'We've got a bit of a surprise waiting for them, don't you worry. You won't go into the darkness alone.'

Neferata heaved herself to her feet. She heard a sound like the growling of a pack of leopards and Ratcatcher made a gesture like a man hearing a familiar melody. 'The boys got a bit eager there, but no matter.' He tapped the side of his hooked nose. 'Artillery crews are like beardlings – give 'em a target and they just can't resist firing.'

His eyes narrowed to cruel slits. 'You shouldn't have killed Razek, blood-drinker. He was my friend. And you definitely shouldn't have tried to take my mountain.' He aimed his handgun. 'Back to the shadows with you, witch.'

'Why don't we go together, ranger?' Neferata said. Still crouched, she raised her fists and smashed them down with every ounce of strength her immortal frame possessed. The crack was small at first, but then the ice ripped with a sound like a melon being chopped in half. Cracks spread outwards from the point of her fists' impact, zigzagging across the surface of the frozen river. The rangers scattered in surprise, but they could not outrun the cracks.

Neferata pulled Naaima to her feet as the ice slipped and shifted beneath them. Together, the two vampires dived into the freezing waters. Neferata arrowed herself towards the struggling dwarfs, who were sinking like stones. With her teeth bared she swam downwards towards Ratcatcher, who sank in a cloud of bubbles. He saw her coming and his eyes widened. His movements were slow and awkward as he clawed for a weapon, his eyes bulging.

She hit him like a bolt thrown from a ballista and tore him in two. The dwarf spun aside in two directions, leaving a cloud of blood in both wakes. She pushed herself around, watching Naaima dart around the other dwarfs like an eel, tearing out throats or opening bellies with every graceful pass. The water became thick with dark clouds and Neferata inhaled the heady brew before pushing herself towards the surface.

'What now?' Naaima said, rubbing her chest. The wound had healed, but she still looked pained. The sound of artillery had fallen silent. Whether that implied that the dwarfs had blown her forces back to whatever hell had spawned them or that they themselves had fallen, she couldn't say. Nor, in truth, did she care. She looked back at the river and wiped her mouth with the back of her hand.

'Now we follow the river,' Neferata said. 'But first, we gather the others.'

When they rejoined the others, it became obvious that the dwarf ambush had been unsurprisingly effective for all that it had been a suicide mission. Layla trotted towards them, dragging a dying dwarf by his foot and leaving a trail of red across the snow. 'This wasn't the only ambush,' she said. 'Not according to this one,' she added, tossing the dwarf at Neferata's feet.

The dwarf glared at them blankly, pink bubbles gathering on his lips as snow collected on his twitching form. Neferata kicked him over onto his face and sighed. 'How many of you survived?'

'Most of us, my queen– Sabula was shredded, the slow-witted cow, and Lodi as well. We are maybe a dozen strong now.' Layla gestured to the smoking piles of shattered bone and smouldering armour. 'And our escort fared even worse.'

'They would only have slowed us down in any event,' Neferata said. 'Gather the others. We will proceed.'

'Should we inform the Strigoi of the ambush?' Layla said.

'Oh, I'm quite certain that they already know,' Neferata said, smiling crookedly. 'In fact, I'm quite certain that a certain Arabyan princeling was hoping for just this sort of occurrence.'

'Redzik's scouts couldn't have missed it,' Naaima said, frowning. 'The rangers perhaps, but the guns – never.' She looked at Neferata. 'Humiliation isn't enough for that one, is it?'

'Oh no, he wants me dead, my faithful Kontoi.' Neferata licked her fingers and rubbed a smudge of blood from Layla's face. 'He knows that eventually I will worm my way out of this trap, as I have every other, and that when I do, I will come for him and his ending will be most unpleasant.' She looked at the devastation caused by the ambush and nodded. 'Let him think he succeeded, however.' She looked at them and her eyes lit on Rasha. Something like satisfaction filled her and she pointed to the former nomad. 'Rasha, you and Layla will stay here. Khaled is certain to send out search parties to ensure our deaths.'

'And you want us to make sure they find nothing?' Rasha said, flashing her fangs. 'Just like the old days, my lady.'

'Indeed. Messengers as well,' Neferata said. She looked up the sky, where the snow's incessant tumble had slowed somewhat. 'The blizzard is lessening its hold. See that none of the messengers that either Khaled or Morath send out reach Mourkain.'

'What game are we playing now, Neferata?' Naaima murmured as the two vampires ran off.

'The same one as always, sweet Naaima. The only game that matters,' Neferata said.

❧ SIXTEEN ❧

The Black Gulf
(−900 Imperial Reckoning)

Neferata lounged on the divan on the deck of the black ark, stirring the wine in her goblet with a finger. Khaled and Anmar stood behind her, their hands on their weapons and their eyes watchful. The druchii slave-master examined the line of shivering, weeping people, occasionally lifting a chin with the butt of a coiled whip.

'They are pathetic,' *the white-haired elf woman lying on the divan across from Neferata said.*

'But serviceable enough for the mines,' *Neferata said, setting aside her goblet.*

The elf glanced at it. 'Are the night-grapes of Hag Graef not to your liking?'

'I have little taste for grapes of any vintage,' *Neferata said.* 'You are satisfied, I trust, Megara?'

'Never, Neferata,' *Megara said. The druchii corsair was as vicious and as treacherous a creature as Neferata had ever had the misfortune to meet. Clad in her armour and silks and dragon-hide cloak, the elf presented a lethal picture,* much more so than Neferata herself, who reclined languidly. 'But I suppose it must do,' she continued in strongly accented Sartosan. Lavender eyes gazed unblinkingly at Neferata, who met the gaze without flinching.

'And you will raid elsewhere?' she said.

'My word of honour,' Megara said.

Neferata laughed. One of Megara's guards hissed something in their own tongue and drew his curved, serrated blade and made to threaten Neferata. Khaled drew his own scimitar, but before he could move forwards, Neferata waved him still. Megara did the same to her guard. 'Careful, Neferata,' she said mildly. 'My people take offence easily.'

'But you don't. And it was you I was laughing at, Megara,' Neferata said pointedly. 'Though perhaps I shouldn't have. You do have honour of a sort. After all, you have kept faith with me ever since I rescued you from my greedy-gut servants that day in Sartosa.' Neferata had pulled the mauled corsair from the jaws of her ghouls on a whim, an action which had since paid great dividends.

Megara frowned. She did not like being reminded of her debt. 'We will concentrate our efforts on the far southern coasts. The Arabyans make terrible slaves, but they're better than this rabble.' She gestured to the quivering fishermen. Neferata gazed at them dismissively. She gave little thought to their eventual fate; such things were beyond her concern.

The slave-master was still going down the line. He stopped in front of a young woman, broad-shouldered and big-hipped. Honey-blonde hair tumbled down, hiding her face. The slave-master forced her chin up and she spat full in his face. The elf stumbled back, his narrow features twisting in a snarl. The woman lunged, snatching the hook dagger from the elf's belt. With a screech, she swept it across his belly, spilling his guts onto the deck.

The guards glided forwards, heading off the potential

revolt before it could begin. They stepped over the twitching slave-master and herded the woman towards the deck rail. Neferata sat up straighter. 'What are you going to do with her?' she said.

'We'll toss her overboard. The spirited ones are great fun, but that one will be more trouble than she's worth,' Megara said. She looked at Neferata. 'Why?'

'I would like her,' Neferata said, tapping her lip. 'I can use a woman with spirit.'

'Better to kill her,' Megara said. She raised a hand.

Neferata leaned back. 'Kill her, then.'

Megara looked at her. 'I thought you wanted her.'

'I can get twenty such, should I wish. It was a whim.' Neferata examined her fingernails. Megara did as well, remembering how those delicate-seeming fingers had ripped great gouges in the armour of her fellow corsairs and torn out throats. She did not know exactly what Neferata was, but she knew that she was no mere human, whatever she looked like.

'Take her,' she said, waving the guards back. Neferata rose smoothly to her feet and swayed towards the frightened woman. The guards fell back as she approached, their dark eyes watching her warily. The knife came up, but Neferata placed a fingertip on the bloody tip and pushed it gently aside.

'What is your name?' Neferata said softly, leaning close. The woman's chest heaved and her face was dripping with sweat as she backed against the rail.

'I... Lu-Lupa Stregga,' she said, her eyes going unfocused as Neferata gazed deeply into them.

Lupa was the local word for she-wolf. 'Appropriate,' Neferata murmured. 'Sleep, Lupa. You will be safe with me.' Her will crashed over the woman's, easily battering it down. She snatched the dagger from her slack grip as she slumped. Neferata caught her easily and motioned for Khaled to come and take her. The vampire did, wrinkling his nose as he did so.

'She smells of fish,' he growled.

'So she does,' Neferata said, licking the blood from the knife and closing her eyes as the heady taste of druchii blood burned pleasingly in her mouth and throat. She tossed the knife down, so that it sank blade-first into the deck.

Megara eyed the knife, and then looked up. 'We'll call it a gift, shall we?'

'You are too generous, Megara,' Neferata said.

'Mmm, indeed. For instance, I have another gift to go with that one.'

'Oh?'

Megara smiled and leaned forwards. 'You have spies in Araby, I trust?'

Neferata frowned. 'If I do, I don't see what concern it is of yours.'

'I'll take that as a yes. Have they mentioned Zandri?'

Zandri. The name of what was once the greatest seaport of long-dead Nehekhara sent a chill through Neferata's curdled blood. 'I know it. What of it?'

'My kin say that sails have been seen in the sour waters there,' Megara said, her voice low. 'Tattered sails belonging to ships of wood and bone, they say.'

'What else do they say?' Neferata asked.

Megara smiled. 'They say the dead are preparing to sail, Neferata. And that they are coming for you…'

The Silver Pinnacle
(–326 Imperial Reckoning)

THE RIVER WAS already freezing over as the twelve vampires waded into its depths, their hands clasped. The water closed over their heads, leaving not a ripple to mark the passage of the human chain as it sank into the depths.

The river bottom was rock and silt and clouds of the latter followed them as they made their way down. They fed on fish and, once, on one of the serpent-things that dwelt in the river, draining them of their turgid juices and leaving the husks to float up. Silt and ice collected on their armour and flesh as they moved, but proved little more than an annoyance. The crushing cold was as nothing to beings who had left mortality far behind, and the trail into the dark was easy to follow.

Dwarfs were no neater than men and they used the river harshly. The cold water clutched close the scents that the Silver Pinnacle excreted, and it was this trail that Neferata and her brood followed into the mountain. The walk through the depths was a long one, a tide of endless hours punctuated only by the appearance of the schools of blind fish which swam up from the mountain's deep reservoirs and the pale serpentine things which preyed upon them.

Days passed. Neferata's mind wandered as she walked. She had ever tried to burrow into existing power structures and rise to the top through the meat of the beast, but such was doomed to failure, even as Ushoran's rule over mortals was. Living societies would expel her even as her own flesh expelled bolts and bullets. But a dead society… Such a society she could rule forever and a day.

It was akin to Nagash's vision, and yet not. There was no need to eat the world hollow, not when all she required was a few sips of its life's blood. With a solid power base, without the need to waste her energies fighting rivals and assuring her own safety, there was no limit to what she might accomplish.

Images of vampiric handmaidens spreading outwards from the silent peaks of the Silver Pinnacle, dwarf gold in their saddlebags and her commands in their ears, filled her mind's eye. She could control nations from the safety of this place; an unseen queen, ruling an invisible empire.

The world would be hers. Nations would rise and fall at her merest whisper. Her daughters would craft empires in the west to match any in the east and they would all bend knee to her as she waited in this place, which straddled the spine of the world.

And then… and then… what?

Before she could come up with an answer, something new intruded on the darkness and silence. Sound carried strongly through the water. Down in the dark, Neferata looked up and saw the teeth of a great wheel bite into the water, and heard the thump and thunder of distant mechanisms. She thrust herself upwards, floating high, reaching out a hand. Her claws sank easily into the tough wood and she was unceremoniously yanked upwards towards the orange glow that lit the surface above. Below her, Naaima and the others followed suit, launching upwards to cling like barnacles to the wheel.

Water cascaded down her face and down in rivulets across the jagged planes of her armour as she burst upwards into the light and heat. Neferata crouched on the wheel as it rose towards the apex of its cycle. The mines of the Silver Pinnacle were as different from the mines of Nagashizzar and Mourkain as the day was from the night. They were places of reverence as well as toil and in the light of the lanterns hanging from the support beams she saw dwarfs everywhere, closing off tunnels and lowering grates over sluice gates. They were obviously sealing the mines in order to prevent just the sort of attack she was planning. They simply hadn't done it quickly enough.

Neferata balanced on the moving wheel for a moment, readying herself, and then leapt off with a sinuous motion. As she landed, she bisected a surprised-looking dwarf with an almost playful flick of her sword. As the two gushing halves fell, she was already moving. Naaima and the others followed suit with predatory grace. The vampires spread out like a wolf-pack on the hunt. The dwarfs had noticed them by then and a number of them, carrying mine-tools or weapons, moved to meet the invaders with a loud cry. Others rushed for the exits. If they reached them, the alarm would be raised.

Naaima caught up with Neferata. 'You have a plan, I trust,' she shouted, trying to make herself heard over the roar of the forges and the cries of the charging dwarfs.

'Oh yes!' Neferata said, laughing. 'We will make them afraid of the dark.' Neferata spun towards the river. Through the centuries, the Silver Pinnacle had been besieged a thousand times, but it had withstood each and every attack. The bones of those defeated armies lay scattered across the mountains and the spirits of warriors killed by the murder-make of the dawi clung tenaciously to those bones, wherever they might lie. Savages from the north and orc tribes from the east, raiders from the west and monsters from the deep, all had broken themselves on the Silver Pinnacle.

The bottom of the river that coiled around the mountain like some grim, black serpent was littered with the decaying detritus of some of those expeditions. And more besides, for the same river stretched through the mountains, running like a living vein. There were a million dead clutched to the river's bosom and Neferata intended to rip as many free as she could. As her handmaidens fought the trapped dwarfs, Neferata stared at the black waters. She stepped back and drew the whispering skeins of dark magic to her the way a weaver might pull threads. Black veins pulsed in her pale skin and her countenance became nightmarish as her human seeming died beneath the waves of dark magic washing over and through her.

Morath had been right, in his way. It wasn't that she possessed an aptitude for the magics, but that the thing that she had become was one with that dark lore. Even as Arkhan and Nagash had replaced their humanity with a swirling void of magics, so too had she become a being of those alien winds. They flowed through her altered form more easily than they did through Morath's fragile human shape. She could hear the thunder of a hundred thousand voices, caught in the shifting waters.

They rose from the water like a morning mist, threadbare at first and then thicker, more real. The wraiths were not all human. Orcs and other, unrecognisable creatures wafted silently amongst the cloud of summoned spirits. Their essence had been wrung from the water by sheer force of will and Neferata found the strain almost comforting. It was good to know that her mind's strength was still intact. Hollow eyes met hers and ghostly heads bowed to her will. She gestured without turning. 'Take them,' she breathed. A waft of turgid, freezing wind surrounded her as the spectral forms clustered around her swept forwards, trailing tendrils of sickly light.

The host of spirits flowed towards the dwarfs and swept over them like a hot wind over desert dunes. Where they struck, dwarfs died, and soon enough the tunnel had fallen silent, but horns blew in the deep and alarms sounded somewhere close by. Reinforcements would arrive soon. Neferata scanned the tunnel mouths that gaped all around them, and then spotted a strange mechanism composed of a flat wooden platform connected to a complex pulley system. Her eyes narrowed speculatively. 'There,' she said.

'Do you know how to work that device?' Naaima said.

'No, nor do we need to. We climb,' Neferata said. As she spoke she chopped through the pulley system, slicing the thick ropes and sending parts of the mechanism rolling across the floor. 'And not all of us,' she added as she turned to her followers. 'Naaima, Varna and Therise, you will come with me. Iona and Freja will lead the rest in two groups. Iona, you will take those metal aqueducts,' she said, gesturing to the heavy bronze pipes that were sunk into the river on the other side of the waterwheel. Another strange mechanism, studded with valves and stopcocks, sat high above the water. More pipes led from it into a narrow tunnel cut into the roof of the hall. Neferata suspected that those pipes led throughout the hold. There were likely other reservoirs of water in the mountain, but she suspected the pipes would lead to all of them.

'The dawi prize their beer almost as much as their gold. Follow those to the breweries. Razek once boasted to me that beer flowed from the breweries even in times of war. Destroy them and damage the aqueducts as you go. Thirsty enemies are weak enemies,' she said. Iona hissed in pleasure and gestured to three of her sisters. The vampires sprinted towards the pipes. Neferata looked at one of the others, a blonde former slave from one of the tribes that roamed the northern mountains. 'Freja, find the storehouses. Even dawi need to eat. Destroy their supply lines. Burn them if you can. A fire is as good as an army, especially when they'll have no warriors to spare in putting it out. Go!'

Neferata watched Freja and her sisters run for the doors. In the weeks they'd spent waiting for the Strigoi to locate the point where the river entered the mountain she had tutored her followers in Khazalid. They knew enough to follow the markings to their targets. And if not... if not, they would serve as a distraction if nothing else.

She looked at Naaima and gestured to the tunnel above them. 'Now we climb.'

The spirit host filled the tunnel like smoke, accompanying them as they climbed. Even as the first warriors entered the mine in response to the alarm, the vampires were already gone. Nothing was left behind save dead dwarfs.

Such an occurrence was to become common in the days ahead. Neferata and her handmaidens slunk through the side-tunnels and crooked passages of the Lower Deeps, striking where the dwarfs least suspected. There were many places to hide, for creatures used to seeking the darkness. Too, these levels were thinly patrolled. Most of the able-bodied were on the higher levels, fighting the bulk of the forces arrayed against the Silver Pinnacle.

Despite weathering any number of sieges, the defences of the Silver Pinnacle had never been penetrated to this degree, and the dwarfs scrambled to meet the threat that crept among them, red-eyed and bloody-fanged in the dark. And to their credit, these attempts were not wholly without success. Three of them were caught over the following days, and their screams still echoed through the depths. The dwarfs were not cruel. But they were thorough.

Despite the loss of her sisters, Freja accomplished her own task. A thrown lantern and burst casks of beer set the great storehouses alight and as the dwarfs fought to put the flames out, she had retreated into the darkness, seeking out her mistress.

Those dwarfs who could be spared to hunt Neferata and her followers were ambushed and slaughtered by their prey, their bodies hung up in the corridors to drain. Soon, the dwarfs abandoned the hunt, and instead stayed close to the well-lit and heavily defended areas. As Neferata had hoped, they had come to fear the dark, ceding it to her without realising that she had been moving in a singular direction since arriving. Razek might have put it together, but Razek was dead.

She and her followers moved ever upwards, bypassing treasure vaults and barracks, looking instead for more solemn targets. Namely, the Vaults of the Ancestors: the hallowed halls where the dwarfs of the Silver Pinnacle laid their dead to their eternal rest.

The grand tombs of Karaz Bryn were filled with generation upon generation of dawi dead. There were thousands of perfectly preserved bodies there, awaiting the dark touch of Neferata's magics. And when she woke them from their dreamless slumber, they would march beneath her banner, crushing her enemies – all of her enemies, living and dead – beneath their metal-shod tread.

Eagerness filled her as they drew nearer to their goal. Morath had shown her how to scent the charnel breeze of hidden tombs and she had learned her lessons well. And from Ushoran, though she would never admit it, she had learned the art of hiding in plain sight. Thus, when they at last reached the tomb-hall where the Vaults lay, they entered surreptitiously and soundlessly.

With an abominable speed, the vampires crawled along the ceiling, slithering out of the passage and up among the support buttresses and rock formations of the tomb-hall beyond. There was no darkness in the hall, save that which clung to the ceiling, and dwarfs, much like men, rarely looked up.

The hall housing the Vaults was immense, stretching for what seemed like miles. The great doors that marked the Vaults themselves were only slightly smaller than the gates to Karaz Bryn itself, and even more ornate. Spread across the centre of both gates was emblazoned the scowling face of one of the dwarf gods, though at that size it was hard to tell which. Radiating outwards from that glaring visage was an intricate mandala of words and images and symbols, none of which made any sense to Neferata. Perhaps it was a recounting of the deeds of all of those interred within, or of their clans.

Regardless of the purpose of the decorations which adorned them, the doors themselves radiated the same implacable menace which marked the gates of the Silver Pinnacle. The closer they drew, the more the presence pressed against them.

'Neferata…' Naaima hissed. Neferata stopped and craned her head back to see her followers huddling some distance behind her as if they were rooted to the spot. And even farther back, the spirit host clustered around the top of the archway that marked the entrance to the hall. Immediately, Neferata cursed herself for a fool. Of course the dwarfs would have some form of protection on their tombs! She turned back to the Vaults, squinting. Her flesh crawled at the thought of drawing any closer, but there was no other choice. To turn back now was to admit defeat.

'I will go. When I give the signal, attack,' Neferata called back softly to her followers.

'And what is the signal?' Naaima hissed in reply.

Neferata smiled. 'You'll know it when you see it.' With

that, she continued on, not stopping until she hung over the gates like a cave-lizard. As she crawled, she watched the ceremonial guards below. They wore ornate heavy armour, and wielded two-handed axes. One was smoking a pipe and the stink of the weed within caused her nose to wrinkle in disgust. There were a half-dozen of them ranged out before the doors. That the dwarfs would spare able warriors on guarding such a place when their hold was under attack told her how highly they valued the tombs of the dead.

She froze as the scrape of boots on stone sounded. More guards, these dressed in battle-stained armour and smelling of bloodshed, strode towards the Vault, surrounding a familiar robed figure. Abruptly Neferata recalled the dwarf woman who had stood beside Borri on his throne. What was she doing here?

The leader of the group before the Vaults obviously wondered the same, as he barked a gruff query. 'Who goes there?'

'It is I, Dromble... Hilga,' the priestess said in a clear timbre. Sound carried easily in the vast space of the hall.

'Priestess,' the tomb-warden said, hastily combing at his immaculate beard with his hand. His men followed suit, instinctively preening before the dwarf woman. 'You honour us with your presence.'

'As you honour our ancestors with your devotion to duty,' Hilga said.

'But why are you here? Surely it is not safe for you down here. Several of those zanguzaz are loose down in the depths.' At the word, the priestess's escort looked around warily, clutching their weapons tightly.

'Nowhere is safe, I am afraid. And I am to ensure that the vaults of our honoured dead are proof against the foul magics of our enemy,' the priestess said, stepping briskly past him and placing her hands against the doors. 'In our last war with the men of Mourkain, they dragged the dead from the ground, both theirs and ours. '

'*Uzkular*,' a guard muttered.

Hilga nodded. 'Aye, they wring motion from the dead and I intend to see that our dead stay safely and honourably in their tombs, as the gods intended.' She waved a hand, and a faint glow crept through the contours of the mandala.

The guards shifted uncomfortably, obviously unused to seeing such things. Neferata crept closer, her flesh prickling as the priestess began to speak. A warm glow spread outwards from the dwarf woman's fingers, illuminating the heretofore unseen runes that marked the doors in turn. Neferata felt the urge to flee grip her in the face of that glow, but she forced herself to creep forwards. The bats that were nestled in the nooks and crannies of the ceiling chattered quietly at her approach, and she stretched her mind towards them.

Their minds were like tiny candle flames and they crowded towards her, their hairy bodies covering hers for a moment. Once, such a thing would have disgusted her. Now she welcomed it. She let her hand drop and the bats followed it, circling her arm like a tornado of leather wings and teeth. 'Go,' she hissed. The bats spiralled down towards the guards and the priestess in a squeaking horde.

There were hundreds of bats and only two dozen dwarfs. Neferata dropped from the ceiling, landing on all fours before Dromble, who gaped at her in astonishment before Neferata closed her hands around his head and crushed both his skull and his helmet with one brutal motion. Then, without pausing, she jumped towards Hilga, knowing instinctively that the priestess was her most dangerous opponent. She caught the dwarf's robes and yanked her away from the doors. Hilga uttered a sharp cry and a short-hafted hammer appeared in her hand. It bounced off Neferata's pauldron and she released the priestess.

Hilga scrambled aside as one of the gruff warriors who'd accompanied her attacked Neferata. He swung his two-handed hammer in a mighty blow, and Neferata's skin itched as the silver-threaded head of the hammer narrowly missed her. Her hands shot forwards, her claws tangling in his beard, and she wrenched him into the air and hurled him at the Vault doors hard enough to kill him. Blood splashed over the doors and she hissed in pleasure as the omnipresent pressure emanating from them dimmed. 'Ha!' she said, turning to lunge for another dwarf. A guard staggered towards her blindly, his head trapped in a mask of bats. Neferata grabbed him, crushing his limbs as she hefted him like a sack of grain and sent him crashing against the doors. Blood and brain matter splattered across the decorations and a moment later Naaima and the others dropped to the floor, racing easily through the cloud of bats. Naaima, a sword in each hand, sprang amongst the dwarfs in a violent dance punctuated by streamers of blood.

'Your magic is powerful, woman,' Neferata said, stalking towards Hilga, who had got to her feet. 'But I am more so.' The dwarf woman's reply was to attack. Her hammer's head was inscribed with more runes than Neferata's eyes could discern and it fairly hummed as it flashed towards her. She stumbled back, falling against the doors to the tombs. Her flesh sizzled and she screamed.

She staggered forwards and fell, smoke rising from her. 'No, blood-drinker,' Hilga said. 'You will not desecrate our dead.'

Neferata growled low in her throat and then, as something caught her eye, she smiled nastily. 'I wouldn't be so sure of that.'

Hilga's eyes widened behind her helm and she spun. Dromble stumbled towards her, animated by Naaima's will. The other dead dwarfs were already falling upon those of their fellows who had survived the vampires' attack. 'No,' Hilga whispered as Dromble clutched at her. 'No!'

'Yes,' Neferata hissed, lunging to her feet and grabbing the priestess from behind. 'Unlock it, priestess, and I will let you live.' In the distance she could hear the sound of clomping boots. Reinforcements were on their way. They had no time.

'Never,' Hilga cried out, struggling in Neferata's grip.

'Then die,' Neferata snarled in frustration, shoving the dwarf into the grip of her dead companion. Dromble gripped the priestess's braids in one hand and clawed for her throat with the other. Hilga set her feet and drove her hammer into the tomb-warden's skull, cracking it and the helm protecting it. But not soon enough; Dromble's fingers tightened, cartilage popped and flesh tore, and Hilga toppled backwards, choking on her own blood.

'Neferata, we must go,' Naaima said. As if to emphasise her words, dwarf horns blew, signalling the approach of more warriors. The animated corpses of the guards swayed in place and then, one by one, as if struck by a strong breeze, they toppled. The magic that seeped from the Vaults was too strong to keep the dead animated for more than a few moments.

Neferata glared down at the body, and then at the doors that were forever barred to her. With a frustrated snarl, she led her handmaidens back into the darkness.

≺ SEVENTEEN ≻

The City of Sartosa
(−850 Imperial Reckoning)

The khopesh, its blade pitted and scarred by sand and time, chopped into the marble column, missing Neferata's head by inches. She slid down and lashed out with a foot, kicking the dead thing in its ribcage and snapping its spine. It toppled, only to be replaced by two more. Spears thrust at her, and blood spurted from her cheek and arm. She cursed and smashed a leering skull with a jab of her palm.

As the dead crowded into the plaza, she slithered up the column, avoiding the bronze weapons which sought her heart. She leapt for the aqueduct, splashing into the water. She paused and surveyed her villa. Ghouls spitted on the spears of Settra's legions writhed in the torchlight, reaching vainly for her. She felt neither sympathy nor pity for the creatures, though she had brought them to this sad fate.

The screams of her handmaidens, however, evoked rage. She longed to throw herself back into the fray, but her instincts of self-preservation were too strong. The sound of chariot wheels crunching across the cobbles reached her, and she turned and ran along the aqueduct. In the distance, Sartosa burned.

Megara's warning had haunted her for years, but she had never truly believed that they would come for her. And now it was too late to do anything but run. The Tomb-Fleets of Settra the Imperishable had come to Sartosa, carrying the vengeance of Nehekhara across the sea.

'Neferata,' Naaima called out. Neferata saw her hand-maiden on the roof of the villa with the other survivors. She heard the creak of dusty strings and saw a line of skeletal archers.

'Get down, fools!' Neferata shouted, as the arrows sped forth. She did not look to see who had fallen. Instead, she turned, alerted by the quiet tremble of the aqueduct. The butt end of a staff caught her in the belly, folding her over. She sank to her knees and looked up. 'You,' she hissed.

'Neferata,' Khalida of Lybaras said in a voice like the rustling of ancient silk. Her slim form was bound tight by the ceremonial wrappings and her proud head still wore her funerary head-dress and the mortuary mask that hid the ravages that death had made upon her once beautiful face. 'In the darkness I dreamt of you, cousin.'

'I dreamed of you as well, little hawk,' Neferata said, rising slowly to face her cousin.

'Hawk no longer. My wings are dust and bone,' Khalida said. Her wrists creaked as she began to spin the asp-headed staff. It was the same staff that she had been entombed with. Neferata had placed it in her hands herself. 'I crawl through time now, like an asp.' So saying, she struck out, the serpentine head of the staff cracking Neferata across the shoulder and nearly spinning her around. Khalida slid forwards, the water seeming to part for her linen-wrapped feet as she struck again and left a red gash across Neferata's back.

Neferata fell forwards into the water, agony such as she had never felt spitting through her. She rolled aside, nearly falling out of the aqueduct as the bronze-shod end of the staff came down, cracking the stone. Water began to flow down through the crack.

'You took my wings, Neferata. You made me crawl. Now I will return the favour. Crawl, cousin,' Khalida said, her tone remorseless and empty of the emotion that should have permeated such a statement. 'Crawl.'

'Never,' Neferata snapped, kicking Khalida in the mid-section. The dead woman staggered and Neferata came to her feet, her talons flashing and ripping through the wrappings around Khalida's chest, revealing the leathery flesh beneath. Fingers like iron bands fastened on Neferata's throat and she felt herself hefted, then she was flying down into the plaza. Tiles cracked and exploded beneath her. The dead circled her, but none moved to attack. She was Khalida's prey, and no other's.

Neferata pushed herself to her feet as her cousin approached, her torn wrappings fluttering about her like hissing snakes. The staff snapped out, catching her on the chin, and she was airborne again before landing heavily. 'Nehekhara is dead, Neferata, and all her people with her. Why should you escape the fate of the Great Land? Why should you walk in twilight, while your people suffer in darkness?'

'Because I am queen,' Neferata snarled, lunging up and grabbing the staff. The two of them swung about, struggling. And the suffering of our people is not my responsibility, cousin. I tried to save them!'

'Is that what you call it?' Khalida said, wrenching the staff away. Neferata ducked the blow and her claws scored the beautiful mask. Khalida stepped back. 'Your actions damned them, though they knew it not until the end.'

'No,' Neferata growled.

'Yes,' Khalida said. She struck again and again, forcing Neferata to dodge and back away. The dead allowed her to retreat. 'Your existence dishonours the memory of our people, cousin. It spits on their grave.'

'They dishonoured me,' Neferata shrieked, anger burning through her. 'They forced me out! They burned my beautiful Lahmia! They deserved all that Nagash did to them!' As the words slipped her lips, she felt it again – that dark, watchful presence that had been coiling within her ever since she had set foot on Sartosa's shores. It purred in satisfaction and she saw darkness. She shook her head and Khalida's staff caught her on the arm.

There was a voice in her head, calling out to her as if from a vast distance. It called her to the black, pleading with her to look, to see, to come. The staff cracked against her upraised forearms. Khalida lunged smoothly, as she had in life. A gash opened across Neferata's left breast, and then her claws punched through the paper-thin flesh of Khalida's midsection. Bones crunched and linen tore as she savaged the corpse-woman.

There was a sigh from the ranks of waiting dead, and then they stepped back, opening a path for her to join the others. Neferata looked down at Khalida, lying broken much as she had centuries before. But this time, she was not dead and her tongue was not stilled. 'Go, Neferata. Your master calls.'

'What?'

'Your master calls. Run to him. We will meet again.'

Neferata hesitated, yearning to smash the white death-mask, to eradicate that mocking, solemn expression. Instead, she turned and ran. As she did, she swore that she would never do so again. And even as she swore that, she knew that it was a lie...

* * *

The Silver Pinnacle
(–326 Imperial Reckoning)

TIME PASSED DIFFERENTLY for immortals. It was something that had taken some getting used to; the passage of days was now like an eye-blink and centuries became as days. Even so the time spent in the darkness moved altogether too slowly for Neferata. Patience was not a virtue she possessed in abundance at the best of times and she was fast running out. But as bad as it was for her it was worse for others, whose hungers were stronger for all that they were less controlled.

'We should take them now,' one of the vampires, a cunning creature called Varna, growled, shifting her weight from one bare foot to the other as they crouched in the shadows of one of the interior tunnels that ran between the levels of the hold. A prisoner they'd taken a few days previously had, under the influence of Neferata's mesmerism, confirmed that the tunnels were old ore veins that had been repurposed as doglegs to be used in the event that the Silver Pinnacle was ever compromised. The tunnels explained how the dwarfs had launched their ambushes and counter-assaults in the first weeks of the siege. They had also used them to send messengers to other dwarf holds. None of those messengers had got far.

Neferata didn't reply to Varna's remark, nor did she take offence as she once might have. Weeks with barely palatable blood and the strain of the constant dance of ambush and counter-ambush in these cramped tunnels had rendered even Naaima irritable. For the younger vampires, it was likely a torment. Iona snarled wordlessly at the other vampire, silencing her complaints.

Iona's group had rejoined them after the destruction of the dwarfs' breweries and water supplies. Rather than demoralising the dawi, however, the destruction of their beer supply had only served to incense them. Neferata had lost two more of her handmaidens in the days following, to dwarf ambushes in or around tempting targets. The dwarfs had lost more, however.

Now they crouched within one of the cramped tunnels that crisscrossed the entirety of the hold. From them, one could reach anywhere within Karaz Bryn if one didn't mind travelling in nearly suffocating darkness for days on end. Even the dwarfs weren't certain how many there were these days. Some had been sealed off and forgotten for one reason or another, their iron doors rusted shut. It was on one side of such a door that Neferata and her followers waited.

On the other side, dwarf voices murmured. The dwarfs had been using the ore veins for the last month to launch surgical strikes against the flanks of the Strigoi forces as the dead moved steadily and inexorably through the upper levels of the hold. How he had gotten the interior entry gate open, Neferata couldn't say. Regardless, once inside, Khaled's talent for bloodletting had come to the fore and the dwarfs had been forced into a steady retreat. There were only a few thousand warriors in the Silver Pinnacle, not nearly enough to stem the advance of the dead. With Morath at his side, Khaled had forced the dwarfs back and back, as she had known he would. The dead might not be able to rule the living, but they could grind them down well enough. Gate after gate had fallen.

Now, only one remained.

Just beyond the rusted portal that blocked their way was the vaulted hall that led to the so-called Deeping Stair. Beyond the Deeping Stair were the temples and shrines. The dwarfs had chosen to make their last stand beneath the gazes of their gods. They had hunkered down, prepared to outwait their enemies, despite a lack of food, resources or reinforcements.

Perhaps they thought the runners they had sent along the Underway to request aid from other dwarf holds had escaped. Perhaps they thought that the Strigoi would grow bored. Perhaps they thought neither of these things but could do nothing else save sit waiting stubbornly for the end, whatever form it took.

Neferata stood. The eyes of her handmaidens followed her. She gestured, and felt the cool, damp presence of the spirit-host. It had only grown larger since she had first brought the ghosts from the depths of the river. Dozens had become hundreds as dwarf spirits were wrenched from their bodies and added to the spectral morass which followed the vampires like an omnipresent mist.

'We must get the last gate open,' she said.

'That means revealing ourselves to an entire army,' Naaima said.

'A risk we'll have to take,' Neferata said. She looked at Naaima. 'The time has come. My patience has grown thin and the dwarfs aren't moving any further. It is time to bring this farce to an end.'

'Which end, the one Ushoran envisions, or the one you've been plotting since we arrived?' Naaima said softly. Neferata blinked. Naaima sighed. 'I *know* you.'

'The only one that matters, Naaima. Mine,' Neferata said, after a moment. She looked around, meeting the unblinking gazes of her handmaidens. 'Ours,' she amended. 'Here we will be free. Here, in these halls, we will build a New Lahmia.' She reached out, stroking Varna's knotted and tangled hair. 'Here we will be queens. We will be the queens of the world. Let Ushoran gnaw the bones of Mourkain. Let him have his petty kingdom. When it falls, we will still be here. When all of the kingdoms of the world are footnotes in the histories of scribes yet to be born, we will still be here. We will sit here, astride a throne made from the world's spine, and our subjects will be kings and hetmen.'

'What of Khaled? What of Morath or the Strigoi?' Naaima said. 'What of Ushoran?'

'We will do as we have always done with those who would try and stop us,' Neferata said. Seeing the look on Naaima's face, she added, 'Once the gate is open and the dwarfs are in retreat, you will take the others and bind the Strigoi. They are as few in number as we and they'll be fewer after the coming battle. She hesitated, then, 'Leave Morath for last.'

'What of Khaled?' Naaima said, and Neferata heard the unspoken question – *and Anmar?* – and she looked away.

'I will handle him myself.'

Naaima fell silent. Neferata smiled thinly. The others trusted her, and obeyed her implicitly. Naaima knew better, knew enough to know that Neferata was not infallible. But she obeyed. They lived on the sharp end, and to hesitate was to get cut. She gestured. 'Go, my hungry she-wolves,' she said curtly. Iona and Varna snarled and sprang for the door. Their shoulders struck it, and the iron bolts popped from the stone and the door toppled inwards with a thunderous clang. Dwarf voices were raised in surprise as Iona and Varna scrambled to their feet and to the attack.

'Harry them. Take every alcove and cul-de-sac,' she shouted, raising her sword. The spirit-host boiled around and between the remaining vampires squeezing into the corridor beyond. Neferata loped in its wake, as swift as thought. There was no light within the passageway, but she saw plain enough. The dwarfs there radiated life and heat and saliva filled her mouth.

The dead and the soon-to-be-dying came together in the darkness. The dwarf line held, shields raised and axes high as the vampires rampaged among them. Neferata's sword split a dwarf's helmet and the head beneath even as the doomed warrior struck at her in vain with his axe. She waded into the line, followed closely by the others, the spirits of the hungry dead clustering on the flanks, pulling down dwarfs with ethereal talons.

'Hold steady, lads, it's just an ill-breeze,' a dwarf bellowed. His axe was decorated with runic symbols that burned bright as he swiped at the ghosts. Several shrieked silently and dissipated as the axe blade cut through them. Neferata felt a spike of pain as the spectres vanished and she lunged for the dwarf. He caught her blow on his shield with a grunt, and the force of the impact drove him to one knee. His axe hissed, as if red-hot, as it cut at her and she hastily jerked back. Like the hammers wielded by the king's guard, some enchantment had been worked into the metal.

Neferata traded blows with the dwarf as the corridor floor ran red. Undeterred by the runic axe, the spirits swept forwards, enveloping the dwarfs and sucking the life from them. As each dwarf fell, the face of the one facing Neferata grew harder and harder, and his blows came faster and faster, as if by defeating her he could save those of his men who remained. And perhaps he could have, if she had let him.

He chopped out at her, overextending himself. She rolled around the blow, stone scraping beneath her sandals as she twirled and brought her sword up into his back. His mail buckled, and the sword screeched against the metal as it penetrated and popped out of his barrel chest in a blossom of blood. She withdrew the sword and turned as he toppled onto his face. The dwarfs were retreating now, falling back along the corridor towards the point where it opened up into a balcony that overlooked the great hall beyond. A wide set of curving stairs waited for them on one side of the gate, leading down to the open floor below.

Neferata paused, taking in the scene. The Deeping Stair was a mile across and three miles long and carved from a single plane of rock. In other circumstances, it would have been breathtaking. It was the main artery for travel in the hold, and even now, dwarfs hurried across it, seeking the safety of the temple district located below. She recognised the immense statues of the dawi gods and goddess, watching with blank-eyed sadness as their people streamed for the safety the temples promised. She could feel the same burning pressure emanating from those buildings as she had felt at the Vaults.

With that realisation came an understanding of the pattern to the dwarf movements. They were fighting a rearguard action, trying to give their people a chance to reach safety. She grimaced. If they reached those temples, they would be almost impossible to dig out. Unless they came out of their own free will. Her frown faded and she moved on, still thinking.

The vaulted chamber rang with the sound of weapons as the fight spilled onto the balcony. The large doors that led to the entry hall shuddered on their hinges and ranks of dwarfs waited for the undead without to break in. There were shouts of surprise from their ranks and reinforcements hurried towards the stairs, seeking to halt the incursion.

Of the dozen or so dwarfs who remained on the balcony, a small group of five set themselves to guard the retreat of the others in a display of commendable bravery. Like their commander, they intended to sell their lives dearly. Neferata leapt from the balcony, bypassing them entirely. Her handmaidens followed, leaping and bounding, leaving the spirit-host to deal with the survivors from their entry. As the spectral creatures boiled across the balcony, the vampires descended. Neferata's eyes found the pulley and wheel system that controlled the titan doors and she gestured with her sword. 'Take it! Get it open!' she howled.

Crossbow bolts rattled off the stone and their armour as more dwarfs moved to stop them. One of her handmaidens, a brunette creature called Sabine, was punched backwards, a bolt standing at attention between her breasts. She writhed and shrieked as she squirmed on the ground, clawing at her chest. Neferata ignored her follower's plight as she bounded towards the gate mechanism. She hit the crank with her shoulder, throwing her whole body into the act. The immense chain that raised the counter-weights which would open the door shook as she hit it.

Crossbow bolts sprouted from her back and her arms. She gasped in pain, but resisted the urge to turn on her attackers or retreat. More bolts smashed home, and she slumped, coughing blood. Yet with a grinding roar, the gates to the inner deep began to swing open. Neferata rolled off the mechanism and fell to the floor as the gigantic ghouls that led the Strigoi advance ripped the doors the rest of the way open and admitted the undead host.

The sounds of battle filled the air and she closed her eyes. The crossbow bolts that had pierced her began to fall free one by one as she encouraged her metamorphic flesh to expel them. Hooves clopped close. 'A handy trick,' someone said. Neferata cracked an eye.

Morath looked down at her, his blistered face twisted into a smile. Neferata pushed herself to her feet. 'Was it? I have so many that I lose track,' she said. She turned. The dwarfs were stubborn, but they were outnumbered and unprepared. Their horns were already calling for a retreat.

'Your plan worked, I see,' Morath said, leaning forwards across the pommel of his saddle. He didn't ask how she had survived, or what had occurred since her disappearance.

'Of course it did,' she said, snatching up her sword and sheathing it. 'They'll fall back to the Deeping Stair. We need to harry them, to keep them from regrouping here. I want them running.'

'Easily done, now that we have some room,' Morath said, snatching at his reins and turning his mount. The dead pushed forwards, ignoring the impotent fury of their foes. The dwarfs gave ground grudgingly, but give ground they did. They had been thrown off their guard by Neferata's sudden entry, and the Strigoi's advent had prevented them from reforming the shield wall.

Corpse-wolves and mummified horsemen galloped past her, following the retreating dwarfs. She let them go. The army would be spread out across the hold, if she judged Khaled correctly. There would be more bastions of resistance than just here, but here was the main one. Here, at the heart of the hold, was where Borri would be. And Khaled wanted Borri. Khaled needed the king's head and beard to establish himself as Ushoran's right hand.

Her Kontoi had thrown himself into the snake-pit with his eyes wide open, and he knew well what would keep him from getting bitten. He would rise far. But never to where he desired. Not now. Not with the crown sitting on Ushoran's brow, dictating the commands of a being better forgotten.

She smiled. She had seen the web for what it was, in the end, and seen the crown for the spider it pretended not to be. A trap by any other name; it was the soul of another dead man, trying to force her into his shadow.

Kings, undying or otherwise, had no use for a queen who spoke her mind. And Neferata had no use for kings. And soon, she would have no need to fear them. That was, if she didn't die in the process.

Mounted on skeletal steeds, Khaled and Zandor rode towards her. Trust the Strigoi to stay close to his greatest rival. Both men displayed surprise at seeing her, and the latter showed a certain amount of trepidation. Perhaps it hadn't been Khaled who had arranged for her to walk into an ambush after all.

'Hail, my Kontoi,' Neferata said, plucking a final bolt from her body.

'I thought–' Khaled began as he swung down off his steed. Zandor followed suit, frowning.

'I know what you thought,' Neferata said. 'Yet here I am, my Kontoi, coming to your rescue again.'

'Rescue,' Khaled repeated, glaring at her.

'Oh yes, though you don't deserve it.' She looked back and forth between them. 'Which of you was it, I wonder, who decided to let me walk into a trap? Was it you, my Kontoi? Or was it perhaps you, Zandor?' She leered at the Strigoi, who stepped back. 'Regardless, the dwarfs are falling back to their final redoubt.'

'Ushoran will be most pleased,' Zandor said smugly. 'You have done well, woman.'

Neferata didn't reply. Khaled looked at her. 'They're retreating to their temples, aren't they?' he said, eyes glinting. 'Zandor and I will take several of the Strigoi and cut them off. We can't let them scurry into their damnable holes. I would be done with this.'

'For once, we are of one mind,' Neferata said. 'There will be women and children in those temples. I want them alive.'

'Why?' Khaled said.

'Because I have commanded such,' she said, putting an edge to her words. 'I intend to offer the dwarfs terms–'

'What?' Zandor snarled. 'Who are you to–?'

'I am Neferata of Lahmia,' she snarled, backhanding the Strigoi and knocking him from his feet. She turned her glare on Khaled, pinning him in place before he could draw his sword. 'That should be reason enough to do as I command. I want them alive, Khaled, alive and unharmed.'

Khaled stepped back and hauled Zandor to his feet. The Strigoi glared at her groggily, but said nothing as Khaled hauled him away. Neferata watched them go, and then said, 'You can come out now, Anmar.'

The girl stepped out from the shadows of the gateway, her sword gripped loosely in her hand. 'Who would you have helped, I wonder?' Neferata said, turning to her. Anmar said nothing. She met Neferata's eyes, but only for a moment.

'Have I ever told you about my cousin?' Neferata said. 'Her name was–'

'Yes, you have,' Anmar said softly. Neferata stopped, nonplussed. 'Why would you spare them?'

'The dwarfs?' Neferata said. Anmar nodded. Neferata smiled thinly. 'Spite. Ushoran wants them exterminated. Thus, I will spare them.' That and it would be easier to get the dwarfs to surrender if their loved ones were offered safe passage.

'Is that why you tried to take the crown?'

Neferata hesitated. 'Why are you asking this? Yes, girl, I wanted the crown for spite.'

'Is that why you took me?' Anmar said, shifting her sword in her grip.

'I–' Neferata hesitated again. What had got into the girl? 'Anmar, you are my little leopard. I took you because I wanted to give you my gift.' She stepped towards the girl. 'Anmar–'

'I must go. My brother will need me,' Anmar said, slipping past Neferata and speeding after Khaled.

'What would you have done if she'd helped him?' Naaima said. Neferata turned and saw her oldest handmaiden picking her way across the bodies of the dead. Before Neferata could speak, Naaima continued. 'The others are doing as you commanded, never fear. The Strigoi will never see them coming.'

'Good.' Neferata peered at her. 'You will take Morath.'

'I will be gentle,' Naaima said, flashing a crooked smile.

Neferata nodded. She opened her mouth to speak, but then closed it. 'I wouldn't have hurt her,' she said finally. 'She is as dear to me as my own sister.'

'So was Khalida,' Naaima said. 'And when it was necessary, you snuffed her as if she were a flame.' Naaima smiled sadly. 'We are tools, Neferata. You call us sisters, but we are but pieces on your game-board. You collect us and hoard us, and sometimes you spend us. Sometimes you spend us for ambition. Other times, it is for spite.'

Neferata stared at her, stunned. Naaima stepped forwards and took her mistress's face in her hands and kissed her softly on the cheek. 'And we love you for it, because we cannot help but to do so. You unmake us as easily as Nagash's crown threatened to unmake you, and remake us in your image.' She stepped back and turned away.

Neferata watched her go, part of her wanting to batter the sad smile from Naaima's face. But the other part, the cold, calculating part, merely made her nod. She pushed the distraction of it all aside. She trotted towards the ongoing battle, slowly at first, then picking up speed.

Neferata scanned the stairs with the eye of an experienced general as she ran. She had learned over the centuries to read the ebb and flow of battle as easily as Morath read his mouldy parchments. This was a fighting withdrawal. They had caught the dwarfs by surprise, and there simply weren't enough of them to face a foe that was seemingly limitless, not to mention fearless. It would be a retreat, then, down to the next level where the final defences were likely already being prepared.

The dwarf rearguard on the Deeping Stair fought with tenacity, but the dead noticed only obstacles, not determination. The sheer number of skeletons and dwarf zombies pulled down the defenders, reducing them from a solid battle-line to struggling, fast-consumed knots of embattled heroes. Rune-weapons blazed in the hands of the mightiest warriors of the hold, and for a moment, just a moment, it seemed as if they might be enough.

King Borri stood amidst his bodyguard. He still held Razek's axe and he gesticulated with it in the direction of the relentless legions stalking towards the dwarf ranks. Borri was as canny as his son, and the dwarfs of the Silver Pinnacle had fought the dead before. As Neferata watched, a dozen dwarfs ran forwards at Borri's command, carrying bubbling cauldrons full of pitch. They slung them into the advancing dead. A moment later, crossbow bolts with burning tips were fired over the heads of Borri and his men.

The wide expanse of floor leading to the Deeping Stair exploded into flame. By itself, it wouldn't have stopped the dead, but it did slow them down enough for the miniature catapults that had been dragged into position on the lower landing to be of use sooner rather than later. Irregular chunks of rock were flung into the air and where they struck, they left a trail of splintered bones and gaps in the ranks.

Morath winced at each impact. Neferata looked up at the necromancer as she reached his side, where he was surrounded by a grave-guard of skeletal horsemen clad in rotting leather and bronze armour that had gone green with age. 'Pull them back,' she said. 'Between the heat and the rocks, the barrow-dead are too vulnerable.'

'Then what do you suggest we send in their place, harsh language?' Morath said, not looking at her. The strain of controlling so many dead was plainly visible on his face. Neferata caught sight of Naaima on his other side.

'No, but there are a wealth of troops they might not be so eager to bounce rocks off,' she countered, sweeping a hand out to indicate the dwarf dead. Morath blinked. Then he smiled weakly.

'Ushoran was right to send you,' he said. His smile faded. 'I–' he began, but she waved him to silence.

'Raise them, necromancer. Set brother against brother.

Let's give our hosts something worthy to record in their pathetic book of complaints, shall we?'

Morath squared his shoulders and took a breath. Neferata felt him pluck the strands of dark magic that clustered near the bodies of the slain with his mind. He raised a hand, his fingers hooked like arthritic claws. Morath had changed much over the past few years. Only traces of his previous handsomeness remained; he was a shrivelled wreck now, but more mighty than he had been. With W'soran's flight, the burden of Mourkain's magical needs had fallen on Morath's shoulders. He had kept the kingdom running, but only just.

In comparison, bringing the newly dead to their feet was as nothing. The dwarfs stirred, ruined mail scratching across stone. She inhaled the strange sickly-sweet scent of over-ripened life. Bloody fingers twitched and heels drummed on the floor. Eyelids peeled back from poached-egg eyes and as one, with a groan, the dead sat up. Gripping their weapons with slack necessity, the dead dwarfs turned as a mass towards Borri's battleline.

The dirge, when it came, was something of a surprise: a collective song of mourning, slipping from the mouths of every dwarf still breathing. Neferata watched as the dwarfs faced their dead kin, singing their sad slow song, and she felt a moment of what might have been respect. There was no fear there, only sadness. The song rose in volume until the very stones seemed to reverberate with its rhythm.

The passage of the dead beat out the flames. Still, beards and braids caught alight, wreathing the zombies in halos of flame as they stumbled towards their former companions in a grim parody of martial discipline. Neferata heard the Strigoi howling in mockery and disgust filled her. This was a necessity, not a pleasure.

In another, better world, the dawi would have been her allies. She glanced at Morath, noting the flat expression on his face.

The necromancer liked this no better than she, she knew. They were both prisoners of Ushoran's madness, though Morath had chosen that fate willingly. She had offered him a place, and he had turned away out of loyalty to an ideal. 'I could have been your queen,' she murmured. Morath looked at her.

'What?'

'Nothing, necromancer. Stay back and leave the fighting to those with the thirst for it.' Neferata trotted after the dwarf dead. She drank in the swirling winds of dark magic as she moved, using it to abate the thirst she felt. She felt her features stretch and sharpen and her muscles harden. She broke into a sprint as the first of the zombies connected with the dwarf battle-line. Others joined her – the Strigoi, shadowed by her own handmaidens, and around them, the war-ghouls of W'soran's devising, their mammoth tread shaking the floor as they roared out unintelligible challenges to the enemy.

The two forces connected with a thunderclap. The dead were a wave washing over the rock that was the defenders of Karaz Bryn. Dwarfs fell, pulled down by the hands of their fellows or crushed by the hammers of the war-ghouls. Neferata bounded from the ground to a ghoul's thigh and then off one of the great statues that stood sentinel over the stairs, landing near Borri. She had to force the king to flee. The Strigoi followed her like a pack of ravening hounds, avoiding the press of the fighting in order to reach the king and his guard.

Borri saw her in the instant before she reached him. He pivoted, nearly slicing her nose off with the axe, and then followed up with the hammer he wielded in his other hand, knocking her off her feet. She rolled beneath the feet of the attacking Strigoi as they flung themselves at the king's guard with bestial abandon. Claws and swords clashed with ancient armour and ancestral hammers and the iron wall of dawi guards disintegrated into a melee within a melee.

Borri's hammer shattered a Strigoi's snarling face, sending the vampire hurtling backwards. Neferata ducked under the flailing body and brought her sword around, locking blade to haft with Borri's hammer. He grunted as he realised her strength and crossed the hammer with the axe, glaring at her between them. 'Treachery,' he said. 'You manlings know nothing but treachery.'

'War,' Neferata corrected. 'Your son understood that.'

'Razek had many faults,' Borri said, shoving her back a step. Sweat coated his beard and ran down his seamed face. 'That does not give you the right to insult him.'

Neferata redoubled her efforts. 'Surrender, great king, and this can all end. Your son had to die, but your people do not,' she said.

'You truly know nothing of us,' Borri said. His wrists bulged and suddenly the sword was ripped from her hands. The axe struck sparks from the collar and she cursed herself for underestimating the king. If he would not retreat willingly, she would have to force him. With a roar, she threw herself back, allowing two Strigoi who had been circling the fight to leap on the king and bear him down. Borri fell, bellowing in anger.

Neferata scrambled to her feet as those of the king's guards not already engaged rushed to his aid. Hammers forced the Strigoi back, and a great crest of hair parted the warriors swirling around the king. Grund burst through the press, driving an elbow into a Strigoi's mouth, shattering fangs.

He roared and chopped down, severing the other Strigoi's leg at the thigh. The vampire shrilled and fell on top of the burly dwarf. Grund shoved the vampire aside and crushed its skull with his fist. He hacked at it wildly for good measure before turning to face her. 'I said I'd have your head, witch, and I've only ever broken one oath,' he roared.

'Grund–' Borri coughed as his men pulled him to his feet.

'No!' Grund snarled. 'She's mine, brother. Come, hag! Come, night-stalker! Fight me!'

Neferata wasted no words on the berserker. She didn't want to kill Borri yet, but this creature would be better off dead. She stepped back, channelling the dark energies that invigorated her as Morath had showed her. She spat a stream of syllables and her eyes crackled with energy, which immediately burst forth in twin bolts. Grund swung his axe up and the energy flared, leaving char-marks on the flat of the blade. For a moment, as it steamed, she could see the tell-tale curl of runes.

Grund lowered the axe and grinned. He raced towards her. She stepped aside, avoiding the seemingly heedless charge, but not his hand as it snapped out and grabbed her hair. Grund set his feet and yanked her down and around, sending her crashing to the floor.

With one foot planted on her back, he raised his axe. Neferata scrabbled for her sword, which had fallen just out of her reach. Neferata's fingers dug grooves in the stone as she tried to shake him loose but it was as if the mountain itself was holding her in place. Grund wanted her head and it looked as if he intended to have it.

As the axe fell, she squirmed beneath him and rolled onto her back. Her palms slapped tight on the axe. There was silver in it and her hands blistered as she strained against whatever magics had gone into crafting the blade. With a stifled snarl, she pulled it out of his grip and Grund, off balance, fell off her. His eyes bugged out and he screamed at her and lunged, fingers hooked like claws.

With a snarl of her own, she let the blade slide through her hands and grabbed the haft, swinging as her palms touched the leather bound tight around the wood. The axe chopped into the mad dwarf's skull, bisecting his berserk features. He hurtled past her and fell. Neferata rose slowly to her feet. Borri was on his feet, his eyes solemn as he took in the body. 'It was a good death. Your debt is discharged, brother,' he said. He looked at her. 'Yours is not.'

'You are a hard people,' Neferata said, looking at his guards. They were in the eye of the battle. Dwarfs fought grimly around them, trying to hold back the inevitable for just a few seconds more.

Borri spat a wad of blood and sputum at her feet. 'We endure,' he said.

'Not for long.' She looked past Borri. 'Your people are in a place that I may not be able to enter,' she said, gesturing to the temple of Valaya across the span of the bridge. 'But reach them I will. I will butcher them, King of Karaz Bryn, your rinn and beardlings. Unless you surrender.'

Borri glared at her silently. She stepped forwards, ignoring the weapons of his guards. She stretched out a hand. 'Your hold is lost, King. But a hold can be replaced. Can your people? What debt do you owe them, as king? Is dying here the way they expected that debt to be paid?'

His face hardened, but only for a moment. His shoulders slumped. 'We must speak on this.' He looked at her.

She inclined her head. 'Pull back what forces remain

to you, King Borri. Neferata of Lahmia will see that you have the time you require,' she said haughtily. His guard surrounded him protectively as wailing war-horns signalled for retreat. The dwarf throng, what was left of it, was in full flight. The dead did not pursue. Instead they paused on the stairs in serried, silent ranks, staring ahead as their enemies retreated. A Strigoi – Dragoj, she thought – made to follow Borri's retreating retinue and she stepped in front of him.

'No,' she said. 'Let them go.'

'Are you mad?' Dragoj snarled, his eyes bright with bloodlust. 'We have them here, we must–' He stopped abruptly and looked down at the sword-tip sprouting from his chest. 'What?' he gurgled as he reached out with a trembling finger to touch the blade.

Neferata's reply was a swing of Grund's axe. Dragoj's head bounced across the stones, the startled expression still on his face. As his body slumped, she met Iona's dark gaze. 'Hello, little she-wolf,' she said. The broken hafts of crossbow bolts protruded from Iona's armour and body alike.

'We have them,' she said.

'All of them?'

'Save those few who are with Khaled. The rest are ours.' Iona grinned. 'They never even suspected until our blades were cutting their hamstrings.'

'Kill them. All of them, and strip the fangs from their skulls. Ushoran will not fail to understand that message.' Neferata paused, and then went on. 'But first…' She looked towards the temples. 'First we must bring this to an end.'

She met with Naaima and the others on the edge of the last landing. The dead waited in patient ranks about them. 'Where's Morath?' Neferata said. She still clutched Grund's axe in her hands.

Naaima waved a hand towards the ranks of the dead. 'He's exhausted. I left him with Varna. She knows not to hurt him,' she added quickly, before Neferata could protest. Neferata looked at her remaining handmaidens. She had entered with eleven, but only six remained. Of those, only two had accompanied Naaima. The others were busy with the Strigoi, and the screams echoed hellishly over the Deeping Stair.

Neferata ignored the noise. 'We go. I want to see if our brave Kontoi managed to accomplish the task I set for him,' she said.

'What of the dead?' Naaima said.

'What of them?' Neferata said, starting down the stairs. 'Let them stay as they are, to remind the dwarfs that there is no escape. Borri can't have more than a hundred warriors left, and most of those will be wounded. No. We've won. Let us be graceful in victory,' she continued. Naaima and the others hurried after her.

It wasn't until they drew closer to the temples that they heard the screams. They were not the wails of frightened women and children. Instead, they were the full-throated howls of men driven past the breaking point. Weapons rattled and the howls of corpse-wolves echoed through the streets of the temple district.

Neferata cursed. She broke into a run, her sword in her hand. The four vampires sped through the streets towards the sounds, and Neferata's curses degenerated into shrieks of rage as she saw that Khaled had indeed accomplished his task, and more besides.

The refugees had not reached safety. Khaled and Zandor had been quicker than the dwarfs, and the latter had paid for it. Neferata stalked into the plaza in front of the temple of Valaya. It was carpeted with the bodies of slain. Little bodies, some of them, impossibly little;

and something in Neferata curdled and she was once more in Lahmia, watching as the soldiers of Rasetra and Khemri and Lybaras snatched Lahmian children from their wailing mothers and swung them by their ankles against the walls of houses.

Borri and his men had obviously arrived too late to rescue any of their loved ones. Instead they had been met by the silent menace of the tortured spirit-hosts drawn from the bodies of the dead. The ghosts of women and children and dead warriors swept across the great plaza, surrounding an imposing structure which Neferata thought must be the temple to either Grimnir or Grungni.

'They ran in there, the little fools,' Khaled said. 'Then, who can blame them, eh?'

Neferata spun. Khaled sat on a dwarf cart, his mouth and chest wet with blood. His gloves were soaked in it and he smiled at her. He cut his eyes to the spirit-host and licked his lips. 'You weren't the only one who learned from Morath. I was quite the connoisseur of such things, before... Well.' He gestured to himself. Neferata caught sight of Anmar behind him, and Zandor. Redzik was there was as well, and four other Strigoi. Dead wolves prowled among the corpses and slobbering ghouls squabbled over the choice bits.

'What have you done?' Neferata hissed.

Khaled hopped to his feet. 'What I was commanded to do, by my master,' he snarled. He pointed at her. 'What you were commanded to do!'

'No one commands me,' she said. 'Not Nagash, not Ushoran and certainly not you, princeling!'

'I told you,' Zandor spat. 'I told you she couldn't be trusted. Kill her, Arabyan!'

Khaled hesitated, his expression shifting.

'Ushoran is not here, Khaled,' she said, her voice quiet. 'Can you feel his influence? I cannot. He has no power here. He cannot command us.'

Khaled looked at her. Anmar hurried to his side. 'Brother, if she's right–'

'Quiet,' Khaled snapped. 'I need to think, I–'

'No! No more thinking, no more talk!' Zandor snarled. He leapt for Neferata as the other Strigoi converged on Naaima and the others. As Zandor crashed against her, the doors to the great temple where Borri and his remaining men had retreated boomed open and off their hinges, shattering the stillness of the mountain.

A maggot-infested wolf bounded towards the opening and was crushed by an expertly wielded hammer. A shorn-scalped dwarf stepped into view, his hair and beard shaved. His eyes were wild and red-rimmed. He held his hammer in one hand as he tore feverishly at the clasps of his armour.

Another dwarf, similarly shaved and bare-chested, followed. Then another and another, dozens, the last survivors of Karaz Bryn, their beards shaved and oaths to Grimnir on their tongues as they discarded their armour with ritualistic contempt. Some had daubed strange markings on their flesh in soot and blood and the eerie dirge that swept from them chilled even Neferata's heart.

She knew then that there would be no surrender. No mercy.

'What–?' Zandor began, staring at them in shock. His hands hung limply around Neferata's neck. 'Are they mad?'

'Yes,' Neferata said, and rammed her fist through his chest. Zandor screamed in shock and pain as her fingers sought his heart. She seized it and jerked it free of his chest. The Strigoi staggered back. Neferata crushed his heart before his disbelieving eyes. 'I told you to remember my hand on your heart, Zandor,' she hissed.

Zandor lunged with an inarticulate cry and Neferata brought Grund's axe up and buried it in the Strigoi's skull as he knocked her to the ground. Before she could get up Khaled's sword sank through the meat of her thigh, pinning her leg to the floor. She screamed. Her scream was echoed by the dwarfs as they charged forwards to meet the ghosts and ghouls and dead warriors that sprang into action at Khaled's barked order. The dead and the suicidal crashed together like opposing ocean waves, and hymns to Grimnir buffeted her ears as she grabbed for the sword.

'No,' Khaled said, stepping back, his expression torn between satisfaction and disgust. 'No. You won't wriggle free of this trap.'

Neferata twisted, but the sword was in an awkward place. She couldn't reach it. Khaled, oblivious to the fighting going on around them, squatted before her, grabbing her chin as she had so often grabbed his. 'Was that what I was? A trap?' he sneered. 'Are all men traps, my lady? Is that why you could not accept what I offered you?'

'You're no trap, Khaled. You're simply a fool,' Neferata hissed, grabbing his wrist. 'You offered nothing. You wanted everything and I give nothing.' Khaled jerked back, trying to free his hand from her grip. Flailing for a weapon, he snatched up the axe, jerking it out of Zandor's skull. The silver wept smoke as it exited the vampire and it trailed it down as Khaled lashed out at her. She twisted.

The axe struck her, gashing the flesh of her throat. Suddenly she was choking on her own blood and she released Khaled and squirmed around, leg still pinned to the floor, clutching at her throat. Khaled gave a scream of fury and prepared to deliver another blow.

'No!'

Khaled whirled as the sword gouged across his side. He swept the axe down into the chest of his attacker. Anmar coughed and fell back. 'No,' Khaled said. 'Oh no, no, no...' He stooped and tried to pull his sister to her feet, but the axe was buried to the haft in her heart. Smoke and steam rose from the wound and from her mouth and nose and eyes as she twitched and thrashed. In her final moments, she reached for her mistress as Neferata rose unsteadily to her feet, Khaled's sword in one bloody hand. Neferata's pain-filled writhing had dislodged the blade finally, and now she held it tightly.

'Goodbye, little leopard,' Neferata said, and drove the sword down through Khaled's body, into his sister's and on into the rock below. Khaled made no sound as his sister expired and the rot that claimed all vampires upon death set in, reducing her form to what it would have been had she lived a mortal life. Khaled shuddered, pinned in place by the sword, unable to look away.

Neferata kicked the axe out of his reach and turned. Borri's men were fewer in number than they had first seemed, and though they fought as berserkers, the dead were numberless. Ghostly hands plucked at bare flesh, drawing the last dregs of life from the warriors.

'Neferata of Lahmia, I declare you oath-breaker and murderer,' a harsh voice rasped. Neferata turned. Her handmaidens still battled the Strigoi. She was alone.

'Borri,' she said, reaching for the sword still sheathed on her hip. The king had doffed his armour, as had his remaining warriors, and his barrel chest was streaked with blood. He still carried his son's axe. 'We can still end this without further bloodshed.'

'Your name has been entered in the book,' he said. Then he charged. Neferata barely blocked the blow and spun, dancing around the dwarf as he chopped at her in grim silence. Soon Borri was puffing and stumbling. The exertions of the day had taken their toll. 'You have murdered us,' he gasped, lashing out at her. 'You have torn out the heart of our hold and condemned us to wander.'

Neferata avoided a wild blow. 'You have condemned my son to wander!' Borri roared, flinging the axe at her as she stepped back. She swatted the axe aside.

Borri tensed. His hands clutched emptily, and he glanced at the axe where it had fallen. Neferata shook her head. 'You won't reach it.'

Borri said nothing. Neferata sighed. 'Honour is a burden a ruler can ill afford. It is a weight on the soul and the mind.'

'Kill me and be done, witch.'

'I don't want to kill you, Borri. If I did, I would have let Zandor and his bone-eating cronies do the job for me,' she snapped, gesturing to the mangled corpse of the Strigoi. 'I want you alive. I want your people alive. Together, we can–'

'No,' Borri said.

Neferata stopped. 'What?'

'No.' He looked at her pityingly. 'Your name has been entered into the Book of Grudges, Neferata of Lahmia. There can be no end other than the settling of the debt.'

'I'm offering you mercy, King Borri. I am offering you the lives of those of your people who survive. And all I ask is that you–' she said, bewildered.

'The living do not serve the dead,' Borri said.

'You dwarfs do nothing but serve your dead,' Neferata spat. 'This whole place is nothing but a tomb! It's a monument to a failed race!'

'Then let it be our tomb,' Borri said simply.

Neferata closed her mouth. She looked away. 'Is that your answer?'

'There can be no other,' Borri said. Then, with a grunt, he leapt for the axe. Neferata whirled, reaching for him. Borri ripped the axe up and rolled across the floor, springing to his feet as Neferata swooped over him. He set his feet and swung his son's axe. Neferata screamed as the axe chopped into her shoulder and the silver threads that ran through it burned her. Her fist punched through Borri's torso, erupting from his back in a splatter of blood. Borri grunted and his trembling arm sawed at her shoulder, trying to reach her heart even in his final moments. Neferata gasped and grabbed his face with her free hand and ripped the dwarf away from her, flinging him backwards. He landed in a bloody heap some distance away and she wrenched the axe from her body, screaming again as smoke escaped from the wound. Still holding the axe she stumbled towards him, intending to bury the weapon in his skull.

But there was no need. Borri was dead. Neferata sank to her haunches and placed the axe between his hands. She stood, one hand holding the wound on her shoulder closed.

She turned towards the battle, her face settling into a still mask as she started forwards. The war was over. All that was left was the massacre.

It had all led to this moment, every struggle and every scheme. She had ever sought a place from which to rule, to command. But always they had been taken from her. Always, outside events had interfered. Lahmia, Bel Aliad, Sartosa, Mourkain, memories and false-starts all, she knew that now. The dead could not rule the living.

But she would rule nonetheless. She would rule this place. She would make it a fortress, a temple to ambition and a refuge from a world whose tides and tempests she would set right. A dwarf roared and swung a hammer at her. She caught the weapon and drove its haft into the berserker's belly, rupturing organs and breaking bones. She kicked the dwarf aside and met their hymns with the war-song of lost Lahmia.

She would see to it that that song was sung again, in the years to come. The ghost of Lahmia would find rest here, within these sheltering halls. A dwarf screamed wildly and drove a broken spear into her hip. Neferata broke his neck and threw the body into the air. More dwarfs charged forwards, seeking death and absolution.

Neferata was happy enough to give them the former.

Blood filled her vision, sweeping away all doubt and ambition. She snarled and spat and screeched, less a woman than some great veldt cat driven past hunger into madness. The dead fell around her, their remorseless march stalled and stopped by the berserkers who tangled their dying bodies in spears and among legs, dragging blazing-eyed ghouls down beneath the press with a final spasm of insane strength.

Soon Neferata was alone, a pale wraith stalking dunes of dead flesh, her fangs popping from her mouth, her tongue long and lashing as she drank the thick, heady brew from her blade. One dwarf left, screaming and bulge-eyed, so far gone in shame and hate that he did not realise that he was alone.

She parried his axe and brought her sword up through his barrel chest, lifting him off his feet. As the dwarf's blood gushed down her arm to splash across the stone, Neferata leaned close to one club-ear and whispered, 'I am queen.' The words sounded hollow in the sudden silence.

The dwarf's only reply was a death-rattle.

Neferata stood for a time, looking down at the body. The last defender was dead. The Silver Pinnacle had fallen.

Long live New Lahmia.

⤙ EPILOGUE ⤚

The Silver Pinnacle
(−15 Imperial Reckoning)

NEFERATA SAT BACK and took a sip from her goblet. 'And that was that. I'm sure you know the rest.' Arkhan the Black gazed at her silently. He had remained standing throughout her tale, his undead body knowing neither fatigue nor discomfort. Now, however, his head dipped and his eyes dimmed.

'*That is it?*' he said.

'You wound me,' Neferata said, leaning back. 'And you do me a disservice.'

Arkhan shifted, his bones creaking. '*You make it sound so simple.*'

'It was anything but, I assure you,' Neferata said. She touched her temple. 'I can still hear it, though its whispers have grown ever fainter in these intervening years.'

'*Where is it now?*' Arkhan said. '*Where is the crown?*'

'Your master knows better than I,' Neferata said. She

tilted her head. 'It sits hidden to the west and Nagash is drawn to it. And you are drawn with him.'

Arkhan stiffened. His eyes flashed. '*As you will be as well. Nothing you have told me is of any use, Neferata.*'

'If you think that, then you are indeed diminished,' Neferata said, her eyes narrowing. 'You truly do not see it, do you?'

'*I see a woman hiding in a tomb, cowering from fate,*' Arkhan said harshly.

'Careful,' Neferata said softly. 'And you should know by now that fate is a mocker. There is no fate, save that which we make for ourselves, else it would have been I who wore Nagash's crown.'

'*Are you so certain? How do you know Ushoran was not its intended recipient?*'

'I don't. But it sought the strongest. Not just in body, but in mind. It wanted a sorcerer and a warrior, not either-or,' Neferata said. 'It wanted a strong body to ride into eternity.' She smiled widely, her fangs surfacing from behind her lips. 'So I gave it one.'

Arkhan stood silently for a moment, the glow in his eyes dim. Then, suddenly, they blazed bright. The skull tilted back and the jaws gaped and Arkhan the Black laughed, truly laughed, for the first time in centuries. There was a black joy in that sound, and relief as well.

The great hall of the Silver Pinnacle echoed with the sound of his joy, and the bats that clung to the ceiling stirred, their tiny dreams becoming unpleasant as Arkhan's voice penetrated their thoughts. As the echoes of his laughter faded, Arkhan looked down at her. '*Do you think he realised, at the end, what you had done?*' he said.

'If he had, he might have tried harder to destroy me,' Neferata said. 'Instead, he was content to squander that power on barbarians and orcs and worse monsters.' She gestured extravagantly. 'Then, maybe he did, and maybe this was my reward for it.' She chuckled. 'I suppose it's too late to ask him now.'

'*I suppose you were only too happy to see the crown vanish into the west, there at the end,*' Arkhan said.

Neferata's humour faded. 'Yes,' she said softly, 'poor Morath. He played his part well, in the end, in the last days of Mourkain.' She looked at Arkhan. 'He was right, you know. Ushoran consumed the Strigoi, as we consumed the Lahmians. You were – are – right. The dead cannot rule the living. They can only destroy them. Or perhaps guide them.'

'*Is that what you would do? Guide them where?*'

Neferata laughed. 'Why... I will guide them wherever I wish, Arkhan.' She pointed at him. 'But you did not come here to hear my plans for the future, did you?'

'*I came for vampires,*' Arkhan said.

'Ah yes, because Nagash demands it. He wants new servants; more, he wants servants who can propagate themselves. With our kind, one becomes two, two becomes four, four to eight and so on,' Neferata said, smiling. 'A plague of undeath, a plague that walks and plans and fights, that is what the old king of bones wants, isn't it?'

Arkhan was silent. He knew her well enough to know that she was leading him somewhere. Neferata rose to her feet and drifted close to him, pressing her palms to his cuirass. She leaned close, her lips brushing the chill edge of his skull. 'To beat Nagash, one must give him what he wants. No more, no less,' she whispered.

Arkhan grabbed her wrists with alien swiftness. '*Are you offering yourself, Neferata?*'

She frowned coquettishly. 'Perish the thought. What

use would Nagash have for a mere woman? No, but I can offer you the services of another…'

There was a scrape of metal on stone. Something heavy was being dragged across the floor of the hall. Arkhan turned with one hand on the hilt of his sword. Neferata leaned her chin on his shoulder and pointed, and said, 'And there he is now.'

Arkhan stepped down from the dais, sweeping aside the curtains. Four brawny ghouls dragged forwards an oblong box, crafted from iron and ringed by silver bands. From inside came a muffled howl. Neferata clucked her tongue. 'Even after all this time, he still weeps for her. I do as well, but he was always quite extravagant about such things. Quite the beast for grand gestures, my Kontoi…'

The ghouls set the box down before them and backed away hurriedly, as if they feared what was inside. 'Two hundred years or so. I wonder what he will look like, my handsome warrior-prince,' Neferata murmured, sweeping down from the dais and running her fingers along the edge of the box. It trembled as if something was thrashing wildly within. There was another muffled howl and she laughed.

She looked at Arkhan. 'He is yours, if you want him. Make of him a gift from the Queen of Mysteries to the King of Death. Or perhaps he is a replacement – a lieutenant for a lieutenant.'

'*What?*' Arkhan said.

Neferata laughed. 'You still do not listen! Even after all these years, you never listen.' She flicked her fingers. 'Take him, Arkhan the Black, Arkhan of Khemri. Though all debts were settled between us long ago and I owe you nothing, I give you this last gift. Give it to Nagash, and be free, my gambler.'

'*I don't understand,*' he said, looking at the box.

Neferata did not reply. She simply laughed and stepped past him. Her laughter remained long after she had left, sweeping into the darkness, her courtiers following her. Arkhan was left only with the ghouls and the moaning thing in its silver-banded box. When silence fell, save for the desolate cries of Khaled al Muntasir in his prison, Arkhan shook himself.

'*Thank you,*' he said, the words escaping from his mouth like a sigh. Then, he turned to go.

His master was waiting, and Arkhan had a prize to deliver.

ABOUT THE AUTHOR

Author of the novels *Knight of the Blazing Sun*, *Neferata* and the forthcoming *Gotrek and Felix: Road of Skulls*, **Josh Reynolds** used to be a roadie for the Hong Kong Cavaliers, but now writes full time. His work has appeared in various anthologies, including *Age of Legend* and several issues of *Hammer and Bolter*.

◄ TIME OF LEGENDS ►

MASTER OF MOURKAIN

A Blood of Nagash short story

JOSH REYNOLDS